PRAISE FOR *SUMMIT*

"A **captivating** debut novel that combines grand storytelling with a thorough knowledge of climbing. Harry Farthing is a compelling new literary voice."
—SUSAN SLOATE
bestselling author of *Forward to Camelot*

"**Breathtaking** and **chilling**...Summit really takes you up into the Everest death zone."
—RHYS JONES
record-breaking British mountaineer
and owner of Monix Adventures

"A gripper. Takes you up to the majesty of Mt. Everest and into the single-minded 'madness' of climbers... what a plot. **Fantastic.**"
—SIR ROBERT SWAN
bestselling author of *Antarctica 2041*, and first person to walk to the South and North Poles

"**A wonderful story** that instantly took me back to my Everest days. Many shades of the legends of mountaineering, such as the great Italian Walter Bonatti and, of course, the doyenne of Himalayan record-keeping, Elizabeth Hawley."
—MARTIN ADAMS,
1996 Everest climber and protagonist of
Into Thin Air and The Climb

"Farthing entertains the reader with a taut, **suspenseful tale** of high anxiety…and conveys a message that we should always be on guard because history repeats itself."
—**SOUTH CAROLINA REVIEW**

"Mountain climbing, crime drama, and historical fiction certainly might not appear to be a natural mash-up, but Harry Farthing pulls it off—and quite well at that…The treachery, the splendor, the whole man-versus-nature element, all well done. To compliment, Farthing adds in a historical mystery…an excellent set of characters…
a fantastic read."
—**AS ALWAYS**

"[An] **action-packed** debut thriller…Farthing's firsthand knowledge of Everest paints a vivid picture of the majesty of the mountain and also the hellish rigors climbers face in trying to conquer it as background to an exciting story, part-thriller, part-historical novel… Marries [Farthing's] knowledge of world travel, adventure sports, mountaineering, and modern history to create a gripping action story that is both compelling and thought provoking."
—**MOULTRIE NEWS**

"Farthing has done a remarkable job of telling two parallel tales while weaving them together into a single narrative…the author brings it all together for a most-satisfying ending."
—**CROW RIVER MEDIA**

ABOUT THE AUTHOR

From the moment eight-year-old HARRY FARTHING first saw the famed summit photo of Tenzing Norgay in his school library, he knew Mount Everest would figure prominently in his future. The years took him across the world and up and down many peaks—not least within three hundred meters of Everest's summit—until he found a way to combine his knowledge of world travel, adventure sports, mountaineering, and modern history; the result is *Summit*, his debut novel.

SUMMIT

A NOVEL

HARRY FARTHING

BLACKSTONE
PUBLISHING

Copyright © 2013 by Harry Farthing
Published in 2017 by Blackstone Publishing
Book design by Kathryn Galloway English

All rights reserved. This book or any portion thereof may not be reproduced or used in any manner whatsoever without the express written permission of the publisher except for the use of brief quotations in a book review.

Printed in the United States of America

978-1-4551-1599-0

1 3 5 7 9 10 8 6 4 2

CIP data for this book is available from the Library of Congress

Blackstone Publishing
31 Mistletoe Rd.
Ashland, OR 97520

www.BlackstonePublishing.com

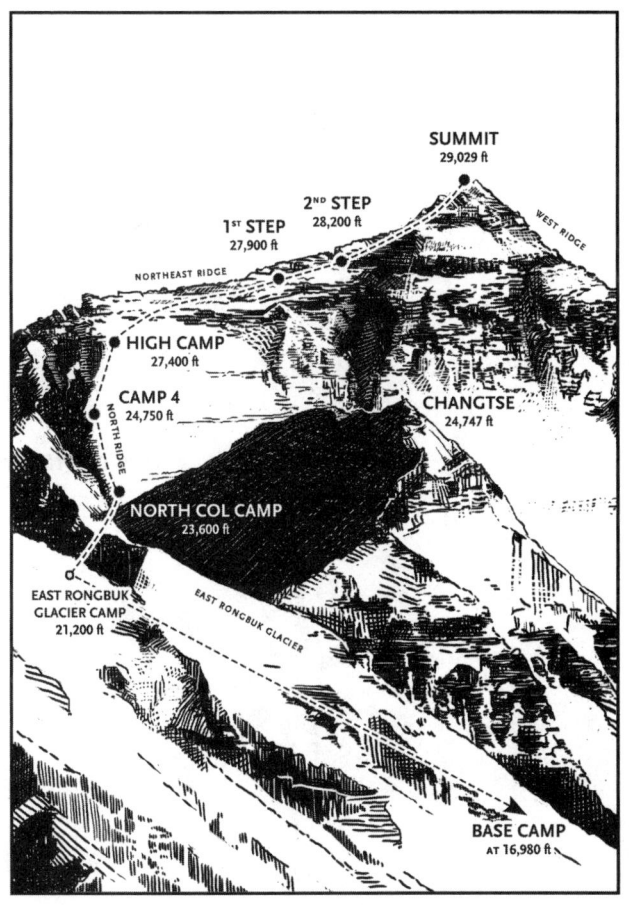

EVEREST NORTH, FROM TIBET

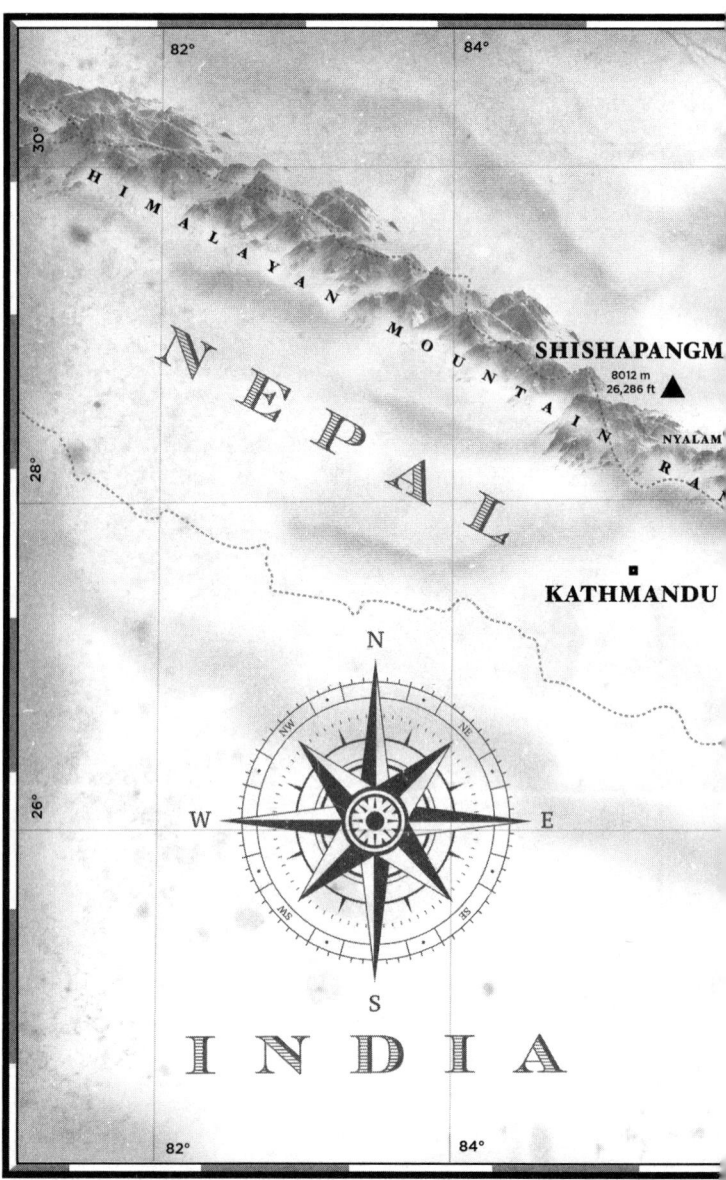

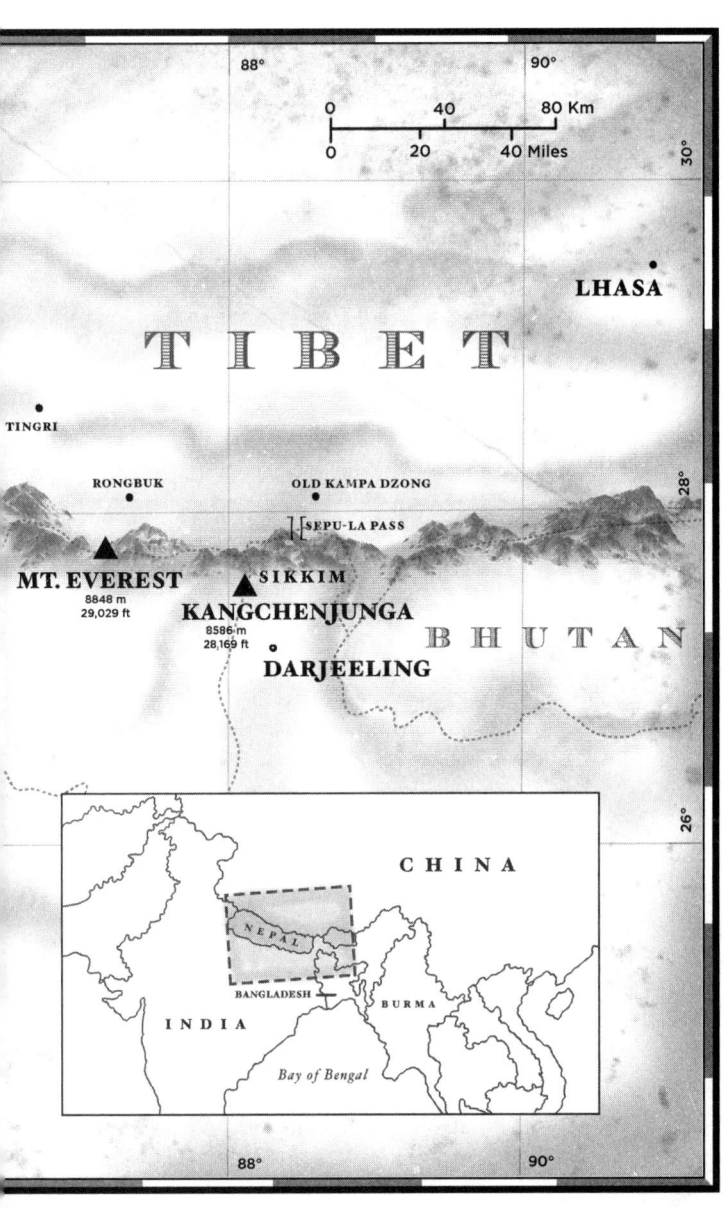

"Berg heil!"

—Traditional German salute to the mountains

PROLOGUE

A filtered crimson light illuminated the windowless room with a visceral glow. The smell of chemicals was toxic, instantly overpowering everyone except the white-coated man already working inside. After a lifetime spent in such environments, the Leica technician no longer even noticed it. Finishing another sequence of adjustments to the skeleton of an archaic negative enlarger, he flicked his head from side to side in silent appeal for more elbow room, mumbling something only to himself. He clearly preferred to work alone.

The man made one further minute calibration then paused, arms dropping to his sides, eyes closing as he mentally counted down some required delay known only to his experience. The instant it was over, he quickly reached for the eight-by-ten-inch rectangle of photographic paper set within the base of the metal frame. Taking a corner of the white card in the long jaws of a pair of tongs, he then deliberately slowed himself to gently slide it into the first of four stainless steel trays of developing fluids he had so fastidiously prepared. He began to bathe the blank paper, lightly agitating it within the clear chemical bath, his soft, rhythmic movements setting the fluids lapping.

A dark smudge dirtied the white rectangle's center. Lines and shadows started to define themselves, growing in twists and turns like an aggressive black vine. The technician, completely and utterly absorbed in his task, carefully tweezered the sharpening image through the next three trays. With each transfer he leaned a little further forward, deliberately hiding it, still, at heart, the small, clever boy at the prestigious Karlsruhe Academy who would shield his impeccable schoolwork from the prying eyes of bigger, slower classmates.

The observers in the room tried to arch around him in response, each desperate for their own first look, but the diminutive man expertly blocked their every move. He didn't care who they were; he had a job to do. Only when he was completely satisfied with what he saw did the technician finally push back to lift the fully developed photograph from the last tray. Reaching up, he clipped it, with two small clothes pegs, onto the makeshift drying line strung in anticipation of that very moment.

The still-wet photograph hung above them all, soft like lychee flesh, swaying a little on the sickly air. No one in the darkroom said a word. They just stared up at it rigidly, as if brought to attention in unison.

The image was black and white, yet to its small audience it shone down through the blood-red haze with all the colors of the rainbow. It showed a mountaineer standing just a couple of steps below the pointed white apex of a mountaintop. The cloudless sky behind was almost black, yet the figure at the center seemed to faintly glow, as if surrounded by an evanescence of a whiter, brighter light.

The baggy hood of the climber's white canvas wind-jacket was thrown back. A pair of round-framed snow goggles were pushed up onto the ice-encrusted front of a fabric-peaked cap. Beneath, a woolen scarf wrapped the climber's head, but it had been pulled down from the mouth to deliberately expose an exhausted yet triumphant face.

The figure's right arm was projecting forward and upward into the sky, its mittened hand gripping the bottom of a long, wood-shafted ice axe in a straight-armed salute. The T-shaped head of the axe was high above, hooking onto the very edge of the atmosphere. Below the axe's long pick was a small flag. At the very moment the photographer released the camera's shutter, the wind must have gusted. In that fortuitous millisecond, the flag was perfectly unfurled, snapped back by the wind, its design unmistakable.

They all recognized it immediately.

PART I

A DIFFICULT DESCENT
EIN SCHWIERIGER ABSTIEG

1

MOUNT EVEREST SUMMIT PYRAMID—29,015 FEET
May 26, 2009
2:04 p.m. (Chinese Standard Time)

Nelson Tate Junior's satellite position tracker was working perfectly. The sixteen-year-old's body was not.

The tracker, a small block of orange plastic no bigger than a pack of cigarettes, was attached, as usual, on the left shoulder strap of the boy's lightweight backpack. Despite being thrust against the hard frozen snow, the unit was still silently and resolutely going about its task of communicating with invisible space hardware orbiting hundreds of miles above. Lacking either the sensors or the programming for humane distractions, it could only ignore the young heart beating as if about to burst, just a few inches behind it.

The tracker signaled relentlessly.

N 27°59'17", E 86°55'31"

The heart pulsated violently.

196 BPM ...

Elsewhere, that latest set of electronic coordinates was being transferred onto a topographical mountain map as a kite-shaped marker. Automatically, the image began popping up onto a number of computer screens around the world, its arrival completing a dotted red line that followed a graceful, linear progression up the Northeast Ridge of Mount Everest to its summit, the highest point on earth. There was still no mention of the frantically beating heart.

* * *

One screen, in particular, had been burning for hours in anticipation of that very moment. On the other side of young Nelson Tate's daytime, five and a half vertical miles lower and many thousands to the west, it was set on a fine English mahogany desk within the warm, softly lit study of his parents' palatial home.

Upon arrival of the latest marker, the pair, clad in silk pajamas and matching monogrammed cashmere robes, began calling out to the family members and guests specifically assembled to share this fantastic moment of unparalled achievement.

Nelson Tate Junior's mother, Amelia, was beside herself with worry. Even if her face had now received a little too much work to fully reveal her emotions, her voice could still betray her. It did so, cracking slightly when she shouted as loudly as she dared, "Quickly, everyone. We think he's on the summit. We're here in the study. He may call. It could be any time now. Please hurry."

The boy's father, her husband, Nelson Tate Senior, was more abrupt. "Come down! Now!

Everyone! It's on!" he bellowed. It was enough to wake the deepest sleeper.

The Tates' family and friends began to obediently shuffle into the varnished world of Senior's wood-paneled study. Ignoring the walls filled with framed photos of their host meeting statesmen and celebrities and the shelves crammed with row after row of glittering trophies recording a career of multimillion-dollar real estate deals and corporate investments, they focused only on the computer screen at its center. Drowsily positioning themselves around the room, they stared at the slowly revolving three-dimensional image of Mount Everest it displayed. In silence the assembled group contemplated the bright red trail that now led to the summit, plundering inadequate memories of ski holidays past, trying to imagine what it must be like to be up there.

How high? How cold? How windy?

None of them could have known that they would have been closer to the answers sitting on the wing of Senior's G5 as it flew them into Long Island.

Mima, the Tates' aging Puerto Rican housemaid, brought in a vintage bottle of Dom Perignon champagne perched in a silver bucket of ice. An unknowing disciple of the "butterfly effect," she gently set it on a side table, seemingly convinced that any disturbance might cause dire consequences on the top of the world. When finished, she loitered just beyond the door with an expression of deep concern, her lips reciting a silent prayer to a god with whom she was familiar.

Excitement, and thoughts warmed by the prospect of vintage champagne, began to enliven the room, generating a buzzing spiral of superlatives.

"Junior's done it!"

"He is standing on the summit of Mount Everest! Just think of that!"

"The youngest person to climb the Seven Summits!"

"The highest peak on each of the seven continents conquered! Can you believe it?"

"A new world record!"

"At sixteen!"

"No one can beat it!"

"Outstanding!"

"Congratulations, Senior."

By summiting his seventh actual mountain, Nelson Tate Junior was indeed ensuring that once again the Tate name would be in the news. The press release was already prepared, Tate Senior's publicists primed, awaiting only his signal to feed it, in a pre agreed hierarchy of exclusivity, to the media. Sitting there in the middle of the assembled group, Tate Senior began to imagine his study walls newly embellished with the framed summit photo in place of honor, flanked by others of Senior and Junior on the covers of magazines or with Letterman, Leno, even the President.

While he visualized the images, Senior's agile commercial mind was simultaneously running the financial mathematics of getting Junior up into space next. Now that was really going to cost. It would make the $500,000 summit bonus he had pledged to No Horizons, Junior's Everest expedition organizer, seem like the chump change it was—for him.

Nelson Tate Senior was looking forward to his only son's "eighth summit"—the one that no one else could possibly afford.

2

While his father contemplated whether his old friend Barney Guttman could make a currency play for him on any payment to the Russian space tourism program, Nelson Tate Junior was actually little more than an unconscious mound of yellow fabric and goose down fifteen feet directly below the highest point on earth. The boy's heavily masked, freckled face was pitched forward into the thick cap of snow, blind to the blue-black dome of unlimited sky above, to the incredible views of the mighty mountains all around him.

Released from reality and reason, his mind had fled. Denying the bitter, tooth-cracking cold; the racing, freezing wind; the rattle of the snow crystals it carried, his addled brain was telling him instead that he was in the beautiful garden of his parents' house. Convinced of soft grass under his feet and a bright sun warming his face, Nelson Tate Junior was, at that very moment, intent only on throwing an old baseball for his bulldog, Buddy …

* * *

Two thick mittens hovered for a moment above Junior's prone body before slapping themselves together and reaching down to turn the skinny kid over in a single, brisk movement.

One hand then gripped the hood of the boy's down suit, the other a shoulder strap of his rucksack, and, with a second hard pull, forcefully wrenched him up into a sitting position.

Nelson Tate Junior came to with a start, hit by successive waves of panic, nausea, and confusion.

What is this alien being, peering down with mirrored eyes, making odd, rubbery noises at me?

If he could have heard the sounds properly, the boy would have understood that Neil Quinn, No Horizons' head guide for their 2009 Everest North Expedition, was shouting, "You've done it, kid. You've done it. No time to sleep. You're on the summit of Mount Everest."

But he couldn't, and as Quinn stopped talking, Junior's head lolled to the side once more.

Quinn gave the kid a shake but to no avail.

He was out cold.

"Fuck!"

The English guide's mind pushed through its own fatigue to start issuing warnings. This was more than someone resting after the final push to the top. This was serious. Reminding himself that he had never lost a client in fifteen years of guiding, Quinn told himself to act fast if he wasn't going to now.

Quickly hunching his six-foot-four frame down from the violent gusts of wind racing over the summit pyramid, the Englishman pulled the fluorescent lime-green oxygen cylinder from the top of the kid's rucksack. He immediately tried to click out the supply wheel on the regulator valve to increase the flow. It didn't move, already screwed out to the maximum. Quinn swore again.

Shaking a gloved hand from within its heavy mitten, he used an index finger to scratch the ice from the face of the regulator's gauge. Pulling his eyes tight into the dial, he saw that it was reading no pressure. Tapping the gauge, its needle started oscillating wildly.

Is it broken or is the cylinder empty? Is there a blockage? Where?

Searching for answers, Quinn saw a heavy ice buildup, translucent and grey, hanging from the bottom of the boy's rubber facemask and encrusting the front of his down suit. The ice continued along the thin, red oxygen supply line and down the thicker corrugated tube that led to the system's clear plastic reservoir bottle. Quickly but carefully he broke away as much of it as he could and then massaged the supply tube hoping that was the problem. After that he followed the red tube back to the regulator to see if it was blocked or split further back, but he could see nothing obviously wrong.

Perhaps the bottle just slipped down within the otherwise empty rucksack and kinked the supply tube?

It was known to happen. One way or another, the boy's precious flow of supplementary oxygen must have been interrupted. Quinn had to restore it.

Pushing the kid's ski goggles up off the bridge of his nose and unhooking the straps of his oxygen mask, he pulled it away. The edges ripped from the teenager's beardless cheeks, taking ice and a little skin with them. The shock of pain, followed by the sudden cold of the freezing air on his wet mouth and teeth, instantly brought the boy back to consciousness. Nelson Tate Junior began to sob and dry-heave alternately. A blister on his lower lip split. A trickle of blood oozed out.

Quinn leaned closely into the small face. It was as white as a sheet, smeared with ice, saliva, and mucus, the only color being the crimson on his lip. The boy's eyes were glazed, lifeless. The guide snapped soundless, gloved fingers in front of them to no reaction. He couldn't understand the kid's decline. He had been going fine, slow undoubtedly, but still making good progress only forty-five minutes before. It had been the Scot on their team, Ross MacGregor, who had been struggling from the moment they left the High Camp until he turned back at Mushroom Rock.

Quinn looked around for Pemba, the Sherpa whose sole task was to accompany the boy.

Where the fuck is he?

He soon saw that Pemba too was down on the snow of the summit, sitting forward with his head between his knees. Dawa, his older brother and the expedition's sirdar, was tending to him. Above them, Quinn could see the other No Horizons client, the Swiss Yves Durand, and his Sherpa, Lhakpa, taking photos on the very summit. They seemed to be fine.

Moving his face back into the kid's, Quinn shouted at the top of his voice, "Talk to me!" The effort winded him.

The kid heaved some more. Then, looking up at Quinn, he said faintly, almost a whisper amidst more shuddering sobs, "Don't let me die."

Upon hearing it, something low in Quinn's stomach squirmed. He recognized it for what it was.

Despair.

The Englishman caught it, releasing an increasing anger to deprive it of room to grow.

"Shit! Shit! Shit! It's okay ... it's okay. I've got you."

Quinn pulled the kid into his chest and, for a moment, just hugged him close. Struggling to catch his breath from the shouting, he ordered himself to get control as he looked back again at Dawa and Pemba, asking himself once more what could have gone so wrong. Many of his clients had made that final, seemingly never-ending push up the summit ridge with little left in their tanks other than willpower, but this was crazy.

Why didn't Pemba see this coming? And what the hell is wrong with him?

Pemba was the strongest young Sherpa they had, a quadruple summiteer before his twenty-fifth birthday. He had already saved three lives on Everest.

That's why he had been assigned to the damn kid, for God's sake!

Quinn began to curse himself. He should have stuck closer to the boy even if he did have other clients up there. He should have done it, not for the money, that bloody $100,000 summit bonus that Jean-Philippe Sarron, the French owner of New Horizons Expeditions, kept harping on about, but because Nelson Tate Junior was exactly what they all called him—*a kid.*

For a second, Quinn wished he were anywhere in the world but there. Immediately acknowledging the futility of such a thought, he laid Nelson back down and went to work.

Stabbing the shaft of his axe deep into the hard, icy snow, he pulled off his own rucksack and hooked it over the axe's head to prevent it from sliding off the mountain. Kneeling between the rucksack and the kid, the guide then extracted his own oxygen cylinder, checked the pressure, and quickly dialed it up to a flow rate of four liters a minute. He pulled off his mask, bracing himself for the effects of giving up his oxygen supply, and put it over the kid's mouth as he warned himself to not be without it for too long.

Holding his mask tightly over the boy's face, he saw Dawa now moving across to him, leaving Pemba alone on the snow but sitting up unaided. At least that was a hopeful sign. Quinn watched him slowly approach, wondering what he would tell him about the young Sherpa, until his attention was pulled back to Tate Junior who was beginning to writhe and moan.

That too was a good sign.

The oxygen was reaching into the kid, bringing him back.

The boy began to mumble something.

Quinn struggled to recognize the words, but when he pulled the oxygen mask back for an instant, he understood.

"My hands. My hands. My hands," the boy repeated.

"What about your hands?"

"I can't feel them ..."

With Dawa kneeling down beside him, Quinn pointed urgently to the kid's hands.

Together they pulled off the boy's black nylon insulated mittens to reveal only the thinnest of silk under-gloves beneath.

Quinn and the veteran Sherpa immediately looked at each other in shared horror as they both understood that the boy wasn't wearing at least another pair of fleece gloves, if not two.

Quinn seized a hand and felt it.

It was rigid.

Peeling off the useless under-glove, he saw that the fingers were soapy white, each one an icicle.

Dawa pulled off the other.

It was the same.

They each began to squeeze a hand, desperate to get some movement, some warmth back into the fingers.

They remained locked solid.

Motioning to Dawa to pull the kid forward, Quinn unzipped the front of his own down suit and forced the kid's hands up and under the fleece layers inside, pushing them up as far as he could get them. He shivered as he felt the bitter cold of the frozen fingers touch his warm skin. Ignoring it, he clamped his elbows inward, squeezing the fingers into his armpits, trying to force every degree of his body heat into them.

Huddled around the boy, Quinn felt the inside of his head suddenly wallow, reality rippling. He recognized it as a warning that the dull floating sensation he was already feeling was becoming a deeper hypoxia. Without his additional oxygen supply, he was entering the gelatinous world of true high altitude where urgency fades, the body slows, and the mind drifts off into the ether.

You need your Os back, Major Tom ...

After asking Dawa to look at the kid's oxygen

system while he continued to warm the boy's hands, Quinn said, "Dawa, Pemba not okay?"

"Pemba sick, I not know, Mr. Neil," the veteran Sherpa replied, momentarily lowering his head as if shamed by his brother's infirmity. "He try for summit without using his Os for big track record, but he sick in stomach so big problem instead. Sorry, Mr. Neil. Pemba better with Os. Good now. You must worry only about boy."

A sharp hiss stopped any further discussion as Dawa broke the seal on a new cylinder by screwing it into the kid's regulator and then concentrated on checking all the parts of the supply system once again.

After several more minutes working on it, the Sherpa indicated to Quinn that it seemed to be functioning. He passed the kid's mask back. Quinn, with one hand, hooked it over his head and pulled it onto his own mouth while Dawa wedged the kid's old cylinder deep into the broken snow above Quinn's ice axe to stop it sliding away down the slope. Taking a series of long, deep breaths from the mask, Quinn felt his head lift and clear slightly. Whatever Dawa had done, it had worked.

"What was the problem?"

"Don't know, Mr. Neil. Maybe ice, maybe bad cylinder …"

"Okay, Dawa. Well done, anyway. Now let's do his hands."

Dawa pulled a white pair of knitted wool gloves from his bag and took some chemical hot packs from the cargo pocket of his bulky, insulated trousers. Tearing them open, he vigorously shook each one to bring it to life while Quinn released the boy's arms from the inside of his suit. Together they both massaged the small hands some more before working the silk under-gloves and Dawa's woolen gloves back over the stiff fingers.

Quinn took off his own heavier, thicker mittens and passed them to Dawa to drop the hot packs inside. As Quinn took the kid's thinner mittens in exchange, Dawa put the Englishman's onto the boy's damaged hands. They both knew well that there was not enough oxygen up there to fully activate the heat pads. There would be even less within the confined space of the mittens, but maybe a little heat and the thicker insulation of Quinn's gloves would reduce the severity of what was well on its way to being severe frostbite.

Tate Junior started mumbling again, more urgently. As Quinn replaced the kid's now-functioning oxygen mask and took back his own, the boy continued to try and force a word through his cracked and blistered lips.

"Pht … pht … pht …"

"Feet?" Quinn questioned.

"No. Pht …"

"What then?"

The word finally emerged.

"Photo."

Quinn's heart sank.

"Really? Just breathe the fucking Os, for Christ's sake." Quinn pushed the kid's mask hard onto his nose and mouth, pulling the elastic straps as tight as possible to secure it, hoping that it might also have the effect of shutting him up.

As Dawa turned away to return to Pemba, Quinn

shouted after him, "Dawa, get Mr. Yves and Lhakpa going down now. They got here a good time before us—too long on summit now. Down. Then you give more help to Pemba. Okay?"

The veteran Sherpa nodded as he slowly moved away.

3

Quinn got out his radio and called down to Base Camp.

"Quinn to NHBC. Over."

Sarron's hard, Gallic voice responded immediately. "Quinn? Talk to me. What's going on up there? Why haven't I heard from you? And Nelson? Are you on the summit? Over."

"We are on the summit. Repeat: on the summit. Nelson and Pemba in bad shape. Yves, Lhakpa, Dawa, myself, okay. Is Ross MacGregor safely back at High Camp? Over."

"Yes, but how bad is the kid?" The heavy French accent snapped back, any radio formalities instantly forgotten.

"Os frozen or blocked. Not sure which. No Os for last forty-five minutes. Exhaustion. Probable severe frostbite to both hands."

"*Merde!*" The shout of rage made the radio crackle and distort. "What the fuck are you doing up there, Quinn? Let me speak to him; I need to patch him through to his family in America."

Quinn looked at the barely conscious boy

slumped next to him. "Not a good idea at the moment, too weak. If he improves, we will call them on the sat phone."

He already knew there was no way he was going to make that call.

"No! You won't do it. We must make the call. I repeat: we must make the call. We need a summit photo and a call. Do you understand me, Neil Quinn? A summit photo and a call home."

"I hear you, but he's in a bad way. It's not the right thing to do."

"Fuck the right thing! You must do it!"

Quinn looked out from the summit, wondering why he was even wasting precious time having the conversation.

"Speak to me, Neil Quinn. Is he standing?" the Frenchman continued, relentless.

Quinn didn't reply, contemplating turning the radio off.

Sarron became incensed at the lack of a response. "Answer me!" he screamed as he swept a laptop computer off the communications table. It audibly clattered onto the rocky floor of the expedition's mess tent. "I said fucking well answer me!"

"No, he is not standing. Descent will be difficult. I repeat: descent will be difficult."

"Put him on the radio now!"

Quinn relented, pulling the kid's oxygen mask back down and putting the radio up to the boy's mouth. A series of uncontrollable tremors ripped through Nelson Tate's body as Quinn said, "He's on. Make it fast."

"*Bonjour*, Nelson, my young friend. You've done

it, boy. Do you hear me? We've done it! You are the youngest guy to have climbed the Seven Summits. It's a world record. We have a new world record. *Ça va? Bien,* huh?"

The kid looked confused before slurring a faint "yeah" in reply.

"We'll get you a summit photo and then get you down, okay? Want to call your parents at home, kid?"

"Home?" the boy questioned pleadingly, looking to Quinn as if he had the power to instantly make it happen.

Before Quinn could say anything in reply, there was a burst of interference from the radio receiver followed by a repeated, "Hello. Hello. Hello."

Sarron had patched them through to the kid's family in America, regardless.

"*Bonsoir*, Long Island. This is Jean-Philippe Sarron speaking, your Everest expedition leader. Are you ready?" There was a pause, then Sarron screamed at the top of his voice, "Well, here it is. SUUUUUMIIIIIT!" He drew the word on and on, in a never-ending howl, as if commentating on a last-minute goal in a Paris Saint-Germain soccer match.

A distant yet equally prolonged cheer went up in staticky reply.

"Neil Quinn, tell us all, *mon ami*, what is it like up there today on the top of the world?"

Quinn groaned inwardly, before being compelled by the return of silence to speak into the radio. "Hello, everyone. This is Neil Quinn here with Nelson, giving you a late-night call from the highest point on earth. We are on the summit of Mount Everest. I repeat: we are on the summit of Mount Everest!"

The radio distorted yet again as another cheer went up from the assembled group in Tate Senior's study. From amidst the cacophony, a deep, languid voice began to speak. "Thank you, Mr. Quinn. Good job, sir. How are you, Junior? What's the view like from up there? Can you see us all down here?" The voice became a self-satisfied laugh as a champagne cork popped loudly in the background.

Against his better judgment, Quinn held the radio up to the kid who, after a long pause, said only, "Buddy?"

"What was that, Junior?" came the immediate reply.

The kid said nothing more.

"Daddy, I think he's asking to speak to his dog," a shrill voice said in the background followed by some laughter.

It abruptly stopped.

"Nelson, do you hear me? How are you, boy? What's going on up there?" Tate Senior's voice tightened with urgency as his questioning accelerated.

The kid, silent, just looked down at the snow as Quinn quickly took back the radio.

Steeling himself to sound confident, he said, "Don't worry. We are doing fine up here. A bit tired but all good. Don't worry. Nelson's …"

Sarron cut back in. "Well, there you are, Mr. Tate: a call from the top of the world. Just some photos now, and then we will get your boy back down safe and sound. I will call you again in a few minutes for a fuller update after I am sure we are getting Nelson some *fantastique* summit photos."

With a sharp click, the line was cut. A second later, Sarron's voice screamed out again from Quinn's receiver, "Get that fucking summit photo, Quinn, then get him down fast! If he loses his fingers, you'll be responsible, all of you up there! I'll fucking see to it that none of you ever work on Everest again!"

The radio fell silent.

Neil Quinn looked at Dawa, who had moved back alongside him to listen to the call.

Slowly shaking his head as Dawa shrugged his shoulders in return, the Englishman asked, "How is Pemba now?"

"He good to go down. I help you do photo quick."

"Okay."

Quinn unclipped his pack from his ice axe, put it back on, adjusted the routing of his oxygen supply tube and then, together with the Sherpa, got the boy to his feet. They each took an arm to drag Nelson Tate Junior to the very top of the world, passing Yves Durrand and Lhakpa Sherpa with a nod of acknowledgement as they began their own descent.

Quinn and Dawa put the boy down amidst the multicolored jumble of prayer flags, tattered climb banners, laminated photos of loved ones, and discarded oxygen cylinders that litter the summit every spring. The Sherpa sat alongside, supporting the boy with an arm around his shoulders. Quinn pulled up the kid's goggles to expose as much of his pale face as he dared before reaching to the side of the kid's rucksack to tug the boy's short, titanium ice axe from the pack's side compression straps. He unwound the small white nylon flag that was attached to it before planting the shaft of the axe into the ice in front of the boy. Dawa reached his free hand forward to pull the flag's one-foot-by-two-foot rectangle taut. Extended, the little flag showed a line drawing of seven ascending triangles across the top with "7 @ 16" written in bold numbers beneath. Below that it read, "Mount Everest, 2009" and, lower still, "www.TatePrivateEquity.com."

Pulling a small digital camera from within the innermost layers of his clothing, Quinn stepped back and took photo after photo until the camera's battery, depleted by the cold, finally gave up the ghost. It was Neil Quinn's ninth time on the summit of Mount Everest, Dawa Sherpa's sixteenth.

4

THE PAZNAUN VALLEY, SOUTHWEST AUSTRIA
October 1, 1938
8:53 p.m. (Mitteleuropäische Zeit)

Fat raindrops started to fall, each landing with a slap on the rough-hewn stone tiles of the cowshed. Pulling up the hood of his army mountain jacket, Josef Becker quickly turned for shelter as the wet splashes accelerated to a continuous drumroll, rods of water stabbing the back of his jacket until he could push himself into the low building's entrance. The young German squatted inside, leaning back against the old door, its iron bolt heads pushing against his spine as he looked out.

The rain is finally arriving. Gunter told us to expect it.

The raindrops splashed and ricocheted, the cowshed's paddock briefly emitting the wet, sour smell of cow dung and straw before all scent was lost to the cold, metallic wash of the downpour. Beyond, the grey opening that notched the black tree line, the entrance to the track from the valley road he had been watching, disappeared, pushed into the darkness behind black sheets of rain. The only things now visible to Josef were the puddles growing in front of him, pooling and merging until they released urgent, bubbling streams of rainwater to race away down the slope of the hill. He knew they would instinctively seek the two wheel grooves of the unpaved track that led up through the woods.

Would the truck even be able to make it up the hill?

It was suddenly colder too. Josef cupped his hands together. Blowing into them, a tattered cloud of warm breath puffed out from between his fingers only to instantly dissolve in the saturated air.

What must be happening higher up?

Snow above fifteen hundred meters was the forecast. Josef shivered at the thought of it—or was it nerves?

Looking at his watch, he saw there were still five minutes to go. Shielding a match in his wet hands, he lit another Stürm cigarette. Inhaling deeply, he savored the bone-dry paper of the cigarette on his lips and the heat of its smoke, even if he disliked the harsh taste. The party leadership claimed to want to stop smoking, yet the SA now monopolized the sale of all cigarettes to the Wehrmacht—more nonsense from Berlin. Trommler, Neue Front, Stürm, they were all the same, cheap and bitter like the people that promoted them. It was no wonder the demand for contraband foreign cigarettes was so strong.

Josef watched his cigarette's orange burn defy the cold logic of the rain. It told him to do the same.

Gunter always said that any man who went into the mountains without being nervous was as good as dead anyway.

A sudden braying from behind the door made him jump.

Too nervous, perhaps?

Settle down, it's only the rattle of the rain disturbing the mules.

Again, Josef looked down at his watch for reassurance.

Maybe they're going to be late.

Perhaps they've already been caught.

It had happened once before. That night, the truck simply never arrived. The three of them had waited for two extra hours, hiding in bushes to the side of the rendezvous building in case their cover was blown. When no one appeared, they still made the trip over the hills to bring the return goods back before dawn. They had really flown that night to make up for the time lost waiting. Josef enjoyed how fast they could go when they were alone. It reminded him of the days when they were boys living in Elmau, and nothing or no one could stop them in the hills above.

The body of the cigarette, absorbing the moisture from his wet fingertips, disintegrated. Josef flicked it away to fizz and die in a puddle still vibrating from the rain. Its companionship lost, Josef let the doorway's small shelter give him a faint sense of security instead, as if he were hidden behind a waterfall, invisible within a place that no one else even knew existed. The sensation settled him and he began to think again about that climb of the Waxenstein he had made the month before, replaying that small patch of unyielding, crystalline rock that had unfolded its upward story centimeters from the tip of his nose.

Even there, crouched in that cramped doorway,

looking out on that slippery, wet night, he could feel his fingers tightly pinching the smallest bumps and folds of the cliff's dry granite, his toes scratching for purchase on the tiniest edges below. No rope, no climbing partner, no possibility for second thoughts, no deciding to simply stop and descend. One way only: up. Just remembering it made Josef's breathing instinctively slow and his mind relax.

He smiled to himself at the memory of the celebrations when he'd returned to the barracks that evening. The men of the 99th Gebirgsjäger, his regiment, had huddled around, congratulating him as he parked his pride and joy, his new BMW motorcycle, and unloaded his small climbing pack from its rear rack. They had immediately walked him into Garmisch to buy tall steins of cloudy *weissbier* and toast him as they recounted how they had followed his every move through their binoculars. They shouted, one over the other, of how it was the most incredible feat of climbing they had ever seen, of how every second they thought he must surely fall, of how, alone, Josef Becker had conquered the one mountain face that everyone had thought impossible. Oberjäger Hubel said that even Generalmajor Ganzler himself had called for a telescope to follow Josef's progress.

It had never crossed Josef's mind that anyone might be watching him. He had only gone out to make that climb because he had a free training day and was so sick and tired of looking up at the sheer rocky wall from the monotony of drill on the 1st Division parade ground. There was only one way to find out if it really was unclimbable. The very same thought he'd casually let slip to the guards that manned the red and white pole across the camp gateway as he left on his motorcycle.

Initially, Josef found the attention slightly alarming, but then, aided by the beer, he started to enjoy it. It was only when he returned to the barracks later and Gunter and Kurt sought him out that his personal spell of glory was broken.

Gunter was furious, growling at him in their Bavarian dialect, "You fool. If you let everyone see you can climb like that then they will always be watching. You know what that will mean for you, for all three of us, sooner or later? I already told you buying that damn motorcycle was a mistake—too obvious that you were making extra money—but now this? You need to get back into the shadows, my boy, or we will all be taking the long fall, not just you."

Three days later, to potentially make matters worse, a small box was delivered to Josef by Generalmajor Ganzler's adjutant. A handwritten note from Ganzler himself accompanied it:

> *To the finest climber in Bavaria. Bravo! Your first ascent of the Waxenstein wall has inspired the entire regiment. Yet more proof that the* Gebirgsjäger *are the finest mountain troops in the world. Wear this with pride—you are worthy of it!*

Josef never mentioned it to Gunter and Kurt, suspending the silver regimental ring that Ganzler had awarded him on the cord of his army identification tag, out of sight.

Thinking about it again, Josef reached down into

the collar of his shirt and felt for the cord to pull the ring up into his fingers. He touched its relief of a single edelweiss flower to bring him luck.

Almost immediately a light briefly flashed in the rainy darkness below. It reappeared to split into two narrow beams that began to intermittently twist and turn within the black of the woods. Through the beating rain, Josef heard bursts of an engine revving frantically accompanied by the helical whine of tires spinning for grip.

They were arriving.

5

Letting his lucky ring fall back beneath his shirt, Josef clenched his fist and thumped backward three times on the door, alerting the other two that it was time. He felt the door move, opening inward a crack. Without turning, Josef quietly said, "The truck is coming up the hill."

"Usual drill, Josef," Gunter's voice rasped in whispered reply. "Check the driver; seven-two-four, remember? Then get the travelers inside as quickly as you can. There will be nine. As little noise as possible. Don't forget to cover your face."

The three-ton Opel truck burst from between the trees out into the rain. A flash of lightning, higher up the hill, illuminated its driver wrestling with the steering wheel, trying to gain as much momentum as possible to make a fast, splashing loop around the clearing before the mud and wet grass could catch the truck's wheels and stop it from turning back down the hill. Tires spinning, windshield wipers beating frantically, a jet of grey smoke thrusting from its exhaust, the dark vehicle almost toppled over onto its side before it came to a rest, facing back down the hill at the edge of the woods, engine running.

Josef pulled his scarf up over his nose and felt his heavy, studded mountain boots squash into the wet mud as he stepped out from the doorway to run down to it. At the mountain soldier's approach, a shadowed head hidden beneath a black fedora leaned from the truck window.

"Are you a true German?" the driver instantly demanded.

Josef knew the routine.

"Yes, I am blond like Hitler—*seven*—slim like Göring—*two*—and strong like Goebbels—*four*." He shouted the answer back quickly, projecting his voice up through the scarf and the rain to be heard over the loud engine. The joke was easy to remember; it was Gunter's favorite, but he had to be careful to insert the numbers correctly as they were different every time. Even as he spoke, the driver stroked the accelerator, keeping the engine's revs up, primed to immediately escape if a single word or number of the response was wrong.

"How many travelers are you expecting?"

"Nine."

Satisfied with Josef's replies, the driver quickly turned off the engine and stepped down from the cab. Without looking Josef in the eye, he shook his hand and together they splashed around to the double cargo doors at the rear. A hidden colleague from the other side of the cab met them there, the two of them unfastening the rear cargo doors and pulling them open. Inside, Becker saw nothing but a wall of stacked wooden crates that gave off an overpowering smell of goat's cheese.

The driver pulled himself up onto the edge of the truck body and started pushing at the lowest row of boxes. A small opening appeared. Taking an electric light out of his pocket, the man removed his hat to push his head and shoulders deep into the little tunnel. There was a brief flash of illumination and voices from within before the driver awkwardly backed himself out again. A moment later, a worn cardboard suitcase jerkily slid its way out of the opening. Following it came the black form of a thin man, squeezing himself out from between the crates on his stomach.

The driver's partner helped the man down from the back of the truck, his feet dropping heavily into the sodden ground. He had difficulty standing, still bent and stiff from the cramped confinement of his journey. With a groan, he reached up and held his forehead. Josef thought he must have knocked it during the truck's violent arrival but he could see no blood. Gradually the man straightened himself up, but when he pulled his hand away from his bruised head, his tired, lined face reacted with horror at the sight of the Wehrmacht insignia on Josef's uniform. He tried to say something, a stutter of fear overwhelming any words.

The driver instantly motioned him to be silent, saying through clenched teeth, "I told you they would be soldiers. It's not important. You need to get moving. We haven't got all night."

Josef nodded in agreement, pointing the man up the hill to the cowshed, its opened door now edged in yellow from a lamp lit within.

The small man didn't move, as if stuck in the mud. Oblivious to the heavy rain pouring onto his thin hair and overcoat, he was completely paralyzed by the sight of the eagle and the swastika on the front of Josef's field cap.

"But you ... you ... you are a Nazi soldier?" he finally said in a Viennese accent, shaking his head in disbelief.

Josef put an index finger up to his covered mouth. "No questions. You need to be quiet from now on. I am here to take you over the hills. Just go up to that building. We will talk inside."

The man tried to say something more but then refrained, visibly diminishing as if the rain were shrinking him. Hanging his head, he pulled his feet from the wet mud and lifted his pathetic suitcase to slog his way up the sodden hill. The man walked slowly despite the downpour, a figure of meek surrender to whatever fate he now imagined awaited him within that shadowy farm building.

Josef watched him go, shaking his head in disbelief at the fugitive's light leather dress shoes and thin, black cotton overcoat. They would be soaked through before he even made it to the building. It was going to be a long, cold night for that man, for them all, in fact.

6

Over the next five minutes, Josef watched eight more frightened faces burrow out from within the packing cases. They were all Austrian Jews. Josef had heard that since the *Anschluss* at the end of March, life was now as difficult for them there as it had been for many years in Germany. In fact most of their transports were Austrian now; the majority of German Jews that could leave had already gone.

Of the nine that evening, two were children: girls, one of about six or seven, the other slightly older, ten or eleven, perhaps. Of the adults, four men and three women, only two were elderly, in their sixties or more. Josef was relieved to see they were still quite mobile. It was the old ones who were always the most difficult to get over the mountains. He wondered if it was an extended family group, but he couldn't be sure. He knew nothing about them. It was Gunter who dealt with the details of each run over the hills. Josef only knew the coded phrase for the driver and the number to expect. He had been told to expect nine, to tell the driver it was nine, and nine it now was.

We must go.

Josef briefly shook the hand of the driver again then watched the truck silently roll away, the driver letting gravity pull it back toward the trees where its engine coughed into life. The sight and sound of the departing truck left Josef with a momentary spasm of loneliness that he had to fight to shake off as he hurried to catch up with the group filing up the hill to the cowshed.

When he reached them, the youngest child shied away from him, slipping and falling sideways out of the line. Josef stepped forward to help her up, but one of the men, possibly her father, got to her first.

"Don't touch her, German," he spat at Josef, stepping in front of him and wrenching the little girl up from the wet ground. Back onto her feet, the child, covered with a thick scum of soil, started to cry, beating at the man with tiny, clenched fists.

In response she was tugged forward roughly, without regard to the fact that one of her feet had emerged shoeless from the sucking ground. This made her cry even more, her screams becoming so hysterical that Josef instantly pushed past the man to snatch the struggling girl up under one arm. Clamping his other hand over the little girl's mouth, he hissed at the man, "Get her shoe and follow me quickly!"

Josef ran with her up the slope toward the cowshed, the tiny, muddy girl flexing and coiling in his grip like an earthworm in the beak of a bird until he could thrust her in through the doorway. Released inside, she started wailing again.

"Shut up!" Kurt shouted from the back of the

shed, breaking his customary reticence to speak. It did no good until one of the Jewish women arrived to seize the little girl, telling her to be quiet and pulling the child tightly into her wet clothes to smother her sobs.

The remainder of the group entered the simple stone building. When the man handed back her shoe the girl turned to him and, taking the shoe, lashed out at him with its muddy heel, starting to howl all over again.

A different, rougher voice commanded, "*Silence her. Immediately,*" prompting the woman to say forcefully, "Ilsa Rosenberg, that's enough," and clamp her own hand over the distraught child's mouth.

The Jews clustered, fearful of the dark silhouettes before them. Gunter Schirnhoffer was deliberately standing in front of a kerosene lamp set in an alcove in the rear wall of the shed, his long shadow slicing into the dirt floor at their feet. Kurt Müller was crouched to his right, also in outline, hunched over, angling his own masked face downward, using the light of the lamp to cut a tent canvas into long thin strips with a hunting knife. Its razor-sharp edge caught the reflection of the yellow light as it scythed through the material. On his other side were two mules, already in harnesses, shuffling from side to side in one of the cow-milking stalls, twitchy and skittish at all the disturbance.

Josef quickly moved alongside Kurt and squatted down into the shadows as Gunter began to address the new arrivals.

"You must all listen to me very carefully."

Standing in a wide-eyed semicircle before him, the travelers did as they were told.

"There is no time for long speeches or even for me to repeat myself. We are three. We are neither your enemies nor your friends. You will never know our names or see our faces. We are dressed as soldiers, but to you we are simply mountain guides who will lead you into Switzerland. All you need to think about is that you are just ten kilometers away from freedom."

The Jews looked at each other, nervously excited at the thought of such proximity to escape, until Gunter broke the spell with his customary warning.

"But, mark my words, they are not easy kilometers. We will be going over the border on an old smugglers' track. It is long, always steep, at places narrow, and difficult. At the top, if you fall, you will have time to wish you were dead before you hit the ground."

Gunter paused for effect.

"Follow our steps, and make them your own," he then continued. "We are good climbers. We know the way like the backs of our hands, even in the dark. We will help you as much as we can. You will need to grit your teeth and suffer in silence. For the oldest or the smallest—you choose—we have two mules to carry you at the beginning, but the mules can't do the final section over the rocks. At that point everyone will be on their own feet. Let me look at them."

The nine were momentarily confused, forcing Gunter to raise his voice.

"I have already said that I don't want to have to repeat myself. Each of you, show me your feet, your shoes. I need to see what you have got on your feet."

The Jews looked at each other again, this time quizzically, until one lifted his leg and pushed forward a foot. The others followed his example as Gunter took the lamp from the wall behind him to look along the row of thin, smooth-soled shoes and low, leather ankle boots caked in wet mud that were now pointing at him.

"*Scheisse!*" he swore. "As always. Every time I tell him they must send you in boots, in something heavy, and every time it is like this. It is a bad night out there. The ground will be very wet. There will be fresh snow higher up. *Scheisse!* These shoes are useless. Each of you must take two strips of canvas from that man there."

Gunter pointed to Kurt, who was sheathing his knife, gesturing him to throw a strip of the cut canvas, which he caught in one hand. Holding it out in front of him, he began to twist the length of material tightly. "Watch what I am doing. Twist the strips tight like this until they make a cord, and then bind them around your feet. It will help your feet grip, protect them a little. Adults, help the children. They need to be tied tightly."

He turned to point to a corner of the shed. "You will find some long sticks and blankets there. Adults take one of each, and two extra blankets for the children. Keep them rolled up for now to keep them dry. You will need them higher on the hill when we move above the rain into the snow. It is going to get cold up there. When it does, you must keep moving your fingers and your toes all the time to keep the blood flowing, like this." He held out one hand, rapidly opening and closing his fingers in demonstration. "The sticks will help you keep your balance. If you have brought anything that you can't carry on your back then you will leave it behind—but not here. We will throw it into the woods on the way up the hill."

The group remained motionless, rendered mute

by the brisk instructions, equally afraid of the coarse soldier in front of them and the unknown journey ahead. Ilsa, the little girl who had fallen into the mud, was quiet now, instead staring intently at Josef, concentrating every hatred her small mind could conceive onto his hidden face. He winked at her in return as Gunter told him and Kurt to help the travelers get ready. The girl snapped her head away with a grimace of disgust.

While the three mountain troopers worked to ready the Jews for the arduous journey ahead, Gunter continued to brief them. "Once we leave this hut, there is to be no talking, no lights, no flames, no cigarettes, nothing but walking. We will go at a slow but even pace. We will stop every thirty minutes for five minutes. Every hour we will stop for ten more. You cannot stop in between, or we will take too long. On the top of the ridge is a small chapel. There we can stop for a longer rest, to warm up and prepare for the final, most difficult section. The entire journey will take about six to seven hours if you do as I say. If you have any questions, save them. There is nothing more that is helpful for you to know. Just concentrate on putting one foot in front of the other, and take comfort in the fact that we are paid much less if we don't get all nine of you to the other side. We will go in five minutes."

7

THE SUMMIT OF MOUNT EVEREST—29,029 FEET
May 26, 2009
2:41 p.m.

The dead camera terminated the summit-photo farce.

Quinn burned with a fury at the whole performance but it gave him no warmth.

The cold was biting hard now.

As he zipped the small silver camera back into an inside pocket of his thick down suit, he imagined instead just flinging it off the summit. He visualized it spinning out into the wispy air and then plummeting ten thousand feet straight down into Sarron's thick skull. Although the thought was faintly pleasing, he ordered himself to stop wasting precious energy, and time, on nonsense.

Pushing into the layers of fabric around his wrist, Quinn sought the familiar face of his battered Rolex. It was nearly 2:45 p.m., Chinese time, a little past midday if you used the more logical Nepali time zone for exactly the same place, the border of the two countries meeting as they did beneath his feet. It was hovering on being the latest that you would want to be up there but not crazy. Still, they needed to get going.

Helping the semiconscious Nelson Tate Junior back down from the very top, Quinn sat him on the snow and went to work again, trying to prepare him for a fighting chance at the descent.

There wasn't much more that could be done for the boy's fingers. That would have to come later at a lower camp and, when it did, it was going to be excruciatingly painful. No, for now it was all about mobility, about just being able to put one foot in front of the other.

High oxygen flow, a dribble of juice from the only unfrozen bottle Quinn and Dawa could muster between them, and a handful of ibuprofen seemed to perk the lad up a little.

Quinn hoped it would be enough as he moved away to radio Sarron that they were about to head down.

Hearing Quinn's call sign, the Frenchman immediately responded with another tirade of insults.

"Shut it," Quinn spat back into the radio, his patience exhausted. Turning his back firmly on the boy, he added in a quieter voice, "I suggest, Sarron, that you save your crap for if we get down, and use your energy to focus on the word *if*. We are talking about the boy's survival now, not his bloody fingers. You need to get to work on mobilizing all the help you can get for us from anyone you can find up at High Camp."

There was a long silence followed by a slow,

precise reply. "Okay, Neil Quinn, so be it. I will do what I can for the sake of the boy, but understand me, and understand me well: if it is as you say then this is a disaster for me, and your problems will most definitely not be over even if you do make it down."

Quinn switched off the radio. He'd done what he could with Sarron.

Standing there, he instead took stock of himself for the coming descent. He was cold, slightly too cold, in fact. Summit-tired also, that was inevitable, but reasonably fit and lucid now that he had his own oxygen system back. Sucking in some more deep breaths, Quinn tried to run some mental estimates on how much oxygen they had left between them on the summit and cached further down the ridge at Mushroom Rock. A precise answer eluded him— *maybe not so lucid*—but he thought it was enough.

He looked out from the summit. The cloud that earlier had been hanging lower down the North Face had thinned. To his left, Changtse peak was now almost totally clear. Beyond it, he could see clearly down into the widening valleys of the Rongbuk Glaciers, highways of broken white ice and rocky brown moraine that curved away from the mountain like wide rivers of foamy, milky coffee. They were all good signs that the stable weather was going to hold. He looked back up and across to the huge mass of Cho Oyu, the sixth-highest mountain in the world and, still further, to a white bump on the curving horizon, Shishapangma, the highest mountain in Tibet. He had climbed both.

Will I do so again or will this be the day when I don't make it down?

The unwanted question shocked him. Quickly turning away from the two mountains to put such doubts from his mind, his eyes trailed down the Northeast Ridge. As he did so, the cold made him shudder violently, or was it the thought of having to get the boy all the way back down that narrow path of loose rock, slick ice, and broken snow? It had never appeared more exposed or treacherous.

Shit, this is going to be a difficult descent.

From his vantage point high above, Quinn could easily pick out the biggest obstacles to their survival, the three places, or *steps,* where the layered slabs of the mountain broke free, jutting out from the line of the hill before stepping down abruptly.

Each was a barrier to their safe return, particularly the second. Situated at just over 28,200 feet, the Second Step was the northern guardian of Everest's summit, a place always in shadow, dark and therefore bitterly cold, riven with ice. It jutted out over the rocky North Face like a section of shattered roof, an explosion of exposed beams and loose tiles.

The crux was near its top—a twenty-foot-high, nearly sheer face of rock split by a vertical crack that had become littered with a spaghetti of fixed ropes and an old ladder. For the Everest climber loaded with an oxygen system, vision obscured, hands muffled, feet numb, mind deadened by the extreme altitude and exertion, it was the most difficult moment of the entire north-side climb—a challenge to the fit and motivated on the way up, an accident waiting to happen for the exhausted and careless on the way down.

Pushing thoughts of having to descend the Second Step out of his mind with a hasty we'll-cross-it-when-we-come-to-it resolution, Quinn looked instead for Dawa, to tell him that it was time to go.

The Sherpa was taking his own final moment on the summit. He stood out against the bright sky, the front of his old climbing jacket patched like New York asphalt with the sponsors' badges from countless previous climbs, each paid for by some corporate desk jockey seeking to brand this man's hard, dangerous career as somehow representative of his own. It wasn't.

Quinn watched as Dawa knelt to tie a string of prayer flags. When released, they immediately flicked out in a dancing trail of color, snapping and twisting in the air, flying out over the immense Kangshung face, energetically ignorant of the immense void below. The Sherpa then stood up and cast a hand to the wind, throwing rice to bring luck to their descent.

Boy, are we going to need it.

That rice would have been blessed by a Buddhist monk; maybe even by the Dalai Lama himself. With each cast, Dawa would be chanting, *"Tse tso. Tse tso,"* beseeching the Mother Goddess of the mountain for a long life still to come. He would then settle into the mantra, *"Om mani padme hum,"* for protection. Quinn often heard the Sherpas reciting it over and over again on the most difficult sections of the mountains. They would mumble it without pause, pushing its continuous sound up into their noses so that it sounded like the faint buzzing of bees.

Seeing Quinn looking at him, Dawa signaled that he should go before pointing to himself and then across at Pemba, giving a thumbs-up sign to show they would be okay. Reassured, Quinn quickly turned his attention back to the kid. Starting his own less spiritual mantra of descent, he said to himself, "Concentrate. Concentrate. Concentrate," as he pulled Nelson Tate Junior up onto his feet.

To his relief, the boy remained standing.

He checked the kid's oxygen system once more before grabbing him by the shoulders and staring closely into his masked face.

"Look at me," Quinn commanded. "Now's the time. We are going down. You can do this. You are going to get down. It isn't a summit until you get back down, do you understand me? Just concentrate. Concentrate on every step. I'll be close to you all the way. Concentrate. Concentrate. Concentrate. Have you got it?"

The kid nodded weakly.

"I said, 'Have you got it?'"

"Yes," came the faint reply.

"Good."

Quinn bent down to retrieve his ice axe, pushed deep into the snow at the spot where he first tended to the boy, the kid's empty oxygen cylinder still pinned underneath its pick.

A tug on his arm suddenly stopped him.

He turned back up to see the kid slapping at the zip of his own breast pocket with his mittened hand.

What the hell is it now?

Quinn freed the pocket's zip of ice and reached a gloved hand inside to find what felt like a wide-studded strap.

Tugging it out, he saw that it was a collar—a thick, studded, leather dog collar.

The kid looked up into Quinn's face and said, "For Buddy ... for the summit ... I promised."

"Christ, there's no time for any more of this crap," Quinn replied, shaking his head and glancing up at the heavens as if making a direct appeal to Him for help. A glimmer of optimism returned in the thought that the kid was at least functioning enough to remember his promise. It told Quinn to humor him.

Maybe it will inspire him to get down, Quinn told himself as he moved as quickly as he could back up toward the summit pile to hang the collar over an aluminium snow-stake jutting from the snow. Looping it over the metal spike, Quinn noticed it already bore the pale blue rosary beads of a previous summiteer. Even though the new pairing seemed faintly sacrilegious, he pointed to the kid where the collar was now and then downward, urging him to really get going this time.

Nelson Tate Junior slowly turned down the slope.

Quinn followed.

The kid made it about ten steps before he crumpled into the snow.

Quinn pulled him back up.

After fifteen more steps, he stopped again and just sat.

Quinn dragged him to his feet once more, this time starting to bully him. "Stay on your feet, whatever you do. Move slowly if you have to, but don't fucking stop. Don't sit either. Every time you have to get back up, it'll tire you more than if you just kept going. Think of your family. Think of your bloody dog. Think of anything you fucking want to get off this hill, but do not think about stopping unless I tell you to. You have got to keep moving or ..." He stopped himself short from finishing the sentence with, "*you will die.*"

While he berated him, Quinn pulled a coil of purple rope out of his pack and tied it between their waist harnesses. He looped as much excess rope as possible over a shoulder and then tied that off too, in order to keep the kid on the tightest rein possible. Holding him on such a short rope would at least give Quinn some control over the boy's movements.

The combination of the talk and the rope seemed to work.

The boy stayed on his feet as he shakily descended the remainder of the final snow crest. From there they slowly made their way down and around the exposed thirty-five-degree rock traverse that led down to the next steep snow section.

As they stepped heavily from the rocks back onto the snow, Quinn remembered with a jolt like an electric shock that he had left his ice axe on the summit.

Fucking dog collar.

There was no going back for the axe. He immediately tried to radio Dawa, hoping he could still bring it, but there was no reply.

His next hope was to God that he wasn't going to need that axe, but he already knew that, sooner or later, he would.

8

Despite a few knocks, Neil Quinn and Nelson Tate Junior descended the Third Step in reasonable shape. The smallest of the three, it was only about thirty feet high, more of a scramble down over jagged rocks than an actual drop.

The rock-strewn plateau beyond was wider, easier going at the expense of being much more exposed to the wind. Quinn pushed them both on, over the uneven gravel and stones, his eyes fixed on the swaying yellow form stumbling ahead of him on its umbilical cord of purple rope. The kid's sharp crampons, in their wayward struggles to find grip on the rocks of the Third Step, had caught and ripped the gaiters on his boots, the metal teeth slicing into the legs of the down suit beneath. With each heavy step, Quinn watched as feathers curled from the tears like toothpaste before fluffing out to be torn away by the wind. Above, he could see the boy's hands hanging heavily to his sides, fingers frozen and useless. He was probably going to lose most of them.

Not good. Not good at all.

Putting aside thoughts of the inevitable mess that was going to cause, Quinn concentrated instead on the approaching Second Step. This time he had no choice but to think about how they were going to down-climb it.

On the way up, Dawa and Lhakpa had fixed it with a new length of yellow nylon rope. Normally on descent, it would just be a case of clipping onto that line and slowly rappelling down, using the rungs of the old ladder that lined part of the route as steps. It required good hand control to manipulate the metal descender on the rope, leg strength to make good each step, and an ability to concentrate on the job at hand despite hanging over a ten-thousand-foot drop. It didn't take the blast of fierce wind that slammed the kid to his knees once more to prove to Quinn that Nelson Tate Junior no longer had any of these abilities.

Struggling to pull the boy onto his feet, Quinn looked back up the hill for help, searching for any sign of Dawa and Pemba. There was none. Dawa's radio was still silent. Perhaps Pemba was struggling once again. Perhaps the batteries of the radio were dead. Whatever the problem, it was too cold to wait, especially with the kid already suffering frostbite.

What particularly worried Quinn was that he had no confidence the boy could work a descender down that length of fixed line. Any slip would be fatal. His only option was to hold the boy on the end of the purple rope and lower him from an anchor until he reached the small ledge that jutted out below the rock wall. Once there, the kid could wait while Quinn followed him down. It was not elegant, but at the very least it would give him some control over where the boy was going. He knew he was pushing his luck, but he had little alternative; it was time to improvise.

Carefully Quinn helped the boy down over the dangerous, broken rock slabs that led to the top of the Second Step before stopping him at the edge. There, clipping the kid tightly to the yellow rope and making him sit, Quinn pushed himself out to look down the upper part of the cliff to check the line down. The world below fell away, a never-ending plunge down the scaly black-and-white slope to the glacier far, far below. It took what remained of his breath with it.

Turning back into the hill, Quinn focused on fixing a secure anchor from which to suspend the boy. To one side he saw an old metal piton firmly driven into the rock. The rough-hewn nail was as black as the ages-old rock that held it, as if it too had been there forever. He hooked a carabiner into the eye of the piton. However hard he pulled, it refused to move. It was solid.

While Quinn assembled the rope's anchor, the kid lay slumped on the ground beside him. The Englishman began to bully him with the details of how he was going to get down, shouting at the boy about how this was it, the only real obstacle now between him and his home, his parents, his dog, and this time he said it—*the rest of his life.*

When everything was ready and Quinn signaled that he could go, the kid weakly got to his knees and then his feet.

Swaying, he slowly turned around to look back at Quinn, leaning out on the rope until it tensioned.

"Concentrate, okay?"

With a nod, Nelson Tate Junior began to step blindly back, slowly vanishing from sight over the edge.

Gusts of wind ripped at Quinn, drilling the cold into his core as he waited above the sheer rock, gently paying out the rope.

Time passed.

When Quinn felt a light tugging on the rope, he knew that the boy was maneuvering himself onto the top of the ladder.

Slowly, he let more of the purple rope slip through the locking device secured into the old piton so the boy could keep descending.

It's working.

Quinn willed the kid on, telling him to go, repeating the word between every labored breath.

"Go. Go. GO!"

About halfway down, Nelson Tate Junior caught his right crampon on some old rope that was wound around the ladder.

He tried to kick his foot free.

Once.

Twice.

On the third kick, the sudden momentum of the crampon's release caused the kid to lose his balance.

Toppling to the side, he swung out and to the right of the ladder, crashing hard into the side of the mountain and dislodging a fall of snow and loose rock.

Quinn saw none of it but felt it all.

The purple rope slammed downward, ripping through his mittens until jamming in the viselike grip of the belay anchor.

All he could do was lean back against the side of the mountain and hold the stretching rope with all his remaining strength, heart pulsing in his throat as if tugged up into it by the purple cord.

Quinn tried to see what was happening, but he couldn't move forward enough to see down to the suspended boy. He shouted out to him, screaming at him to answer, to tell him what was happening, but there were no sounds in reply, only the rasp of his own frantic breathing shooting backward and forward like a hacksaw through metal.

An eternity passed in minutes.

Quinn began deliberately sucking in more air, preparing himself to move so he could help the kid.

But, to his surprise, just as he readied himself to get up, the tension on the rope relaxed a little.

It felt as if the boy was pulling himself back onto the ladder.

The rope tensioned once more.

The boy was actually continuing to descend.

Quinn couldn't believe it.

He paid out more rope until it stopped again.

This time Quinn felt a faint yet distinct series of pulls that told him that the kid must have made it to the small snow slope that lay at the bottom of the rock face.

Double-checking that he was clipped into the yellow fixed rope that ran down over the step, Quinn unhooked the purple rope from the security of the old metal piton and moved to the edge of the step.

Directly below him the boy was indeed standing on the ledge, leaning in against the sheer rock, waiting.

Quinn started to make his own way down, gathering in the purple rope as he went.

When he too reached the ladder, snow and rocks,

loose from where the kid had swung against them, started to fall to the side of him.

Each time, Quinn instinctively huddled against the metal frame, pushing his face into its worn rungs, close enough to see the scratches and scrapes from the hundreds of pairs of sharp crampons that had worked their way up and down it over the years. When the falls stopped he slowly continued, focusing everything he had on getting to the bottom of that rock face.

Finally sensing he was near, Quinn began to prepare for the uneven step down off the ladder.

A sharp skidding noise from above caused him to momentarily look up.

Then there was nothing.

* * *

When Neil Quinn came to consciousness, he was lying facedown on the sloping snow ledge.

His goggles and oxygen mask were pushed from his face, his mouth and nostrils plugged with freezing snow.

Raising his head, an unlikely warmth leaked down his forehead.

Blood?

It began to run into his right eye.

His brain began to pound.

How long have I been out? Seconds? Minutes?

Weakly lifting his spinning head, he wiped his face and pushed his oxygen mask back up over his mouth.

For a while, it was all he could do to breathe.

Eventually he was able to roll over onto his side to see down the mountain, scanning the debris from the small avalanche that must have caused his fall. It tracked away from him down the sloping strip of snow and over the edge.

His blurred, bloody vision made out the length of purple rope still tied to his waist harness.

He knew he was searching for something.

What?

He traced each twist and turn of the wavy purple line until it stopped at the sharp slice of rock that had cut it.

Contemplating the end of the rope, senseless, not connecting, Quinn was just surprised at how perfectly that rock must have severed it as it sliced into the snow.

Suddenly he felt as if he had been slammed by another rock, but it was only his aching head recalling what should have been at the end of that purple rope.

9

THE PAZNAUN VALLEY, SOUTHWEST AUSTRIA
October 1, 1938
9:30 p.m.

The rain had eased a little by the time the mountain troopers and the Jews set off up the path that began behind the cowshed. Slippery and narrow, it followed the steep side of the wooded hill with an animal's natural respect for gradient, taking long, looping switchbacks up through the dripping trees.

Gunter led the way, as always. He put the oldest adults at the front of the line. He always did that too, taking his pace from them, slow but steady. Halfway along the tramping line, Kurt was leading the first mule bearing the older of the two girls. At the rear Josef followed with the second. On the mule's back sat little Ilsa, her skinny legs jutting out over the animal's wet flanks, tiny feet encased in bulbous bandages of canvas that bounced upward from the mule's rib cage whenever it made a sudden movement up one of the many steps in the path.

Every now and again someone slipped or stumbled. It would cause a pause in the line before it restarted, as if by instinct. There were occasional sickly coughs, muffled into sleeves so as not to incur a hissed rebuke from Gunter, who demanded silence at the slightest sound. At one point, Josef thought he could hear Ilsa faintly crying. When he quietly asked her how she was faring, the noise stopped, but he received no reply. Josef felt for her, for them all, in fact. Over the last few trips, their charges had become so hunted and afraid, particularly the children, that it was no longer enough to remind himself that it wasn't sympathy that spurred the three of them to lead these desperate collections over the hills. It was habit, and money.

Gunter, Kurt, and Josef were all from a little hamlet situated high in the Bavarian Alps where the men took their living from the surrounding hills, not as soldiers, but as shepherds, hunters, guides, and smugglers. Josef had been five, Kurt six, and Gunter eight, the day a pale limestone mountain in the Dolomites was mined during the third year of the Great War. It had taken the Italians three months to bore the intricate blast tunnel beneath the German hilltop position and load the massive charge. The morning the Alpini finally set the fuse to the thirty tons of tightly packed gelignite, they could smell the Kaiserjäger troops above cooking their breakfast, the mouthwatering scent of bacon seeping down through the natural fissures in the chalky, soft rock. It was the last thing that any of the Germans would smell. In the valleys below, they said it was as if the entire mountain rose up and spilled over into the sky like boiling milk.

The boys' fathers, all infantrymen in the 71st, died

without breakfast that day, exchanging hunger for death in an unknowing instant that left their equally unknowing young sons with the obligation to grow up quickly. As soon as they could, the boys went to work in the high hills to support their stoic yet tired mothers and protect their defenseless sisters. Josef had two, Trudl and Ava, eight and two at the time of their father's death. Everything he did from that day on, he did for them. When, in 1935, the boys, now men, were conscripted into the 99th Gebirgsjäger, one of the reformed German infantry regiments instructed by Adolf Hitler to ready itself for new glories, they went without enthusiasm, mumbling the oath of loyalty to the führer without conviction. Already successful providers from time-honored mountain trades, the unfair exchange of their days and abilities for a poor soldier's wage offered little appeal. The three of them had no interest in the politics of the city, in the building of empires, or the supposed perfidy of other races. Not one of them had even seen the sea.

At the barracks in Garmisch, the three unhappily settled into a dull military regime of training ever-younger recruits in mountain skills that they had known since childhood. They became somewhat happier, however, when they realized that their uniforms and Wehrmacht passes provided opportunity to continue their other, more lucrative, alpine trades. Whenever they could, they would lead climbs for the growing National Socialist cult of alpinism, they would track for Nazi dignitaries and businessmen in hunts for trophy chamois, boar, even bear, and, most profitable of all, they would secretly cross into Austria to make runs over the high passes into Switzerland, smuggling people out and foreign cigarettes and currency back in. To do so, they used the high, hidden routes known only by their fathers and their fathers before them, lost smugglers' paths that ignored arbitrary lines and frontiers on maps and showed little respect for the extremes of natural geography. The Treason against the Reich Act might well make being caught with either cargo punishable by death, but then again, falling off a rock face or being gored by a wounded boar had always offered them such possibility.

Of the three, Gunter was the natural leader, Kurt, the taciturn hunter, and Josef, the agile mountain goat that could climb anything. They combined these skills to form a team that prided itself on being able to get anyone or anything over the highest mountain. As the Nazis' prohibitions increased, so did the demand and price for their services. Their recently issued Heeresbergführer badges, officially classifying them as army mountain guides and instructors, provided yet more license to roam the hills of the newly joined Germany and Austria under the cover of "training." This run was the eighth of that year, the third using that secret route above the Paznaun. They rotated them to keep the Austrian border police guessing, but sometimes they wondered why they bothered. The police rarely ventured into the highest hills, particularly if it was snowing.

That night was proving no different than usual. They walked. They stopped. They walked again. No words were spoken. The hours passed, each person retiring from the wet, the cold, the constant exertion, into their own individual hopes and fears, memories and dreams. Josef, as always, lost himself in thoughts of mountains he wanted to visit, of climbs he had made, of others still to do. He could daydream about them for hours. It was his way of shutting out the world, of enduring the boredom of the barracks, of diverting his attention from the risks they ran, and, more and more, of ignoring the frightened people, particularly the young girls that reminded him too closely of his own, once helpless sisters.

10

By the time the file of twelve stepped out from under the last, stunted pine trees to move up onto the steep grassy slopes above, the skies were clear. The rainclouds had pulled away to the north, leaving behind a black sky punctured with bright stars, the occasional flicker of lightning edging the high, mountainous horizon that bound it. With each flash, the high, narrow ridge they were bound for faintly shimmered, white from the first snows of the autumn.

Out in the open, the group soldiered onward and upward, stretching out a little but still moving well. Occasionally Josef thought he heard the little girl on the mule behind him singing softly to herself. At least she wasn't crying now. He didn't have the heart to tell her to be quiet. At the next stop, he quickly pulled out her rolled-up blanket and showed her how to hold it over her head to keep warm. She listened to him silently, eyes large in her tiny face, before he lifted her back onto the mule. Five minutes later, there was a hesitant, whispered, "Thank you, man."

As the narrow path rose ever higher, it straightened to traverse above a huge grassy bowl that dented the flank of the steep mountainside below. Ahead they could see the faint trace of its line rising up diagonally before them, and below they could feel the increasing emptiness of the long slope that was growing beneath them. Patches of snow crystals began to appear, lightly resting on the thick tufts of grass that edged the narrow trail. A cold wind started to gust down onto them, chilling their faces and burning the tips of any exposed noses or ungloved fingers. Josef knew well that this was the moment when the travelers really began to suffer the strain of the trek even if there was still some way to go before the point where the path turned straight up for a final, brutal slog up onto the ridge itself. That was the steepest, hardest section, cut into the side of the hill like a huge, never-ending staircase. It always exhausted the travelers and made the tiny chapel set high on the ridge not only a convenient but a necessary resting point.

The kapelle St. Christoph must have been up there, in one form or another, for more than three hundred years. A simple stone structure used more often by shepherds and hunters than pious pilgrims, the three of them found it a useful, if temporary, escape from the elements in order to prepare for the final, most difficult part of the journey. It was also a good place to leave the mules as the way beyond was soon blocked by a wall of granite over which they could not pass; the final barrier to Switzerland. There was no need for border fortifications up there; those jagged, towering rocks were natural frontier enough, impassable to anyone who didn't know the tiny, hidden goat path that wove its way through them. On the other side, it was straight down as fast as they could go to meet the Swiss connection and exchange the Jews for the three big wicker back-baskets awaiting them. Each would be loaded to overflowing, weighing a measured forty kilos, packed and ready to be lifted up onto their shoulders. It was always a backbreaking pull to carry them back up to the chapel, but at least there they could transfer some of the tightly bound packages the baskets contained onto the mules and lighten their loads a little for the last leg back down to the valley below.

Josef never knew how much money and merchandise they were carrying. He never even got to see it. It was always immediately handed over, placed, still bundled and sealed, into the open trunk of the black Mercedes with the Munich district registration that would be waiting for them down on the valley road. Only when they closed the trunk would cartons of foreign cigarettes and a thick envelope of *reichmarks* be handed from the driver-side window to Gunter in silent return. He often wondered how much more Gunter did know but whenever Josef asked him, the reply was always the same: "It's safer for you not to know."

* * *

The path finally made its abrupt turn.

They all started to grimly make their way straight up. Josef instantly fell into his habit of counting every step up to one hundred before starting at zero all over again. As his hundreds multiplied and the path got steeper still, Josef knew they were nearing the final crest before the little chapel. It would be good to have a rest and smoke a cigarette. Even his legs were aching.

He looked at his watch. The faint outline of its luminous hands said 1:45 a.m. They were making reasonable time. Josef searched upward for the edge of the ridge and, to his surprise, saw it clearly outlined for an instant by a faint flash of light. "More lightning," he whispered to himself. It was closer now they were higher and warned that they were going to be hit with more bad weather before the night was over.

The mule that Josef was leading began to slow as if struggling with the more direct, steeper route. To urge it on, Josef gave a hard tug on its bridle, just as something moved in the dark above them.

A large rock thumped out of the night, pounding in and out of the snowy grass as it bounced violently down the hillside to their right and disappeared into the darkness below.

The group froze as Josef and Kurt fought to hold the two mules, both startled by the falling stone.

Josef was fortunate. Having just taken a tight hold on his mule's bridle, he was able to strong-arm its head down and calm it with soft sounds, all the time holding little Ilsa onto its back with his other hand so she wouldn't fall. Kurt's mule however was on a looser rein. It reared with fright and toppled sideways off the path, throwing the older child from its back and struggling desperately as it tried to get a footing on the steep, slippery slope.

Kurt and two of the men in the party had to move quickly to stop the animal from sliding further down the slope. They got the beast under control but not before the frightened braying of the mule and the screams of the thrown child had shattered the silence.

An uneasy stillness returned. Then, from above, there was more movement in the dark.

Three mountain goats sprang out into the night air, one of them a huge ram with thick, ridged, perfectly curved horns that seemed to glow white in the blackness. They, like the rock, leapt directly down the steep hillside in giant bounds before veering off to the side, as if steered only by a flick of their stubby tails. They passed so close to Josef he could smell them through his face scarf, more bestial and pungent than the stink of the cheese in the back of the truck.

The mules panicked again. This time Kurt and the two Jewish men restrained their animal. Now it was Josef who battled for control.

Pulling little Ilsa off its back with an outstretched arm, he held her to his side as he wrestled with the harness to stop the beast from bolting. It pulled and stamped, but his grip was strong and slowly he steadied it.

Once again a nervous silence returned to the hillside.

The two children were shaken but unhurt.

The group waited, unsure what to do next until Gunter's voice broke the night.

"It's all right. It's only *steinbock,* mountain goats. Keep going. You have got to keep going. We are nearly at the chapel. You can rest there."

The group started trudging upward again, hearts beating loudly in their ears from both exertion and fear.

The mules were still nervous so Josef pulled Ilsa up onto his back instead. She held on to him tightly as he climbed the final section and tugged the mule after him. The small child was as light as a feather. For a moment, it reminded him of his own childhood when he would carry his youngest sister, Ava, on his back in those rare moments of playtime when all their chores were done. He thought he heard another whispered "Thank you," but he couldn't be sure. Even if she hadn't said it, Josef had already decided that he was going to continue carrying her on his back until he delivered her to Switzerland. She was nothing compared to the return load.

II

The slope, now covered with a thick layer of snow, finally began to level off. After turning right along a narrow rising ridge, they eventually arrived at the doorless entrance of the chapel.

The exhausted group quickly filed inside.

Josef set Ilsa down. After giving him a quick look, she too darted in, leaving him to tie the mules onto a rusted metal loop set to the side of the doorway, while Kurt broke the ice in an ancient stone drinking trough of water with the hobnailed heel of his boot. With a pat on his friend's shoulder, Josef then followed Kurt into the building.

Inside, Gunter had relit his lamp, putting it up onto a bare altar made of granite slabs that filled the end of the narrow, single room. It produced a soft, flickering light, illuminating the simple crucifix pinned above and the nine Jews collapsed onto the earthen floor and leaning back against the rough stone walls.

The three mountain troopers began to move amongst them, asking how they were, checking the bindings on their feet, telling them they were going to get half an hour's rest, that they had earned it. They offered them bread, some water or wine to give them a little more strength for the final climb over the top.

There were appreciative mumblings in response. Josef could see they were still frightened from the surprise of the goats, but even the older ones had a faint gleam in their eyes now. They knew they were getting near.

When Josef came to Ilsa, who was huddled to the side of the altar, he produced a red tin of Scho-Ka-Kola, his army chocolate ration. It was strong and bitter, heavily caffeinated, not really for a child but it would give her some energy for the final leg over the border.

He unwrapped the round cake from its silver foil and broke it into pieces. The girl looked at the small sections with hunger but when Josef offered them to her, she struggled to pick up a piece, fingers fumbling. Josef took her hand and felt its thin woolen glove. It was soaking wet, very cold.

Peeling it off, he held the tiny hand tightly in his to warm it and with the other lifted a piece of the chocolate to her mouth so that she could eat at the same time. The chocolate was hard and he heard her small teeth trying to crack into it.

Before he could stop her, the girl suddenly reached up her other gloved hand and pulled down his scarf.

In the half-light, she studied his face intently as her mouth contorted into an exaggerated grimace to crunch the bitter chocolate.

Josef smiled back at her, but careful to keep his exposed face twisted away from Gunter's sight.

"It's nasty, isn't it?"

She nodded.

"The chocolate, not my face!"

Ilsa gave a tiny, gentle laugh.

"But it's good for you. Make you strong for the next part. You're going to make it, little Ilsa Rosenberg."

When she heard Josef say her name, the girl seemed a little taken aback. Her small eyes met his and she asked, "What's your name then?"

"That's a secret," he replied.

"Is it Adolph?"

This time Josef couldn't help but laugh at her question as he replied with a soft yet exaggerated, "No!"

Ilsa smiled in return to show that despite her tender age she was playing with him.

Completely disarmed, Josef whispered his name.

Before Ilsa could say anything in return they both suddenly heard the cascading sound of rifle bolts being actioned.

Raising his index finger, Josef motioned Ilsa to be perfectly still.

A sharp voice outside shouted, "You are completely surrounded. You will all come out now."

Gunter instantly extinguished the lamp.

The adult Jews began to panic.

In the darkness, Josef seized the small girl by the wrist of her exposed hand and pulled her closer to the side of the stone altar, keeping her down.

Feeling the narrowest of gaps behind the heavy stone slabs, he instinctively pushed her inside.

A shadow stepped into the faint rectangle of the chapel doorway, blocking it.

A bright light then blasted the entrance, the incandescence burning into Josef's blinking eyes the silhouette of a man, the outline of a stick grenade hanging from his right hand, an officer's cap on his head.

"Out! All of you! With your hands in the air or I will throw in this grenade!" the figure shouted.

One by one, the Jews slowly stepped out of the chapel into the blinding light.

There, they were met by a dark line of soldiers standing on each side of the spotlight, the glinting metal of rifles and machine pistols pointing back at them.

When Gunter, Kurt, and Josef came out, a number of the soldiers pushed forward to seize them, separating them from the Jews.

Kurt immediately started to struggle, rolling his shoulders and ripping his arms from their grip. In an instant, one of the soldiers thumped the butt of his rifle onto the side of Kurt's neck. Another delivered a sideways stamp to his right knee. Josef heard a distinct crack of bone or cartilage as Kurt crumpled to the ground, the two soldiers falling onto him, pushing him, writhing and groaning, further into the snow. They quickly stripped him of his hunting knife and papers, which they passed up to the officer.

At the same time, the ends of cold gun barrels were shoved hard up under Gunter's and Josef's chins to stop them from trying anything similar. The pair of them were tugged closer to the light, a leather-gloved hand snatching at the scarf that still covered Gunter's face, ripping it down as Josef's and Gunter's weapons were also removed.

Josef could smell the stink of stale coffee and tobacco on the fetid breath of his captors as they worked. It was worse than the goats. He recognized the skull-and-crossbones badge that adorned the officer's cap and caught glimpses of the double sig runes on the side of the soldiers' helmets as they rifled their pockets:

⚡⚡

Finding Gunter's and Josef's *reichpass* books, the soldiers immediately passed them to the officer, who held them to the side of the light, studying them against a notebook. When satisfied with what he saw, he folded the *reichpass* books inside, standing back to address them in formal, Berlin-accented, high German. "I identify you three as Obergefreiter Gunter Schirnhoffer, Gefreiter Josef Becker, and Gefreiter Kurt Müller, serial numbers abt.1651/99-1, abt.1659/99-1, and abt.1663/99-1 respectively, all soldiers of the 99th Gebirgsjäger. I hereby place you under arrest for the crime of Treason against the Reich. You are to be returned to Germany for court martial and punishment. Start taking them down."

The guns pulled away from beneath their faces, only to return with a jab to their spines, signaling they should start walking away from the chapel, back down the snowy, narrow ridge.

Two other soldiers pulled Kurt back onto his feet. His right leg immediately gave way under him and he collapsed back onto the snow with a cry of pain. Observing the fall, the officer ordered the soldiers to stop. Pointing at Josef and Gunter, he shouted, "You two, come back. You will carry your colleague down to the valley."

Turning back for Kurt, Josef looked at the illuminated chapel, willing the tiny girl inside to stay hidden. Then, each taking an arm, he and Gunter had to lift Kurt once again. Together they began to all but carry him down the slope, his right leg dragging uselessly.

At the turn onto the steep path from the ridge, they submerged once again into the inky dark below.

Some minutes later, a rifle fired. The shot's retort raced over them to collide with distant, invisible hills before springing back in multiple echoes.

There was another, then a third.

Josef counted four more as he struggled with Gunter to help Kurt down the steep, narrow path, all the time their captors goading them to keep moving.

With each echoing shot, a feeling of nausea grew in his stomach.

After the seventh, Gunter shouted, "You SS bastards."

It earned him a punch in the face, but it didn't put him down.

Gunter just scoffed at his attacker.

From behind, another soldier struck him on the back of the head with the pistol grip of his MP38 machine gun.

This time Gunter did go down. Kurt and Josef fell with him.

From somewhere far above as he lay in the snow to the side of the path, Josef heard their two mules begin to bray wildly.

A man's voice screamed, "Ilsa! Ilsa! Ilsa!"

The desperate cries were silenced by a long burst of machine-gun fire as, under a barrage of kicking jackboots and incensed screams of "Get up! Now!" Josef was forced to pull himself up from the snow.

Standing, he looked back uphill to see the flash of an

explosion illuminate the entire ridgeline bright orange.

An avalanche of masonry hurtled down the mountainside.

The sound of the blast ripped all sense from Josef's brain, its echo continuing to sound in his numbed heart all the way to the valley floor.

12

THE SECOND STEP, NORTHEAST RIDGE, MOUNT EVEREST—28,133 FEET
May 26, 2009
5:07 p.m.

The realization of what was missing paralyzed Quinn. He lay there, able only to visualize Nelson Tate Junior's young body being struck by the rockfall, seeing it sweep the boy off the ledge to cartwheel down the sheer face below like a rag doll, the rucksack releasing, the oxygen system spinning away, the yellow down suit ripping and bursting in explosions of blood and feathers at every contact with the razor-sharp edges of the mountain …

Stop!

Breaking his mind from the image, Quinn told himself to put his ski goggles back on. But, as he wrenched them back around to his eyes, he found that the hard plastic lens was split cleanly in two. They were useless. Pulling them up over his head, he tossed them away. When his gloved hand returned, he saw that it was covered in blood from his bleeding forehead. He pushed it back, applying pressure to the wound to try and staunch the flow, involuntarily imagining the boy's fall all over again until a new sequence of thoughts finally intruded:

You need to move.
You can make it through this.
You've got to try.

With his other hand, Quinn reached for a frayed and faded length of red rope that was projecting from some hard ice at the foot of the rock wall.

He tugged on it.

It held.

He waited a little and then pulled on it with all the remaining strength he could muster.

Slowly, Quinn brought himself up onto his knees, then his feet.

His head spun like a gyroscope as he straightened himself. Winded from the exertion of getting up, it was all he could do to lean into the rock to stop the spinning.

Breathe.

His dry mouth pooled with saliva. He was going to vomit.

Instinct made him push his oxygen mask out of the way. He needn't have bothered. Nothing came out as he dry-heaved painfully. It was a long time since Quinn had eaten anything.

The vomiting only winded him more.

Still continuing to retch, he pushed his mask back up onto his mouth as the rock in front of his face replayed Nelson Tate Junior's body rolling to a rest, far below, smashed to a bloody pulp.

Quinn screamed at himself to stop thinking of the

boy's fall, to start thinking about saving himself instead.

FOR FUCK'S SAKE, DO SOMETHING!

He began to pull in the purple rope that had linked him to the boy. When he arrived at the finality of its tufted end, Quinn felt disgusted with himself.

Untying the remnant from his waist harness, he let the severed rope fall to his feet.

Immobile, he stared down at the hopeless coils until an inner voice said he wasn't going to find the boy's body there.

LOOK FOR IT!

Grasping the end of the rope with which he had righted himself, tugging on it once more to be sure that it really was hard frozen into the side of the mountain, he gradually inched himself toward the edge of the snowy ledge. There he stopped, tentatively leaning out, craning his head to look down into the cavernous black and white drop below.

Almost immediately, Quinn made out the forms of two dead bodies, one clad in blue, another in green, partially snow-covered and folded into the rocks directly below the step, but of the yellow-suited boy, there was no trace. As he searched further, an understanding of the boy's unhindered drop down the sheer side of the mountain reawakened a forgotten—or was it just heavily suppressed?—sensation from long ago.

Jump! a crystal-clear voice suddenly seemed to command.

His legs started to tremble, his eyes fogging.

JUMP! JUMP! JUMP! it repeated.

Quinn's insides spiraled into nausea once more.

To beat the vertigo that was threatening to overpower him, he forced himself to step away from the drop and back into the mountainside.

Turning, he saw a dark shape flick out from the rocks to his right until a cloud pushed up the face, obscuring the area.

Quinn kept his eyes fixed on the spot until the cloud thinned and he saw the darting shape again.

The small black form leapt out, tumbling and twisting madly on the buffeting wind until it could break free with a flick of wings and disappear back into the rocks.

It was a *gorak,* a mountain crow.

Quinn's first reaction was to consider its presence as inevitable.

Years of expeditions with the Sherpas had ingrained his subconscious to automatically offer up their superstitions, whether he believed them or not.

The Sherpas said gorak came to collect the souls of lost climbers…

The bird was slow to reappear a third time.

While Quinn waited, a baser, more sickening realization of what it was really doing there ousted the mystical. Unlike humans, gorak are not interested in achieving incredible feats of survival at high altitude. They are motivated to break avian records for one reason and one reason alone: food. Even though a rock buttress blocked Quinn's view beyond the end of the snow ledge, he grimly understood what must have attracted the crow.

Continuing to look across the length of the narrow ledge, he noticed some new marks in the snow, tight into the rock face.

His heart jolted.
The kid went that way!

The thought offered a moment of alternative, but not of sustained relief. The route down from the Second Step ran in the opposite direction. Quinn already knew the direction in which he was looking was a dead end in every sense, a projection of crags and buttresses that offered no prospect of safe descent.

The bird appeared again, as did the thought of what it might be feeding on.

No. You can't permit that.

Cursing the absence of his ice axe to give him some support, Quinn cautiously began to make his way along the exposed traverse toward the bird.

In the beginning, it did indeed seem to lead nowhere. Only as he finally reached its visible end, the point where the rock buttress jutted out, did he understand that there was something beyond.

Gripping the buttress for support, he saw that the ledge narrowed to a width of just a few inches but actually continued around the small promontory. Hugging the rock, his oxygen mask blocking any downward view of his feet, he blindly forced the sharp points of his crampons into every groove he could feel and edged his way around, constantly fighting the magnetic pull of the massive void he knew was below.

13

On the other side, Quinn saw a small, roofed alcove that pushed darkly back into the rocky cliff.

He moved to step down toward its small opening.

Immediately the black bird, forgotten during the difficult climb around the buttress, flew up into his face.

A claw snagged on his oxygen mask, stopping the bird in midflight. Hooked, the crow violently beat its rigid wings against Quinn's exposed eyes and wounded forehead in wild desperation to free itself.

Instinctively using his arms to push the frantic, pecking bird away, Quinn lost his balance. Tumbling from the side of the buttress, his body fell onto the edge of the little alcove.

His hands were unable to grip the icy lip of the cave floor; his crampons scratched desperately at the steep face below, their points breaking away loose ice and rocks to start the immense drop to the glacier ten thousand feet below.

Quinn began to slide down the face after them.

With a lunge, he reached an arm back up into the

cave to get a hold on something, anything.

His right hand slapped onto the shaft of an ice axe.

The kid's?

With all his might, he seized it.

It held his fall for a split second only to explode from the ice.

Instantly Quinn started sliding downward again.

Really falling now.

Dragging the axe after him, its metal head banging against the mountainside above, Quinn dropped ever faster, caught by gravity—the only thing up there that altitude couldn't slow.

The axe's long steel pick caught.

It broke away.

It hooked again, this time slotting into a horizontal crack in the rock.

It stopped instantly but the force from Quinn's dropping body ripped his hand down the shaft.

Still falling.

Just before his hand could slip off the very end of the shaft, it momentarily gripped around the raised metal collar of the axe's end-spike.

Simultaneously, a crampon toe-point keyed into a small crack in the rock.

Two points of contact.

Two points of contact that held.

Stopped.

Quinn wedged his other foot into a bigger crack and spread-eagled across the vertical rock, face pushed hard against the cold schist. He could do nothing more than wait for his shattered nerves to settle.

Shit.

When finally recovered enough to be able to

move, he slowly pulled himself up alongside the axe. Resting his face next to its shaft, his blurred vision slowly took in that it was not the kid's. The shaft was made of wood, not titanium. It was an old axe.

Whatever, it had saved his fucking life.

* * *

Kicking in and pushing up from below with his feet, feeling with his free hand for every edge he could find, reaching ever higher with the long axe, Quinn continued his climb back up.

Eventually he dragged himself into the cave. Panting and shaking from the exertion, watering eyes adjusting to the darkness, Quinn began to take in the small area. It was only about eight or nine feet deep, not much wider either, the roof just high enough to permit someone to stand. Slowly he made out the body of Nelson Tate Junior lying to one side, pushed tight against the left wall of the little cave, curled in the fetal position. A mound of snow and ice rose up to fill the remainder of the small chamber, looking like the treacherous mountain in miniature.

While Quinn looked at it, a spontaneous feeling of dread sent a shudder through his body. Shaking it off as a residual effect of his near fall, Quinn crawled further in between the boy and the frozen mound. Fighting a desperate need to just stop and rest, he laid down the old axe and pulled the boy's body over onto its back to check for signs of life.

To his relief, he found a faint pulse in his neck, but no amount of shaking was bringing him around this time. He knew well that the boy desperately needed water, heat, oxygen, but, in that small cave, he had none of these things. There was only one option left to him to get the boy moving again. Immediately, he reached into the innermost pocket of the fleece jacket inside his suit and pulled out the expedition's small high-altitude medical kit. Ripping the Velcro cover open, he searched for the preassembled syringe he knew would be inside. Uncapping the needle, he squirted a little fluid from the end and compressed the puffy down over the kid's thigh as much as he could with his other hand.

Quinn stabbed the needle through fabric and feathers, deep into the muscle below, depressing the syringe's plunger as far as it would go. Discarding the syringe, he then pulled the boy up into a tight embrace praying that the steroid might revive his charge. It was his last chance, a slim one.

The kid twitched once.

Quinn then felt a growing tremor run through the boy's body. It culminated in a violent spasm as if the kid had been subjected to a massive electrical shock.

It was all Quinn could do to hold on to him.

The boy began thrashing wildly, throwing his head from side to side, his frozen hands jerking up and clawing bluntly at his face. Desperately they pushed off the oxygen mask and goggles as if they were suffocating him. Freed, his mouth began alternately coughing up foamy sputum and drawing in desperate groaning breaths that racked his whole body.

A second spasm flung the boy's whole body backward before arching his spine so intensely that his head began to push painfully into Quinn's sternum. His eyes, white, bulging from their sockets, stared up at Quinn from a face set in a rictus of terror.

His spiked feet began scraping against the ice floor to try and push himself away as he spat individual words up at the Englishman.

"But ... you ... blood ... dead."

A different voice, deep within Quinn, admonished him to get moving or they both soon would be.

Reaching for the head of the old axe and with his other arm still under the kid, he struck the axe's long metal point into the icy floor. Pulling down hard on the T-shaped head of the vertical axe, he forced himself and the squirming, panicking boy back up onto their feet. Still looking down, for a moment, Quinn caught sight of a deep gash in the side of the mound of snow, the place from where the head of the old ice axe must have originally broken free. Within the hole, he saw something blacker than shadow.

The kid started to move, snapping Quinn's eyes back to him instead. Grabbing at the boy's suit and rucksack, Quinn used Nelson Tate Junior's growing momentum to direct him out of the cave onto the side of the stone buttress. There, utilizing his much bigger body to surround the boy completely, he pushed him face-first, tight against the rock and, with the old axe, pulled them both slowly back around to the other side. All the way he had to fight in order to pin the flailing, squirming boy into the mountainside, to stop him from pushing them off.

On the other side they fell onto the snow ledge together. Quinn, exhausted from the exertion of pinning the kid onto the buttress, could do little more than hold on to the still straining boy who actually began dragging them both, inch by agonizing inch, along the ledge to the foot of the rock wall of the Second Step. There, they finally stopped in the bloodstained snow where the kid had first gone missing. Looking up at the darkening sky above him, unable to move any further, Quinn gave in to a black inertia, welcoming the solitude it brought.

Flickering images began to strobe his failing mind. Mere hints of faintly remembered feelings, faces, places flashed and vanished.

He began to plummet downward again.

Above him now, the images lingered and merged, growing like time-lapsed crystals into recollections, vivid and real.

He clutched desperately at the memories to try and stop himself from falling. But, fading to white, they offered no holds.

Quinn continued to drop, revolving now, down into a black hole.

Looking back up at that receding circular patch of light far above him, he saw that a gorak had alighted on its edge.

The black bird was staring down at him, angling its head as if in question.

He knew what it was waiting for.

He no longer cared.

A voice began to call a name.

His name.

"Quinn. Quinn. Quinn."

Over and over until ...

"Quinn? Mr. Neil?"

Neil Quinn forced his eyes open to see Dawa's face inches above his. "Dawa?"

"It's okay, Mr. Neil. It's okay."

With a spike of adrenaline, Quinn twisted his head from side to side, searching once more.

"The boy? Where's the boy?"
"Gone."
"What? Down? Down with Pemba?"
"No, he here with you but …"
"What is it, Dawa?"
"Mr. Neil, I sorry, but boy dead."

14

PRINZ-ALBRECHT-STRASSE 8, BERLIN, GERMANY
October 5, 1938
4:54 p.m.

SS-Untersturmführer Goerdeler was seated opposite Reichsführer-SS Heinrich Himmler. Every single word issuing from Goerdeler's full, wide mouth was a study in precision. With equal resolution, he was ignoring the painful ache in his lower back that came from the constant effort of compressing his tall body down into the chair. Franz Goerdeler never questioned that the smaller man to the front of him was the bigger man and never let his large physique imply otherwise. Their weekly meeting on miscellaneous domestic matters, a one-hour review where he personally briefed the *reichsführer*, accompanied only by a secretary to take shorthand notes, was an outstanding opportunity for a junior officer to impress. A little back pain could not be allowed to jeopardize it.

The *untersturmführer*'s task was clear: bring to the reichsführer's attention any minor matters or inquiries that he considered his office might have otherwise overlooked. To Goerdeler it was yet another reflection of the precision and attention to the smallest detail that his punctilious superior brought to every facet of his leadership. He knew that it was also his first step on the ladder to a position of trust and responsibility within Himmler's personal staff—the dream of every young SS officer. Perhaps he could even be his next adjutant; surely SS-Obersturmführer Jurgen Pfeiffer was soon to be destined for a command position.

The neat pile of eighteen manila files stacked on the table to Goerdeler's right signaled the day's briefing was coming to a close. He had raised more matters than normal. The reichsführer had been in Munich for the week previous, present at what all the Berlin newspapers were heralding as a German triumph, the final laying to rest of the humiliation of the Great War and the perfidious Versailles *diktat* that followed. Goerdeler had heartily complimented the reichsführer on that great success before they opened the first file and the meeting seemed to have proceeded satisfactorily thereafter, even if he could never be totally sure. It was not an easy job to decide what he should bring to the reichsführer's attention and often even more difficult to gauge his superior's true reaction to what he did present.

The reichsführer always listened to every matter raised with equal attention, each time closing his eyes and resting his face forward on the tips of his index fingers and thumbs as Goerdeler read out the salient points of the matter. He would then quietly request the file, studying the supporting documents himself, applying his keen eye to every page before handing it back. Only then would he issue concise, precise instructions as to how to proceed, leaving SS-Untersturmführer Goerdeler to feel nothing but awe at the reichsführer's mastery of all matters. The success of the meeting was so important to Goerdeler's burning ambition that if he thought it had gone well, the young SS officer would reward himself with a surreptitious small cigar during his four-block walk back to his quarters followed by a brandy after dinner. If he felt that he had not impressed, he would be unable to eat or sleep for the disappointment.

The nineteenth and final file of the day was now in Goerdeler's big hands. He had resisted some pressure in the office to leave the matter off that day's agenda. Others had advised that perhaps it lacked the gravity worthy of the reichsführer's attention, that it was just a piece of journalistic bombast. One fellow junior in the office even warned him that not all the Nazi leadership liked the weekly *Der Stürmer*, that Reichsmarshall Göring actually forbade his staff to read it.

Goerdeler had, however, persisted, believing that due to the reichsführer's known interest in the region mentioned and the amount of correspondence that the matter generated, it should be raised. He told them all, in turn, that it was exactly the sort of thing that should be included, something that at first sight appeared trivial but was actually much more serious, easily overlooked given the attention that week on Munich. Petulantly, he had even added that his colleagues would do well to remember that the newspaper in question was the führer's favorite, and what the führer liked, so did the reichsführer.

The young officer opened the file before him. On

seeing the newspaper clipping within, he hesitated for a moment, wondering only then if he should have listened to the others. Raising such a matter might well be a waste of his superior's time, a mistake that would not go unnoticed.

But it generated so many letters from the general public to the reichsführer's office, it must be right to raise it, surely?

"This is the final matter on our agenda for today, Herr Reichsführer."

"Proceed."

"It is a brief editorial from a recent edition of *Der Stürmer* accompanied by a selection of the correspondence it generated to this office. I hope that you do not consider this to be frivolous use of your valuable time, Herr Reichsführer, but the people see you as their protector and guide in all matters relating to the honor of the Fatherland, and I am aware of your keen interest in Asia. As a result, I … we … we considered that you should be made aware of this matter as the last item on today's agenda. I apologi—"

Himmler held up his hand, stopping Goerdeler midsentence. There was a pause as he looked directly into the junior officer's eyes, his own hidden by the reflection of the ceiling lighting on the small round lenses of his pince-nez.

Only when the silence had grown into a buzz of white noise in the young man's eardrums did Himmler break it. "Then, Untersturmführer, I suggest you quickly read to me what Editor Streicher has to say, as your allotted time is nearly over."

Goerdeler swallowed and glanced furtively at his watch to confirm the time remaining. It was indeed just a few minutes. Feeling his heart beating heavily, he took the newspaper clipping from the final file, careful to hold it in both hands so as not to permit the slightest tremble. For a brief moment as he looked at the dense, black blocks of heavy print thumped onto the coarse grey paper, he struggled to make out any words at all.

Blinking his eyes twice nervously, he forced himself to start. "Of course, Herr Reichsführer. The editorial for your attention is taken from the fifteenth of September issue of *Der Stürmer*. The title of the editorial is 'An Insult of Mountainous Proportion.'"

Franz Goerdeler had to moisten his lips and swallow before he could continue.

"The editorial reads as follows:

> The role of the German weekly newspaper that fights for the truth is first and foremost to reveal the cancer that is the Jewry within our midst.

He gulped again.

> As *Der Stürmer* always says, "The Jews are our misfortune!" and so we remain unsleeping in our desire to rout out their debilitating wickedness from within our great Reich.

> However, a true watchdog is attentive not only to the wolf, but also to the fox. A fox that sometimes lurks within the most innocuous situations, hiding behind cunning platitudes as it intends instead to wound and steal.

Reading the newspaper article out loud, Goerdeler suddenly heard for himself how ridiculous the opening paragraphs sounded. Worse still, how little they actually said. He wondered if he had already lost the reichsführer's interest.

He couldn't tell. There was no trace of a reaction, not a flicker of movement from the top of the pomaded crop of parted black hair angled toward him. A wave of nervous panic shot up the inside of his rib cage and branched out into the tops of his arms. The others were right; it was an error to raise this issue. But he had started now. There was no alternative. He must finish it. Fighting a still-drying mouth, Goerdeler continued:

> We have been alerted by our many friends in the DÖAV, our august Alpine Association, to a recent inquiry received from two British Alpinists, named Smythe and Shipton. A request that might have gone unnoticed by many in this proud country, were it not for the keen eyes and ears of this proud newspaper!
>
> So, once more inspired by the twin flames of devotion and duty that burn, ever present, in this vigilant editorial office, we reveal a shocking British request for what it really is, nothing more than a shameful insult, yet another bitter slight from a fading nation that wilts daily in the shadow of the Third Reich.
>
> What is the crime of Messrs' Smythe and Shipton, you ask? It is none other than to have the effrontery to ask the German Alpine Authorities for their "blessing" to climb the mountain of Nanga Parbat.

Do these fools understand nothing of history? Do they not realize that this is an approval that can never be given? Nanga Parbat is the German mountain of destiny, the scene of our greatest alpine tragedies, the future place of our greatest Himalayan triumph.

With a justified sense of outrage, we respectfully call upon our leadership to respond in the strongest terms and forbid such a ridiculous idea. A response that says unequivocally, "Do not dare to approach our mountain, you, who once again have weakly succumbed to failure on the mountain that you cannot conquer, namely Mount Everest, in the country you cannot possess, namely Tibet!"

How many feeble British Everest expeditions has it been now? We count at least seven since 1921. And how many of your sons have you lost in these pathetic attempts? We think it is only two or three, of the tens, or is it not now hundreds that you have sent to try and bully that great mountain into submission? Such a litany of failure and cowardice in no way qualifies such people to even walk near the graves of the eleven alpine martyrs of the Fatherland who sleep in eternal rest beneath the slopes of Nanga Parbat.

Do the British invite us to climb Mount Everest? No, they do not! They jealously guard it for themselves in the manner of spoiled, weak children desperate that no others might—

"Enough!" said Himmler.

He gestured to be handed the file.

With a visibly shaking hand, Goerdeler passed it over the table. Himmler opened it and, with no regard for time, studied the editorial and then the reams of supporting correspondence from an equally outraged readership. He read every page, slowly, as if hunting for hidden meaning in every word. Then, keeping hold of the file, the reichsführer stood. The young SS-untersturmführer barely had time to do the same and salute, hearing only the words, "This is indeed an insult," as the figure departed the room.

When Goerdeler turned back to the now-empty table to collect the other files, his notebook, and fountain pen, he noticed that the shorthand secretary, seated silently at the side of the room, was looking at him with something akin to sympathy in her eyes. There would be no cigar and brandy for SS-Untersturmführer Franz Goerdeler that evening, little food or sleep either.

15

APARTMENT E, 57 SUKHRA PATH, KATHMANDU, NEPAL
May 28, 2009
9:00 a.m. (Nepal Time)

Henrietta Richards first came to Kathmandu in 1969, but she was no hippie. In fact, she couldn't have worked any harder to complete her degrees in politics and history at Oxford University the previous summer. During those long pleasurable days of intense study backdropped by a murmuring radio that promised a world beyond her academic cocoon, a world that finally had young, sharp edges, Henrietta had felt ready to take her place in it, fully prepared to experience a little of its excitement and danger. "Dropping out" would be for others.

She was as determined and thorough in her pursuit of a job in the British Foreign Office as she'd been in earning her double degree with honors. With an outstanding academic record and a respected high court judge for a father, it was inevitable that Henrietta would be successful even though she was a woman intent on entering what was still very much a man's world. Her first posting was as junior diplomatic secretary to Portugal in September that very same year.

Once there she found the British Embassy in Lisbon crumbling and quiet, like the city itself. While her more senior colleagues constantly slipped away to Estoril to play golf or tennis, she remained, mindful of her lowly status and keen to prove herself. Henrietta diligently typed daily summaries of generally dull Portuguese current affairs and promptly dispatched them. She suspected no one in London even read them.

Henrietta Richards herself had little weakness for diversions such as golf or tennis or even the eager-eyed men who, attracted by her tall, slender form; dark, glossy hair; and piercing blue eyes, continually knocked at her office door inviting her to play. Her only weakness was for the truth. She believed rigidly in it. Detesting the lies of others and utterly unable to deceive herself, she quickly concluded that she was little more than a prisoner in a seaside paradise. With dreams of living more challenging, relevant days in Berlin or Moscow or Saigon, Henrietta applied for a transfer. It didn't take long, nor was it a matter of choice or discussion. A quick-talking, fruity voice called from London to say simply, "Kathmandu, in the mountain kingdom of Nepal, is suffering from a plague. The British Embassy there needs urgent assistance. You are to go at once. Travel details to follow in the next diplomatic pouch. Good luck."

Henrietta knew little about Kathmandu beyond its name, which, like Timbuktu or Ouagadougou, conjured in the mind as somewhere hopelessly remote, exotic, exciting. As she hastily packed, she thought about what sort of plague could be ravaging her next destination. Was it disease or infestation? Cholera or TB? Locusts or rats? What precautions should she take in each instance? She had no clue. It was only when she got off the BOAC Boeing 707 at Tribhuvan International Airport and rode with the deputy ambassador into town in his battered Morris that she began to understand. The city's plague was not some rampant disease or unending swarm of voracious insects. It was a "plague" of people.

While the deputy expertly wove the little car through potholed streets teeming with pedestrians, bicycles, rickshaws, and sleepy, freely wandering cows, he explained everything to her in a mellifluous voice that instantly took her back to the lecture halls of Oxford. He told of how, a few months after the Battle of Waterloo and following its own smaller-scale yet surprisingly persistent war with the British, Nepal had agreed to the Treaty of Sugauli. A concession of much of the country's lush Terai lowlands, the hillier territory of Sikkim, and the supply of an annual quota of fierce Gurkha troops won the tiny mountain kingdom little more than the right to be left alone.

It was a splendid isolation that lasted for nearly 150 years. When Nepal finally reopened its borders in 1951, it did so as a medieval time capsule, an untouched land of old ways and beliefs that looked out onto a new world it had no hope of understanding. To the south, the once all-mighty British, bankrupted and diminished despite victory, had left India after the Second World War. Mohandas

Gandhi assassinated, Nehru was now trying to lead the populous new nation through the complexities of independence. To the north, China was now an equally huge communist republic under Mao Zedong, particularly as the chairman had moved quickly to expand his already massive borders by "liberating" Tibet from its own people. Like a baby rabbit caught between two fierce headlights, Nepal did not know which way to turn, so all it could do was crouch and stare as people started arriving from all sides: Tibetan refugees from the north, Indian traders and migrants from the south, and then, most confusing of all, the hippies from everywhere.

These "freaks," as they preferred to be called, were young and had little money but saw neither as limitations to seeking a different world. In army surplus Bedford trucks, battered Volkswagen Kombis, even old London double-decker buses, they turned their backs on the postwar America and Europe of their parents and headed east in a self-perpetuating spiral of spiritual interrogation and narcotic experimentation. The journey quickly became a mythical search for the perfect source of both, and the word was that it could be found in Kathmandu.

It was true at first. The myriad of gods and temples, the distant, all-seeing, all-knowing snow-covered mountains, the shops that sold charas, the sweetest and strongest hand-rolled hashish of all—"I mean, can you imagine that, man?"—all magnified the ancient, smoky city into a continual and wonderful kaleidoscope of the senses. There was no need for any onward destination from there, and the word quickly spread.

What began as a trickle became a river, a river that flooded and left a swamp, a human swamp. By 1969, five thousand freaks were crossing into Nepal every week—each day more embittered about the Vietnam War, more reckless in their pursuit of the biggest high, more impoverished, if that was possible, by the army of con artists and rip-off merchants that now lined the magic way east. They shopped at the Eden Hashish Center, joined the herd on Jochne's "Freak Street," then, to the electric sounds of Janis and Jimi, let it all go. And, for some of them, it did exactly that, leaving them in the city's squalid hospitals or jails or just catatonic on a hippie skid row. No way out, no way home. Sooner or later their respective embassies had to come and clear up the mess.

From the minute she arrived, Henrietta's days and nights were filled getting her countrymen freed, getting them better, getting them home. She threw herself into the task, enjoying its many challenges after the torpor of Lisbon. The only thing she didn't like was the fact that, in their stoned ramblings, her charges lied to her continually. There was little that she could do about it—most of them were so addled they could barely remember their names—so she resigned herself to seeking the truth in her second task at the embassy, which was to monitor the inflow of the Tibetan refugees and report to London every snippet she learned about the Chinese occupation. This time, the people in Whitehall did read her reports. The Chinese were missile testing; they had "gone nuclear." The Himalayas were a frontier of interest once again, just as they had been in the heady days of Younghusband and the Great Game.

The job was not what Henrietta had imagined, but she was busy, very busy, and time flew until, in the '70s, the hippie tide started to turn. President Nixon, increasingly cognizant of the fact that he was losing the war in Vietnam, decided to start another—that he had even less chance of winning—on something much closer to home: drugs. He formed the Bureau of Narcotics and Dangerous Drugs and sent Henry Kissinger off to meddle with the rest of the world all over again. Nepal was an easy, early stop for him, drugs quickly banned in exchange for greenbacks—seventy million of them, some alleged, that never left the deep pockets of the royal family, who, others said, already controlled their country's now-illegal and therefore more valuable drug trade. Nice.

By the time the next generation of proto-hippies in Woking or Waco had read Billy Hayes' *Midnight Express*, rather than *The Electric Kool-Aid Acid Test*, the ayatollahs had taken Iran, the Russians had invaded Afghanistan, and the "hippie trail" east had become a no-through road. A few stragglers stayed on in Kathmandu, but most went home to get haircuts and mortgages, resigning themselves to changing the world by endlessly reinventing the computer or the coffee bar, their future revolutions confined to new washing machines.

Henrietta didn't miss any of them. She had always sought her company elsewhere. She loved the Nepalese who adopted her as someone altogether more honest and serious than her bombed compatriots. She was respected by the diplomatic corps of the city for her incredible powers of insight and analysis—even if she'd already realized the many spooks and spies that inhabited its fabric were even bigger liars than the hippies. She also increasingly enjoyed the company of another group that now continually passed through the city: the climbers and mountaineers. Her deep knowledge of the bureaucracy and intricacies of getting things done in Nepal made her a much-sought-after fount of information whenever they got into town.

Intrigued by their stories and still a history student at heart, Henrietta in return became fascinated with their quests to climb the world's highest mountains. She read the little she could find on the subject and began to keep records of everything she heard. The simple black-and-white truth of whether someone made it to a mountain's summit or not seemed to fill a need within her. She quickly learned that climbing had its liars too, and for some reason she found that to be particularly unacceptable. There were brief romances with a few of them, and then there was love with one. He was a blond, curly-haired American at the forefront of a new breed of climber who, rejecting the huge siege-style expeditions and obvious routes of the first Himalayan summiteers, instead sought to go lighter, faster, and more elegantly up the hardest faces to reach the top.

Henrietta's relationship with him became as intense and severe as the climbs he made. When he wasn't in the mountains, he stayed with her in Kathmandu. They would sit together analyzing maps and photographs, studying her growing collection of expedition notes and books, designing the most perfect routes up the fiercest mountains. He would then leave her to climb them with a ragtag group of climbing gypsies who all followed the same creed. She had no desire to go with him. Her only desire was for him to return, but always she knew that, one day, he wouldn't. It was statistically probable that he would be killed. She couldn't even lie to herself about that—after all, they were her statistics—so she just chose not to think about it until that inevitable day arrived in 1981 and she was left with no choice. When her American was hit by a falling rock during a desperate, freezing descent of the West Face of Makalu, something in her also froze, so hard she knew there would be no thaw. Henrietta Richards should have gone home, left that place the next day, but she didn't. He would be there for eternity, and so would she.

She quietly continued her work at the embassy. She studied the Nepali and Tibetan languages and many of the dialects in between, becoming fluent in them all. She watched as the tiny, antique city she loved grew into a brown-brick sprawl that scabbed the once-green Kathmandu Valley. The old city's infrastructures crumbled around her, unable to cope with one million people. Legions of small motorcycles and cars replaced the cohorts of bicycles. Their pollution unchecked, Kathmandu's once-blue skies receded behind a metallic smog that Henrietta could taste on her tongue by midafternoon. The country's royal family corroded further from within, finally self-destructing when Prince Dipendra, heir to the throne, murdered nine of its members, including the king, before turning the gun on himself. The king's brother Gyanendra took over, but, unpopular and mistrusted, he only accelerated the final fall of his house. Narrowly avoiding a revolution, he stepped aside at the very last minute, just as the Maoists prepared to come down from the hills and take power by force.

Kathmandu should have collapsed under it all, but surprisingly it didn't. Nor did Henrietta. Her dark hair greyed, her back bowed a little, but her piercing blue eyes stayed focused on the truth as she observed mountaineering change once again, this time into a multimillion-dollar industry that offered every type of trek or climb to every level of climber. Summits were packaged and priced, and public perceptions, conditioned by those dark, dangerous first climbs, lionized anyone who reached them. Everest became the biggest, most sought-after prize of all. Henrietta eyed it all with a caustic acceptance. She knew it was a rare source of income for the impoverished country she loved, and that much of it was a sham. However, she insisted that its participants at least be honest in what they claimed. Night after night, she applied her now huge knowledge to every climb that claimed a summit, to every climber who published a summit photo. Her records grew to fill twenty filing cabinets crowded with details of over fifty thousand ascents. They said she had every Himalayan expedition report ever written, some going back to the nineteenth century. It wasn't true, but she did know more about every route, every lofty summit pyramid than most of the people who actually visited them.

When she finally retired from the embassy in 2006, there was still neither tennis nor golf in her plans. The only change Henrietta made to her life was to move her recordkeeping into the daytime, juggling it with the freelance consultancy she continued to provide the city's diplomatic corps. Her free evenings she now used to channel her encyclopedic, obsessive knowledge into writing books about Everest, particularly George Leigh Mallory and Sandy Irvine's ill-fated attempt in 1924. After forty years in Kathmandu, Henrietta Richards was still no hippie.

16

For Henrietta, that morning in May was much like the rest at that time of year. She got up at 6:30 a.m. precisely and turned on her aging, vinyl-covered radio to listen to the BBC World Service, its languid eloquence one of the last reminders of her youth as she prepared herself for another busy day. She then made a cup of tea with milk, some toast and marmalade, and ate her breakfast, reading, as always, the previous day's copy of the *Daily Telegraph* and that day's *Kathmandu Times*.

Sanjeev Gupta, her assistant, would arrive promptly at nine o'clock, and that was her signal to start work. Until then she enjoyed the slow solitude of her morning ritual, calling it her "calm before the storm," a particularly apt choice of words during the premonsoon season between late May and early June. It was always her busiest time of the year and she knew when it was coming.

From the window of her apartment, she would watch the monsoon's arriving rainclouds be momentarily halted by the barrier of the world's highest mountains. They would stack so high into the sky above Kathmandu that they themselves formed another barrier to block the fearsome jet-stream winds that pummeled the heights of those same mountains for the rest of the year. The resulting "window" of calmer conditions on high was when the expeditions made their summit attempts and, as soon as they did, Henrietta would vet every single expedition that claimed success.

Given the season, it was no surprise that her first call of the day came in on the dot of nine. Just as Sanjeev was letting himself in through the front door of Henrietta's apartment, she picked up the phone on its second ring and said simply yet imperiously, "Richards."

The speed and brevity with which she answered seemed to fluster her caller for a moment, much as intended. After a pause, a voice said, "Henrietta? Jack Graham speaking."

"Hello, Jack," she replied, tone warming to the familiar sound of the longtime British ambassador to Nepal, a colleague and close friend of many years. "Bit early for you, isn't it? To what do I owe this honor?"

"Yes, I know. Sorry to disturb, but I have top brass from the Department for International Development here with me all morning so I needed to speak to you first."

"Not a problem. How can I help?"

"Edward Shay, the new US ambassador, invited me to dinner last night, wanting to pick my brain about something. As I am sure you know, he's only been here for a few weeks, first ambassadorship for him and all that. Solid chap, actually, I think he'll do well. Anyway, yesterday he was being absolutely hammered by DC because a sixteen-year-old American has been killed on Everest. The boy is or, should I say, was the son of a Mr. Nelson Tate, billionaire, big political donor, you know the type, and evidently the man has been raising merry hell at the highest levels ever since. Have you heard anything about this?"

"Yes, I did hear some early chat yesterday about a death on the north side of the mountain but no details as to who it was." She wearily sighed to herself before continuing. "I really wish they would stop this ridiculous record-breaking to be the youngest or the fastest or whatever it is going to be next. I mean sixteen is just too young to be up there. The death of such a young climber is going to be a major tragedy for the mountain. It'll be a big story."

"Well, that's the point actually, Henrietta. We need the full story. Shay has told Washington he is going to compile a detailed report on precisely what happened to the almost inevitably named Nelson Tate Junior. It won't bring the boy back, of course, but it may bring some closure to Tate Senior—and we both know that the preparation of a bloody good report always buys some time. He was asking me who I thought was the leading expert on Everest in Kathmandu and, naturally, I said you. They'll pay you for it, of course."

"But if it was a Tibet climb, isn't this something for the US authorities in China to pursue?"

"You know as well as I that the Chinese have long denied the US request for a consulate in Lhasa. They have no one officially on the ground there and whilst the US Embassy in Beijing is evidently kicking up a fuss, the Chinese will undoubtedly respond to it by just hiding the facts of the matter behind some simple statement until it all goes away. I told him that the only hope they had of really getting to the truth would be through you from Nepal."

"I can't disagree with that. The truth is definitely my game. Do you know who the younger Tate was climbing with, Jack?"

"Yes, it appears that Nelson Tate Junior was with No Horizons. Sarron."

Henrietta shook her head at the news. The mere mention of the name made her skin crawl. The Frenchman's narrow, hateful face, with its taut, permanently tanned skin and silvering, curly hair pulled back into that irritating ponytail instantly appeared in her mind's eye.

"Really? Most definitely not my favorite person—or anyone's, in fact. Did you say anything about Sarron to Shay?"

"No, I thought better not to at this stage. He's picked up that Sarron is difficult, 'an Everest maverick' he'd been told. However, I don't think he's fully aware of what a complete piece of work that damn Frenchie really is. Surprisingly our links with the Indian Intelligence Bureau are currently better than the Yanks', who, I guess, are slightly more focused on the Muslim than the Maoist these days."

Henrietta nodded to herself. "Yes, probably for the best," she said pensively. "We don't yet know the details of Tate Junior's death. I don't want to sound callous, but if it was the result of just a fall or an avalanche then why stir up a lot of trouble involving Sarron? It will only make his parents' suffering worse."

She paused. "However, Jack, if it proves to be not as simple as that, make no mistake, it will all come out about Sarron, and then the Tates will have some very serious regrets as to what their son got into."

"I know," Graham replied.

"Tate Senior can't have done much due diligence before the climb. What a fool!" Henrietta continued waspishly. "It so annoys me when people don't look further than an expedition company's success rate. Sarron's always been smart at selling his expeditions on his summit stats and leaving the nasty surprise of his absolutely loathsome personality for when everyone gets to the foot of the hill. I bet he really laid on the charm at the thought of Tate's billions. Did Shay give you the names of any others involved?"

"Yes, an English guide called Neil Quinn."

"Mr. Quinn, indeed," Henrietta said, stopping to think about what Jack Graham had just told her.

"What's he like?"

"Nice enough chap, good Everest man. Big guy, strong, must have been on the top eight or nine times now. He's no idiot either, told me once that he gave up a possible career as a London lawyer to become a professional climber. I have always thought he could have been one of the best in the world, but he's a bit of a journeyman these days. It's pretty common really. They start out young and hungry but over time find themselves compelled to pay their bills doing the same old hills time and time again. In Quinn's case it's just that the hill happens to be Mount Everest. I am surprised, though, to hear that he was working for Sarron. I would have put him above that. Did Shay say who the sirdar was?"

"I wrote it down actually. Let me look … Dawa Sherpa, could it be?"

"Yes, that would make sense as he often works with Quinn, although I must say he's another I wouldn't have foreseen in Sarron's Base Camp. Dawa's a legend on Everest and even I would approve the use of such hyperbole in his case. Ho hum, Quinn and Dawa, more bees around the Tate honeypot perhaps? Well, how do we proceed?"

"Shay would like to meet you for lunch to brief you on what he needs and by when. He said he'd send a car to collect you at midday if you were up for it."

"You can tell him I'll be waiting."

"Good. I'll leave you to agree the rest with him. Don't forget it's the Americans. Think of a number for the report and double it. Oh and, Henrietta, one more thing. I have just finished your last book, the one you sent over at Christmas, and I must say, I thought it was excellent. If I read it right, it seemed to suggest that you believed George Leigh Mallory did reach the summit of Everest before he died, an unusually romantic conclusion for someone as scientific in their approach as you."

"I have my reasons, Jack. I'll let you know how I get on with Shay and the report."

Putting down the phone, Henrietta turned to Sanjeev, who had already switched on the computer and quietly started to work. "Sanjeev, as a priority please let me have anything you can find on the 2009 No Horizons Everest North Expedition and, particularly, Jean-Philippe Sarron, Neil Quinn, and Dawa Sherpa. Print it all up as I'll need to take it with me for a meeting at twelve. I'm also going to put the answering machine on now as I suspect we might be getting more than a few calls from the newspapers today and we've got a lot of work to do."

17

EAST RONGBUK GLACIER CAMP, MOUNT EVEREST—21,200 FEET
May 28, 2009
1:45 p.m.

Since awaking at 11:00 a.m., finally released from a revolving, repeating dream of being trapped in the gorak cave on the Second Step, Quinn had just lain there in that small tent, completely stunned. Cocooned in someone else's stinking yet warm sleeping bag, with no feeling in his fingers or toes, it was all he could do to drink endless cups of warm, sugary tea and watch a series of strange cartoon animals acrobatically climbing the tent's zip.

Or had I?

Are the tiny animals just a hangover of my dream-racked, tormented sleep?

Whatever, they were gone now, leaving only the bright light illuminating the tent's thin yellow canvas to burn his nearly snow-blind eyes, and the wind howling down off the North Col to stir his pounding headache. If he shut his stinging eyes to try and rest them, he saw instead his painful descent from the Second Step. It had taken thirty-six hours of stumbling, staggering, and resting to make it down the North Col and then to the relative safety of their camp on the East Rongbuk Glacier. The starting, the stopping, the constant drifting in and out of reality anchored only by the dreadful fact that Nelson Tate Junior, his responsibility, was dead. The creatures were preferable to that. Anything was preferable to that.

Isolated and alone, Quinn took no comfort from the realization that if the animals had gone then the rest and rehydration were returning him to normality. Some kind of normality that was going to be anyway; it might not feature the surreal daydreams of an exhausted mind, but his biggest nightmare was now going to haunt him forever: he had lost a client.

Why did Dawa save me? I should be the one still up there.

But Dawa had saved him and Quinn should be grateful. He hoped there would be a day when that would be so, but he couldn't imagine it anytime soon.

Dawa Sherpa.

Unbelievable really. Despite struggling down from the summit with Pemba, who had never properly recovered from his own collapse, Dawa had found Quinn and brought him back to life too. Physically pulling him away from the boy's lifeless corpse, he had got him moving down again as soon as he could, saying over and over to him, "There is nothing you can do."

Even Dawa had started to flag as they made their tortured way down through the Yellow Band, toward the pinpoints of light slowly moving up the hill to meet them. Bearing fluids and fresh oxygen, three Sherpa, one of them Lhakpa, despite the fact he had already been to the summit with Durrand, and two strong Czech climbers, who knew full well that they were throwing away their own summit chance by making a rescue, had met them at the very last moment to lead them down via the High Camp.

There is nothing you can do.

The words continued to ring inside Quinn's aching head as if bouncing between the immense walls of a cathedral.

But there was nothing more he could have done for the boy.

Quinn had done everything humanly possible.

But the boy is dead and I am alive.

His stomach churned just thinking about it.

And it didn't even make sense. Nelson Tate Junior had still seemed strong after they made it around the buttress. If anything it was Quinn who had been the weaker. The boy had almost pulled him along the snow ledge ...

Didn't he?

Am I remembering it right or am I the one not making sense?

He couldn't be certain.

You are never really sure of what happens up there.

* * *

Quinn's painful soul-searching was interrupted by the curved tent above him bowing inward twice under the gentle push of a hand. The arched doorway then zipped open and Lhakpa stuck his head inside to pass another thermos of tea to Quinn.

"How are you, Mr. Neil?"

"Recovering, I think."

"Okay, Mr. Neil. Drink more bed-tea. Good for you. We also make noodle soup. Ready soon. Also good as you must go Base Camp tomorrow. Sarron insisting. He wait for you before go Lhasa to make report of climber death with Chinese. Boy's father making big noise. Chinese officials in Lhasa involved now. Rest of team will return to Kathmandu with expedition kit."

Quinn thanked the Sherpa and took in both the tea and the new information. With every new flask of restorative tea, accompanying snippets of news had also been delivered to unintentionally counter the effect:

> "Sarron is crazy insane with rage. Even Old Dorje, who has worked as his camp cook for years, has never seen anything like it."

> "Pemba is recovering. He is saying to everyone the No Horizons oxygen was bad. Dawa telling him to be quiet."

> "No one is getting paid."

> "Nelson Tate Senior want us to retrieve boy's body. Sarron refuse, saying too high, too late in season now, not possible anyway. He right, Mr. Neil. Not possible from Second Step."

> "Dawa say you do everything—not your

fault. Sarron saying is your fault, all your fault. Dawa, Pemba, also."

"Big mess, Mr. Neil."

Yes, on that last point they were all agreed.

It was indeed a big mess, one that was only going to get worse when they arrived back at the No Horizons Base Camp.

18

PRINZ-ALBRECHT-STRASSE 8, BERLIN, GERMANY
October 10, 1938
7:58 p.m.

His meal finished, Heinrich Himmler left the officers' dining room in a meditative silence. Seeing him to be deep in thought, his chief of staff, SS-Grupenführer Karl Wolff, and his personal adjutant, SS-Obersturmführer Jurgen Pfeiffer, said nothing.

Silently, they walked behind him to the room where they habitually took their after-dinner coffee. Only when they were sat in the black leather armchairs of the salon did Himmler, turning directly to Pfeiffer, speak.

"Did you look into that newspaper article as I requested?"

Pfeiffer, a tall, thin man whose choirboy complexion and soft flick of backswept blond hair belied the fact that he was the most ambitious and ruthless young officer within the elite *Leibstandarte* SS Adolf Hitler regiment, replied in the affirmative.

"Yes, Herr Reichsführer."

Pfeiffer reached into the inside breast pocket of his jet-black uniform and extracted an envelope, opening it to take out two pieces of paper and a folded map. He smoothed the map open on the coffee table and put an annotated photograph of an immense black mountain on top of it. The other paper, a page of handwritten notes, he rested on his knee. He said nothing more, only awaited his next instruction.

Himmler nodded in approval at his protégé but quickly turned over the photograph to obscure the map, remaining silent as a white-jacketed orderly approached and poured coffee. After the orderly had left the room, the reichsführer revealed the map and the photograph once more and spoke.

"From the moment that my SS Tibet expedition set foot in India earlier this year, it has been continually insulted and harassed by the British authorities in the region. Five of our finest SS scientists treated as if they were some sort of invasion force rather than a legitimate visiting delegation from one sovereign nation to another. You will recall that this behavior has necessitated I write to Admiral Domville in London a number of times in order to request the group's unhindered onward passage to Lhasa, the capital of Tibet."

As the two officers nodded in acknowledgement, Himmler took a sip of the black coffee before speaking again.

"Even now Dr. Schäfer and his team remain blocked in the British-controlled territory of Sikkim to the northeast of India with only one short reconnaissance over the border into Tibet to their name."

He stabbed at the map with his stubby index finger. "About there, I think. Anyway that brief visit was more a by-product of Ernst Schäfer's resourcefulness than the result of any improved cooperation by the British. Sir Basil Gould, their political officer in Gangtok, seems determined to obstruct us at every move. Likewise, I understand that the British Cadre in Lhasa is using every opportunity it can to poison our name within the Tibetan Council of Ministers."

His voice accelerated to keep pace with a growing anger.

"The British disgust me. They behave like snakes, appeasing us at the negotiating table without the guts to resist our demands, exactly as we saw at the Munich Conference, yet out of our sight, winding and worming behind our backs to hinder us in every way they know how."

Himmler stopped, his face taut, lips pursed, straining to control his temper. Taking off his pince-nez spectacles, he began to clean them with a white silk handkerchief. Rapidly polishing the crystal lenses, squinting down at his short, fast-working fingers, he slowly relaxed until he could speak calmly again.

"Some days ago Untersturmführer Goerdeler, in a commendable display of initiative, showed me a recent editorial in *Der Stürmer* about two British mountaineers inquiring of our own alpine association as to whether they could have their approval, 'blessing' was what they called it, to climb Nanga Parbat. We all know, of course, something of the tragic losses incurred in our country's many attempts to climb that accursed mountain in India. As always, Editor

Streicher was admirably passionate in his anger at what I now understand is considered to be a huge insult in German alpine circles. I too will admit to being moved by the emotions of the correspondence that the editorial generated."

He paused to reposition the pince-nez on the bridge of his nose.

"Normally, I would say that we have more important things with which to concern ourselves. However, given the trouble the British have caused my Tibet expedition—an SS Ahnenerbe project that you both know is close to my heart—I could not help myself from thinking, as young Goerdeler read me Julius' editorial, how magnificent it would be to send a team of Germany's finest alpinists to climb Mount Everest and have them plant a swastika on its summit, right under the noses of the damn British."

The two staff officers looked at each other in an instant of surprise before their eyes were drawn back to the reichsführer, who was looking again at Pfeiffer.

"Please, my dear Jurgen, given that you now have had a few days to read Goerdeler's file and learn something about Mount Everest as I requested, explain to me why that would not be a good idea so that I might return my mind to where it is better needed."

Pfeiffer leaned forward and, with a faint smile, responded. "Actually, Herr Reichsführer, I think it is a most interesting propaganda idea but one that would be very difficult to effect. I have discussed Streicher's editorial at some length with Professor Markus Schmidt, the senior mathematics professor from Munich University, who, you will recall, led our recent study into the possible human freight capabilities of a unified Central European railway system."

"I remember the man."

"Evidently Schmidt is quite the enthusiast of alpine sport. He was able to tell me a great deal about the Himalayas and the background to the comments made in the editorial."

Looking down at the piece of paper in his hand, Pfeiffer continued. "It is correct that since 1921, the British have sent seven expeditions to try to climb Mount Everest from the Tibetan side, as the mountain is shown in this photograph that Schmidt gave me. The most recent was earlier this year in the spring, as they always are. Every expedition has met with failure. In 1924, two of their climbers, a George Mallory and a Sandy Irvine, did get very high on the mountain's Northeast Ridge." As he spoke, his well-manicured fingernail traced a line up the photograph's mountain only to stop just short of the top. "But they were never seen again. Some say they could have actually made the summit before they died, but there is no proof, and until someone does come down with such proof, the British persevere."

Pfeiffer's cold eyes glanced at his paper once more.

"They have got close a number of other times. Over the years at least four of their men have gone higher than twenty-eight thousand feet, which is over eighty-five hundred meters, only a few hundred meters below the summit. One of them was actually the same Mr. Smythe mentioned in Streicher's article—probably good reason in itself to keep him away from Nanga Parbat."

"But have any other countries even tried to climb Mount Everest?" asked Wolff.

"No. As you can see from the map, the mountain straddles the frontier between Tibet and Nepal. The Kingdom of Nepal is completely closed to the outside world. Only diplomats can visit its capital, Kathmandu, and no one may travel beyond. Tibet is a slightly different matter. Some foreigners, such as the famous Swedish explorer Sven Hedin—a great supporter of the führer as we all know—and your own Dr. Schäfer have been able to visit the country sporadically in the past. However, Tibet only provides regular formal access to the British under an agreement that dates to what were little more than surrender terms imposed on them by Younghusband after the British invasion of the country in 1904. As long as Everest remains unclimbed, it can be assumed that the British could and would demand that Tibet prevent any other country from having access to the mountain."

Pfeiffer's mention of British control contorted Himmler's face once more into a look of anger. The younger officer carried on, regardless, intent only on his precisely assembled facts.

"It is evident that the British do treat Mount Everest as their own. Other nationalities are permitted to climb other mountains in their sphere of influence—they let us go quite freely to Nanga Parbat—but Everest, the highest, remains theirs. Given that Himalayan expeditions are generally huge affairs with tons of supplies and hundreds of porters, and the British control the approach routes to Tibet through India and Sikkim, it is impossible to envisage any other country assembling such an expedition and then passing unnoticed and unhindered to Everest, even if a secret permission could be negotiated with the Tibetans."

Himmler motioned Pfeiffer to stop talking. "But why could it not be a small team of two or three of our most expert alpinists?"

"Yes, couldn't we just parachute them in?" Wolff added.

"No. Tibet is too big, too remote. It has no air facilities," Pfeiffer replied. "Planes can fly above the Himalayas, but the current range and altitude ceiling of our existing transport, the Junkers JU-52, is insufficient, even if able to refuel in India without the British knowing, which would be impossible. As for parachuting, well—"

"The only way is by land then," Himmler interjected, reluctant to waste time on the merits of parachuting.

"Yes, and interestingly, Professor Schmidt told me that four years ago a British man called Maurice Wilson did make it to the foot of Everest in what was an unofficial, clandestine attempt to climb the mountain alone. He traveled across Tibet in disguise with three porters, so it is possible." As he said the last sentence, Pfeiffer drew their attention to the approximate route of Wilson's approach, which had been drawn on the map with red pencil. "Evidently his original plan was actually to crash an airplane into the side of the mountain and then get out and climb to the top, but the British impounded his plane in India to stop him. Cruel, really."

"Why? What happened to him?"

"He died a slow death from exhaustion beneath the mountain long before he got anywhere near the summit. If the British had allowed him to take his plane, it would at least have been a quicker suicide."

"So you are saying, Jurgen, that any such attempt is little more than a suicide mission?"

"Yes. But we should recognize that the lone Englishman who died, whilst undoubtedly determined, had no real climbing experience at all."

"So, I repeat myself, why don't we send a small team of our finest alpinists but in disguise? Those men who climbed the Eigerwand perhaps? Heinrich Harrer, I think, was one of them. That was a suicide mission and they survived it. Surely they could do it."

Pfeiffer smiled at the reichsführer's joke. "Possibly they could, but our best climbers are very famous now, not only in the Reich but also in England, France, and Italy. They would be unlikely to pass unnoticed in British India. No, for me, the only way might be to find some good yet unknown climbers that could be—how should I put it best?—'motivated' to climb the mountain yet are somewhat expendable and deniable should it go wrong, which it most probably will. It would be a very long shot, but something along those lines could possibly be imagined."

Himmler stood and began to pace the room.

"Very good, Jurgen, as always," he finally said. "However hard I try, I cannot get the image of a swastika flying from the top of Mount Everest from my head. Imagine a photograph of such an achievement: the undeniable evidence of our noble black order reaching the world's highest summit before all others. What power such a picture would have. It would be the ultimate inspiration for the SS—the entire Third Reich in fact—and, at the same time, there could be no greater humiliation for the British, particularly those very diplomats and spies who have worked so hard to hinder me in Tibet."

The reichsführer stopped to stare at Pfeiffer.

"I have heard enough. SS-Obersturmführer Jurgen Pfeiffer, you will do the following two things: One, prepare a communication from me to the office of the Reich Minister of Propaganda, Josef Goebbels, that states, with immediate effect, any matter relating to the ascension of any mountain now comes under the complete control of the SS. No debate is to be permitted. I don't want that man involved in any way. This is to be our gift to the führer.

"Two, prepare a preliminary operation process that develops your idea with details of personnel required, suitable timetable, and estimated costs. Codify it as an SS Wewelsburg/Ahnenerbe project with security classification 12WBB, restricted. In your detail, always have regard for the fact that we must be able to completely terminate this operation at any moment of my choosing."

Taking out a small note pad and silver fountain pen from an inner pocket, Himmler jotted a note to himself.

"I myself will speak to Reinhard Heydrich of the SD and the acting heads of both the gestapo and the kripo to obtain details of any current detainees that might have the necessary skills for the type of project you suggest. Once we have a list, you will obtain the dossiers on them and their families and select the most suitable candidates. We will review progress of this project in two weeks. Now let us move on to other matters."

"*Berg heil!*" said Pfeiffer, invoking the traditional German salute to the mountains as he began to neatly refold the map.

The light glinted off Himmler's spectacles, hiding the eyes but accenting the faint smile on the lips below, as he picked up the photograph of Everest. With his still-open pen, he slowly and carefully inscribed the two sig runes of the SS on its very apex before blowing gently on the photograph to dry the ink. Handing it back to Pfeiffer, he said, "*Sieg ... heil*, my dear Jurgen. Sieg heil!"

19

EVEREST NORTH BASE CAMP, RONGBUK VALLEY, TIBET—16,980 FEET
May 29, 2009
8:54 p.m.

Ahead, the large geodesic tent at the center of the No Horizons Base Camp glowed with yellow light, an illuminated blister on the moonscape of the Rongbuk Valley. Slowly, Quinn, Dawa, and Pemba continued to pick their way toward it through the dark, careful to avoid tripping over the guy ropes of other tents, wary of the vicious mastiff dogs of the Tibetan yak herders that always lurked around the edges of the camp.

Every muscle and joint in Neil Quinn's body was aching as if he had been pulled apart on some medieval torture rack. He had experienced the heavy fatigue that follows an Everest climb many times before. Usually he ignored it, brushing it aside with optimistic thoughts of home or the next trip, but this time it was different. The exhaustion and the pain were extreme, unlike anything he had ever felt before, amplified still further by other feelings—feelings of shame, regret, and failure. It had taken him all day to walk back down the glacier. Dawa could easily have gone on ahead quicker, but Quinn had insisted the Sherpa stay with him and Pemba. Not because he needed his help, but because Quinn wanted to be the one to meet Sarron face-to-face first. He had to be the one.

Quinn stopped for a minute to catch his breath in anticipation of what was going to happen next. Nothing in Sarron's habitually aggressive demeanor suggested that it was going to be an easy or a civilized encounter. Breathing deeply and slowly as if in preparation, he looked around at the other groups of tents that dotted the valley floor. Many of them were also lit; most of the teams were off the mountain now. A post-climb party was underway in one of the larger mess tents. He could see people spilling out of the tent, despite the bitter cold, drinking and dancing to the loud hip-hop music being played inside. They were rapping along to it, shouting words about being on "top of the world" at the top of their voices, raising beer bottles and glasses toward the summit, ecstatic that they had been there, that they had survived, that they too were now Everest summiteers.

There would be no such party in the tent to which Quinn was headed, summit or no summit. The thought spontaneously made him turn back to the mountain, almost vainly hoping the kid was going to be there, just walking up the trail behind him, one more Everest summiteer ready to celebrate.

But the trail was empty.

The kid is dead.

Accepting it meant it was time to face very different music.

Quinn painfully walked on.

I did everything I could.

* * *

Finally arriving at the mess tent, they dropped their rucksacks outside and Dawa unzipped the curved fabric door to let the three of them in. Inside, the big domed tent was empty except for Wei Fang, the team's Chinese liaison officer, and Phinjo, the expedition's youngest cook boy. Fang, technically from the Chinese Himalayan Association and there to assist the expedition with its logistics as part of the CHA's expedition permit, was really a low-pay-grade spy with the mission to prevent anything that might harm Chinese control of the region: no smuggling refugees into Nepal, no "Free Tibet" propaganda, no displaying the illegal Tibetan flag—particularly not on the summit of Qomolangma, most supreme of Chinese mountains.

Fang was completely drunk, face pitched forward on the large trestle table that stood in the middle of the tent, its incongruous flower-patterned vinyl tablecloth littered with opened Pabst beer cans and half-full bottles of whiskey and vodka. The little cookboy was trying to clear the empties without disturbing the comatose Chinaman. Seeing the three of them enter, Phinjo stopped and looked at them as if he were seeing ghosts.

"It's all right, Phinjo. Can you go and tell Sarron that we are here?" Quinn said to the lad who instantly put down the tray and left the tent. To break the silent wait that followed, Quinn said to Dawa and Pemba, "Let me do the talking, okay?"

Before the other two could even answer, the rip of the zip announced Sarron's arrival.

Ducking into the tent, the Frenchman looked first at Quinn and said, "Damn fucking right you're going to be doing the talking." He turned and shouted at Dawa and Pemba, "You two, get out!"

The two Sherpa didn't move, looking only at Quinn for instruction until he nodded that they should go. But before Pemba could step outside, Sarron pushed in front of him, blocking his way and shouting into his face, "Don't think I've finished with you yet, you little fuck. I haven't even started. You fucking want to sit up there in the Glacier Camp telling everyone my oxygen is bad. That it was all because of my fucking Os. You think you're going to get away with that?"

Instantly irritated, Quinn pushed between them. "Look, all Pemba was saying was that something felt wrong up there." Even as he spoke, Quinn could smell the alcohol on Sarron's heavy breath. He must have been keeping Wei Fang company.

Staring back at Quinn, Sarron said only, "What?" Seemingly winded with rage, the Frenchman began to bite his lower lip, fixing his wild eyes on the Englishman until he could finally shout at the two stopped Sherpa, "Dawa, Pemba, I thought I said 'Get the fuck out!'"

"Mr. Neil?" Dawa asked.

"It's all right. Just wait outside for now," Quinn answered.

Trying to defuse the tension, Quinn raised both

his hands as the Sherpa left and said slowly, as calmly as possible to Sarron, "Look Jean-Philippe, be calm. We had a bad day, a terrible day, I'll admit it, but you know how it is up there; things can and do go wrong. I did everything I could to save that boy from the moment he went down on the summit. All Pemba was saying was that something was off, we don't know what but there was something, maybe the kid had a heart condition, I don't know, but make no mistake, it shouldn't have end—"

Before Quinn could finish, Sarron moved in close, angling his enraged face up at him and screaming, "*TA GUEULE! C'EST DES CONNERIES!*"

Quinn, clearly unable to reason with the incensed Frenchman, shrugged his shoulders and shook his head.

"What the fuck does that even mean? Look, I'm trying to explain what happened up there."

"IT ... MEANS ... 'QUINN, ... SHUT THE FUCK UP WITH YOUR BULLSHIT!!!' I don't want to hear about your bad fucking day, about Pemba being sick, or the oxygen, or the kid's shitty gloves, or your lost ice axe, or any of the other pathetic excuses that have been filtering down from the Glacier Camp for the past twenty-four hours because you were too shit-scared to come and tell me yourself. I may have listened to you this morning but it's too fucking late in the day now. It's done. The kid is fucked. And now his rich papa is going to see that I am also. He won't pay me what he owes on the expedition. He won't pay any of it. I needed that fucking money. It was important. Getting that boy to the top and back safely was why I employed you, one of the reasons that Tate Senior chose my expedition above so many others, and you screwed it up completely."

For a second, what he was hearing reminded Quinn of the $100,000 summit bonus—all that Sarron could talk about before the climb. Wondering if such an amount of money could really be that important or if it was the drink making Sarron so crazy, Quinn told himself, once more, to try and stay reasonable. "Well you obviously don't want to hear me out but I'm telling you something was wrong. Maybe we should try and do this tomorrow. You are clearly in no condi—"

Again Sarron interrupted him, this time apoplectic, shouting so loud that the whole Base Camp must have heard.

"THE ONLY THING THAT WAS WRONG UP THERE WAS YOU, YOU IDIOT! YOU KILLED MY CLIENT! YOU AND YOUR FUCKING SHERPA FRIENDS ABANDONED NELSON TATE JUNIOR ON THE SECOND STEP! YOU MUST HAVE! THAT BOY DIDN'T WEIGH MORE THAN A FUCKING CHICKEN. A GUY LIKE YOU—YOU COULD HAVE CARRIED HIM DOWN BY YOURSELF!"

"You know that's not true."

Sarron stopped and looked at Quinn, then said with an apparent relish, "It's what I have already told his father this evening. You should have got back quicker."

Quinn was stunned. "You can't have. But if you did then obviously you do have something to hide. Maybe Pemba is right about your oxygen."

Something in Sarron snapped. Without warning he launched himself at Quinn's throat.

Together they fell, crashing back onto the table, sending bottles, cans, and the Chinese liaison officer flying to the floor.

Hitting the ground hard, Wei Fang came to, shrieking like a stuck pig as he scrambled on all fours to the side of the tent.

Quinn, weak from the climb, struggled to hold the rabid Frenchman above him as Sarron snatched up a fallen vodka bottle and, holding the neck, smashed it against the hard ground. It broke in an explosion of glass and clear spirit.

Sarron thrust the jagged remnant of the bottle at Quinn.

Desperate to keep the stabbing, razor-sharp edge away from his face, Quinn jerked his left hand up to grab Sarron's wrist. But however hard he tried to push it away, the glass spike kept getting nearer and nearer. Sarron, strong and rested from being only at the Base Camp, was simply overpowering him.

Just as the glass edge sliced across his cheek with a spurt of blood, the Frenchman was suddenly wrenched up and away from Quinn.

Pemba had the arm with the bottle, Dawa, the shaft of the old ice axe under Sarron's chin and across his neck.

Together, the two Sherpas pulled him back and over onto the ground.

Other Sherpas and Tibetans began pouring into the tent as Quinn got up.

Lhakpa and a Sherpa Quinn didn't recognize joined Pemba in holding Sarron down as Dawa stood, resting the steel end-spike of the axe on Sarron's throat, saying only, "Stop."

The Frenchman wrestled once against the hold of his captors, forcing Dawa to jab the spike tighter into his throat.

"Stop," he repeated.

This time Sarron did.

"I suggest you go now, Sarron," Quinn said, getting up from the floor, holding his bleeding face.

Sarron said nothing, immobile, just staring back up with hatred.

Slowly Dawa pulled the axe tip back. As he did so, the Frenchman began to speak, softer now, all the time staring at the spike of the old ice axe Dawa was still pointing at him. "*C'est ma maison ici*. You really think you can do this to me here and get away with it?"

Shaking his arms from the grip of the other Sherpas, Sarron got up and, looking at Quinn, said, "Someone told me that you were crying during the descent, saying it should be you still up on the Second Step, not that kid. Frankly, my friend, it would have been better if it were. Don't think that I have finished with you or your two Sherpa saviors yet." Pushing through the onlookers, he left the tent.

With the show over, the mess tent emptied as Dawa organized for Quinn's face to be butterfly stitched and then disappeared into a group of Sherpas and Tibetans. An agitated discussion started amongst them all just outside the tent's door. When it finally quieted down, Dawa reappeared alongside Quinn to say that between them all they were going to keep a watch for Sarron so he couldn't try anything more that night.

Quinn thanked him yet again for everything he had done.

Dawa just nodded in silent response before raising up the old axe once more.

"Mr. Neil, I keep this for you. I bring it. For you," he said, pushing the axe toward him.

Quinn had totally forgotten about the old axe from the gorak cave until he had seen it at Sarron's throat. Having it in front of him now brought it all flooding back. "Sorry, Dawa, but I don't want that thing."

"No, Mr. Neil. It save you twice now. I know you meant to have it," Dawa insisted, pushing the long wooden axe into his reluctant hand.

Quinn took it, if only to humor the veteran Sherpa. As he did so, he noticed the moon-faced Wei Fang was still there, staring intently at them both. Quinn walked across to him and, with his free hand, snatched the whiskey bottle the Chinaman had salvaged from the floor.

"I need that more than you."

20

Using the long ice axe as a walking stick, Quinn gradually left the battleground behind. A canopy of bright stars now filled the night sky curving over him and, although even colder, there was not the slightest breeze to carry away the intensifying noise from the summit party in the other, distant mess tent. It was still in full swing, probably recently reinvigorated by news of the fight in the No Horizons Tent. Everest Base Camp thrived on two things: summits and gossip.

The cut on his cheek stinging, Quinn stopped, trying to shake off the pain and the shock of Sarron's attack. He had always heard that the guy was difficult, a tough guy, a bit of a crook even, but there were many of those on Everest and he had worked well with a lot of them. Even when people had particularly warned him about Sarron he had thought that he could deal with pretty much anyone. But he couldn't handle this guy. He was absolutely crazy.

But isn't it really your own hubris that walked you into this nightmare?

Quinn knew it was. He had told himself that after eight summits he had Everest's number, that he could get a sixteen-year-old boy up and down it, even when inside he had serious reservations about getting involved with such a young client.

And yes, it was also about the money.

The expedition company that originally booked him for 2009 had folded just a few months before the season began. When he had made it known to the other outfits he was available, he thought he'd already missed out for that year, but almost immediately Sarron had jumped at the chance of hiring him. Quinn had actually been slightly flattered that the Frenchman had been so keen. Like him or not, Sarron was an important player on the mountain and the fact that he was also offering to pay him twenty thousand dollars to be the head guide, more than he was usually paid, with a bonus of another ten thousand if one client in particular was successful, made it better still. Until that season Quinn had always accepted that he was never going to be paid enough for the task of guiding on Everest. It hadn't mattered. He made up the shortfall in his wallet in his head, with thoughts that April and May were lean months elsewhere in the mountains and that he would be doing what he loved on the greatest mountain in the world. Yes, it was true. The combination of his hubris and Sarron's—or should he say, Tate Senior's money—had pushed his normal standards aside.

Unscrewing the cap of the whiskey bottle, he took yet another long swig, letting it burn, hurt even. When he pulled the bottle back down, he noticed the music from the party again. An older rock song was playing. It was called "Photograph."

Of course it was.

The word immediately took him back to those chaotic moments on the summit with Dawa and the boy—dangerous, absurd, little more than a soulless business transaction.

All for a bloody photograph.

Quinn was still surprised and disgusted with himself that he had gone along with it. With everything that had happened since, the fact that he hadn't even looked at his camera put the futility of that summit photo into even greater context.

But why am I so surprised?

One way or the other, it was always about a photograph.

Even for him.

A photograph had brought him to that place, to mountaineering, in fact.

Standing there, alone in the cold, drinking more whiskey, he recalled the tall-ceilinged school library where he had first seen the fateful picture. In the beginning that library had just been a place of sanctuary, a book-lined alternative to the hard walls and fickle *Lord of the Flies* atmosphere that otherwise pervaded the old English boarding school he was sent to at seven years old. He would hide inside its realm of utter silence, forensically working his way through the literary fads of young boys in the '70s: hand-me-down paperbacks by men like Dennis Wheatley, James Herbert, Sven Hassel, Erich von Däniken, that weren't even to be found on the library's shelves but bartered and borrowed in the dangerous corridors outside.

Whenever he finished his latest contraband text, he would be drawn to the rows of *National Geographic* that blocked a wall of shelves with decades of fading yellow.

Those compact, solid journals soon became his reason to visit the library. Quinn would study them for hours, diving into the rich, glossy photographs and reading the elegant descriptions. He let them transport him far from that place, to the top, the bottom, the hottest, the coldest, the wettest, the driest, even the nothingness of outer space. He didn't know it then, but those magazines ignited a wanderlust that would never leave him, a desire for adventure that could never be satisfied, however much he tried.

One image appeared often. It was the perfect photograph, one of the most famous of the twentieth century. Every time he came across it, it would hold him transfixed within its sublime instant. The picture showed a man in an almost jaunty "one foot up, one foot down" pose, as if triumphantly stepping onto the shoulder of some huge beast he had hunted for years and finally felled with the perfect shot. A tight snow pyramid beneath his feet cascaded down like newly opened champagne. To each side of its sloping, white shoulders, a distant horizon was lined with the tops of other mighty, yet clearly lower, mountains. It was unequivocally the "top of the world."

The climber, standing in the photograph's center, was completely swaddled in thick, gaitered boots, bulky grey trousers, and an all-covering navy blue parka. His face was masked and hidden, but the oxygen mask and dark goggles seemed to disappear the more you looked, until it revealed a white-toothed smile of utter joy. Above, reaching up into a clear yet darkening sky, was an ice axe raised in triumph. A number of flags were attached, mostly hidden behind the axe's shaft, being torn back and away from the photographer by what must actually have been a violent, constant wind—the only clue in the photograph that the conditions were anything less than perfectly serene.

Only one flag was clearly visible: the red, white, and blue of the Union Jack. It branded the photo, soaring away from the fact that neither the person bearing the axe, Sherpa Tenzing Norgay, nor the person so expertly using the camera, Sir Edmund Hillary, was actually British. It overpowered such details with the weight of its history to shout, "Great Britain, first to the summit of Mount Everest, May 29, 1953." Even a young boy could see that the Britain that now lay outside his school gates was no longer great. It made crappy cars and put up ugly concrete tower blocks. It went on strike continually and sent its once-glorious soldiers no further than Northern Ireland, where they were reviled and executed by the Provisional IRA under a continual grey rain. But to young Quinn that Everest summit photo was British, and it was great. It made him believe in his country and also a little in himself as he wondered if, just maybe, one day he too could accomplish such a fantastic feat.

That famous photograph quickly directed him to the dry explanation of John Hunt's *The Ascent of Everest* and then accompanied him onward to many other mountains through the vivid translations of Maurice Herzog's *Annapurna*, Hermann Buhl's *Nanga Parbat Pilgrimage*, Heinrich Harrer's *The White Spider*. It even pushed him out of the library to pull him eight feet up onto the top of the wooden wainscoting that ran around the inside of the old, exposed walls of the gymnasium. Once there, it left him all alone to the backbeat of a thumping heart, dry-mouthed with vertigo, edging breathlessly along its two-inch-wide lip, knees trembling, small fingers continually searching for handholds within the rough-shaped stones and crumbling mortar. The first time he completed a lap of the entire gymnasium, he shouted with joy, feeling taller and stronger when he climbed down. He never stopped climbing back up, higher and higher, until in the end he turned his back on all the privilege and security his expensive education could have provided and headed for the hills instead.

Quinn lifted up the old axe that Dawa had returned to him. It was almost identical to the one he remembered in that original photo. It felt balanced in his hand yet so heavy when compared to the smaller, modern axes made of titanium and carbon fiber they now used. As he looked at it, the whiskey suggested to him that it could indeed be the very axe that Tenzing had raised that fine day. It was that vintage, maybe even older. In different circumstances he would have considered it to be a good find. He often came across old equipment high up on Everest. Most of it was junk really, bits of old canvas, tent pegs, tin cans, discarded pitons, once a hammer, but rarely something interesting, something like this. Only one other time had he found something its equal when he stumbled across a discarded brass oxygen cylinder from one of the British climbs of the thirties. He had transported that cylinder all the way back to England as a souvenir, despite the fact that it was desperately heavy, only to reluctantly later sell it on eBay for twelve hundred pounds to a collector in Germany. He had been sad to let it go, but, as always, money was tighter than sentiment.

Increasingly chilled by the cold, Quinn let the axe fall and returned to the small tent that had been his Base Camp home for the past six weeks. Nearing it, he passed through the harsh, acrid smoke of a yakherder's dry-dung campfire. Sat around the glowing embers were four hooded shadows, pushing themselves in close for warmth. One of them looked up and nodded at Quinn. It wasn't a Tibetan. It was Lhakpa Sherpa. "Don't worry, Mr. Neil. We take turns. Watch for Sarron. You sleep easy. Need rest. All better in the morning."

Unzipping his tent, Quinn pushed the ice axe and then his pack inside before reaching for a small gas lamp, which he lit. Once he had crawled in also, he collapsed onto his sleeping bag for a few minutes to recover. Then, putting the old ice axe inside the biggest of the two kit bags at the back of his tent, he told himself to start repacking the rest of his gear for the long journey back to Kathmandu. But it was too cold; he was too tired. He'd do it tomorrow.

Instead, he pulled his sleeping bag around his shoulders and sipped more of the whiskey from the bottle. He'd drunk enough to no longer feel the pain it caused his split lips and sore throat, the sharp heat loosening his tired mind instead. The song "Photograph" was still caught in it, looping relentlessly. He drank to its beat.

Photograph.
Photograph.
Photograph.
He told himself not to do it but he did.
Reaching into his pack, he pulled out his camera

and, from his kit bag, another battery pack. With fumbling, cold-deadened fingers, he put the charged battery into the camera and turned it on.

Neil Quinn began to scroll through the pictures it contained, following the one-way journey a sixteen-year-old boy had made to the roof of the world.

No amount of whiskey could help him after that.

21

REICHSAUTOBAHN 7, DIRECTION NORTHWEST, GERMANY
October 16, 1938
1:21 a.m.

Trying to ignore his left index finger, Josef listened to the steady hum of the truck's heavy tires on the smooth pavement beneath his feet. He wished the noise would lull him to sleep, but it didn't, asking instead the continual question, "Where are they taking us?" The engine rumbled in reply but gave no answer as the bloody end of Josef's finger seared in pain once more.

How could one finger hurt so damn much?

The pain seemed to have layers to it. The sharp, cutting sensation of the nail having been ripped away now lay above a secondary pulsing that felt deeper than the thickness of the finger. Rhythmical, like the relentless ticking of a clock, it told him that the ointment, smeared on hastily before the finger was bandaged, was already losing the battle with infection.

If this is only one finger then what the hell must Gunter be feeling?

Josef looked down at the shadow of his friend stretched out on the floor of the truck. Even in the dark he could see the white of the bandages that entirely covered both of his mutilated hands and hear the occasional moans that accompanied his constant drift in and out of consciousness. Reaching out to him with his still-intact right hand, Josef felt once again the hot fever on Gunter's clammy forehead. He wondered if he was dying.

The thought frightened Josef. He and Kurt, his hands untouched by the gestapo but his damaged knee having suffered particular attention throughout their interrogations, had already done what little they could to try and aid their broken friend. They had given him sips from the water bottles the guards provided. They had made him as comfortable as possible, propping up and covering him with the three old blankets that awaited them in the back of the otherwise empty truck. They had wiped his brow. But their best efforts had made no impression on his suffering.

It appeared to Josef to be more than just the torn and ripped fingers. He suspected that Gunter had sustained some unseen internal injury in one of the earlier beatings. The gestapo had known from the start that Gunter was the ringleader. They'd singled him out, dedicating the most time to him, hoping to extract what they were so desperate to find out. Josef didn't know if Gunter even knew the true identity of the people in Munich who were behind the smuggling operation, but, looking at those bandaged hands, in the end he must have told his torturers everything. No one could resist the gestapo, not even Gunter.

Again Josef wondered where they were being

taken. They were back in the hands of the SS now and the only conclusion he could come to was a desperate one; they were being taken somewhere to be shot. It couldn't be for more torture. The gestapo were masters at that and had already extracted every detail. No, the SS would simply want to silence the three of them. They had been there on that hill, they knew what the SS had done to those nine Jews, including women and children—Josef himself had complained about it during their interrogation. In the darkness of the truck, Josef saw it all again, hearing once more the shots and the explosion that had killed them. With every murderous echo that night, a bit more of his old, carefree life had been wrung from him. By the time they had reached the valley road, Josef knew that he was no longer young, no longer a free person who lived without consequences. Ever since, the memory of those sounds had denied him the right to even hope for his own survival.

Why couldn't the SS just have arrested us?
Is this really what happens now?

Gunter began to moan, then screamed once, horribly, before falling silent again. The cry made Josef recall his own screams when the gestapo had set to work on his hand only for that tall, blond SS-obersturmführer to suddenly barge into the room, waving a fistful of official-looking documents and demanding they immediately release him.

At first, his interrogators had refused to unbuckle the heavy leather straps that bound Josef's wrists to the deliberately spoon-shaped wooden arms of the chair. On the left one, in a pool of red blood that spewed from the end of his finger, the rough pliers, his fingernail still within its teeth, was set down alongside his trapped hand. With a taste of bile in his mouth, eyes stinging with dirty tears of pain, Josef had flicked the pliers onto the floor, only to receive a punch in the side of the head from one of his torturers.

The SS officer responded by instantly pulling his Luger from its holster and shouting, "Do not touch this man again, any of you. These documents show that your most senior officer, the reichsführer of the SS, Heinrich Himmler, orders that you release him into my custody immediately. Do so now, or I will shoot you myself!" The man had jabbed the pistol toward the face of the nearest gestapo officer and passed the documents to another. Within seconds, Josef was out of the room. His finger hastily covered, he was put into the awaiting lorry, Kurt and Gunter already inside. They had left immediately.

Another cry from Gunter made Josef, once again, tell the two SS guards seated between them and the rear of the truck that he needed their help and, once again, they said and did nothing. A terse "you should save your breath" had been their single response for the entire journey. There was nothing Josef Becker could do but sit in silence as his friend failed, waiting for arrival at what he was sure would be his final destination.

* * *

Their first stop after the arrest had been their own regimental barracks in Garmisch. For a number of days a visiting officer from the SS, accompanied by officers from his own regiment, had individually questioned them. The interviews were thorough yet formal, almost civilized in their adherence to military protocols.

Josef hadn't told them much because he didn't know much.

Yes, he was a qualified Heeresbergsführer, an official mountain guide of the army.

Occasionally they did guide people over the mountains and bring contraband back.

Yes, they did get paid to do it, always in cash when they handed over the goods at the end of the return journey.

He sent most of the money to his mother and two sisters who lived in Elmau.

Yes, he had also bought a new BMW motorcycle with some of it. He used it to get back to his home village to visit his family.

They were a close family, had been since his father was killed in the Great War.

Yes, he used the motorcycle to go climbing as well.

Yes, he did like to climb. He had climbed many routes.

Everything: rock, ice, snow, whatever necessary to reach the top.

Germany and Austria. Switzerland also when he got some leave.

No, not always alone, but often.

No, he didn't know who organized their smuggling runs. He had never met them, never even been told about them. He was only a guide. It was what he did before the army; it was what he did in the army; it was what he would do after the army.

No, he didn't understand that there would be no "after the army" now.

No, he wasn't a communist.

No, he didn't love Jews. They were people. He was a guide. He had guided a lot of people in the mountains.

The interviews went on and on. Josef saw no reason to be devious. The only thing he knew for sure was that he climbed, he soldiered, he worked with Gunter and Kurt on whatever mountain work came up. His captors knew it also, so why deny it?

On the fourth day, Josef had been taken from his cell back to the interview room once more. As he walked there, he wondered what use it would be to ask the same questions all over again. However, this time when he stepped into the room he was confronted with the back of the commanding officer of the 1st Gebirgs Division.

Generalmajor Ludwig Ganzler was looking out of the frosted window and up at the sheer, spiky rock faces of the Wetterstein Mountains that towered over the barracks. Ganzler's adjutant was already sitting to the side of the questioning table, a leather file of papers open in front of him. The generalmajor turned to contemplate Josef as he entered. He was smoking a meerschaum pipe with an ivory bowl carved in the shape of a ravenous wolf's head. The room was clouded with the smoke of the pipe's aromatic tobacco. It irritated Josef's eyes as he stood to attention and saluted, yet its smell was faintly comforting. His father's pipes still hung on the wall of his mother's house.

Ganzler gestured Josef to a chair. As he also sat at the table, Ganzler placed the pipe down in front of him on a silver dish that his adjutant must have brought into the room for that precise purpose. The wolf's smoke dwindled and then stopped. It was the first time that Josef had ever been so near to his commanding officer. He was a long-faced man, grey-haired. He spoke like a gentleman. Josef had taken many like him hunting in the hills but never the generalmajor. At his neck, behind the Iron Cross First Class, hung a distinctive enameled blue star, the "Pour le Mérite." In the regiment they said that the generalmajor had won his Blue Max, the highest decoration of German valor, as a young lieutenant on the Italian front in 1917, the week before another young officer by the name of Erwin Rommel had done the same, and that they had become lifelong friends as a result.

The two medals trembled a little as Ganzler began to speak. "You know that I watched you make that solo climb up the Waxenstein?"

Josef nodded.

The officer glanced at Josef's right hand.

"I don't see the regimental ring I sent to you in recognition of your feat. Did the SS take it?"

"Yes," Josef replied, recalling the moment before they were placed in the cells, when they had torn the identification tag from his neck, taking his ring with it.

"A pity. Whatever trouble you may be in now, Gefreiter Becker, you earned that ring that day. Do you know I followed every move you made through a telescope I had brought to my office? It was a beautiful thing to see, a perfect demonstration of bold, fluid climbing. I wondered how you could do it, so alone up there, without ropes or pitons. You were hugely exposed. One slip. Imagine."

Ganzler stopped, waiting for Josef to say something.

"I never think about it, Herr Generalmajor. I just concentrate on climbing."

"So you do, to very great effect. Watching you that day made me proud of our regiment. I thought to myself it is not only the SS who can conquer the great alpine north faces, but we, the Gebirgsjäger, the true troops of the mountains, can also climb like spiders. With men like you, I said to myself, it is true; Germany can be truly great once again.

"Your officers tell me, and I believe them, that you are the finest climber in the entire division, one of the very best in all Bavaria. I wondered if I might watch you fall that day, but I didn't, and I was glad of it." He paused and then said slowly as he stared at Josef, "It goes against the grain of any decent commanding officer to watch helplessly as good men die."

Josef hung his head a little to escape Ganzler's piercing look.

"You should know, Gefreiter Becker, that I have tried to keep this as a military matter—a regimental matter, in fact. I and others like me believe that we should be able to deal with our own. However, I fear that this may no longer be possible in your case. The gestapo and the kripo are fighting between themselves to have you three delivered to Munich. You must understand that there are other agendas at work in this country now that go far beyond simple soldiering. They make matters such as this much more complicated than they once might have been."

The generalmajor waited to let what he was saying sink in before he spoke again.

"The reason that I have called you here is to ask you one last time, as one soldier to another, if there is anything that you can tell me that might make it possible for me to keep you in Garmisch, to give you a life behind bars here rather than a wasteful death in Munich.

"War is coming, sooner or later, Gefreiter Becker. When it does, a man like you would not stay in any jail of mine but would be free to serve his country, to take his chance alongside the rest of my soldiers. I think that you earned that right as I watched you climb.

"Tell me, Becker, who organized the smuggling? Was it Obergefreiter Schirnhoffer? Who in Munich was behind it? Give me something, a name, anything that I can put on the record to permit me to keep you here."

Josef wanted to say something, but he only knew one name and Ilsa was dead. In silence, he found himself looking directly at the officer's Blue Max medal. It was a thing of beauty, delicate and fine, chivalrous when compared to the blunt, black Iron Cross that hung to the front of it. It spoke to Josef of a time when innocent children weren't shot like rats.

"The only thing that I can put on the record, Herr Generalmajor, is that the SS soldiers who captured us murdered the nine Jews that we were transporting over the hills," Josef said, looking at the generalmajor.

Ganzler stared back into Josef's eyes for a second. "And I think they will murder you too, Gefreiter

Josef Becker. I have given you a last chance, and now, whether I like it or not, I must accept that I am watching you fall. You just haven't hit the ground yet."

He stood up, saluted, and, with a final glance at Josef, took up his pipe and left.

Within an hour, the three of them were being moved to Munich in two black Mercedes cars. Through the rear windows, the snowy Bavarian mountains had silently watched them go. Two hours later they arrived at Gestapo Headquarters in the center of Munich, immediately leaving the surface world of night and day for a small cell in a basement.

Down there, Josef understood immediately that his life was now the possession of others, to do what they would with it. Almost immediately, new interrogations began, interrogations that became beatings, and beatings that became torture, always Gunter first. When Gunter was thrown back into the cell that last time, his fingers bleeding, and they pulled Josef out, he already knew what they were going to do to his precious hands.

The arrival of the SS officer may have stopped it after the agony of just one finger but it couldn't have been for compassionate reasons. There was no compassion in the SS. It had to be because they wanted the prisoners for themselves. They were going to be silenced.

* * *

The monotonous sound of the truck's engine suddenly changed, the sound jerking Josef back to the moment as he felt the vehicle turn off the long highway it had been following. The engine started to rise and fall, the lorry slowly working its way along what felt like narrower, windier roads. A deeper chill cut into the truck, an invisible mist moistening his clothes and bringing with it a smell of damp, earthy farmland. It made Josef wonder if they were going to have to dig their own graves.

The truck slowed even more, changing down to its lowest gear, protesting as it climbed slowly up a rippling gradient before finally stopping. One of the SS guards immediately pushed a sacking hood over Josef's head and pulled him toward the back of the truck where unseen hands roughly pulled him down onto his feet. Through the bottom of the hood Josef caught a glimpse of damp, rounded cobblestones, shiny yellow with reflected light.

Standing there, Josef could feel his heart pulsating in his chest, beating like a massive drum. He tried to calm it by thinking of the mountains but instead could only recall the face of little Ilsa in that godforsaken chapel above the Paznaun and the sound of the rifle bolts from outside.

He waited to hear that sound again.

22

HOTEL SHAMBHALA, LHASA, TIBET
May 31, 2009
4:50 p.m.

Sarron stared up at the asbestos-paneled ceiling of his hotel room in Lhasa. He had stopped the plump Han Chinese hooker from dressing. Even if her high-pitched squeals of faked appreciation had reminded him of a yak calf with a hoof caught in barbed wire, he wasn't finished with her yet.

Watching her dimpled backside wobble to the bathroom, he reached for his cigarettes. He had seen her hanging around the hotel when he returned from the airport and thought she might distract him. It hadn't worked. His body was still tense with rage, violently seething. He had debt up to his eyeballs, contacts around the world that no longer returned his calls, the Indian Intelligence Bureau investigating him for arms trading, and now this fuckup on Everest.

He lit a cigarette and watched its smoke twist and turn upward as he told himself again that the summit bonus, his ticket out, was gone. The closing words of his last telephone conversation with Tate Senior burned once more in his ears. "Sarron, don't expect another cent from me. Understand also that my lawyers are going to find everything there is in this world that has your name on it and tie it up in such a storm of endless legal bullshit that it will be frozen harder than my s—" The incensed American had been unable to complete the word "son."

Lying back on the stained nylon bed cover, Sarron felt the walls of the small room closing in on him. The feeling made him tremble with anger and aggression, his mind raced, flicking involuntarily between thoughts of violence and pain. Struggling to suppress the urge to smash both the cheap room and the slovenly whore to pieces, he snatched the glass ashtray from the nightstand and perched it on the center of his chest over his tattoo of the *1er Bataillon de Chasseurs Alpins* regimental badge as if it might pin him to the bed. Telling himself to calm down, he drew heavily on the cigarette, filling his lungs with smoke.

Now exhale.

Slow.

Inhale again.

The cigarette burned as Sarron steadied his thoughts.

Looking down to ash the cigarette, the old tattoo, distorted and magnified through the thick glass, caught his eye. It resembled little more than an ugly black bruise now. The sight of it made him think back to a time when it was crisp and new, to the lull during that vicious fighting in Chad when it had first been inked. He was going to have to fight like that now for his survival.

Inhaling deeply again on the cigarette, feeling his lips curling back against his teeth, he told himself if that was to be the case then the people who had let him down were going to be the first casualties.

Quinn.

Pemba.

Dawa.

They were all up there with the boy.

They should have done better—that fucking Quinn, especially.

Brooding about the Englishman, Sarron was reminded of what Wei Fang, the Chinese liaison officer, told him happened after he had left the tent. How Dawa had handed Quinn that old ice axe, insisting that he take it even when Quinn tried to refuse.

Why did Dawa do that?

Why did Quinn seem so spooked by the axe?

What is its significance?

Something inside Sarron cautioned that he needed to know the answers to those questions, and that he should limit his opening salvo of the coming battle to stun, not kill, until he did. Even if it was nothing, Dawa and Quinn had used that axe to humiliate him and, in return, he would make sure that it would be used to punish them when the time came.

Stubbing out the finished cigarette in the ashtray, he got up from the bed, retrieved his cell phone from his discarded clothes, and called a number in Kathmandu. He issued a stream of instructions before throwing the phone back onto his clothes and motioning the returning Chinese girl facedown onto the bed.

Just as he was saying, "Bitch, you are going to fuck me silently this time," and reaching to the floor for her underwear to stuff into her gap-toothed mouth to ensure she complied, his phone rang again. Seeing the same Kathmandu area code on the screen, Sarron answered, shouting, "What now? Haven't I made myself clear?"

"I don't think so. Well, not yet anyway," said the refined English voice on the other end of the phone.

"Who is this?"

"Sarron, it's Henrietta Richards. I have been asked to look into the death of Nelson Tate Junior by the US Ambassador to Nepal. I have some questions for you."

"FUCK OFF!" Sarron screamed.

The hooker flinched on the bed as the cell phone flew across the room to shatter against the far wall.

23

APARTMENT E, 57 SUKHRA PATH, KATHMANDU, NEPAL
May 31, 2009
3:05 p.m. (Nepal Time)

On the other side of the mountains, Henrietta was not the least bit surprised by Sarron's reaction to her call. The honest and the intelligent had always seen her as the undisputed historian, the guardian even, of Himalayan mountaineering. They actively sought her confirmation of their successful summits as a necessary endorsement of what they had achieved. The braggarts, the frauds, and the crooks, on the other hand, saw her only as a potential threat. There were many reasons for Henrietta Richards to dislike Jean-Philippe Sarron, and the fact that he had always refused to give her the time of day was confirmation of them all.

In the beginning Henrietta had come across Sarron, as she did most people, because of his climbing achievements, but in the latter years of her time at the embassy, it was more due to his other activities.

There were many myths and legends about Sarron but even when she found that the truth was different, it was, ultimately, no less tawdry or dangerous. It was said, for example, that Sarron had been in the French Foreign Legion—he sometimes said so himself—but Henrietta knew from her investigations that he had actually served in the *1er Bataillon de Chasseurs Alpins*, the French Army mountain troops. He had only been seconded to the FFL when the intense fighting that took place between Chad and Libya in the mideighties moved into the Tibesti hills. What was undoubtedly true though, was that using accumulated periods of long leave, he did undertake some of the toughest climbs of that time. For a short period, Henrietta was even developing an admiration for his abilities, but when he showed absolutely no interest in respecting hers, she placed him under a more critical eye.

After one of those climbs, Sarron had somehow acquired a hotel in Kathmandu with a small trekking business. In the bars of Thamel, it was said that he bought them for when he was going to leave the army, but Henrietta knew they were actually given over under some duress in lieu of a nonexistent payment for a wayward shipment of French military oxygen. When Sarron did finish with the army in 1988, he moved to Nepal to take up the ownerships. The hotel was quickly sold as the man clearly had little aptitude for hospitality. However, trading on his climbing reputation and his ruthless streak, Sarron built up the guiding business, assisted in this by two brothers.

Oleg and Dmitri Vishnevsky were wild Russians from the mountainous Caucasus, who, as teenage conscripts to the OKSVA in Afghanistan, deserted by escaping over one of the highest passes into Pakistan during the winter. With no prospect of a welcome home from Mother Russia, they spent the next few years traveling onward, stealing and cheating their way along the tourist trails of the Indian subcontinent until caught one night breaking into Sarron's equipment store in Kathmandu. The pair told Sarron, during their subsequent beating, of how they had crossed the Dorah in January in little more than army fatigues, that they were Russian and nothing he could do would break them. Sarron, tempted by the challenge but suspecting they might be right, decided instead that they should work for him. He paid them very little, told them to drag his clients to the summit if necessary, and regularly tapped their psychotic streak if anyone crossed him.

By the midnineties, No Horizons, his unruly yet effective expedition company, had become increasingly successful at getting people up the highest peaks, even Everest if they paid enough. His heavy French brogue and constant cursing were ever-present features of those base camps where the majority of the occupants were paying handsomely for the often questionable pleasures of being there. As the number of climbers to the eight-thousand-meter peaks increased exponentially, so did the demand for bottled oxygen. By renewing some old military contacts and, quite literally, breaking some new local ones, Sarron started to feed off this market as well.

For a time, he appeared to be living well off it all. Too well to make sense, a few even said, despite the obvious facts that he paid his two head guides next to nothing, suffered no mark-up on his own oxygen, and was clearly one of the principal ringmasters of what was fast becoming a high-paying Everest circus. More recently however, everyone was in agreement that things seemed to have been turning against the Frenchman. A demand for higher standards and quality was making both the expedition and oxygen businesses more professional and competitive—a competition that increased still further when the global recession significantly reduced the number of punters able to pay the $65,000 Everest admission ticket. Sarron's problems were further compounded when his two guides, the "Vicious Twins" as they had become known, vanished after their sideline of importing crystal meth and MDMA from Thailand turned sour when a bad batch killed three backpackers in a Thamel dance club. Since Sarron had then been compelled to pay market rates to the more respected guides, he needed to try and win back the business he was losing.

That was enough of an explanation for most, but Henrietta knew the true extent of Sarron's other activities—and losses. Diplomatic circles had long suspected that No Horizons was also a "front" for profiteering from the Maoist insurgency in Nepal, primarily through the sale of stolen French army weapons to the rebels and general thuggery for hire in Kathmandu. The fact that the Nepalese Maoists had come in from the hills to political respectability in 2006 had also killed that side of Sarron's dealings, leaving only the Naxalite rebels in India as customers. From what Henrietta had heard, the Indian Intelligence Bureau were also now onto that. A failed, somewhat bizarre attempt in late 2008 to sell two containers of Chinese counterfeit climbing clothes through the port of Naples had even traced back to Sarron to show how desperate he had become.

Yes, it was hardly surprising that Sarron was not going to speak to her about such a disaster for his operation on Everest.

Calling over to Sanjeev Gupta, she asked, "Sanjeev, can you find out what hotel the No Horizons team uses in Kathmandu? It's probably the Peak or the Khumbu, most climbers tend to stay at one of those two. When you do, please give them a call and find out when the No Horizons team will be arriving back from Tibet. I want to organize one of my post-climb chats with Neil Quinn as soon as possible."

Feeling strangely irritated that Quinn should have gotten himself mixed up with someone like Sarron, Henrietta stood and readied herself to leave.

"I'm off now, Sanjeev. I think it might be useful to have one of my little lunches with Pashi the barber to hear what the gossip is on the No Horizons expedition. Can you warn him I'm coming? Back later."

24

WEWELSBURG CASTLE, NORTH RHINE-WESTPHALIA, GERMANY
October 16, 1938
3:21 a.m.

Josef, the burlap bag still covering his head, stood blindly in the cold awaiting his fate. But no guns were loaded, no shots fired.

The only sounds were remote noises of other people echoing from an unseen building he sensed was surrounding him.

They must have been delivered to a prison.

Finally hands gripped his shoulders and started him walking.

Another thought came to his mind.

Their prisons have guillotines.

The realization made him nauseous as through the bottom of his hood, Josef dizzily watched his feet slowly step up three steps, cross over a heavy stone doorstep, then follow a smooth-floored corridor, newly tiled in highly polished red, white, and black squares.

They walked far into the building before turning and entering what he thought must be a large room—unlikely in its overpowering warmth and rich smell of food.

Despite his fear, Josef's mouth instantly started watering.

The guard pushed Josef down onto a bench and removed the hood to reveal a heaped plate of steaming potato and sausage placed on the table in front of him. A ceramic mug of hot wine was set alongside it. It too steamed with a smell of mulled spices. To Josef's side, Kurt was also sat at the table, his leg propped out straight to the side of him, but there was no sign of Gunter.

The pair of them looked at each other, shrugged, and started eating hungrily.

When Josef drank from the mug, he noticed a small design on it. It was also on the plate, even engraved into the cutlery. Words within it read: "*SS-Schule Haus Wewelsburg.*"

Josef had no idea what that was. He didn't care; he hadn't been shot and he couldn't imagine he was going to be if they were letting him eat and drink like this.

Those were his last conscious thoughts.

* * *

Josef awoke to find himself lain out on a blanket on a wooden floor. His head was aching, his mouth dry, his tongue swollen, as if he was suffering the consequences of an evening mixing liters of wine and beer before a heavy yet too brief sleep.

Lifting his head, the daylight shining in through

a single-dormer window above him bleached his eyes.

With some difficulty, he stood up. Head reeling, he pushed out a hand to stabilize himself against a wall and looked around to see Kurt lying on another blanket. Gunter was on the only bed. Both were sleeping. Gunter's bandages seemed new, but blood was already seeping through them. He looked at his own hand and saw that the dressing on that had also been changed.

He checked his watch.

3:47

But it was stopped.

He asked himself, *When, a.m. or p.m?*

He didn't know.

The spinning in his head subsided a little so he moved over to Kurt, crouching down to give him a shake. Slowly he too began to wake.

Moving on to Gunter, Josef saw that he was breathing slowly now. Laying his undamaged hand on his friend's forehead he felt that his fever had receded a little.

Deciding to leave Gunter sleeping, he looked instead around the little room. It had few identifying features. The bare wooden floorboards were smoothly polished, the white walls newly painted. The dormer window had been recently reglazed. It was little more than another cell but cleaner and brighter, more monastery than prison.

Josef went to the window and looked out over rolling countryside. The land appeared hard and frosty, rendered colorless by a pale autumn haze. A roundel of white light hung low in the sky. Josef wondered if he was looking west or east, if the almost hidden sun was rising or falling. Trying the handle of the window, he was surprised to find that it clicked open readily. He pushed his head out into the cold air. The chill brought some precision to his befuddled brain as he understood that they were in a room high within the roof of a castle or country house, a tall building positioned higher still on some cliff or promontory that raised it up far above the surrounding countryside.

Directly below the window, Josef could see only the fall of the roof. It ended abruptly and barred him from seeing what was directly below. He could only look diagonally down at a distant wood and, further on into the distance, at a wide valley with a brown river that meandered through barren, buff-colored meadows punctuated by copses of tall, leafless black trees.

Holding on to the side of the window frame, Josef stuck his head and shoulders out further still. With a twist backward, he saw that the window projected out from a very steep, pitched roof that rose up to a high ridge. The covering was almost new, tiles of black slate, perfectly square, smooth to the touch, and tightly lapped together. His climbing instinct instantly questioned the grip they would offer and told him that that the unbounded edge below was unforgiving. One slip would send him down and out into the open air as efficiently as the ski jump his regiment had built in Garmisch for the '36 Winter Olympics.

To each side of him, more dormer windows punctuated the fall of the roof. The line of five to his right finished in a single, massive circular tower of a pale limestone that dominated that end of the castle. The tower's flat, round top with only a shallow battlement gave it an incomplete look, as if still awaiting some tall spire to give it further height and drama. From the windows that ran down the tower's side, Josef could see that it was at least five or six stories high. As he studied it, he noticed that the low sun had fallen a little from its first position. It was going down. His window was looking due west; the tower pointing directly to the north. The setting sun told him that whatever had been put in their food or drink the night before had knocked them out for the best part of a day.

Why?

Josef's eyes were drawn back to the top of the tower. There were two tall white poles rising up from the top. Each held an immense flag, one scarlet, the other jet black. Both were too big to be more than faintly disturbed by the weak breeze that was blowing from the northeast. Within the blood-red flag, Josef could see the familiar black and white of the circle and the swastika. The black of the other was broken only by two white blazes, the SS insignia. The sight made him recall again the "*SS-Schule Haus Wewelsburg*" embossed on the crockery of his last meal.

What is this place?

Turning back into the room, Kurt was now sitting up. He asked where they were. Josef tried to describe what he had seen but was distracted by Gunter, who was mumbling unintelligibly. At first they thought he was still asleep, but as Josef moved closer, he understood that Gunter too was now awake. He was asking for water.

Knowing already there was none in the room, Josef banged on the door to demand some attention. Almost instantly it unlocked, and a white-jacketed orderly entered as if they were at a hotel. Josef told him that they needed water. The man quickly left to return with a pitcher and some glasses. He waited as Josef gave some to Gunter. While he held the glass to Gunter's lips, Josef asked the hovering orderly where they were. "Wewelsburg, Westphalia," came the reply. "It is the castle of the reichsführer-SS, Heinrich Himmler, the academy and home of the SS. Now that you are all awake, I will get a doctor for your friend."

A little later, an SS officer with a medical bag came in. He introduced himself as a medical doctor but gave no further name. Diligently and slowly, he examined Gunter, who was drifting in and out of consciousness again. Then he administered an injection from a nickel and glass syringe into a vein on Gunter's inner forearm, saying only, "It will help him sleep," as he gently laid the arm with its bandaged hand back down on the bed.

Finished with Gunter, the SS doctor surprised Josef by asking to look at his finger. He stripped off the new dressing and thoroughly cleaned the ragged tear where his nail had once been with a strong disinfectant. The contact of the spirit with the bare flesh burned so much that Josef had to grit his teeth not to scream with pain. As the hole started to bleed again, the doctor quickly put on another new dressing, binding the individual finger so tightly that it throbbed intensely. After, he said, "I need to stitch that finger; the wound is still open. But now is not the time to anesthetize your hand, maybe later. It will hurt, but covered like this you can still use it."

The man then turned his attention to Kurt's damaged right knee. He unwound the bandage and released the splint to slowly try and bend the limb, feeling, as he did so, the patella—the action of the joint. It could barely move. Just the doctor's touch made Kurt flinch with pain. Rebandaging it, the doctor said only, "This knee is very badly broken," and left the room without further comment. Alone again, Josef and Kurt said little, confused by the medical visit. Uncertain as to what they should or could do next, Josef leaned against the side of the window and watched the light of the dull day fade to darkness until, unannounced, a single electric light went on in the small room and the orderly returned to set down a tray that offered them a simple meal of bread, cheese, and ham. This time there was no mulled wine, only another carafe of water. There was also no cutlery.

Instead of leaving immediately, the orderly joined Josef by the window. Standing alongside him to look out at the night, he said gently under his breath, "I don't have time to explain what happens here, but if you can get out, I would. It would be better to take your chance rather than wait for what they are going to do to you when the reichsführer arrives." Saying nothing more, the man quickly left the room. Josef heard the door key turn behind him even if the window remained open.

"Did you hear that?" Josef whispered.

Kurt nodded, looked at Gunter, and then pointed at his own knee as he shook his head.

Josef understood.

"Is he getting any better?"

Kurt hopped on his left foot over to the bed and sat on the side of it as he touched the side of Gunter's cheek with the back of his hand.

Gunter didn't move.

Immediately Kurt rushed his fingers down onto the side of his neck, feeling for a pulse.

He pushed once, then twice, in search of it, before stopping and turning back with a look of disbelief to say, "Josef, I think Gunter's dead."

Josef rushed over to them.

It was true. Gunter was dead.

He replayed the visit of the SS doctor over in his mind.

What was in that injection?

What is happening to us?

They both looked down at their oldest friend in silence, transfixed to the spot until Kurt said simply, "We will go when it's darkest."

"But what about your leg?"

"I would rather fall than wait here and let them play with us anymore."

25

Josef felt the mountains call to him, offering escape, as he crept out the narrow window. Outside on the sill, he could see a light burning within one of the tower windows to his right and the twinkling constellation of a small town in the far distance; but everywhere else, the main part of the castle, the other dormer windows, the surrounding countryside, was pitch black.

The cold night air blew across his face as he sat there thinking about the dead childhood friend he was going to leave behind. Unsought, the face of little Ilsa suddenly replaced Gunter's in his mind. Seeking to banish the ghosts from his head, Josef quickly climbed around the window frame, holding on to it tightly with both hands, his wounded index finger stabbing with pain from the tension of the holds. To relieve the strain on his hands, he tried to get some purchase with his feet on the steep tiled roof to the side of the window but the studded soles of his boots slipped and slid as if on black ice.

It wasn't going to work.

With his upper body strength, finger howling in protest, Josef pulled himself back up onto the window frame and into the room.

"Kurt, the roof's very steep and slippery," he said when inside. "We will need to do this in bare feet to have any chance of getting some grip. Take your boots off and lace them together to hang over your neck. I think it's too difficult to go straight up such a steep roof. We must get up onto the top of the dormer window and then move sideways across the fall of the roof using the others. In this way, we can reach a rain gully to the left where two parts of the roof join. It will give an easier line up to the ridge and from there we can see where to go next. Take a look out and see."

Kurt hopped to the window and, using his arms, pulled himself up to lean out and see the route Josef had described.

When he moved back in, he looked at Josef with a grim expression but resolutely said, "We go. Help me get this boot off."

"Okay, but you must watch exactly where I go. Keep your weight on your hands and your good leg," Josef instructed, as he unlaced and removed his friend's boots before climbing back out of the window.

Slowly and carefully, Josef stepped down onto the steep tiles once more. Chilled and damp to the touch, he pushed his toes against their thin edges to steady himself and moved one hand up, gripping the projection of the window. Tensing himself, he brought the other hand up, and below slowly began to edge his feet up the sloping tiles. Even as he was telling himself to move faster, that he must pull harder on the window structure to get his weight off his feet however much his hand hurt, they slipped away out from under him. His body instantly jerked downward from the side of the window to fall fully onto the steep roof.

Josef began to slide down the sharply angled roof toward the edge, an internal voice shouting, *This is it!*

The slide accelerated, his hands slapping uselessly against the slick tiles, feet scrabbling for purchase.

How long will I fall before I hit the ground?

Just as he anticipated answering his question, Josef's right toes touched something: a vent pipe projecting up through the tiles.

It jarred Josef to a momentary halt. A stop just long enough for him to find another tiny edge with his other foot and smear his body hard against the roof to arrest the fall.

Spread-eagled on the tiles, feeling their stone freeze his burning cheek, Josef desperately tried to regain his composure.

When he looked up again he saw the outline of Kurt leaning out of the dormer window watching him.

"Stay where you are," his friend said before vanishing from the window.

A few minutes later the end of the blanket that had covered Gunter was lowered to Josef's outstretched hand and gradually it pulled him back up to the window.

Shaken by his near fall, Josef rested inside. When he had recovered his breath, he said to Kurt, "I'm not sure we can do this."

"We must," came the reply. "Out there if we die, we at least die free. In here, who knows? Go again."

* * *

This time Josef was much quicker in his movements and he did make it up onto the top of the window's dormer roof, pausing there before making a darting sideways pass on all fours across to the next one and resting again. In this fashion he reached the guttered valley he had noticed before. To his relief he found that its two roof edges did give good purchase for his hands, and his toes slipped less on the rough lead sheet set between them, enabling him to rapidly monkey-climb up to the very ridge of the roof as he had anticipated.

High above the castle, released from the concentration it took to get up there, he looked down to see Kurt's dark form edging out of the window. However, almost the instant he was on the roof, his broken knee gave way beneath him and he vanished downward.

Josef heard the beginning of a shout and then only silence. Horrified, he recklessly slid back down the gully between the two roofs to get nearer. Reaching the edge, he looked across to be confronted with the silhouette of Kurt hanging from rain gutter that lined the bottom of the roof.

"Hold on. I'm coming," he shouted as loudly as he dared.

"No. Go," came the reply.

"You did it for me, I can do it for you," Josef said as he extended a foot down into the gutter, gently pushing his weight down onto the narrow trough to test its strength. To his relief it felt strong. When he kicked into it a couple of times, it still didn't move a fraction. It too seemed newly installed. It would hold them.

"Keep holding on!" he called across to Kurt again. Then, using the gutter to hold his toes, he turned inward, placed both hands flat on the roof tiles, and started to crab sideways across to his dangling friend as fast as he could. Desperate to get there, he was oblivious to the sharp edge of the roof tiles cutting into the fronts of his shins as he shuffled them from side to side.

Finally reaching his suspended friend, Josef leaned down, outstretching his left arm to reach him. His wounded finger stung viciously as he closed his hand around Kurt's wrist.

Leaning down further to try and tug it upward, Josef's heavy boots, still slung around his neck by their laces, suddenly slipped off and fell.

The boots hit Kurt's upturned face hard in its center. The surprise caused him to lose his fingerhold on the gutter, spurring Josef to squeeze the wrist he was clutching as tightly as he could. His wounded finger exploded with pain but he didn't let go, his grip holding Kurt who, after two attempts, managed to get his hands back onto the metal edge of the gutter. But however hard Kurt tried, he couldn't pull his body up. He needed both feet to try to walk up the wall as he hung there; but his right leg was useless, leaving only his left foot to scratch hopelessly at the side of the smooth, newly repointed wall.

Kurt struggled in vain to raise himself up using only the strength of his arms. Josef, still gripping his right wrist, encouraged him to keep trying, tugging on the wrist he was holding each time as he did so. With each painful pull, more blood oozed from his finger; seeping from the dressing into the grip he had on Kurt.

Josef could feel the wrist beginning to slip through the bloody wetness of his fingers.

Then Kurt felt it too.

He looked up at Josef one last time, shook his head, and released his hold on the gutter.

Kurt's full weight instantly wrenched his hand through Josef's bloody grip, ripping the dressing with it as it went.

With a scream of pain, Josef watched Kurt's body silently fall into the dark until, from somewhere deep below, there was a sudden crash through tree branches followed by a dull, heavy thump.

Stunned by what had happened, Josef just lay there, straddled across the bottom of the roof, awaiting the shouts of guards, the beams of spotlights from below, the rifle shots or machine-gun fire that must surely follow. He didn't even care. When those lights came on, he decided that he would jump too.

Panting, shivering, he prepared himself for the inevitable. But no lights did come on. The silence, returning quickly after the sickening thud of Kurt hitting the ground, sustained, as if only a single stone had been dropped down a deep well.

Orphaned by his friend's fall, Josef slowly twisted himself back up the roof and, using the gutter once again to hold his feet, worked his way back to the diagonal rain groove.

Still there were no noises, no lights, no shots, only the intense pain in his hand, so he climbed on back up to the central ridge of the main roof, where he stopped to rest. Straddling the crest as if on a horse, he sat there, taking in deep breaths of the cold night air while his desperate brain struggled to formulate his next move.

From up there the first thing that was apparent was that the castle was not square. It was a narrow triangle shaped like a spearhead. The bigger tower to the north was the tip of the spear point, and the two other corners each had a smaller tower. The three flanks of the castle were set under steeply pitched roofs, and within Josef could see an illuminated triangular courtyard. He found it strange that the courtyard was so well lit, yet the outer walls of the castle were so completely dark.

More pain from his ripped finger stopped him thinking about it. Tearing a strip of material from the bottom of his shirt, he bound his wounded, bleeding finger as tight to the next as he could. Josef then started moving along the ridge of the roof toward the first of the two smaller towers. When he reached its side, he felt the surface. The stone was smooth and well-fitted. It would have been difficult to insert a pocketknife blade between the blocks, let alone fingers. It offered no possibility of a descent so he edged around the upper wall of the tower and down the next section of roof as far as he dared to study that face of the castle.

It was as high and sheer as the one he had come from. His best option was beginning to look like climbing back into the castle through a window and trying his luck at getting out from the inside. But with the likelihood of a confusing maze of corridors and staircases all inhabited by SS soldiers, that didn't appeal. Climbing quietly down the outside, if possible, had to be the better alternative. Josef moved back up onto the very ridge of the roof again and across to climb around the back of the next tower and on to the castle's third side.

This time he found that he didn't have so far to

climb up to get onto the crest of the roof. The third side of the building was at least two stories lower. He also saw that halfway along, it was breached by a cobbled bridge that gave access into the castle's internal courtyard. Where the bridge met the wall of the castle, a tall yet narrow enclosed structure with a small roof projected out. It must once have housed a portcullis or drawbridge mechanism. The structure was buttressed to the sides and decorated with filigrees of ornate stonework, its construction older, rougher than the other parts of the building. Upon seeing it, Josef felt his heart leap. He knew he could down-climb it.

Climbing along the ridge until he was directly above it, Josef slowly slipped down the roof to arrive directly above the entranceway. There, he hung from the gutter and dropped onto the top of the small parapet roof that projected out from the main wall. He crouched there for a while, studying the best way down. Then, considering each hand and foothold one at a time, Josef began to climb down the right side of it.

The cobbles of the road bridge started to come up to meet him. He could see no guard but told himself that when he reached the bridge he was going to have to move quickly and silently to get to the dark woods beyond. He cursed the loss of his boots, but there was nothing he could do about that for the moment. Foot down, hand down, foot down, hand down, he went, until, preparing himself for the dash he would have to make when he hit the bridge, Josef stretched his left foot down to make contact with the top of the wall that lined the side of the bridge.

His bare foot pawed the air.

"If you move your foot about five centimeters to

the left and a little lower, you will find what you are looking for," a crystal-clear voice said from the dark.

The sound made Josef start.

His immediate thought was to chance a jump to the side of the bridge, into the unknown below.

"If you jump, Gefreiter Becker, you will fall about ten meters. It probably won't kill you, but it is somewhat rocky down there. It would likely shatter your legs, and I could ensure you quite some time without treatment so that it did end up killing you. I suggest you step onto the bridge and put your hands up instead," the voice continued, as if reading Josef's mind.

Josef followed the instructions, stepping onto the parapet wall and down into the middle of the cobbled roadway as a floodlight somewhere beyond the bridge flicked on to wash Josef in a blinding white light.

An SS officer clad in a peaked cap and a long, black leather overcoat calmly stepped out of the shadows at the end of the bridge and walked toward him.

"Time to stop now, I'm afraid. No more climbing for tonight," the officer said, pointing a pistol directly at Josef.

The officer's face slowly appeared beneath the peak of his black cap. It was the same blond SS-obersturmführer who had released Josef from the gestapo. Four more SS officers appeared behind him and began to walk across the bridge back toward the castle entrance. They were chatting and laughing amongst themselves. Josef also recognized one of them immediately.

"Most impressive, my dear Jurgen, even if only one of your candidates has successfully passed your audition. Gentlemen, it is late; we will speak further in the morning. Good evening to you all," said the man that Josef knew from photographs in the newspapers to be the reichsführer-SS, Heinrich Himmler. He left the group to stride quickly back into his castle. He stared into Josef's eyes as he passed but without uttering another word.

26

THE KHUMBU HOTEL, THAMEL, KATHMANDU, NEPAL
June 5, 2009
8:45 a.m.

The note had been waiting for him at the reception when they checked in late the night before.

Its scrawl of ballpoint read:

> *Mr. Neil Quinn,*
> *Telephone message from Mr. Sanjeev Gupta:*
> *Miss Richards would like to see you.*
> *She suggests at midday, tomorrow.*
> *Usual place.*

Quinn had met Henrietta Richards enough times to know that it was not a suggestion in the slightest. She would expect him, seated in the lounge of her apartment on Sukhra Path, at precisely twelve noon. No time would be wasted on any other arrangements.

It was not the first time that he had been summoned. If you trod enough summits in the Himalayas, then, sooner or later, you would also be stepping into Henrietta's apartment to explain yourself to her satisfaction. Never having felt a need to be anything less than honest about his achievements, he had little to fear from her inquisitions. He actually used to quite enjoy them, always awed by her incredible knowledge of the mountains, even if recently they had begun to leave him with the faint feeling that she thought he was selling himself short, that he could do better than the repetitions of the traditional climbs by which he made his living. He never left an interview without a recommendation of some old climbing book he should read or some obscure route that he should "try if he had a bit of time to himself." It got under his skin a little because he knew she was right.

This time, however, her intense scrutiny of his failure was the last thing he needed. He had other things to do. Most of all, he had to communicate with Nelson Tate Senior, tell him what really had happened up there. Quinn had tried to telephone when they stopped at Xangmu on the way back but couldn't get through. In a way it was a relief. He wondered how such a call could work anyway. The Tates' pain, probably also their anger, and his own still-raw emotions, would undoubtedly get in the way of proper explanation. By the time they had made it back to Kathmandu, he had decided the correct thing to do was to first prepare an email and set down all the facts. He had to get his side of the story to them before the shouting and crying started.

Stepping out from the calm of the hotel into the vibration and fumes of the busy street, Quinn could feel the prestorm heat and humidity already pushing down on the frantic city, the heavy rain clouds churning above. Waiting on the side of the road, alert for the first free rickshaw or tuk-tuk, he realized that maybe it wasn't such a bad thing that he was seeing Henrietta after all. She was a stickler for the truth of a matter, and he could also give her a copy of the email for an unbiased opinion. Thinking of the nearest Internet café where he could sit quietly and write, Quinn pushed his hair away from his still-bruised and battered forehead. That first long shower when he arrived back at the hotel always rendered it completely unruly. He needed to get it cut, particularly if he was going to see Henrietta later that day; everyone knew she was not fond of hippies.

* * *

Quinn finally waved down an empty bicycle rickshaw, shouting, "The Annapurna Café" over the traffic noise. The small Tamang rider wearing an Inter Milan soccer shirt, a pair of cutoff denim jeans, and flip-flops stopped, gesturing for Quinn to get on the ripped bench seat behind him. The thick, tanned muscles on the man's right thigh then bulged as he stood forward on a pedal and pushed down with all his modest body weight, no further instructions needed.

Cogs reluctantly caught, the chain clattered in protest, and the rickety contraption arced out in slow motion to join the suicidal ballet of vehicles already competing for space in the road. Gathering speed, it threaded its way through Thamel, the tourist center of Kathmandu, rattling down the crowded roads and pavements, passing the neon-bright shops overflowing with colorful souvenirs and pounding with music, occasionally swerving to avoid opportunistic street kids loudly offering eclectic alternatives such as tiger balm or wooden flutes.

Soon, the wheezing, twanging rickshaw pulled up at the Annapurna. Thrusting some dirty rupee notes at the rider's outstretched hand, Quinn got off. He entered the café, buying a coffee and time on a computer at the back. There, with numb frost-nipped fingertips, he began to slowly type. He wrote and wrote for nearly the next two hours, digging as far into what happened as his tired mind would permit, questioning everything he remembered. It wasn't easy. There is no such thing as perfect recall of what happens at over 27,000 feet. When finished, he felt spent, empty-headed, as if he had just put down his pen at the end of a three-hour university exam.

Quinn printed a copy to give to Henrietta Richards, and saved the email in his account as a draft. Rather than sending it to her and then to the Tates, he thought he should wait just in case something else came to him as he was explaining himself to Henrietta. Also she had a habit of picking up on anything that didn't sound right and he wanted to be sure that his note was correct. Exchanging the five printed pages for the lightweight Gore-Tex jacket in his day sack, Quinn stepped back out into the street. It was even busier than before as people hurried to get things done before the rain came.

Pushing through the crowds, he walked quickly to the alley that led to Pashi's Barbershop, ducking his head to pass beneath the rows of embroidered souvenir T-shirts that hung across the entrance like prayer flags.

They swayed above him, their fantastic multicolored threads a last nod to the hippies, hundreds of pairs of exquisitely stitched Buddha eyes looking down at him. Before he could even leave their rainbow glare and enter the barbershop, the proprietor greeted Quinn in the passageway like a long-lost friend. Pashi immediately pointed to the fresh dressing on Quinn's forehead and, with his habitual friendly smile, asked directly, "What is this, Mr. Neil?"

Suddenly reminded of the falling ice and rocks on the Second Step, Quinn made an exaggerated wince. "Oh, that. It was a rock, Pashi. A close one."

"And this?" Pashi pointed to the gash on Quinn's upper cheek from the broken vodka bottle.

"Cut myself shaving."

"But you still have beard, Mr. Neil," Pashi said too quickly. Trying to correct his error, he continued, "Bad joke. I'm sorry to hear that you have difficult climb this time, Mr. Neil. Come in. Hair long. I think you will also need shave and head massage if seeing Henrietta Richards later."

Taking his place in front of the cracked mirror, feeling faintly irritated that Pashi already knew that he had been summoned to see Henrietta Richards, Quinn took in the place once more. Most definitely not a hair salon, it was an old-style barber's, third-world Spartan. The unfinished shelves were scattered with skinny, pointed scissors and homemade cutthroat razors that ended in old-fashioned safety blades, murderous in their efficiency, questionable in their sterility. To each side of the dirty mirror before him were pictures of American beefcakes from the '70s, modeling mullets or perms, all with thick, droopy mustaches. It was like being eyed up by the John Holmes fan club.

Covering all the remaining wall space were hundreds of expedition postcards, stickers, and pennants. All the climbers went there when they got back into Kathmandu, and Pashi, customary fabric topi perched on his head, always wanted to talk. It was said that the by-product of all his chatter was that he knew nearly as much mountain gossip as Henrietta Richards. Usually Quinn entered into the spirit of it, but this time as he sat in the old swivel chair, a wave of fatigue and sadness hit him hard, prompted by the knowledge that his disaster on the mountain was now seemingly common fare for all. It rendered him silent.

The barber, seeing something darker in Quinn's face than the wounds, took the hint. He set about his work quietly, clicking scissors the only sound. While Pashi's fast fingers hovered around his head, Quinn looked at himself in the grimy mirror. The bruising from the impact of the rock was spreading beyond the edges of a new dressing to show darker purple and blue, a hint of yellow even, within the tan of his forehead. The cut on his cheek was heavily scabbed, still criss-crossed with the butterfly strips now curling up at the ends from the moisture of his morning shower.

Thinking again of the fight with Sarron, Quinn tensed and then exhaled so deeply that Pashi momentarily stopped, asking if everything was okay. Quinn nodded that he was fine but pointed to the cut, warning him to be careful of it when he did the shave.

When the shave was done, the little man covered Quinn's entire face with a cold, damp towel, pushing it down onto its contours and massaging the jaw to clean off the residual soap. It felt as if he was being suffocated. Quinn flashed back to the Second Step. He was there again, within that tiny cave, but this time alone, trapped inside its mound of ice, freezing but alive, desperately clawing at it to get out …

Pashi pulled the towel away with a flourish, leaving Quinn staring at his naked, beaten face as if it were that of a stranger. He began to make out the skull within. His shadowy eye sockets darkened to become black holes. His nose and lips burned away, leaving only a hollow grin.

What the hell is happening to me?

"Head massage, Mr. Neil? Head massage?"

The words sped up with urgency, snapping Quinn back. Still shaken from the tricks his mind had been playing, he stammered a little as he replied, "Yes, Pashi, yes, but not near my forehead."

The little man went to work first on his neck, kneading deep into the muscles, electric shocks of relief springing up Quinn's spinal cord into his head. Pashi's small, strong fingers then manipulated his skull, rotating thumbs pushing in tight under his ears. With it, a welcome clarity returned and Quinn began to think instead of how he was going to handle Henrietta Richards.

"All finished," Pashi eventually announced.

Quinn got up from the chair, rolling his head around his shoulders, while the little man fussed over him, attentively brushing off any stray hairs. It made him feel guilty he had been so silent and abrupt.

"Sorry I wasn't very talkative, Pashi. A lot on my mind," he said and, in consolation, paid Pashi a good tip.

The barber smiled as he took the money. "Don't worry, Mr. Neil. I understand completely. I am only sorry that you don't have haircut before you climb. I could have told you many reasons why not a good idea for you to go to Everest with the Frenchie. Be careful, Mr. Neil. Be very careful."

Ducking back out into the street, Quinn noticed that the rows of staring T-shirts had gone. The traders had brought everything in and were closing the doors of their shops in anticipation of the grey sky unleashing the first rainstorm of the day. Feeling the first drops when he crossed the main street, Quinn stepped straight into a bar to wait out the worst of it, telling himself he needed a stiff drink before the even greater scrutiny of Henrietta Richards. Drinking his first whiskey, he watched through the window as the deluge began, thinking again about that gorak cave on the Second Step.

27

DURBAR MARG INTERSECTION, KATHMANDU, NEPAL
June 5, 2009
11:26 a.m.

Pemba died not long after the third car hit him.

His new 150 cc Hero Honda, his pride and joy, was now little more than a twisted piece of metal blocking the road. A laptop computer, thrown from the Sherpa's satchel, lay to one side of it. Shattered by cartwheeling down the tarmac before being crushed by the many car wheels that drove over it, the laptop had shared the same fate as its owner when the out-of-control motorcycle had reared up in the rain and flung them both into the path of oncoming traffic.

A crowd of onlookers on the pavement watched as the heavy rainfall pummeled the young Sherpa's broken head, the cheap Chinese motorcycle helmet that surrounded it split cleanly in two like the shell of a walnut. His lifeless body was propped up against the high curb of the street, bright red blood flowing from his soaking T-shirt into the torrent of monsoon rain that cascaded along the side of the road. The crimson stream mixed with the dirty water and the refuse it carried, slowly dissolving into its filthy grey.

Fixated despite the driving rain, the bystanders stared at the scene, sharing the macabre fascination of yet another motorcycle accident. When the ambulance finally took the body away, they also drifted off, content in the collective observation that the number of motorcycle accidents always increased when the monsoon came. There would be more tomorrow and the day after. No other conclusion was necessary.

No one had seen what really occurred anyway. That first downpour of the day hid it all. Not a single person witnessed the car pulling alongside the small red and chrome motorcycle as it tried to accelerate its way home through the rapidly increasing rain. Nobody noticed the passenger door slam outward into the bike and its rider, causing him to lose control as the motorcycle bucked wildly into the oncoming traffic, handlebars flicking from lock to lock. No one had been watching anything until they stopped to watch Pemba die on the side of the road.

The stolen Maruti Suzuki car had vanished before the motorcycle even came to a rest, its two occupants satisfied that the nasty fall the Sherpa undoubtedly suffered was suitably within their orders from Sarron. It had been opportunistic, quick, and convenient. They had a busy afternoon and evening ahead with two more to deal with, particularly after missing the first one at his hotel that morning.

The car's passenger handed the driver a photo of Dawa and shouted an address. The small car immediately turned to the left, across the oncoming traffic, to head for the other side of Kathmandu.

28

APARTMENT E, 57 SUKHRA PATH, KATHMANDU, NEPAL
June 5, 2009
11:55 a.m.

Quinn ducked into the entrance of the old Rana Palace building, shaking himself like a wet dog before taking off his jacket. Ascending the stairs to the third-floor apartment, the taste of Japanese whiskey still on his tongue, the post-climb ache burning in his shins and thighs the higher he got, he slowly left the deluge behind. Arriving on the coconut mat in front of the white gloss-painted door with the brass "E" in the center, it was as if he had also left Asia behind.

The instant he knocked, Sanjeev Gupta opened the door and let him in, taking the soggy jacket from Quinn's hand in the same deft movement. Inside, as always, the apartment was an oasis of English calm. The flower prints, the shelves lined with colorful mountaineering books, the dishes of potpourri, the stark line of alphabetized grey filing cabinets that ran along one wall, the aloof black cat skulking in a corner, they all combined to make it feel like the headmistress' rooms at some elite girls' school in Surrey.

Henrietta Richards looked up at Neil from her upright chair in the center of the main living room, her lap covered in papers. To her side was a table laden with bound notebooks and loose-leaf files. In a corner on a desk, Quinn could see her computer; its screen burned vividly with a report that she and Gupta must have been working on. Observing him over the top of her half-moon reading glasses, taking in his battered and bruised appearance alongside a faint smell of whiskey and rainwater, Henrietta said, "Hello, Neil. Excuse me if I don't get up, but as you can see, I am rather in the middle of something. You can sit there. Would you like some tea? Milk, no sugar, isn't it? Sanjeev will do the honors."

"Henrietta, yes. Thank you," Quinn said, sitting in the empty chair in front of her. When Sanjeev handed him the tea in a flower-patterned porcelain cup and saucer, it looked ridiculous in his big hands, still calloused and raw from the climb.

"Neil, I'm sorry to drag you here so soon after your return to Kathmandu. I'm sure you need to rest but I have been asked to look into what happened to Nelson Tate Junior by the US authorities in Nepal," Henrietta said, changing her tone and quickly getting to the point.

"I suspected as much, Henrietta. I understand the need for clarity," he replied. Setting down his tea, Quinn then pulled out the draft email of explanation from his day sack. He passed it across to her. "I thought it best to try and write the whole damn mess all down."

Henrietta took the pages. When she saw there were five, all filled with type, she turned to Gupta and said, "Sanjeev, can you pass me a copy of my book?" Sanjeev quickly handed her a thick hardback book. The dust jacket read, "*From Picadilly to the Sky: The British Quest to Climb Everest, 1921–1953* by Henrietta Richards."

She passed the heavy book to Quinn almost as if in return for his note, saying, "Neil, I want to carefully read your email while I have you here, so why don't you take a look at my latest while you're waiting."

Beginning to read, she quickly stopped and looked at Quinn.

"Have you sent this already?"

"No. It's just a draft at this stage."

"Good. My advice is to hold it back. From what I am hearing, Nelson Tate Senior is not a particularly reasonable man and anything you send him is likely to be little more than fodder for his lawyers, who are going to twist your words in any way they can. I already know that Sarron is saying you abandoned the boy and I can understand your desire to explain yourself, but you should let it be through an independent source like me rather than directly, however uncomfortable that makes you. Obviously that assumes you didn't desert the boy, something your note will confirm I presume?"

"Of course, Henrietta. Frankly I would rather it was me still up there, not him."

"That's a noble sentiment, Neil, but you're not, so you need to get ready for the legal onslaught that is undoubtedly going to come your way. You won't be the first guide to be sued for losing a client on Everest."

"I know. Ironically I studied law at Bristol

University and worked at Peckett, Cross & Avon in London for six months in 1990 before I quit to become a mountain guide."

"Yes, you told me that once before. I suspect it's not going to be much help. Tate is telling the US ambassador that he is going to be utterly relentless in punishing whoever was responsible for his son's demise. I also know that Sarron has already filed a report in Lhasa with the Chinese, and, whilst I am unable to get my hands on it, I am sure it is consistent with what he has been telling anyone who will listen—that the responsibility is yours. This whole affair is going to get even messier than it is already, so given that Sarron is really not my favorite cup of tea let me read this carefully now and see what I can do to get to the truth. Have a look at my new book while you wait—it might restore your faith in the mountain a little."

At first Quinn found it hard to concentrate on the meticulously detailed hardback, distracted by the intensity with which Henrietta was studying his email. With a red pen, she was making notes and marks next to every paragraph, leaving him feeling as if he was having his poorly done homework marked in front of him. Wishing his life was still that simple, he reopened the thick book to the section of photographs in the center.

Quickly flicking through the images of tweed-jacketed English gentlemen backdropped by mountain monasteries or taking tea in the shadow of Everest, he arrived at the final picture to see that it was the classic image of Tenzing on the summit in 1953. As he looked again at the very picture that had started him on his own journey to the mountain, it struck him painfully that his Everest career was over, whatever the outcome of that meeting. The thought made him shut the book and wait in silence instead.

When Henrietta finally finished studying his note she said, "It's thorough, I'll give you that. Can you send it to me electronically?"

"Given what you have already said, should I do that?"

"You can trust me, Neil." Holding up the note, she asked, "Dawa and Pemba will corroborate all this I assume?"

"Yes."

"Well that's good, because I will be seeing them also. I must say that the thing that worries me is that Tate Junior's death is not clear-cut. Do you think that Sarron's oxygen was defective?"

The question shocked Quinn because he hadn't mentioned Pemba's speculation about it in his report, focusing only on the hard facts and the timeline of their climb as best he could recall.

"I didn't say that in my notes."

"No, Neil, you didn't. But that is what they are saying on the street."

Quinn shrugged his shoulders. "I'm really not sure. Something was wrong with the kid's system on the summit even if I must say that mine was working perfectly. When we got down to the Glacier Camp, Pemba was saying he thought some of the cylinders were defective but as you'll have read in my email he didn't actually use his on the way up, trying for a summit without Os when he wasn't feeling that well which really didn't help matters. I rather put his comments down to trying to deflect attention from his own error. Dawa wouldn't say much on the subject but maybe the Sherpas did talk more about it amongst themselves. You know how they are. Anyway we left the kid's cylinder on the summit next to my ice axe so there's no way to get it now and check. Personally, I think it was more a case of one of those days when little things start to go wrong and slowly but surely everything snowballs out of control."

"Do you think the summit bonus might have clouded your judgment at any point during the expedition?"

There it was again—another thing he had made no mention of in his email.

Quinn began to feel uneasy.

"No, even if Sarron did become slightly obsessive about it, but I suppose it was a lot of money."

"How much money, Neil?"

"One hundred thousand dollars; Sarron promised me ten percent."

Henrietta tutted once loudly at him and then very deliberately shook her head.

"Actually, Neil, you are on the low side with that. Tate Senior is a billionaire. The Kathmandu rumor mills, whose sources, I assume, are predominantly Sarron's many creditors, think that the summit bonus was actually five hundred thousand dollars. Even Pashi the barber could have told you that."

She watched Quinn as the information sank in. His eyes closed a little, and his face stiffened, revealing to her that only then did the whole performance on the summit finally make sense to him.

"Well, however much it was, it won't be paid," Quinn replied with a grim shake of his head. "The kid is dead and I'm sure that Tate Senior is going to want his pound of flesh from all of us in return, as you say. Frankly, I wonder if he isn't right too."

Henrietta paused and then angling her head slightly said, "Tell me about that old ice axe you mentioned finding on the Second Step."

"It's just an old axe. Lucky for me, I guess, that I found it when I did, but beyond that I can't see it's really relevant to the big picture."

"It's not George Leigh Mallory's, is it?"

Quinn shook his head quickly, revealing his disbelief, a little frustration even, that she was thinking about details like that given the greater scheme of things.

The woman really is bloody relentless.

"No, Henrietta. I don't think it is. It's just an old axe, anyone could have left it up there."

29

WEWELSBURG CASTLE, NORTH RHINE-WESTPHALIA, GERMANY
October 17, 1938
1:27 a.m.

Standing at gunpoint on the bridge, Josef was swamped with the realization that his whole escape had been a sham, an amusement for Himmler that had killed both his friends. While he was being directed back into the castle's triangular courtyard at gunpoint, Josef even heard one of the other officers behind him say, "Yes, I know I lost my bet. I will pay up in the morning, but it was worth it for the entertainment. It was quite impressive, just as Jurgen predicted it would be."

The other officers dispersed to leave Josef with only the man who had stopped him. "On the premise that you understand your escape is impossible and would involve you being shot before you set one foot outside the castle, I am going to put away this pistol and ask you to join me for a conversation inside," the SS-obersturmführer said as he opened the flap on his pistol holster. Waiting for a nod from Josef, he put his Luger away as two guards appeared, falling in alongside his prisoner. The officer then turned on his heels to lead the way across the cobbled courtyard and enter the castle's most imposing entrance.

Inside they followed a banner-strewn corridor lined with polished suits of armor and thick brocade curtains drawn over unseen windows until they entered a large baronial hall. A log fire was raging in an open hearth at the end of the room. A simple yet massive fireplace surrounded it, the heavyset stone carved with swastikas and other symbols. On the mantel was a wrought-iron candelabrum, twisted and hammered to resemble entwined oak branches, that supported twelve red candles burning with smoky, yellow flames. A set of large golden SS runes, cast into the center of the black candelabra's tree, shimmered beneath their candlelight.

A long, highly polished table ran the length of the room. Pfeiffer pointed Josef to sit at it.

In its center were Josef's boots still tied together by the laces. Observing Josef notice them, the SS officer said, "Your boots. They survived their fall, I am pleased to say. Sadly, your friend was not so fortunate. Please excuse me a moment while I go and get some things. Try not to let your hand bleed on the table in the meantime." He passed Josef a folded white handkerchief that he took from inside his jacket and left the room.

The two guards moved behind Josef in silence as he wrapped the handkerchief around his blood-soaked, bound finger and rested it inside the top of his shirt, trying to keep it upright. To take his mind off its throbbing pain, he contemplated the three immense tapestries that were hung on the wall opposite him. Newly woven, threads still brightly colored, the first panel to the left of the wall depicted helmeted, black-clad SS troops fighting furiously behind a barricade as two helmetless comrades, one with his head swathed in a bloody bandage, administered aid to a wounded SS officer at their feet. The officer was lying back in a scarlet pool of his own blood, his Luger pistol still at the ready in his hand.

The next panel, in the center, showed the same SS soldiers but this time stripped down to baggy black trousers, jackboots, and white shirts with rolled-up sleeves as they tilled the bloodstained soil that stretched into the distance until blocked by a range of fierce-looking, snow-covered mountains. The third and final panel was a pastoral scene of a smiling, happy family. The father, recognizably the wounded SS officer, healed and out of uniform, was standing alongside his blond wife and four perfect children in front of a thatched, whitewashed farmhouse. The family was linking arms as the father pointed proudly across the same land, its acres of golden corn ripe for harvest, toward the mountains in the distance, now a soft purple, their snows receded to the tops of the highest summits.

Josef's attention was brought back to the table by the return of the SS officer who sat opposite, placing a leather folder and a sheathed SS ceremonial dagger to his front. Lifting the knife, he drew its deep blade from the black and silver sheath. Reaching forward, he inserted the point under the laces of Josef's boots and with his other hand pulled them back to him. The instant he applied pressure on the blade, it sliced through the heavy laces as if they were made of silk. Looking at Josef, he then laid the knife down in the center of the massive table that separated them; the tip of its blade pointed directly toward Josef. The flickering glow of the fire picked up the Gothic script engraved down the center of the knife's polished blade:

𝔐𝔢𝔦𝔫𝔢 𝔈𝔥𝔯𝔢 𝔥𝔢𝔦𝔰𝔱 𝔗𝔯𝔢𝔲𝔢

The officer's pale eyes stared into Josef's. "Gefreiter Josef Becker of the 99th Gebirgsjäger, I should introduce myself, as there was no time for such pleasantries in Munich. I am SS-Obersturmführer Jurgen Pfeiffer of the Leibstandarte SS Adolf Hitler. I am the personal adjutant to the reichsführer of the SS." He paused to let his introduction sink in before continuing. "Gefreiter Becker, what do you notice about the knife you see before you?"

Josef looked at it and back at the officer. "It's sharp."

Pfeiffer studied Josef a little longer then said with a slow, exaggerated nod, "Yes, it is, isn't it? It could kill you in a second. What else do you see?"

"The blade says, 'My honor is my loyalty.'"

"It does. Do you have any loyalties, Gefreiter Becker?"

"Yes."

"Given that you have committed crimes against your führer, your race, and your country, to what, then, or to whom, perhaps, are your particular loyalties?"

"My family and my friends."

"Of course. Family and friends, those ever-convenient refuges of self-justification invoked, without conscience, by every petty criminal and gangster the moment he realizes his pathetic little game is up. As this evening's events have substantially reduced the number of your friends, for the purposes of this conversation I must ask then that you give further thought to your family as we speak."

Pfeiffer looked once again at the knife. "What else do you see, Becker?"

"The blade is double-edged."

"Yes. What does that make you think of?"

Josef was drained, exhausted. He'd had enough games.

"Nothing."

"I know climbing can be tiring, Gefreiter Becker, but I do advise you to humor me."

Pfeiffer gestured to the two guards to leave.

In an instant they were gone, the door shutting behind them.

Josef was now alone with the SS officer. He looked at the cold, unblinking eyes before him, seeing a faint reflection of the fire burning in the hearth.

"That there are two edges to the blade," Josef replied pedantically.

"Exactly. Two. Sharp. Edges." Pfeiffer stated each word individually as he stared at Josef. "Hence, it cuts both ways, a concept that you should focus on as you listen to what I am about to explain to you. Shall I begin?"

"Do I have a choice?"

"No." Pfeiffer picked up the knife and started to gently stroke one edge of its blade with his thumb. "You forfeited that right when you took it upon yourself to smuggle Jews. Crimes such as yours against the Reich are automatically punishable by the death sentence. Fortunately for you, I have the power vested in me by the reichsführer to override that sentence in order that you might do something for us. However, the task still has an edge to it. It could kill you, although that would only happen in the moment of your own failure, which is therefore more up to you than to us, so it could be seen as a slight improvement on your current situation."

Pfeiffer turned the knife over and repeated the movement on its second edge, then with the flat of the blade he opened the leather folder in front of him. Inside was a thin stack of white cards.

"To ensure that you quite literally apply your heart and soul to the operation I have selected you for, we also have the other edge of the blade. Do you like playing cards? I am sure you do, isn't that how all Wehrmacht *gefreiters* pass the time?"

With the tip of the knife, the SS officer slowly arranged the white cards in a row of seven as if laying out a hand. Inserting the knife blade under each card, he began to turn them over revealing that they were photographs. He stopped after the first three, the faces of Gunter, Kurt, and Josef.

Lifting the knife, Pfeiffer stuck the point first into the face of Gunter and lifting the photo, then laid it down on top of the photo of Kurt. Pushing again on the knife, it stuck through into the second photo and again he lifted them, both impaled on the tip of the blade as he coldly looked at Josef.

Getting up from the table, Pfeiffer said nothing but walked to the fireplace where he pulled the two photographs from the end of the blade and tossed them into the flames. Returning to the table, he used the knife again to turn over the next three photographs.

Josef found himself looking at the faces of his mother and his two sisters alongside his own photograph until Pfeiffer blocked his view by laying the knife blade over the top of them.

"Forgive me if I am being a little melodramatic, but I assume I am making your situation clear?"

Looking away in horror, Josef glanced up again at the three tapestries behind Pfeiffer, wishing with all his heart that the SS officer before him was the one bleeding out in the first panel. If Josef could have anything to do with it, this man wouldn't survive to look at any mountains with his family.

His eyes traveled into the mountainous distance of the tapestries, and then all the pieces suddenly fell into place. With utter hatred, he returned his eyes to the SS officer. "So what is it you want me to climb?"

Lifting the knife once again, Pfeiffer used it to flick over the final photograph.

"This."

30

THE KHUMBU HOTEL, THAMEL, KATHMANDU, NEPAL
June 5, 2009
2:35 p.m.

Entering the Khumbu Hotel, Quinn was quickly pulled aside by the doorman who said breathlessly, "Mr. Neil, you must watch out, sir. Two men looking for you this morning. I say you not here, not know where you are. They are bad men, Mr. Neil, very bad men. The type that is fucking the mother."

Quinn was more amused by the man's anxious turn of phrase than concerned about his visitors as he bumped into Ross MacGregor and Yves Durrand walking out. With a slightly apologetic look, Durrand said, "Neil, I know things are not great, but we're on our way home tomorrow, so would you have a drink with us later? I've got a table at the Rum Doodle booked for eight. Some of the Sherps will be there too. I told Dawa this morning when he brought round the other bags. Despite everything, it would still be nice to get together one last time, and we must give the Sherpas their tips if

Sarron is not going to be paying them anything."

Quinn was in no mood to party, but he liked the Scotsman and the Swiss and he needed to catch up with Dawa and Pemba, particularly as Henrietta was going to be speaking to them, so he agreed. Back up in his hotel room, he tried to take a nap. Despite being still exhausted from the climb and additionally drained by Henrietta Richards' interview, he could only sleep fitfully, a staccato of bad dreams pushing him repeatedly back to wakefulness. In the end, he resigned himself to just lying there and resting. After a while he couldn't even do that.

He picked up Henrietta's book that she had insisted he take with him and turned to the section about George Leigh Mallory and Andrew "Sandy" Irvine's final attempt on the summit in 1924. He already knew well the story of how the two climbers had set off one last time for the summit and never returned, leaving the world guessing whether they actually summited before they died, making it to the top of Everest nearly thirty years before Hillary and Tenzing. He was also aware of the search for their bodies, motivated by the thought that one of them might still bear the borrowed Kodak Vest Pocket camera that they took with them, the hope being that frozen within would be undeveloped film that might finally reveal the truth of the greatest climbing mystery once and for all.

In her book Henrietta had thoroughly assembled all the known facts, including the details of Irvine's ice axe being found in 1933 and then Mallory's body in 1999. Mallory's axe and Irvine's body were still missing and, unlikely as it seemed, it did make Quinn wonder about the old axe that Dawa had returned to him. He got up and pulled it from his dusty duffel bag. Taking a facecloth and a glass of water from the bathroom, he started to clean and, for the first time, study the axe seriously.

It was slightly more than thirty inches long. The shaft was ash, the wood still tight, light tan in color, crosshatched with black grain lines, varnished with age. Only in one place, near the bottom, was it damaged, the wood pockmarked and gouged as if a wild animal had chewed it. On one side, near the head of the axe, he saw that the wooden shaft bore the faint stencil mark of two numbers:

99

On the other side, he made out a rougher carving of two capital letters, lightly cut into the wood, trying for a Gothic elegance yet slightly irregular and amateur:

J. B.

Resuming his study, Quinn saw that the bottom end of the axe shaft was clad in a round steel collar from which projected the steel spike that had stopped Sarron in his tracks. At the opposite end, there was an almost flat steel head that divided into a shallow triangular adze for digging and a long, almost straight pick with a row of serrations that ran partially along the bottom. The edges of both showed the axe had been well used. New silver scratches into the metal of the pick reminded Quinn of how it had arrested his own fall on the Second Step.

Around the wooden shaft was a tarnished steel ring that slid up and down. A small metal screw projected out from the wood about six inches above the bottom end to stop the ring from sliding off. He knew that the ring had once held some form of leather or canvas hand strap.

Beneath the neck of the axe was another ring, but this was made of a white cloth tape. The material was browned with age and exposure, fragile even if its knot was still tight. Quinn understood that it must once have been attached to some form of flag. It chilled him a little to think that the owner of the axe had anticipated reaching the summit.

He began to scrub the metal head of the axe with the dampened facecloth.

On one side of the long pick he identified a tiny serial number: DRGM No. 1496318.

Turning it over, he saw that an oval had been engraved into the metal on the other side. There was writing within it.

Quickly licking a fingertip, he rubbed at it. The spittle picked out the faint lines cut into the steel, darkening them against the dull sheen of the metal. He pushed the head of the axe up close to the bedside light. It read, "MODELL ASCHENBRENNER," across the center of the oval. Arched under the top were the words "GARANTIE-PICKEL" and, beneath, "WERK FULPMES."

To the left of the oval, Quinn noticed another, much smaller engraving. He wet his finger again and rubbed some more.

The tiny design revealed a faint line drawing of what he thought was a bird with outstretched wings.

A feeling of urgency took him, and, spitting directly onto the metal, Quinn continued to wipe at the faint incision.

It was a bird, a simple line drawing of an eagle. Its two wings were made up of four linear blocks, one stacked above the other to give a rigid, stepped shape that stretched out to either side. The head of the bird between the outstretched wings was looking to the left. Its square profile tapered into a sharply hooked beak. The small design was imperial, almost Roman at first sight.

The eagle was perched on a tiny circle. To the left of the circle was the letter *Z*, to the right the letters *Fg*. Within was an ancient Asian symbol with a much more modern European familiarity.

A swastika.

31

TRIPURESHWAR, KATHMANDU, NEPAL
June 5, 2009
4:45 p.m.

Up a narrow alley leading down to the refuse-strewn north bank of the Bagmati River, punch after punch was being driven into Dawa's midriff. His lungs, stomach, and bowels had all emptied by the tenth pummeling hit. The crude metal knuckle-duster being used was now tearing the stomach muscle and splitting the internal organs within, snapping ribs when the punches landed high.

When it was clear that Dawa could no longer stand on his own, sprays of blood replacing the vomit that accompanied the first blows, the taller of Dawa's attackers motioned the other to stop holding him from behind and let him fall. The Sherpa crumpled down onto the dirt and mud of the unpaved side street.

Immediately the pair started kicking the motionless body, each impact breaking the Sherpa some more. The two Gurung were enjoying their work. They missed their old army days spent interrogating Maoist suspects—and anyone else, for that matter—who irritated their masters. Too much had changed since the threat of the communists in the hills had finally ousted their king, forcing them out of the army and into the dark underside of the city. At least Sarron still gave them the occasional opportunity to relive old times.

They particularly hated the Sherpas. As the pair kicked, again and again, they reminded themselves how the climbing Sherpas thought they were such big men in Kathmandu, flashing their dollars around, riding their new motorcycles, always kowtowing to the foreigners. It felt good to be able to bring a couple of them back down to earth and get paid for the pleasure.

Reluctantly heeding the instruction from Sarron to wound, not kill, the tall man stopped the other. He stood above the inert body and paused for a few moments as he slipped the knuckle-duster back into his pocket and looked down, coldly studying their violent handiwork, impressed at how they had reduced the strong Sherpa to a broken, bloody mess. They still had it.

After another minute or two to regain his breath, the man raised his knee and brought his heavy boot down as hard as possible on Dawa's right ankle. There was a snap of tendon and bone. It produced little more than a dull grunt from the unconscious body. He picked his leg up again and repeated the action on the left knee. With that, the man said in Nepali, "That'll put an end to your climbing, you monkey. Hope you enjoyed your 'summit bonus' from Sarron."

Laughing to himself, he turned to his colleague. "Two down, one more to go. Let's get out of here." They returned to their stolen car, the passenger door bearing the vivid scratches from its contact with Pemba's Hero Honda. As it sped away, wheels spinning on the dirt, a skinny, black, feral dog wandered over to Dawa's contorted, immobile form and started licking at the blood and vomit covering him. He didn't move.

32

THE KHUMBU HOTEL, THAMEL, KATHMANDU, NEPAL
June 5, 2009
7:30 p.m.

The shower beat down on Quinn as he still tried to make sense of the swastika on the old ice axe. But however hard he thought about it, he could produce little more than a simple statement in response: the British had Everest, and the Germans had Nanga Parbat, a well-known, well-documented mountaineering fact from the early days of Himalayan climbing that he had learned as a boy—two countries, two mountains, two completely separate prewar histories of trying to climb them.

The earliest Quinn could remember reading of anyone other than an Englishman even going near Everest was the solitary Canadian, Earl Denman, in 1947, and then maybe a similarly solo Swede, or was it a Dane, a few years later. Whatever, they made valiant but strictly personal efforts long after the days of the swastika. They also hadn't even gotten high on the mountain, certainly nowhere near to the Second Step. He squeezed his brain to think some more about the bigger teams of Swiss, French, Chinese, the rumored Russians, even, who all joined the race among countries to try to be first to the top by one route or another in the '50s and '60s, but still, there were no Germans, even without swastikas.

Perhaps it was one of the Russians that left the axe up there?

He recalled again the old climber's legend that in 1952 a Russian team led by a Dr. Pawel Datschnolian had tried to snatch a first summit of the mountain from the British who, still unsuccessful, were due to return to the mountain the following year. It was said that they took the north-side route but that the entire summit party of six was simply blown off the mountain, never to be seen again. Even with the fall of the Iron Curtain and subsequent opening up of Russian records to the rest of the world, no one had ever been able to prove the veracity of the story one way or the other.

Did I find evidence that the story is actually true?

Nineteen fifty-two was only seven years after the end of World War Two in Europe—the axe could easily have been a returning Russian soldier's souvenir from the rubble of Germany.

Well, it's my souvenir now. An ice axe with a fucking swastika!

Given the current circumstances, it seemed in some way appropriate, Quinn thought, as he dressed quickly and checked his wallet for the little cash remaining to him. He then rummaged in another of his duffel bags to pull out some locking carabiners and a new set of four ice screws. As he held them in his hands, they seemed to offer a poor return for saving his life but they were the best he could do to tip Dawa. At least the Sherpa should be able to sell them for good money to one of the many trekking shops in Thamel. Putting them into the deep side pocket of his cargo pants, Quinn set off on the short walk to the Rum Doodle, the Thamel restaurant named after the imaginary forty-thousand-and-half-a-foot peak made famous in the 1950s novel of the same name.

The Rum Doodle was a well-known place of celebration for all the tours, treks, and climbs that finished in Kathmandu. If you summited Everest, you even ate there for free, after the restaurant owner had quickly verified the fact with Sanjeev Gupta, of course. He had little to celebrate this time, but for the sake of his two clients, Quinn told himself to put his troubles aside and make an effort. Walking into the bar, Quinn saw the pair already propping it up. The Sherpas weren't there yet.

Yves handed Quinn a large, fiftieth-anniversary bottle of Everest beer, wet and cold. It tasted good as they rather halfheartedly toasted Durrand's summit. As Quinn continued to drink from the oversized bottle, the gold-rimmed oval label featuring that same summit photo of Tenzing loosened and shifted in his hand as they always did. Quinn peeled it off. Everyone always did that too—some intent on sticking the label in the diary of their trip, others on the backs of unknowing teammates where they dried and loosened their grip to slip to the floor, leaving the most famous image in mountaineering to stare back up through the lesser feet that unknowingly trampled it. Quinn put his onto the bar counter, smoothing it out flat with still-numb fingertips. Whenever he looked at it, he felt the stab of pain from the thought that he was most probably at the end of the long road that photo had first set him on. It soured the beer in his stomach.

The three of them continued to wait at the bar but still the Sherpas didn't arrive. In the end, they moved to their table and ordered. When the dinner was finished, Quinn reluctantly agreed to give up on them ever arriving and to continue on to the Tom & Jerry, one of Thamel's best-known pubs. Tipping the waiter more generously than usual in compensation for the fact that he had to leave two steak dinners off the bill and that half their party hadn't turned up, they left a message for the Sherpas that they had gone on and left.

The Tom & Jerry was even more crowded than the Rum Doodle, but they were eventually able to take one of the red vinyl-covered booths. There, the three of them drank and talked some more, until Quinn was interrupted by a small face at the end of the table frantically beckoning to him. "Mr. Neil, it is me, Phinjo. The cook boy. Lhakpa sends me to find you. You must come now, Mr. Neil, now!"

With some difficulty Quinn pushed his way out to the young Sherpa. Putting a big hand on Phinjo's small shoulder, he directed him to the relative quiet of the street outside. "Phinjo, what is it?" he asked.

The boy started crying uncontrollably.

"Phinjo, tell me," Quinn demanded.

Through sobs, the boy blurted out words that slowly became sentences.

"Pemba ... it's Pemba. He dead ... Motorcycle.

His motorcycle crash ... on Durbar Marg. We think it because of the rain. Killed. He killed by fall."

Quinn struggled to take in what he was hearing as the boy continued to speak.

"Then people find Dawa by the river. He beaten. Very bad, Mr. Neil, beaten very bad. Maybe he die too."

All Quinn could manage in reply was a shocked, "What?"

"They break his legs, Mr. Neil, so he can't climb. Now we think maybe also Pemba killed. Not accident. Lhakpa say Sarron."

The little cook boy broke down, once more crying hopelessly.

Quinn looked back over his shoulder, his horror at the news developing into a chilling recognition that it must be connected with the two men who had tried to find him at the hotel earlier that day. Sarron really was coming after them as he had threatened.

Phinjo regained some control. Wiping the back of his hand across his eyes, he stuttered, "Lhakpa send me to say to you, 'Be careful.' They think Frenchie Sarron mad, mad for long time now, and he pay killers to hurt you and Dawa and Pemba. Lhakpa hiding. He safe. He say you be safe too, Mr. Neil."

Quinn pulled some notes from his wallet and pushed them into the boy's hand. "Thank you, Phinjo. Now go home quick in a taxi. Don't stop for anything or anyone. Do you understand me?" Wiping his sleeve again across his nose and mouth, the boy hugged Quinn then ran off into the Kathmandu night.

Quinn hurried back into the bar and quickly forced his way to the booth.

"Yves, we've got to go now. I can't explain here.

Just get Ross moving. Come on. Now."

MacGregor was drunk and unsteady on his feet, forcing Quinn and the Swiss climber to pull him outside and into a passing taxi with them. As they traveled the few blocks back to their hotel, Quinn explained to Durrand what the cook boy had told him, the Swiss climber sobering up in front of his eyes.

At the hotel the little doorman was nowhere to be seen.

Quinn looked into the darkened lobby. He could see no one, so, with Durrand's help, they moved the wasted Scot inside and up to the door of the small cage elevator.

"Yves, if they're here, I don't think they will be after you two—only me. Get Ross up to his room and leave him on the floor in the recovery position. You know it, right?"

"Of course." Yves nodded.

"Then if you hear anything else, please get help—whatever you can, just get it, okay?"

The cage door of the old elevator closed with a screech, and after a dull thump and a whirr, the car elevated slowly upward.

Watching it rise, Quinn wondered what to do next. He searched the lobby for something with which to defend himself. There was nothing.

A hint of panic was stopped by an idea. Reaching into the pocket of his cargo pants, he took out the two longest of the ice screws he had intended to give to Dawa.

Each one was about ten inches long. He ripped off the sleeves of blue plastic webbing that covered the tubes' sharp threads and uncapped the ends to reveal the four razor-sharp points with which each chromoly tube finished. The sharp, steel edges glinted in the light as, taking one in each hand like a dagger, Quinn slowly and silently began to ascend the stairs.

Creeping up to the top-floor corridor, he then approached the door to his room at the end of the hall.

Nearing it, he thought he heard a faint noise from inside.

Inching closer, he saw that the door was very slightly ajar, yet the room was pitch black inside.

Quinn paused, took a deep breath, and then, touching the tip of the ice screw in his right hand against the door, slowly pushed it back.

When the door was almost open, the head of the old ice axe swept down from the dark interior, crashing onto the ice screw, causing Quinn to instantly drop it.

A figure leaped forward from the dark to grab him by both shoulders and pull him headlong into the room.

The shaft of the ice axe smacked violently down a second time, hitting Quinn across the back as he fell forward.

His face smashed into the floor, and the hands on his shoulders forced him down into the funk of the carpet as the side of the ice axe slammed across his back, again and again.

Every time the flat side of the axe's metal head beat on his spine, bolts of white lightning flashed up through his body and into his brain.

The Englishman squirmed, trying to free himself, but the weight of the man holding him down kept him hard against the floor as more blows from the old axe beat his body.

Amidst the explosions of pain, Quinn had crystal-clear images of Dawa helping him down from the Second Step. With all his might, he responded to them by twisting his body up from the floor, thrusting his left arm wildly upward at the unseen attacker restraining him.

He felt the ice screw that hand was still gripping push into something soft.

The man to the front of him howled horribly, immediately releasing him.

As the man pulled away, Quinn felt the motion tugging the ice screw.

He let it go, still lodged in his attacker's right eye socket.

Freed, Quinn scrambled to get up only to see the head of the ice axe, this time with its sharp pick facing downward, hurtling toward him.

He rolled to his side just as the axe crashed down, scraping across his chest in a rending tear, hooking the fabric of his shirt and sticking point-first deep into the carpet and wooden floor beneath.

The figure above tried to pull the axe back up, but it was stuck fast. He lifted a foot to stomp down on Quinn's head only to be knocked backward by the other assailant making crazily for the door.

Screaming in agony, the figure ran out, holding his blood-spurting face from which the long, steel ice screw still protruded.

The other attacker released the embedded ice axe and chased after him.

Quinn blacked out as another heavy monsoon rain started to hammer on the flat concrete roof of the hotel.

PART II

AN EXPOSED TRAVERSE
EIN AUSGESETZLER QUERGANG

33

WEWELSBURG CASTLE, NORTH RHINE-WESTPHALIA, GERMANY
February 15, 1939
8:30 a.m.

Josef was almost finished preparing his pack for his daily training march when Pfeiffer entered the guardroom. Immaculately dressed, as always, but with the hint of a rare smile on his face, he appeared to be holding something behind his back. *Probably his damn SS dagger,* Josef thought, looking up without bothering to hide the hatred that came naturally to his face whenever he saw or even thought about the SS officer.

Pfeiffer had been absent since Josef had returned to Wewelsburg. The last time they had met was when Pfeiffer collected him from four weeks' basic training with the Liebstandarte SS Adolf Hitler at Berlin-Lichterfelde only to deliver him for a further month's combat and survival training with elite Waffen-SS troops in the Harz Mountains.

Josef wondered what the murderous man wanted;

his appearances were never casual. He moved to get to his feet to find out, but the officer stopped him. "Continue. I have no wish to interrupt your training regime," Pfeiffer said, looking down at Josef kneeling on the cold flagstones and cinching his heavily weighted pack.

Beyond the heavy oak and iron door, the castle grounds had been blanketed with a thick covering of snow since the winter solstice, the New Year bringing a persistent, freezing north wind that had encased everything with ice. As he studied the man preparing to head out alone once more into that frozen world, Pfeiffer approved of what he saw. Although reportedly sullen and silent throughout, Becker had been classified as "excellent" at both Lichterfelde and Bad Harzburg, despite the instructions to single him out and push him to his very limits. Since his return to Wewelsburg, Becker's guards reported that every day, whatever the weather or temperature outside, the man hiked for six or seven hours with a pack that weighed forty kilos, pounding himself up and down the steep sides of the hills that surrounded the castle. After, he would shower and change, eat like a horse, and spend the rest of the day in the library studying everything he was given about the mountain they wanted him to climb. Even if he said little to anyone other than the librarian, Josef Becker gave every appearance of having wholeheartedly followed every order Pfeiffer had given.

"I bring good news," Pfeiffer said. "Ernst Schäfer's team has finally been permitted to cross into Tibet. It is now an official and internationally accredited Reich expedition. Legitimate diplomatic contact with it therefore permits us to also secretly furnish you with everything you will need when you arrive at the foot of the mountain as I have always envisioned. Given that things will soon be accelerating, I am here to review progress and advise you of the next steps. We will talk further when you return from your training session. In the meantime, I have brought you some things in recognition of the efforts I hear you have been making."

With a deliberate flourish, Pfeiffer pulled his arms from behind his back. He was holding Becker's ice axe, his Gebirgsjäger mountain cap, and his army identification tag, Ganzler's edelweiss ring still attached to it.

"I understand that these were taken from you when you were first arrested. I think you have earned the right to have them back. I have taken a small liberty with your cap, as you will see."

Becker stood up and said nothing as he pulled his heavy backpack first up onto his knees and then up and around onto his back. Reaching for his axe, he gave its metal head a sweep with his gloved hand before spinning the wooden shaft back over his right shoulder. He inserted its point between the pack and his back, letting the axe slide down until the head hooked. It always lived there when he wasn't using it. It felt good to have it back. Still silent, he took the tag, the ring, and the cap from the SS officer.

The tag and the ring he retied around his neck and pushed back down under his clothes. Touching the ring, he felt no luck in it now, only shame and loss. Bending the peak of his cap in a little on both sides, as was always his habit before wearing it, Josef saw what Pfeiffer had been talking about. The small colored roundel beneath the German eagle to the front had been replaced. He looked at the new, polished metal badge in its place.

It was the *totenkopf*, the death's-head insignia of the SS.

Death. Yes, that, rather than the edelweiss, is the correct talisman for me now.

Josef put the cap on, pulling it down tight over the woolen scarf that already bound his ears and chin. He then covered his eyes with black-lensed snow goggles that pushed Pfeiffer into the dark shadow where he belonged.

Pulling the hood of his white jacket up and over his head, Josef said only, "I will start now, if I may, Herr Oberst."

"Of course," Pfeiffer replied, opening the heavy door to the outside. The bitter cold instantly slammed them both, Pfeiffer gritting his teeth against it to watch Becker step out into the monochrome winter morning without the slightest hesitation.

"Halt!" Pfeiffer commanded. Josef did so, turning to look back at the SS officer, the freezing draft racing around him to invade the castle through the still-open door. "You hate me, Obergefreiter Josef Becker, I know. But understand that is good. Hate is a strong emotion. It makes us capable of anything and, for what lies ahead of you, that is going to be very necessary. We will meet again later. Until then, berg heil!"

Josef shook his head, feigning an inability to hear through the layers of his headgear, but he understood every word, acknowledging even the promotion from *gefreiter* in the title Pfeiffer used. That man said nothing by mistake.

Striding away from his captor without a second look, feeling remote from the world within his many layers, Becker concentrated instead on the huge weight of his loaded pack bearing down onto his back, pushing the shaft of his returned ice axe hard against his spine, cutting its straps into his shoulders. Usually he would ignore it, savoring instead the relief of at least a temporary escape from the castle, but that day he welcomed its burden, letting it squeeze pain, anger, and, yes, utter hatred into every part of his body. Quickening his pace, he crossed the castle bridge, hobnailed boots clattering over the rounded, icy cobblestones.

At the cleared roadway beyond, he quickly turned down into the steep-sided wood. His legs immediately sunk into snow up to his shins, feet slipping and sliding under the pack's weight as he began to descend, forcing him to grab at small evergreen bushes and naked saplings to stay upright. They shook their coverings of new snow onto him until he arrived, as he did each morning, at the spot below the castle where Kurt's body must have landed. There, shaking off the snow and ice, Josef stopped, calling to mind the thudding sound of his friend's death fall, the silent passing of Gunter before, the terrified faces of the nine Jews he had guided to execution, particularly the tiny girl he pushed into her own stone sepulchre. He said no prayer, just remembered what he had done and contemplated what their murderers now wanted him to do.

Hate, indeed.

From there, every day he would push himself as hard as he could up and down the steep slopes of the river valley beyond the castle's promontory. He would do it for hours, punishing himself under the backbreaking load, forcing himself on until his lungs heaved and he could taste blood in his mouth. With every step he would fight the urge to just keep going in one direction. If it would have meant a single sniper's bullet for him, there were days when he would have gladly taken it. But he knew there would be more bullets for his mother and sisters and that thought would reel him back to the castle as effectively as a fishhook through his cheek on an unbreakable line.

However far he went, he could always feel the building's sinister presence. It brooded over the surrounding countryside as if it alone were responsible for the desolation of winter that lay on the barren, hard-frozen land. Josef knew a lot about the *SS-Schule Haus Wewelsburg* now. The only person within the dark castle that he regularly spoke to was the librarian, a captain called Waibel, charged by Pfeiffer with providing everything Josef needed to plan the climb ahead and supervise his studies.

A nervous man in his late fifties, Waibel hid behind a well-tailored SS uniform and medal ribbons that told of time, and wounds, in the trenches of Flanders. In breathless, lyrical sentences, he described Wewelsburg as part university, part fortress, the spiritual "axis mundi" of the SS, a new Camelot for the reichsführer's Teutonic order of Black Knights that was going to conquer the world and never grow old, not even in a thousand years. With eyes misting, he eulogized the reichsführer, describing him as a mystical man, a spiritual man who understood more than anyone why the Aryans were the master race destined to rule all others. He whispered of a prison camp nearby that held only Jehovah's Witnesses, the best builders, engineers, and architects deliberately selected to restore the castle, compelled by their beliefs to work to the best of their abilities and not even try to escape. Jews could never be allowed to touch such a hallowed place. The castle, he said, doomed them to death instead.

Yes, that is what they do to them now.

Josef shut the horror of the place and its inhabitants from his thoughts as he did everything: by thinking of climbing instead. It was not so difficult to do. Ever since Pfeiffer had turned over that photograph and given his next climb a name, Mount Everest, he could let it rise up before him at will. Never-ending and colorless, it was as if the black-and-white images Josef had been poring over for months were now developed directly onto the inside of his skull. Its vast size could easily fill his mind to push everything else aside, and he let it. With every leaden step of his training, he would mentally tackle the details of a route he had now learned by heart. Whenever exhaustion stopped him in his tracks, he permitted the thought of what it would be like to take that final magnificent step to the very summit to push him forward again.

The desire to climb the mighty mountain grew stronger every day, however much he told himself that to do so served his enemies and betrayed his friends.

Even when he thought of his own family and told himself that he had no choice in the matter, Josef knew that it was no longer as simple as that. Everest was beginning to possess him as much as the invisible bonds that held him within the dark, almost medieval world of the castle. He risked losing his soul in the contradictions of its companionship.

34

Entering the castle library that afternoon, Josef was immediately met by Waibel stuttering, "G ... g ... guests. You have guests."

Looking across to the table to where he usually sat, Josef saw the backs of two black-uniformed officers sitting before the many maps, books, and photographs that covered his reserved study area. As Becker approached the table, one stood and turned to face him. It was Pfeiffer, of course.

"Good. You are here precisely when Waibel said you would be. Come and sit with us, Obergefreiter Becker."

The other officer remained seated. He was signing letters and orders, each sandwiched between the pink blotting pages of a large, black leather-bound folder. With a wave of his fountain pen, he motioned to Josef to sit down but said nothing, continuing to study and sign each document with his spiky signature. Every time, it was identical, an even row of jagged points that cut across the page like teeth:

H. Himmler.

Turning the last page of the blotter to reveal no further letters, the reichsführer closed the folder and slowly screwed the top back on his fountain pen. Satisfied that it was properly closed, he put it inside his black jacket, passed the leather folder to Pfeiffer, and looked directly at Josef. His slightly puffy, undistinguished face—despite the small Y-shaped dueling scar Josef could see on his left cheek—twitched slightly as he spoke.

"So you are our Sisyphus? I see you the mornings I am in my office in the North Tower. I watch as you slowly move up and down the sides of the river valley under your heavy backpack. I find it somewhat inspiring, a daily reminder of cold determination."

He stared intently at Josef before turning to Pfeiffer.

"Obersturmführer, please update me on the progress of this operation."

Pfeiffer reached down into his attaché case resting on the floor and put in the leather folder. His hand returned with a buff-colored file and a small package. Placing them on the table in front of him, he opened the file and looked at the typed notes and memoranda bound within. Josef could see, clipped to the inside cover, Pfeiffer's photographs of him, his mother, his sisters, and the mountain.

"Certainly, Herr Reichsführer. Obergefreiter Becker has been our guest at Lichterfelde, Bad Harzburg, and here at Wewelsburg for four months now. From his very first briefing on the objective of our operation, I am pleased to say that he has embraced the possibilities for preparation we have offered. He has impressed our training officers and exceeded their requirements. He has worked diligently on his fitness, as you have witnessed, and studied the mountain in detail. In addition, we have enabled him to become fully conversant with modern photography so that he might properly record his actions. He has also learned some English so that he can at least understand a bit of the dominant international language of the countries he will be passing through. With still a few weeks before he leaves, I consider that he will be more than adequately prepared for what lies ahead."

Himmler looked back at Josef as if considering him anew. "Good. Refresh my memory as to how he is going to get to the mountain undiscovered."

"He is joining a climbing expedition to Sikkim under the auspices of Professor Markus Schmidt, who is to lead a group of seven climbers and scientists in tackling some of the lower peaks of the Kangchenjunga as well as studying the geology and fauna of the area. The expedition has been Schmidt's dream for some years, and, in order to assist our own objectives, we have facilitated it. Given that its mountaineering objectives are relatively modest, it has the full approval of the local British authorities. That is not to say that it won't be monitored by the presence of one of their army officers, but that should not cause us too many difficulties."

"Does Schmidt know the objective of Operation Sisyphus?"

"Professor Schmidt is within our confidence. A long-standing party member and member of the

Freundeskreis Reichsführer SS, he is utterly loyal and will do everything in his power to assist Obergefreiter Becker until the first ascent of his expedition. Following completion of that climb, Obergefreiter Becker will be deemed to be suffering from 'mountain sickness' and ruled unable to continue. He will then, with a local porter already identified as suitable, be ordered to return to Germany. In reality, however, they will instead secretly make their way into Tibet. Once they arrive at the mountain, they will be met by a member of Schäfer's Tibet expedition, who will furnish additional equipment and give support for Obergefreiter Becker's climb of the mountain. As you know, we favor the solo climb as by its very audacity and lack of huge resources, it will show the entire world what one determined German can do. Such an achievement would also be an even greater humiliation for the English, who always send armies of people when they try to climb it."

"It sounds thorough. When do they leave?"

"The second of March on the SS *Gneisenau* from the Port of Venice to Bombay. It's the same ship that Schäfer's team took to India."

"That is quite soon." Turning back to Josef, Himmler asked, "It is said you have the ability to climb anything. Do you feel honored to have such a chance to prove it?"

Josef looked back at the glass lenses of Himmler's omnipresent pince-nez seeing only multiple reflections of the mountain and his family from the inside of the open file on the table.

"I do, Herr Reichsführer. I look forward to placing a flag on the summit knowing that it will bring pride and happiness to my family for years to come."

Even as he said the word "family," Josef's eyes flicked at Pfeiffer who instantly cut back into the conversation.

"On the subject of flags, I have had these prepared. I think they will work well."

Opening the package set on the table, Pfeiffer took out two new, small flags. He carefully unfolded them, smoothing each one out. The first was a red triangle, a swastika within its white central circle, the second, a black square with the two white sig runes of the SS. From one side of each flag hung two white strings of cloth tape, which Pfeiffer pointed out to the reichsführer.

"I have had the two flags sewn and sized so they can be tied one above the other on Obergefreiter Becker's ice axe when he places it on the summit. As already mentioned, I have ensured that he is fully trained in the use of the Leica thirty-five-millimeter camera so that he can properly record this glorious moment for us to present to the world. What a photograph that will be."

"Yes," Himmler responded as if slowly tasting every word of Pfeiffer's explanation. He fixed his stare once again on Josef. "If we meet again, you will be the man who first climbed Mount Everest, a German hero. No longer the traitor and criminal you are today. That's quite a thought, wouldn't you say?"

Josef said nothing in reply as Himmler reached back inside his jacket to retrieve his fountain pen. Taking the operation file, he wrote something across the back of a piece of paper. Folding it, he passed it to Pfeiffer.

The younger SS officer read the note while Himmler got up from the table and left, saying nothing more. Pfeiffer carefully put the piece of paper into a pocket, refolded the two flags, and, with a forced smile, said, "Good. Becker, do you have any questions?"

"Yes, only one."

"Tell me."

"What is 'Sisyphus'?"

"Not what, Becker, but who. Sisyphus is a character from Greek mythology. You would do well to read about him before you set off. You will soon understand why it is such an appropriate code name for this operation."

35

THE KHUMBU HOTEL, THAMEL, KATHMANDU, NEPAL
June 8, 2009
10:30 a.m.

Quinn stepped up into the passenger seat of the decrepit old Land Rover, sharp pains stabbing his spine. Wincing within the tight bandage that bound his midriff like a corset, he sat forward on the edge of the ripped grey seat, hands pulling on the vehicle's old metal dash to avoid any contact between his beaten back and its disintegrating foam and protruding metal frame.

Babu Sonam, the president of the Nepal Sherpa Climbers organization, got into the driver's side and tried to start the old four-by-four. It was reluctant, needing five attempts before it finally wheezed into life with a triumphant fart of sooty black smoke to further pollute Kathmandu's air. Gunning the engine before it could change its mind, Sonam immediately thrust the vehicle out into the road saying as he did so, "Dawa is at the Sagarmatha Zonal Hospital, not the Bir that treated you."

The old Sherpa spoke in a clear, fluent English that surprised Quinn.

"He is still in a coma. He was very severely beaten. If he had not been found so soon, he would have died where they left him." Sonam concentrated for a moment on grinding the reluctant Land Rover into another gear before he could continue. "The surgeons had to remove his spleen to save him. One of his lungs was punctured, a kidney ruptured, many ribs and both a knee and an ankle badly broken. I think what was done to him is called 'kneecapping' where you come from. Well, that is what my cousin says. He was a Gurkha in your British Army for many years. When Dawa comes out of the coma, his recovery will take a very long time. Maybe one day he will walk again, but he will never return to Everest. His climbing days are over."

Quinn slowly processed the information as the Land Rover bullied its way through the dense Kathmandu traffic. "Who's paying the medical bills? They must be huge," he asked.

"Part of it will come under the public health care system, and our organization will try to cover the rest. We can't do it really; we don't have the money, but we will seek donations from the many foreign climbers that Dawa has worked with over the years. I know they will be generous. Dawa Sherpa has the respect of many people." With a look of obvious concern, he added, "It is his future after the hospital that will be more difficult. He has a wife and three children. He will also have to help his brother Pemba's wife and young son. How can he do this if he is unable to work the high mountains? It's all he has ever done."

Quinn looked out through the scratched, yellowed

side window of the noisy vehicle. Against the news of Dawa's wounds, the stacked bare-brick buildings, the spiders' webs of exposed cabling, the speeding cars and motorcycles, the jay-walkers all struck him as even more dangerous and precarious than normal. For the first time, he truly felt the fragility and violence of trying to survive in that ramshackle city, day in, day out. He thought back to the attack that he had suffered, shuddering a little at what he had done with the ice screw to defend himself. "Have you heard anything about the two who attacked us? I assume that they—"

"No. No. No. Nothing at all," Sonam answered briskly, before Quinn could even finish his sentence. Swallowing twice, the old Sherpa stopped talking, suddenly becoming very intent on the road ahead.

They traveled on in silence, Quinn's back and ribs howling in protest at every pothole and lurching traffic-light stop until they reached the chaotic forecourt of the hospital. Leaving the Land Rover double-parked without hesitation, Sonam showed Quinn inside to the hospital's waiting room. It was crowded, sweaty, hot. Rows of grubby orange plastic seats were filled with bloodied men looking dazed, pregnant women contracting and shrieking, and small children holding their stomachs and whimpering. While Sonam signed them in, Quinn absorbed the collective misery around him, awaiting anesthetic and debridement; it reeked of pain and infection. His beaten back throbbed in sympathy with them all.

* * *

A nurse finally appeared to lead them deep into the

hospital's sweltering, shadowy warren. At the door to Dawa's room, Quinn met the Sherpa's tiny wife. He towered over her. Through tearstained, bloodshot eyes rimmed in smudged kohl, she looked pleadingly up at him, bringing her hands together with a meek, "*Namaste.*"

Quinn repeated the gesture in return, adding, "I am so sorry," unaware if she even spoke English. When she opened the door for him to come into the room, the sight within spiked tears into his eyes. It was not at all what he expected. He had prepared himself for the "coma" of Hollywood movies, anticipating a perfect person lying gently asleep, hands neatly arranged over crisp white sheets, a discreet bank of life-support machines bleeping confirmation of a regular stability.

Dawa's coma was nothing like that. It was tormented, tortured. He appeared trapped beneath a thin ice of consciousness, desperately trying to break up through to stop himself from drowning in a hideous, accelerating nightmare. His broken body twisted and writhed amidst a network of plastic tubes through which raced small trains of amber fluids and feathery clots of blood. Snippets of words, pleading sounds emerged from a clear plastic oxygen mask, the viciously swollen face behind it almost unrecognizable. Occasionally his whole body would violently jerk up from the bed. Although unconscious, he screamed from the pain.

The sight shattered Quinn. He wanted to run from it, to instantly get out of the room.

Unable to control himself, he pushed backward only to find his way to the door blocked by Sonam.

"I know it is difficult to see, Mr. Quinn, but you must stay and talk to him. The doctors say that he might respond to familiar voices. It could, at least, help to calm him. He has been with you a lot over the past months on the mountain, in fact, with you many times on the mountains. Please try, Mr. Quinn, please try."

Ashamed of his flight instinct, Quinn steeled himself, pulled up a chair and sat. Dawa's wife moved in behind him. He heard a faint humming noise begin, her chant of *"Om mani padme hum,"* while he struggled to find anything to say. His tongue suddenly tied, his few clumsily chosen words sounded trivial and inappropriate to the scene in front of him. Only by closing his eyes and telling himself to "Concentrate. Concentrate. Concentrate," could he start properly.

Gradually, Quinn got into his stride as he talked about the climbs the two of them had been on together, about the moments they had shared, the people they both knew, the summits they had stood on. He continued to talk about England. About the places he had lived. About the pubs he had frequented. About the women who had given up on him ever loving them more than he loved the mountains.

He even talked about the motorcycle he owned. The Sherpas always loved to hear about that. Even though it was nearly thirty years old and had over forty thousand miles on it, to them it was fascinating: 150cc was a super-bike to them, 1000cc unimaginable. He described the old BMW to Dawa once more. He told him about the trips he had made on it, his words riding it again to Scotland, to France, to Switzerland, to Austria. On arrival, he parked it and described the mountains climbed, the foods eaten, the wines drunk, the languages spoken, the friends made.

His voice went on and on, soft and low, reciting a never-ending mantra of his life while Dawa's wife's faster buzz of incantation played its continual, higher harmony.

* * *

A gentle touch on Quinn's shoulder interrupted him.

"Mr. Quinn, I am sorry, but we must go now. It is Pemba's funeral soon," Sonam whispered.

Quinn looked at his old Rolex Explorer. He had lost all track of time.

It was a shock to see that he had been talking for two hours. He was surprised also to find that his face was wet with tears.

He took off the watch. Its metal bracelet folded in on itself, reducing it to a tight lump of steel in the palm of his hand, solid and warm as he clenched it. He recalled his late father giving it to him on the day of his twenty-first birthday. He'd wanted one ever since he'd seen it advertised in those *National Geographic*s in that library so long before. It was the best present he'd ever received.

Quinn turned to Dawa's tiny wife and handed her the watch. "Sell it," he said simply as he closed her small, hennaed hands around it.

She looked quizzically at Sonam, and after he said something in Sherpali, she looked back up at Quinn and murmured, *"Thuchi che, Quinn-baba."*

Quinn nodded and turned back to look again at Dawa. He was slightly more at ease now. His movements were slower, his breathing more regular. Perhaps the talking really had calmed him.

"Get well, my friend. Get well," he said, leaning close into the Sherpa.

Dawa's face turned very slightly to his, his bruised and swollen eyelids prizing themselves slightly open.

The bloodshot eyes within the gummy slits fixed for a moment on Quinn. From beneath the plastic oxygen mask came a single word, "Axe."

The eyes closed only to flicker open again as Dawa said, "Ang ... Noru."

The Sherpa sank back into unconsciousness.

Quinn turned to Sonam. "Who is Ang Noru?"

Sonam shrugged and obviously asked the same question of Dawa's wife in Sherpali.

She responded instantly with a screeching howl of sound, a wail that rose and fell without break, as if her whole explanation consisted of one convoluted word of pain. Then she started crying, crying uncontrollably, heavy tears cascading down her face onto her hands, bathing Quinn's watch that she had pulled up tight to her sobbing mouth.

Sonam paraphrased her desperate response. "She says Ang Noru was Dawa's great-uncle on his mother's side, a tiger taken by the mountain demon long ago. She says that it is bad karma that Dawa should speak of him now. It means that the tiger has returned to feed Dawa to the same devil."

Quinn could only stare at the small, trembling woman, shocked and confused by her sudden outburst of lyrical mysticism. He tried to say something more to calm her, but at a loss for any real words, could only clasp his hands around hers, saying, "I'm sure he'll be okay." Leaving with Sonam, Neil Quinn wondered how that could possibly be true.

36

STEAMSHIP *GNEISENAU*, PORT OF VENICE, ITALY
March 2, 1939
3:45 p.m. (Ora Italiana)

From the top deck, Josef observed the SS *Gneisenau*'s roster assemble. On the wharf below, black cars and carriages shuttled to and from the distant arches of the Port of Venice railway station like beetles. With every arrival, another group of passengers would emerge, momentarily uniting to take their first excited look at the great steamship until the unexpected chill of the easterly wind pushed them quickly into the offices of Norddeutscher Lloyd.

Josef had been on board since the morning. The day before, Pfeiffer had delivered him to Professor Schmidt in Munich, departing with a pat of a leather-gloved hand on the side of his face to reinforce his final words. "You know the rules, Josef Becker: summit or die in the attempt. Those are the only circumstances that will let your family live. Good luck. I will await the news of your success."

Left alone with the professor, the corpulent man was quick to establish his own complicity in the threats of Operation Sisyphus. "Soldier, mountain guide, smuggler, prisoner, whatever it is you really are, let us be clear about one thing from the start. If you go missing at any time during our long journey ahead, I am instructed to telegram the information directly to Obersturmführer Pfeiffer. We are both aware of what instructions will be given as regards your mother and sisters should you not return. You should know that it has taken me three years to organize this expedition, the last ten to earn the trust and respect of the superiors who now reward me with its leadership. I will do everything in my power to assist Operation Sisyphus, and you in return will do nothing to jeopardize the opportunity I have been given."

During the preparations for the departure of the 1939 Combined German Universities Himalayan Expedition on the night train to Venice, Schmidt had introduced Josef to the rest of the assembled team, describing him as a noncommissioned army mountain guide assigned to the expedition by the reichsführer-SS. He pompously embellished Josef's cover story by saying it was a clear demonstration of the esteem in which the reichsführer held both him and his expedition, before warning there could be no further discussion of Becker's role with anyone as any military presence on a civilian expedition was classified. Soon after the train departed, Josef excused himself to sleep, silently irritated by the group's boisterous braggadocio; the loudmouthed Schmidt always at the center of the selection of smug, self-satisfied students from elite Nazi families. Josef didn't think there looked to be a climber amongst them.

He slept well despite the sleeper carriage's cramped cot but awoke early to a misty Italian dawn, feeling anxious for his family yet unable to remember the details of the dream that caused it. Trying to shake off his anxiety, Josef watched the passing flatlands of the Veneto emerge into another day, envying the freedom of the farmers already tending the wide tracts of land. With a heavy heart, he mourned simpler days when he too worked in the high pastures and climbed for amusement, not mercy.

The train reached Venice at 9:00 a.m. precisely. With all the equipment on board by lunchtime and the rest of the day to enjoy before the ship set sail, Schmidt loudly invited the team to visit the watery city with him. Under his breath he said to Josef, "You, on the other hand, will remain on board until we leave port." Josef didn't care; he was glad to be free of them. He unpacked and then set off to explore the ship, the first he had ever been on, finally settling against that rail on the highest deck to smoke and watch the preparations to sail.

* * *

His last cigarette finished, Josef grabbed the polished brass handle of the door to return inside.

Opening it, he found his path blocked by a woman. Seemingly a few years younger than him, she was wearing a long, dark blue coat with a bright scarf tied over her glossy, dark brown hair. On a thin leather strap around her neck hung a silver Leica camera.

The surprise of the girl's beauty combined with

the shock of seeing a camera identical to the one that he had been supplied with for his mission stopped Josef in his tracks. Unable to pass, his thoughts returned from a momentary recall of being relentlessly drilled in photographic techniques at Wewelsburg to consider the gentle contours of the face before him, the soft curls pushing forward from the red and gold silk scarf, the jade green of the eyes looking back.

Moving aside to let him enter, the girl said in Italian, *"È freddo là fuori?"*

Josef stepped inside, missing the question but excusing himself in German as he entered.

"I asked you if it was cold outside," she replied, switching to fluent German. She smiled as she spoke, thinking to herself that he had a kind, handsome face, but one that looked tired, heavy with cares.

Her eyes met Josef's, pulling his glance into hers for a split second. "Yes … it is," he replied, rendered unsure of himself by the girl's scrutiny.

He could feel the details of her face—the long eyelashes, the gentle downward curve of the bright eyes, the fuller upward sweep of her mouth—etching themselves into his brain as she responded, "Good. Then I must make the most of it. I think the cold is going to be one of the things I will miss most where I am going."

"And where are you going?"

"Hyderabad, India."

"That's a long way away from Germany."

"It is," she replied, a little pensively at first before seeming to remind herself of something happier, "but it is for the best. My father is building a factory there with an English business partner. We are moving there permanently so that he can supervise its operation. Hopefully the light is good enough for me to take some last photographs to remind me of chilly old Europe?"

"It is," Josef replied, well aware of the conditions necessary to take the perfect photograph.

Looking directly at Josef again, the girl asked, "So were you saying farewell to the cold as well?"

"Not exactly." He paused before adding, "I don't think I am destined to escape it so easily."

37

Josef continued to spend the first days on board largely alone, compelled to look out at a dull winter sea from a lower side deck or the porthole of his cabin. He had tried to return to the upper deck where he'd spent that afternoon before the departure but it was closed to all but first-class passengers. The exclusion was a disappointment because he wanted to meet the girl again. She had told him her name was Magda von Trier, and, in his mind's eye, he constantly reconstructed the picture of her face saying she hoped to see him again during the voyage.

It was beginning to look unlikely. Only Schmidt was actually traveling first class. On the train to Venice, he had revealed his first class ticket, waving it proudly like a flag, loudly delighted in the fact that the expedition's benefactors had justly mandated that he travel with the status befitting the führer of a German expedition. Josef had listened to the team member nearest him mutter to another how his family could easily have afforded for him to travel first class but that he had decided against it to avoid upsetting Schmidt and risk being excluded from such a jaunt. The other had just nodded in sly agreement.

Whatever the reasons, the remainder of the team was booked into second class, but Josef could find little fault in that. It was as luxurious as anything he had ever experienced. He even had a cabin to himself. It was comfortable, quiet, and filled with the new clothing and equipment he had been given before leaving Wewelsburg. Although Schäfer was going to supply him with the additional materials needed once he arrived at the mountain, Pfeiffer had seen that Josef was issued with the best mountain clothing available to take with him. His new, reversible, grey-white winter camouflage jacket and trousers were the latest SS issue. Insulated and windproof, they were better than anything Josef had ever used before. His goggles, crampons, gaiters, gloves, sweaters, woolen undergarments, and boots were also totally new. The only old equipment that now remained to him was his field cap and his ice axe. When Josef got bored, he would lock himself in his cabin and try it all on for size. Feeling the anticipation of the climb ahead, the mountain would rear up before him until his conscience reminded him of the price of his new wardrobe and he guiltily put it all away again.

By his bunk, he stacked the books, maps, and notes on Everest that Waibel had given to him to continue his preparations during the voyage. On top, in pride of place, was a copy of George Finch's *Der Kampf um den Everest*. Whenever he read the Englishman's firsthand recollection of the 1922 British Everest expedition, oddly first published in German, the rare voice of its experience made Josef's heart beat faster. He studied its recollections endlessly, imagining their climb, experiencing its difficulties, and worrying at how much the man believed in the necessity of using additional oxygen high on Everest. He already knew that the equipment Schäfer was sending to meet him at the mountain was not going to include oxygen cylinders. "If, by my count, four different Englishmen have been able to get to within three hundred meters of the summit without it, then one good German can do even better," had been Pfeiffer's only reply when Josef raised the matter. He hoped he was right.

The specter of the climb that Finch conjured also pushed Josef to continue his fitness regime in the ship's otherwise empty gymnasium. Using dumbbells and medicine balls, he worked his body as long and as hard as he could to keep the condition that his winter stay at Wewelsburg had provided. With every exercise he would tell himself, *It's just another climb*. He said it so much he almost believed it, letting his thoughts be consumed all over again by the task ahead, forgetting, for a while, all else, even the girl with the camera.

* * *

On the third day of the voyage, a knock on Josef's cabin door interrupted his afternoon reading.

Waiting at the door, a white-jacketed steward handed in a note that read:

> *The sun is now shining enough for even you to escape the cold. Come and join me on the top deck. The steward will bring you. MvT.*

The invitation gave Josef a jolt of excitement that sent him rushing for his hat and jacket without any thought for the consequences, mountain books instantly abandoned.

Joining Magda on the top sundeck, they took tea together. The conversation was light and pleasant, but also wary. Intent on avoiding too many personal details, Magda focused their attention, and her ever-present camera, on the moments of brilliance that only a sea voyage can provide: thin shafts of sunlight piercing the clouds and spearing distant circles of sea, the surprise of silver fish flicking out unexpected wings and launching themselves from the top of waves, the mystery of distant white islands that served as brief, anonymous reminders of land.

Josef looked at the things she pointed out and, in each, saw a new world denied. In return he re-created for her some of the incredible things he had seen in his old world of the mountains until, the tea long finished, he said he should leave even if he wanted to stay.

Magda walked him back to the second-class level, saying nothing until she said softly, "Let's do this again tomorrow."

The next time they met, their conversation was faster, more eager, fueled by the break in their company. Magda spoke more personally, describing her interests in photography and ballet, but primarily of her love for the medicine she had studied at Leipzig University.

While Josef was listening to her describe becoming a junior doctor, she suddenly diverted his attention to the very end of the deck. There, an overweight man in undersized white exercise gear was doing loud, exaggerated calisthenics as he looked out to sea.

"I didn't know Hermann Göring was on board," Magda said to Josef in a deliberately wry fashion while they both watched the grunting, bobbing man. The sight was comical, the fat buttocks threatening to overwhelm the seams of the white shorts every time the preposterous man bent or squatted. Magda said nothing more but lifted her Leica toward the appalling sight, raising her eyebrows at Josef as, with mock horror, she feigned taking a photograph. Suppressing giggles that threatened to turn into tear-streaming laughter, Josef realized that it was the first time he had laughed since being captured five months before. There was a time when he used to laugh a lot.

However, Josef's amusement ceased the instant the man finished his elaborate exercise regime and turned to leave. With genuine horror, he saw that it was Schmidt. Knowing full well he was playing with fire by merely being there on the first-class deck, let alone sitting next to a beautiful girl, Josef instantly tilted his head forward to hide behind the brim of his hat. His disappearing act spurred Magda to gently poke him in the ribs as the professor strutted past. Each touch was like an electric shock but still Josef kept his face down.

Only when the deck door had slammed shut, did he risk looking up once more. Magda poked him again and made a little snorting noise like a piglet. This time Josef laughed until the tears ran off the end of his chin and that she did photograph.

Finally able to pull himself together, Josef said without a word of a lie, "You're dangerous."

"You sound like my parents," Magda said seriously,

before asking with her smile renewed, "Now tell me, Josef, am I to assume from your behavior that you know that fine example of German physical perfection?"

He looked back at Magda and, with all the credibility he could muster, recited his rehearsed reasons for being there with Schmidt's expedition.

It was not the truth, and the more he spoke, the more he wanted to tell it to her.

38

DAKSHINA MURTI ROAD, KATHMANDU, NEPAL
June 8, 2009
1:25 p.m.

As the rattling Land Rover neared Pashupatinath, the traffic increased exponentially until finally the manic flow of trucks, buses, old four-by-fours, motorized rickshaws, small motorcycles, bicycles—all headed in the direction of the holiest Hindu temple in Nepal—ground to a halt.

From the paralysis, a cacophony of car and motorcycle horns began to blare, drowning out the spirited ringing of hundreds of bicycle bells as, with difficulty, Sonam forced the old Land Rover up onto the side of the road. There, he gestured to Quinn that they should get out.

"Many people are coming to the cremation, Mr. Neil. There is a lot of anger and grief about what happened to Pemba and Dawa. We can walk. It's not far. This traffic is not going anywhere until the funeral is over."

Abandoning the vehicle, they started on foot. Quinn was actually somewhat confused as to why they were even going to Pashupatinath. As they pushed between the crowds on the pavement, he asked Sonam about it. "I thought the Sherpas were Buddhists. Pashupatinath is a Hindu place of worship, isn't it? Why would they do the cremation here?"

"It is often difficult to draw lines between religions here. Many Nepali are Hindu and Buddhist, sometimes a little Christian as well. They combine many gods into a single devotion to the holy. Kathmandu has always been a place of many gods. In fact, they used to say Kathmandu had more gods than people, more temples than houses. That is sadly, and obviously, not true now, but Pashupatinath is still a most important holy place suitable for everyone to show the greatest respect to Pemba Sherpa."

Following the flow of jostling humanity filing along the pavement, Quinn spied a little Mini Clubman car almost hidden in the traffic. About thirty years old and showing its age, the microscopic British car appeared utterly incongruous, sandwiched as it was between a dirty bus and a huge Tata truck covered in painted slogans and mirrors. Behind the driver's wheel of the tiny Mini was Henrietta Richards with Sanjeev Gupta seated alongside her. The sight was almost comical. Quinn pushed out between the stationary vehicles to knock on the side window, beckoning Henrietta and Sanjeev to get out and join them. As he opened the door, Henrietta unfolded herself from the low seat of the small car, pulling a long golf umbrella from behind it. "Thank you, Neil. I was hoping that I might run into you," she shouted above the continuing racket of the traffic jam. Then with a sigh she looked back at her car. "I suppose I will have to leave my baby here for now. It better be there when I get back."

The expanded party setting off again, Henrietta said, "Neil, I am glad you are back on your feet. It was a brutal attack. I have always thought Sarron was unstable, a horrible explosion waiting to happen, and I'm sorry that you and the two Sherpas got caught in it, particularly after the death of the boy on the mountain. Evidently Sarron's instructions were that the three of you be taught a lesson but not actually killed. Unfortunately the two goons he used, ex-army sadists, were sloppy in their desire to continue freelance careers of torture and mayhem, something that wouldn't have happened if he still had the services of the Vishnevskys. I must say, I do find it particularly interesting that, in your case, they were specifically told to beat you with that old ice axe you found and then bring it to Sarron."

"Probably in return for the axe being used against him when we fought in the mess tent," Quinn offered in explanation.

"Yes, possibly. I understand they weren't able to take it, making off instead with one of your ice screws."

Quinn shook his head, thinking, *How does she know all this stuff?*

The same words must have come out of his mouth.

"I know nothing," she replied in a faintly humorous voice, "just as no one else in this town seems to know how your two attackers ended up doing a good impression of a Tibetan sky burial on exactly the spot where Dawa was found."

"What?"

"You must know what a sky burial is, Neil?" She didn't wait for his reply, seeming to relish answering the question herself. "It's when the Tomden or Yoginbutchers, Tibetan outcasts who answer only to the monks, take big meat hatchets to a recently deceased corpse. They slice it from head to toe, exposing the flesh and bone within, cutting it into small pieces that they then place out for vultures to devour. It is a very effective disposal system for dead bodies in a land with little wood to burn and where the rock-hard ground is not exactly amenable to the digging of graves.

"Actually in this case it seems that your two assailants might not have been dead when the process started, and that it took quite a long time for them to become so. It appears also that the feral dogs that run the banks of the Bagmati River got more of a meal than the vultures. Unnecessary details perhaps, but you know me, I always seek the devil in the detail."

I'm sure you do, Quinn thought but asked instead, "Where's Sarron now?"

"Well, not in Kathmandu and no longer in Lhasa, I suspect. A lot of people are very keen to see him and likely to be none too gentle when they do. I doubt he has even gone back to France, for now. It's much more likely that he will lose himself in India, Goa maybe, or perhaps one of his former French army hangouts in Africa. Not many could get to him in somewhere like Djibouti. However, Neil, you are going to need to be very careful. Sarron's behavior strikes me as a vendetta almost as much as him simply having something to hide about the climb. I know his back was to the wall for a number of reasons before the climb and he was counting on the Tate summit bonus. Anyway, enough about him, how are you?"

"I'm actually okay considering everything. Even sorer than I was from the fun and games on the mountain, but nothing major broken. I'll mend." Quinn's voice trailed off as he thought instead of Dawa's still— desperate condition. "I did, however, visit Dawa this morning. Now that's a different story. He really is in a bad way, but they seem to think he will recover to some degree. Won't climb again though."

"Neil, what those two thugs did was horrific even if I am sure that they came to regret it in full. It will be very difficult for Dawa to support both his and Pemba's families." Her voice slowed. "I remember you mentioning that Dawa saved your life on the Second Step. You do know that if there is more to the story of you finding that ice axe there, and let's say, for argument's sake, that you might also have found the body of Sandy Irvine, then there would be a lot of interest and not a little financial upside possible from such a discovery. Probably enough to support Dawa for a very long time."

Quinn knew what she was driving at before she even arrived.

"I mean, if you could find the camera that revealed a picture showing Irvine and Mallory on the summit all those years before Hillary and Tenzing, then you too could probably retire. When they displayed just the small items that they found on Mallory's body in 1999 in America, they were insured for nearly half a million dollars. Neil, we are not talking the contents of Tutankhamen's tomb here, just some old climbing gear really, but there is value in this stuff to the right people. Even I will confess to the fact that I would love to have that blue and red paisley handkerchief they found Mallory's letters wrapped in. It was still perfect. It even had his initials, GLM, stitched into it. Perhaps if you did find the camera, you could buy it for my climbing archive with some of the proceeds?" She smiled at her own flight of fantasy.

"Perhaps I would, Henrietta, no one deserves it more, but isn't that whole Mallory and Irvine camera thing just a piece of nonsense? I mean, if it still exists, it'll have been up there for nearly a hundred years now. High altitude is not a perfect time capsule. Things break with freezing; they can rust up there even. I've seen it. Surely any film would have been destroyed long ago?"

Henrietta tutted, shaking her head a little. "You'd think that, but it's not impossible. I heard that Mallory's watch, even if the glass crystal had broken and the hands had fallen off, still ticked when wound some seventy-five years later. I am not sure if that's really true, but it is clear that things do survive up there for a long time. It is so high the atmospheric conditions are almost unique, particularly if the item has been well hidden inside a pocket or a jacket. One of them had the camera, and it wasn't on Mallory when his body was found, so it must be Irvine; I am also damn sure that if they got to that summit before they died, it would have been used to record the moment."

"So you really do believe in the possibility that it still exists and the film could be developed?"

"Neil, it's not only Everest that has its share of doomed eccentrics and frozen relics. In 1897, a Swede by the name of S. A. Andrée set off for the North Pole with two colleagues in a hydrogen balloon.

They were never seen again. Thirty-three years later, seal hunters found two of the bodies, and then a later search found the third with a tin containing the expedition's undeveloped photographic plates. The developed pictures revealed to the world the story of the trio's ill-fated three-month attempt to walk home over the ice after the balloon had failed.

"The film in that case had survived at a far lower altitude where moisture would have been a much greater factor, so it's not impossible that one left high on Everest might last longer. Who knows really? But anyone who loves the Everest story has a natural appetite to learn the details of that final summit attempt by Mallory and Irvine and whether they might actually have made it to the top. Any news, concrete information one way or the other, would be massive. I imagine *Time, Newsweek, National Geographic,* you name them, would all bid through the nose to be able to reveal to the world that they really had made it to the top before anyone else. A photograph proving it would become one of the most famous and valuable of all time."

Quinn understood her need to hang on to the hope that he had found something related to Irvine and that the mystery of all Everest mysteries could be solved in her lifetime, but he hadn't. Just as he prepared to say so, wondering whether he should mention instead his suspicions that the axe might actually be related to the Russian mystery as he'd first thought, Babu Sonam cut in. "Miss Richards, have you ever heard of a Sherpa called Ang Noru?"

"No, Sonam, I can't say I have but, at last count, there were about fifteen thousand Sherpas working in the Nepali climbing and trekking world. Not even I can keep up with them all. In fact, if he's anyone in the Everest world, I am surprised that you don't know him already."

"Oh, no, Miss Richards, I think this Sherpa has been dead for many years. It is possible that he was a Tiger."

Henrietta's face creased with curiosity as Quinn deliberately put his big frame between her and the old Sherpa to prevent the conversation going any further.

"We are at the entrance," he interjected. "Let's go in quickly before this crowd gets any worse."

Henrietta and Sonam stopped talking and filed in, but as Quinn waited for Sanjeev Gupta, he saw that he had already taken out a short pencil and was scribbling something down in his notebook. Quinn knew it was the name Ang Noru and the reference to "Tiger."

It hadn't crossed his mind until Sonam had mentioned it, but then, watching Gupta, the connection struck him like a lightning bolt.

39

Entering Pashupatinath's historic, sprawling complex of temples and ghats, any possibility for further discussion of the matter was lost. Street vendors beckoned and pawed at them from all sides, desperate to offer bright garlands of marigolds, powders in every color of the rainbow, thin guidebooks in English, Spanish, or Mandarin Chinese, even see-through rain macs branded "Monsoon Proof." Quinn shooed them away to permit their party to slowly wind its way down the crowded, slippery street toward the river, noses increasingly overwhelmed by the smell, an unholy mixture of incense, crushed flowers, sewage, wood smoke, and, god forbid, burning bodies.

With every downward step, Quinn wanted to kick himself instead. Firstly, because he had missed the link to a history he knew well, and then secondly, because the old Sherpa had instantly publicized it to Henrietta Richards, the one person who would most definitely connect the dots. The devil in the detail, as Henrietta put it, was as much in Dawa's wife's reference to a tiger as in the actual name that Dawa had uttered. Quinn had stupidly ignored the pertinent detail of the tiny woman's outcry, automatically assuming that any tiger stalking Dawa was simply the inevitable boogeyman that would haunt the nightmares of a desperately wounded Sherpa. It was only as Sonam mentioned it to Henrietta that Quinn instantly remembered that the word, title even, "Tiger" had a far more specific significance when linked to the Sherpa.

At first, it was little more than a nickname of appreciation, an accolade bestowed on the fifteen mountain porters, out of the original mixture of fifty-five Tibetans and Sherpas selected, who remained fit enough to assist in the preparation of the high camps for that ill-fated 1924 British expedition to Everest. Over subsequent expeditions as the Sherpas particularly excelled on the great mountain, it became something more: a stamp of undisputed excellence. By the midthirties, Bill Tillman, who along with Eric Shipton and Frank Smythe had taken up the British torch of being the first to summit Everest, was awarding "Tiger Badges" to the handful of Sherpas able to carry loads to their Camp VI set at 27,200 feet—higher in itself than the summit of the sixth-highest mountain in the world. The British Himalayan Club, based in Darjeeling where all the early expeditions set out from, soon followed this example by formally minting "Tiger Medals" for any porter who successfully carried through to 25,000 feet. Few were given, and the recipients, the "Tiger Sherpas" became well-known in the prewar mountaineering world of their day.

By the time he had made it down to the bank of the river, Quinn knew it spelled more questions about the axe. Dawa had clearly referred to it before he mentioned Ang Noru, and if he had been a Tiger, then that could date it to well before the Russians, if they had ever existed. But, just as quickly, Quinn reined himself in with the reminder that another famous Tiger Sherpa had summited Everest a year later than those legendary Russians in 1952, and that man was Tenzing Norgay.

Thinking about it all, he asked himself whether he shouldn't just share his find and his thoughts with Henrietta; after all, she was helping him with her report. But something held him back. Dawa had wanted him to have the axe, was even now trying, from the depths of his own misery, to give him clues about it. He couldn't make Dawa well, he couldn't settle his financial problems, but he felt that he should respect Dawa's wishes—wishes that seemed to suggest that he wanted Quinn to keep it.

Crossing over a narrow bridge, they filed up a flight of worn stone steps before turning right onto a terrace that looked across at the jumble of temple buildings, their stacked pagoda roofs the originals of the style that now defined the Far East. Below, on the opposite riverbank, were the burning ghats, seven heavy granite daises that projected from the greasy slabs that banked the slow-moving, khaki-colored river.

On one a fire already raged. Bright orange flames feasted on a pile of rough-hewn logs, the faint shadow of a blackening corpse within. The funeral pyre's pale smoke plumed up into a sky filled with darker clouds, slate grey and heavy in anticipation of the afternoon's coming monsoon downpour. Quinn watched a monkey artfully and carefully climb up the side of the ghat, intent on the crumbling edges of the fire and the burning body within, only to be violently beaten away by a skinny man with a long bamboo pole. As it fled, the man screamed at it, outraged at an intention of theft that insulted the laws of nature.

While they stood there waiting, a file of Sherpas paid their respects to Henrietta Richards as if she was as venerable as Pashupatinath. The Everest spring season now finished, they were all back in Kathmandu. Quinn saw among them those incredible men like Dawa who each had ten, fifteen, or even twenty Everest summits to their names. Each saluted Henrietta with a bow and the greeting "*Namaste.*" A number draped long, cream-colored silk *kata* scarves around her neck. After, they passed Quinn and looked straight into his eyes, as if in silent understanding, nodding their heads as they went. "The good thing, if there is any good to come out of all this, is that Sarron is finished in this town," Henrietta whispered to Neil. "The Sherpas will never let him return. They've known for a long time what sort of person he was but had to suffer it for his employment." She turned and looked at Quinn intently. "They know so much more than they ever let on, don't you think, Neil?"

"I'm sure they do," Quinn replied, slightly unsure at what she was hinting at, uncomfortable with the question. He changed the subject quickly. "Talking of which—without Pemba's and Dawa's testimonies, have you been able to complete your report about the climb?"

"I have, even if subsequent events have somewhat overtaken it. I can't explain the boy's death—I have no hard evidence—but I have set out what seem to be the pertinent details, both of the climb and its aftermath, and it suggests that you should have the benefit of the doubt. I suspect that will not be enough for Tate Senior; he seems to be a man who is very black and white in his approach, so I hope that Dawa will at some point be able to speak to me about what happened up there as that will back up your story to no end. So what now, Neil?"

Quinn shrugged his shoulders. "I don't know really. I'm broke, physically and financially. The only thing left in my wallet is my return ticket to London. I guess I'll use it and try to scrounge enough money to put some gas in my bike to get me to Chamonix so I can work the Alps for the summer."

"You'll be on French soil then and you know what that could mean?"

"Possibly, if he wants to find me."

"Oh, he will, Neil. Sooner or later, he will. You can be sure of it."

"Well, I have to take that risk. I know people there and hopefully it will get me back on my feet, even if I have to accept that my Everest career will be finished by all this."

"Look, Neil, I'll make you a deal. I'll email you a copy of my report so you can show it to anyone who questions your suitability to guide. In return all I ask is that if you come to any conclusions about that old axe, you'll let me know." She hesitated before adding, "But only when you're ready. And in the meantime, I would recommend keeping one eye looking over your shoulder."

Before Quinn could thank her, a scuffle broke out in the crowd assembled behind them. From its center, a small DVD camera curved up into the air, hanging there momentarily like a fly before landing with a soupy plop into the middle of the dirty river. A rotund, orange-faced man in a transparent pink waterproof jacket that encased him like a condom was then ejected off the viewing terrace with a well-placed kick up the behind from one of the Sherpas.

The rest of what appeared to be a Korean or Chinese tour group, each in their own matching sausage-skin jacket, swiftly followed, wailing in alarm, hands pawing the air in panic. The assembled group of mourners gave a loud cheer at their exit, clapping and whistling, forcing smiles onto their concerned faces.

The incident seemed to slightly lighten the mood. Quinn mentioned as much to Henrietta, who whispered in reply, "Neil, it is a Sherpa custom to try to not be unhappy at funerals. They believe if you are it brings bad luck, and a rain of blood will follow."

Too late for that, Quinn sadly thought as a quiet descended on the crowd.

A solitary bell began to toll.

Four men arrived on the opposite riverbank holding a stretcher supported by two thick green bamboo poles. On it was a loosely swaddled body. They stopped before one of the ghats, the raised stone slab already stacked with huge logs, all space between stuffed with tinder.

After other bystanders had restrained a crying woman who desperately tried to fling herself onto the laden stretcher, the four men gently laid it on the funeral pyre. One of them then pulled back the folds of orange sheet arranged over the body to expose a young, dead face. It was Pemba. The sight set off a hideous wail from the young woman, who was now being physically held back from the body and the platform.

Taking a long, lit taper from a brass pot, another man draped its curl of flame across the Sherpa's lifeless face and then in and around the orange material covering his dead body. It seemed to almost kiss and caress it. A small plume of smoke was the only clue that the fire was catching until it suddenly roared into a conflagration that quickly sucked the swaddled remains from sight.

The pyre burned for what felt like an age.

Everyone stood silently, lost in their own remembrances.

Quinn thought about Pemba, about Dawa, about Nelson Tate Junior left behind up there, frozen in eternal death, denied the chance for such an instant, fiery dissolution.

He thought also of the old ice axe, how it strangely seemed to link together everything that had happened from the moment it was found, how it seemed to save, but also punish, of how he just couldn't seem to get away from it whatever happened.

When the flames finally began to dwindle and the fire collapsed in on itself, attendants stepped forward to push the still-smoking logs and glowing ashes over the side of the platform and into the river. The burning embers spat and popped as they made contact with the dirty water, the bigger, still-burning logs caught by the river's slow current to float off twisting and turning gently, puffing thin trails of smoke behind them like small steamers.

Watching them go, Quinn told himself that he would find out the true story of the ice axe. He couldn't explain to himself why but he knew that the answer was important: important to him, to Dawa, to Henrietta, and also, the memories of Pemba and Nelson Tate Junior. It seemed, at that moment, to be the only thing he had left to offer anyone.

40

STEAMSHIP *GNEISENAU*, BAY OF BOMBAY, INDIA
March 9, 1939
5:45 p.m. (Deutsches Reich Zeit)

Josef and Magda's daily meetings continued as the *Gneisenau* steamed east and the days grew hotter. Connecting Josef's need to avoid Schmidt with a necessity for the both of them to stay out of an increasingly strong sun, Magda conjured times and places where they could quietly pass the time together. Shaded by umbrellas or hanging lifeboats, they continued to watch the ocean flow by, telling each other truthful details of their lives that carefully avoided the real reasons why either of them was on that great ship.

Despite the fact they came from very different backgrounds, it was a comfortable, amusing companionship driven by Magda's keen wit and Josef's kind nature. He enjoyed telling her about his home village, his family, his friends, carefully reconstructing through his words and memories everything that had been stolen from him. The more he spoke, the more he understood how his had been a simple, honest life based on kindness, friendship, and trust; a way of life doomed to extinction under the Nazis.

The realization made him want even more to tell Magda everything, but Pfeiffer's invisible dagger was still sharp. The stab of its point stopped him every time, leaving him instead to take in the beauty of the girl and the precious moments they shared.

When the ship passed through the Suez Canal and into the Red Sea, they met after dinner on the rear middle deck to look across the inky water at the faint outline of the shore, seeing little detail in the dark but feeling the warm desert wind on their faces and imagining the hidden, mysterious kingdoms it had passed over to reach them. Magda, immaculately dressed, having come from dining in the first-class hall, yet tense and exasperated by the politics and pomposity of its elaborate assigned seating that rotated the wealthiest passengers around the ship's captain and senior officers, would visibly relax as they spoke.

Josef knew that Schmidt was requesting individual team members join him to dine at his table each evening but he was never invited. It didn't concern him. He was happy to keep his distance from Schmidt, from the entire expedition in fact. His days now revolved entirely around the time he spent with either Magda or preparing for the mountain. He began to concoct an elegant fantasy that perhaps if he was successful in climbing it, the prestige and glory that would come after might allow him to return to her.

* * *

The day before they were due to arrive at the Port of Bombay, an orderly approached Josef with a handwritten card from Schmidt inviting him to join his table that evening. Josef was surprised at the invite but immediately hopeful that it might give additional opportunity to be with Magda. He dressed carefully in the suit that Pfeiffer had instructed him was for formal occasions with Schmidt. It was tailored to fit him perfectly and Josef felt a shiver of anticipation at the possibility that she would see him in such fine clothes. Walking to the first-class lounge to meet Schmidt for his predinner cocktail, an electricity of excitement coursed through Josef's body.

The professor was already there, holding a martini, his little finger faintly twitching as it projected into the air. He looked Josef up and down with a mixture of amusement and surprise.

"Obersturmführer Pfeiffer certainly equipped you well for your little adventure. Let's hope that clothes do indeed make the man," he said with a smirk, finishing his martini in a gulp. "There is, however, one thing missing, boy."

Schmidt produced a small enamel badge from his pocket. Without pause he pinned it onto Josef's satin lapel, its red and white vivid against the black of the suit, its swastika surrounded by the words "*National—Socialistiche—D.A.P.*" there for all to see.

"Good. Now you are ready for your first dinner in first class. I know you will enjoy the company at the table, well, at least some of it." Schmidt gave Josef a sly look before standing back and grinning to himself as he smugly surveyed the assembling dinner guests and called for a second cocktail.

The professor's cheeks were flushed by the time he had finished a third and dinner was announced. While the diners began to file in from the bar, Schmidt leaned in close to Josef and said in a blast of alcoholic fumes that hinted at a deeper foundation than the three martinis, "*Bon appetit!*"

Josef didn't reply, rendered speechless by the sight that opened up before him as they entered the dining room. Beneath elegant crystal chandeliers, the plush red carpet was studded with polished round tables, each laden with sparkling glassware, lines of silver cutlery, and floral centerpieces interspersed with gleaming silver candlesticks. With the first-class passengers, their guests, and the ship's senior officers, more than 150 people were sitting down to dinner. Josef had never seen anything like it.

Perhaps this is how it will always be when I am the man who first climbed Mount Everest.

The ship's purser headed Schmidt's table. The other guests were diplomats and businessmen heading to India or further east—polished, well-dressed men with silent, cold-looking wives who stood slightly behind them as they made their introductions. The last three guests to arrive were Magda von Trier and her mother and father. Schmidt turned to look at Josef as they appeared but his eyes were so caught on Magda that he didn't notice the almost triumphant leer on the professor's face.

* * *

Magda smiled back when she first noticed Josef, but then, as her father was presenting her as if it was the first time they had met, her eyes dropped to linger on the party badge that Schmidt had stuck into his lapel.

Josef immediately felt any force disappear from the soft squeeze of her handshake, a look of disappointment hardening the gentle curves of her face as she quickly moved away to take her seat.

The start of the dinner was restrained and Josef felt totally excluded from the conversation. Even Magda said nothing to him.

Josef noticed that Schmidt was constantly looking at Magda and her mother. He asked himself repeatedly what the hateful man was so intent on, until, with a chill that squeezed ice water through his veins, an answer came to him in the form of another question.

Is Magda's mother Jewish?

It had never crossed Josef's mind but now that it did, it suddenly explained so much left unsaid about her family's journey to India. Continuing to eat in silence, Josef's fantastic, ridiculous fantasy of climbing Mount Everest to claim Magda collapsed inside him as if punctured by the swastika pin.

At the end of the first course, the ship's captain got to his feet and, calling for silence by tapping the side of his glass, welcomed the assembled diners, saying that sadly for some it would be their last as the ship would be arriving the next day at the Port of Bombay.

The news was met with a round of applause. As it died, Schmidt, by now on his second glass of wine, stood up and shouted loudly to the assembled room, "Heil India! Heil Hitler!" His salute was met with a resounding repetition from most of the assembled diners and more applause. As that too subsided, Josef noticed Magda's father whisper something under his breath to his wife. She glanced at him with a flicker of alarm, faintly shaking her head before looking back down at her food.

Their daughter had stopped eating and, putting down her cutlery, was now staring directly at the still-standing Schmidt with a look of utter loathing. Schmidt, oblivious to her gaze, was inspired by the success of his toast. Calling for another glass of wine, he sat back down and began to loudly lecture the table on how it was an honor and a privilege to be able to lead fine young Germans to the mighty Himalayas, how wise and generous was a regime that supported such a venture.

Some of the table's guests murmured approval at what Schmidt was saying until Magda, with an obviously forced smile and knowing full well from Josef the stated objectives of the expedition, said, "Professor Schmidt, please do tell us some more about your expedition. Is it to try to climb the mountain of Nanga Parbat once again? I imagine it is about time that some more fine young Germans died for the honor and privilege of placing our beloved führer's proud flag on the top of that dreadful mound of snow and rock." Undisguised sarcasm oozed from her precisely chosen words. Magda's mother visibly tensed as her daughter spoke. Her father angled his head downward before looking up at her through greying eyebrows, lips pursed as if willing her, through his stare alone, to be silent.

The question flustered Schmidt for a moment before he responded abruptly, "No, young lady, it is not! How …" He checked himself, explaining to the rest of the table in a more magnanimous tone,

"Actually it is as much a scientific expedition as it is a mountaineering venture, although, that being said, we do hope to visit the summits of a number of the still-unclimbed peaks of the Kangchenjunga massif." Looking directly at Magda and her mother, he then said, "And when we do, I can assure you all that it will be my pleasure to see that our proud swastika does indeed fly from each. Who knows, you might even be able to see them all the way from Hyderabad."

Josef was instantly concerned that Schmidt seemed to already know the von Triers' destination, sure it hadn't been mentioned during the dinner. A sense of unease took him, bringing with it the thought that perhaps his invitation had been deliberate when Schmidt had seen the von Triers were going to be at his table that evening.

Magda, with a look of unconcealed scorn, spoke to Schmidt again. "Do you not think it is somewhat frivolous, Professor Schmidt, to be sending young men up dangerous mountains instead of considering what is really happening in Germany? There is daily talk of war, visible evidence of murder, persecution, theft, and yet here you are"—she glanced again at Josef—"marching up mountains, waving your little flag without a care in the world. Your hubris is larger than any of the mountains you seek to climb. In fact, I find it to be greater than Mount Everest, the highest of them all. Actually my only real surprise is that you do not have that mountain on your pathetic list of planned conquests."

Her words dropped onto the table, where the other guests slowly digested them in an anxious silence until Schmidt stood up and leaned across the table and stabbed a finger toward Magda to reinforce every word of his angry response. "There is absolutely nothing frivolous, young lady, about demonstrating to the world the superiority of Nazi Germany and its fine Aryan youth!" Retracting his finger, eyes scanning the other guests with an imploring look for support, he said to them in a more moderated tone, "I have read that the British climber George Leigh Mallory, when asked why he wanted to climb Mount Everest, would only say, 'Because it's there.' Well, I say to you all, we, the Third Reich, should climb mountains because we are here, and the entire world should both see it and know it!"

The ship's purser instantly shouted, "Bravo!" and, holding aloft his glass said, "Guests, we should drink to that!" Offering up, "Because we are here!" as a toast, he took a heavy swig of wine. The other diners drank, clinking their glasses, nervously laughing to shake off the discomfort of the exchange.

Schmidt continued to speak after emptying his own wineglass. "I have not the slightest doubt that just one good German could climb Everest itself if he set his mind to it, such is the strength of the Nazi will. Do you not agree, Josef Becker?"

The question jolted Josef.

Filled with alarm at Schmidt's angry hint about his secret project and embarrassed at being drawn into the argument, he was not sure how to reply.

Magda quickly removed the need by standing up from the table and saying, "Mr. Becker, when you step on your summits on behalf of yourself and your Nazi colleagues, I only ask that you please be mindful of those who have been walked over in order to raise your flag of shame."

Watching her stride away from the table, Josef could say nothing in return, stunned.

Schmidt's face swelled with a red rage. He stared at Magda's father before blurting in a spray of spittle, "That was an outrage, von Trier, an absolute outrage. A wayward daughter is most definitely not an asset, sir, particularly given her racial heritage. I will expect a full apology, or I will demand satisfaction of you."

Von Trier, a proud, educated man who reminded Josef of the generalmajor in Garmisch said nothing as he looked back at the blustering Schmidt. In the absence of any response, the professor repeated, "An apology or satisfaction, do you hear me, sir?"

Magda's father's eyes narrowed. Then for all the table's guests to see, he traced the tip of an index finger slowly down the line of a faint yet long scar on his left cheek, all the time continuing to stare Schmidt straight in the eye.

"Professor Schmidt, it is most definitely not in your best interest to demand satisfaction of a Prussian, whoever he might have married. I was a student at Heidelberg until the eve of the Great War, in which I fought for four long years. As you can see from my face, I bear a dueling scar that proves the stupidity of my university days. What you cannot see are my other scars that prove the stupidity of war. Even if you study only what you can see, you might think again about the wisdom of speaking to me in such a manner."

With a conciliatory smile he turned to the other guests. "I hope that you will forgive my daughter's little outburst. She merely fears for the future, as I think we all do to some degree. She is still young, and sadly her passion sometimes gets the better of her. I will see that she supplies each of you with a written apology. In the meantime, I would suggest to the entire table that we try not to let her behavior ruin this delicious dinner."

Schmidt puffed himself up for a further response, but the ship's purser cut across him with a loud exclamation of, "Hear! Hear! Now then, everyone, a good dinner shouldn't be spoiled." The purser then made a big show of calling for more wine in an attempt to further defuse the situation, his intervention allowing the other diners to return gladly to their food with an intense concentration that permitted little eye contact or conversation. Josef could see that Magda's mother's hands were trembling as she ate. Her father cut into his food, staring at Schmidt as if filleting one of the professor's fleshy cheeks with his knife. Schmidt said nothing more for the rest of the meal.

41

The knock on Josef's cabin door came at 1:00 a.m. As soon as he'd unlatched it, Magda pushed into the little room.

Standing before him, eyes red as if she had been crying since the dinner, she smacked him as hard across the cheek as she could. "That's for deceiving me."

Pushing past Josef, she walked to the porthole of his cabin and looked out at the calm sea and the black, star-filled horizon before hanging her head and resting her hand on the pile of books and notes on Josef's desk. "I should hate you, but I can't, and that makes me even angrier."

"There is no reason for you to hate me, Magda."

"But there is. I thought you were kind and good, just a young adventurer seizing an opportunity to do what he loves. But how can you be, really, if you are accompanying a man like Schmidt on an official German expedition?"

"I can't tell you. You know as well as I that we have both been avoiding reality to pass the time."

"But I have no choice. Mine is one of imprisonment and death."

"And you think you are alone in that?"

"No, I share it with everyone of my mother's blood. Do you also want to kill me because I am a *mischling,* a half-Jew?"

"Of course not. It means nothing to me. It never crossed my mind."

"Well, now it must."

"Magda, it makes no difference to me that you are part-Jewish. I have my own problems."

"Staying alive on a mountain is not a comparable problem."

"Of course it's not. You should leave now."

Magda picked up a book from the desk, looking at its cover. Turning back to Josef, she read aloud the title as a question *"Der Kampf um den Everest?"*

Josef instantly reached for the book, but she pulled it back from his outstretched hand.

"Was I right after all? Is this the opportunity you are really seizing?"

Exhausted, confused, totally disarmed by the soft, proud face before him, Josef sat on the edge of his bunk and, as if betraying an old love to a new one, said simply, "Yes, I am going to climb Mount Everest."

"But how is this even possible?"

"I shouldn't have told you. There are lives at stake here, lives that are precious to me."

"Am I precious to you?"

"Yes."

Letting the book drop onto Josef's bunk, Magda took Josef's hand, feeling the scar of his maimed finger in hers.

"Josef, I am never wrong about people. Tell me. I'm a strong person."

He began to talk.

Slowly, precisely, Josef's words guided Magda up the Paznaun to the coldblooded murder of his nine charges, including a little girl called Ilsa Rosenberg whom he, Josef Becker, had personally condemned to the worst death of them all. He continued to speak, pushing through his pain and guilt, to lead Magda back down again from that snowy godforsaken ridge to captivity, to torture, to more death, and finally blackmail. He explained every detail of his subsequent preparation for Operation Sisyphus as if reading from Pfeiffer's own file. When he had finished, he pulled his hand from hers and said, "So that is it. Now you know everything."

Looking at him with fresh tears in her eyes, Magda could only say, "I'm so sorry, Josef."

Josef moved away from her to the small dressing table in his cabin and took something from its top drawer.

As he turned back to her he said, "Hold out your hands. Cup them together."

Into her trembling hands Josef placed his edelweiss ring.

"This is me. I am the edelweiss, not the swastika."

He closed Magda's hands around the silver ring and then, gently taking her by the wrists, said, "Just as you are holding this ring in your hands, you also now hold me, my mother, my sisters. If you drop us we die, just like my friends, just like your own kind up on that hill. Are you truly strong enough to keep us safe?"

She said nothing, then kissed him tenderly.

Pulling back, she said, "I will hold you forever."

Kissing Josef again with a passion, she pushed him back onto the bed.

Finch's heavy book on Everest fell to the floor with a thud.

42

AVENUE MICHEL CROZ, CHAMONIX, FRANCE
September 12, 2009
6:45 p.m. (Central European Summer Time)

Walking past the Chamonix Alpine Museum, Quinn noticed that the leaves of the larch trees in the gardens were beginning to yellow and the evening was drawing in quicker. Summer was already ending.

Returning from Kathmandu, Quinn had stayed in London only long enough to organize with his bank that he could continue his overdraft and to collect his motorcycle from its lockup in South London.

In a desire to nurse the aging bike, he took a lazy southeasterly diagonal from Calais, across France, to the Alps, seeking out the slower, emptier Route Nationals, avoiding the traffic and the expensive *péage* of the autoroutes. After the tragedy and chaos of his Everest climb, it was refreshing to run the old GS down the straight, tree-lined roads, smelling the French countryside and feeling the moist, fresh air of the mornings change into the warm sun of the afternoons. For Quinn, a motorcycle trip was still the most effective way to put his mind in order. The long hours alone in the saddle allowed parallel journeys through thoughts and memories with enough time to arrive at positive conclusions, to look forward with hope rather than back in anger.

By the time he could see the first lights of Chamonix twinkling through the black silhouettes of the tall pines, the immense snowcapped hump of Mont Blanc glowing in the night sky above, he had convinced himself of a number of things: firstly, one day he was just going to keep going and ride that bike all the way to Cape Town; secondly, he was going to get to the bottom of the story of that old ice axe; and thirdly, above all, he had done everything he could for Nelson Tate Junior on that dreadful summit day.

Quinn had once heard Chamonix described as "the death capital of adventure sports." Whether it was true or not, its outdoor industry,—so obsessed with the mortal pleasures of climbing, extreme skiing, BASE jumping, even wing-suit flying—lingered little on the death of its sportsmen. It seemed to include his recent Everest disaster within that category. Without even having to show Henrietta's report on what happened with Nelson Tate Junior, Quinn was relieved to find that there was a lot of work waiting for him in Chamonix, and he threw himself into it. He led alpine courses teaching wide-eyed beginners to tie knots, to climb up, to rappel down, to use their sharp, new ice axes and crampons without maiming themselves or anyone else. He climbed a myriad of routes with a revolving selection of clients of varying abilities, equal only in the pink-faced exhilaration brought on by the intoxicating alpine cocktail of danger and beauty. He summited Mont Blanc and looked east across the tops of puffy clouds, over the occasional stabbing points of other peaks, toward the Matterhorn and Monte Rosa. A few weeks later, he summited the Matterhorn and looked back at the view in reverse as if studying a negative. On his days off, he teamed with other guides and made harder climbs on the Drus and the Grandes Jorasses, intent on discovering if he still had what it took. He did.

It was only at the end of the day when the payback came. In the evening, he would open his mail to receive the latest legal letter sent by Tate Senior's camp. Aggressive and persistent, they talked of manslaughter and threatened ruin. At night, he struggled to sleep and when he did, it was fitful and haunted, hollowed out by revolving nightmares of death and failure on the Second Step that contradicted his belief that he had really done all he could to save the boy. When he awoke in the dark he would have to reach down from the bed to feel the carpeted floor of his room, tugging at the weave until convinced that he was not still up there. Only occasionally did he enjoy a happier, more colorful dream where he and Nelson Tate Junior summited and then descended, laughing and joking, to a hero's welcome. When that one ended, he desperately wanted to touch the floor and feel the cold rubble of the Rongbuk instead.

Quinn fought back by filling his restless nights with researching the old axe on the Internet. Quickly he found the details of every official national team that had ever gone near the mountain from the Tibetan side and, interspersed with it, the endless speculation as to whether Mallory and Irvine might have made it to the top so many years before Hillary and Tenzing. Digging further, he followed the threads of the other mysteries of the north side: the legend of Datschnolian and that "lost" 1952 Russian climb, the dispute over the veracity of the 1960 Chinese first summit from the north that produced no photographic proof, the lone wolves that went to the mountain, the Earl Denmans and the Maurice Wilsons of Everest lore.

Like a late-night scholar, he noted down the salient details of them all into a moleskin notebook, underlining the references to unexplained old high camps, ancient climbing equipment found abandoned all over the mountain, and the many theories and counter-theories of who might have left it there. Throughout it all, he was continually bounced back to the theories of what might have happened to George Leigh Mallory and Sandy Irvine. It ran and ran to a level of analysis and detail that would have put many doctorates to shame. Quinn even found an essay on how to handle their frozen camera if ever discovered. He scratched a sarcastic note to self across a page: "Keep it frozen at all costs—no airport X-rays either!!!"

However, despite all his studies, he drew a factual blank for Germans or Russians on Everest in those early years, so he decided to bait a few mountaineering forums to see if their chat might throw up something that he had missed. Taking inspiration from a beer mat on the table of the small apartment that Scottish guide Doug Martin was letting him share, Quinn converted its image of a grinning devil greedily eyeing a pint of a brew called Mephisto Ale into an anonymous sign-in of "Mephistopheles." When asked also for numbers, he added "8848," the height of Everest in meters.

Launching some deliberately inflammatory questions about early German and Russian intentions to climb Everest, he moved on to research the old axe itself. There were web images of many that were similar. The axe was pretty much typical of the type used between the early '20s and the late '60s even if the swastika clearly branded it as having been issued to the German mountain troops—the Gebirgsjäger—within a tighter time period of the ten years that led up to the end of World War Two. He read a little about them. They were once based in Bavaria, to the south of Munich, and had fought continually through the Second World War in Poland, Norway, the Balkans, and the Eastern Front. *Maybe a Russian hadn't needed to go as far as Germany to find the axe?*

The mention of Munich rang a faint bell and Quinn recalled that he had sent that old oxygen cylinder he'd sold on eBay to a collector called Bernhard Graf in the same city. The man had been very determined to win the bidding, pushing up the price aggressively, and, when Quinn had subsequently found out that the weight of the cylinder would make shipping it to Munich much more than initially estimated, hadn't balked in the slightest at paying the considerable additional cost.

Quinn dug out his emails from the sale and, in order to reestablish a contact, dropped Graf an email, giving a few hints about an old German ice axe that he might be interested in selling. That done, he moved on from the axe to see if he could find any reference to an Ang Noru, but he found nothing to prove he had ever existed. The Tiger Sherpas were well known and much had been written about them in recent years, but nothing mentioned Ang Noru. It was as if he had been wiped from history.

Frustrated that every which way he turned he seemed to arrive at a dead end, Quinn increasingly turned to another tactic to fill his long nights. Soraya was the barmaid at the Olav Hotel. Half-Japanese, half-Australian, she was an Olympic-standard snowboarder, they said, petite but athletic with a beautiful, pastel-shaded tattoo of lotus flowers that entirely sleeved one of her arms. When Quinn caught her eye in the bar, she told him she found scars interesting and was impressed by Everest summits. He offered her both in abundance. Warning him she wasn't into commitment, he gladly took that in return and began to lose his intense interest in mountain archaeology. Whenever he did tune back in to see how his forum questions were doing, he saw a lot of chat, not a little abuse, but nothing concrete to link either Germans or Russians to the north side of the mountain contemporary with the old axe. That was, until he started to receive messages from a "Schicklgruber666."

He thought the first was a joke. It was a video clip from the Indiana Jones film *Raiders of the Lost Ark* showing Nazis torturing Jones' lost love in her bar in Tibet. A few days later, the second was more serious. It was a grainy black-and-white film of the German explorer Ernst Schäfer traveling through Tibet and sitting at a table with Tibetan elders in Lhasa, the wall behind decorated with SS pennants.

The messages kept coming through late July and August, one after the other, always in some way linking the Nazis to the mountains or to Tibet. Quinn understood that Schicklgruber666 was walking him so thoroughly and elegantly through the largely unwritten history of Nazi alpinism that he even wondered if it might actually be Henrietta Richards behind it. It was certainly someone with the same levels of knowledge and attention to detail.

The final message arrived on the last day of August, pinging its arrival just as Quinn was actually reading an email from Henrietta telling him that Dawa had now left hospital and was euphemistically "helping her with her inquiries." Hoping that meant she would finally get Tate Senior's lawyers off his back, his attention moved to Schicklgruber666's latest missive.

As soon as Quinn clicked on it, it took over his laptop like a virus. To Wagner's "Ride of the Valkyries," the screen dissolved to black. The music then crescendoed worthy of *Apocalypse Now*, but only a single cartoon helicopter appeared. It began to fly in circles around the black screen like a fly on a thread, as a snow-covered mountain pushed up from below.

When the mountain had grown enough to fill most of the screen, and Quinn could easily recognize it as a view of Everest from the north, the helicopter began to hover above its very top. From it parachuted a small, brown-jacketed Adolf Hitler, who proceeded to plant a swastika flag on the summit before goose-stepping around with one arm in the air in a Nazi salute to the sound of a techno-trance mix of the "Horst Wessel Song."

The little Hitler was then collected by the helicopter, which flew away, the display falling black and silent once more. Quinn tried to cancel the screen but it remained blocked.

Slowly, letter by white, Gothic letter, a question appeared as if being loudly typed up onto the screen:

Mephistopheles, have you put 2 and
2 together yet and arrived at 8848?

Despite reluctantly concluding that he had, he heard nothing more from Schiklgruber666 after that.

* * *

That mid-September evening, Quinn could only hunch his shoulders as he recognized the arrival of autumn and walk on, unable to fend off the greater chill that always came with being a freelancer. He only had one more booking left, four days in Saas Fee, Switzerland, with a young English climber who wanted to do the Weissmies Traverse and the Nadelhorn, and then he was out of work again.

Pondering what his next move should be, his cell phone rang. It was the guide Doug Martin, his friend and flatmate. "Neil, I'm in Le Choucas hotel with old Jean Peynard. He told me that there's a rumor that Sarron has been seen."

"What? Here?"

"Not sure. It's probably just bullshit. I'll see what else I can find out but, just in case, stay safe, okay?"

As soon as the call finished, Quinn's phone rang again. An international number filled the screen, his heart jumping at the sight of it.

Sarron?

"Hello, Mephistopheles," a voice said when Quinn put the phone to his ear.

"Mephistopheles eight-eight-four-eight," it repeated slowly, stressing each syllable before adding, "it almost sounds as if I'm asking to be connected to Zorba the Greek, but I am not, am I, Mr. Quinn?"

The use of his forum identity followed by his name gave Quinn another jolt.

"You do know that Mephistopheles is the devil, Mr. Quinn. The devil with whom Faust exchanges his soul for unlimited knowledge. It might be an interesting trade at first but, of course, one that is unlikely to offer much happiness in the longer term."

It was no Frenchman speaking. The voice had a German accent even if the English was perfect.

"Actually I think you might have been slightly mistaken in your hurried selection of a forum name to hide behind. Your sense of irony is to be admired, but I'm afraid you miscast yourself. 'Faust8848' is who you really are. You should read more and climb less, Mr. Quinn. Scale some mountains of the mind perhaps, of which you will find that Everest is still the greatest."

Quinn moved into the warm entrance of a café to be able to better hear what the eloquent voice was saying, replying testily when it stopped, "Okay, very good, but who are you, and what do you want?"

There was a pause on the other end of the phone before the voice resumed. "Forgive me, Neil Quinn, if I play a little. The temptation to immediately cast myself as the true Mephisto to your Faustian tragedy is strong, but perhaps I should keep things simple for now and offer my own forum name instead."

"Which is?"

"Schicklgruber … Six … Six … Six."

Quinn was lost for words.

"Have I surprised you some more? I do think that I have. This really is too much fun. Schicklgruber is such an amusing name, isn't it? Strange then that it should be the maternal name of one of the least comic figures in history, whatever my witty little cartoon might have suggested. Actually, to be truthful, that cartoon wasn't mine but something prepared for me by the rather talented, if slightly right wing, young friend of mine who organizes my business website. Anyway, I digress. Where was I? Ah yes, Schicklgruber. You must know that your own, so droll, Mr. Winston Churchill always used to refer to Adolf Hitler as Herr Schicklgruber to very great effect. Sadly, name-calling didn't assist greatly in preventing the death of six million Jews, but there it is … or was, I should say. But while we are still on the subject of names, why don't we use another I have? It might put you slightly more at ease, so you can at least talk."

There was a long pause.

"Neil Quinn, this is Bernhard Graf speaking."

The collector from Munich, Quinn realized. "But I emailed you months ago."

"So you did, but I thought I would give you the summer to better answer some of the questions that were so obviously troubling you before I invited you to come and compare notes on some things that have been troubling me. You have my address, I believe. I would like you to pay me a visit absolutely as soon as you can. Munich is not so far from where I believe you are currently based."

"But why should I come all the way to Munich. Can't we do this by email?"

"No, we cannot, Neil Quinn. The time for the

Internet is over. There are real things for you to see and understand now. And while we are talking of real things, bring that ice axe you mentioned in your email. While you were somewhat disingenuous about its origin, I hardly needed to sell my soul to the devil to conclude that you must have found it on Everest."

43

GHOOM RAILWAY STATION, DARJEELING, NORTHEAST INDIA
March 15, 1939
3:30 p.m. (British India Standard Time)

The train funneled out of a dark and dripping final tunnel to emerge into an emerald world of tea plants. The cold of the hill's stone heart lingered in the wet mist that floated into the open carriages from the surrounding steeply terraced hills. Josef quickly unrolled his shirtsleeves and buttoned the wrists, wishing for his jacket, until the recall of the long, hot journey across India told him to enjoy it.

Since disembarking from the *Gneisenau* into the chaos and confusion of Bombay, Schmidt's expedition had traveled continually by train across an entire subcontinent that was as hot as an oven. Throughout the journey, broken only by a day's stop in Calcutta waiting for the Siliguri Post train north, Josef had rarely had any idea where they were. There were few landmarks, only desiccated fields scratched into red soil or endless scorched scrubland punctured by stunted thorn bushes that offered no shade, useful only to the type of small, mean bird that impales its prey alive on the spines to keep it fresh. When the occasional building or rocky hill attempted to push up from the flat horizon, it was quickly sliced horizontal by the rippling haze.

Increasingly drugged by heat and distance, Josef let the empty views from the succession of trains become blank screens on which he projected his own vivid thoughts.

Magda's face ...

Pfeiffer's threats ...

The North Face of Everest ...

His mother and sisters alive ...

Gunter and Kurt dead ...

Little Ilsa ...

He watched them focus and fade in a silent agony of separation, confusion, and loss.

He missed Magda most of all. After their last night on the boat, she had pleaded with him to escape, writing her family's new address in Hyderabad in the inside of his Everest book so that he might come and find her when he did. It was an impossible dream. Josef was trapped, pinned to Pfeiffer's plan by Schmidt's swastika pin as effectively as a caterpillar on a thorn.

"Summit or die, Obergefreiter Becker, summit or die ..."

* * *

When the train exhaled to a final halt in Ghoom station, Josef's first impression of Darjeeling was one of faint familiarity. It was an alpine town, the air sharp and thin. He could feel the mountains, even if he couldn't yet see them. It lifted his spirits a little.

A sea of expectant faces awaited the train: a mixture of white sahibs in straw hats, stocky porters with tanned bare arms and legs, and tribesmen in heavy wool clothes. The tallest of the whites, a man with a cadaverous, narrow face above a cream linen suit, raised his hat to catch Schmidt's attention. He shouted his name, "Hans Fischer," in order to identify himself, directing them to a file of rickshaws, simultaneously unleashing a line of jostling porters to pull their supplies from the wagons to the rear of the train.

After a long pull up the hill, Josef's rickshaw, to his surprise, halted in front of what appeared to be a perfect replica of a Bavarian hotel. "Hotel Nanga Parbat" was painted in large, black medieval letters across the whitewashed, heavily gabled front. Fischer's matronly wife emerged from the front door to be introduced by her husband to Schmidt.

The equally stern-looking pair then united to show them all in and begin the registration of their new guests. "Damn the English and their need for endless bureaucracy. It gets worse every year," Hans Fischer said loudly in German as he unbundled a pile of forms and set to work at the reception counter while the team waited, studying the array of maps and pictures that lined the hotel lobby's walls as individual documents were requested and handed over.

The display was mostly of Kangchenjunga, Nanga Parbat, or Everest: precise black-and-white photographs that condensed each mountain into a single, unassailable massif that looked impossibly high and treacherous, or hand-colored illustrations that gave the opposite effect, reducing the very same mountains into benign pastel drawings devoid of any scale or difficulty. While Josef contemplated an image of a particularly brutal-looking Everest, another team member commented loudly, "I'm glad we are not trying for that bastard." The others laughed. Only Josef remained silent, Schmidt watching him intently.

To turn his team's attentions elsewhere, Schmidt directed their gazes over a number of team photographs of past German expeditions, name-dropping as he went, until he tapped on a photo of a solitary ice axe planted in a snowy summit. It was flying two small flags, the German swastika above the British Union Jack. He stood back from it, proclaiming loudly, "Take heart, boys, and study this photo of the top of Siniolchu. It is a peak near our destination that my good friend Paul Bauer's team climbed two years ago. Let it be your inspiration, and let me assure you that our photos will feature only our German flag, whatever our hosts might require." As he said it he caught Josef's eye, before continuing. "Dinner tonight will be at 7:00 p.m. Now let's distribute the keys to the rooms and get everyone settled in. Becker, I need to speak with you and Herr Fischer about some arrangements for the team's equipment before we go any further. Please join me."

Josef walked with Schmidt behind Hans Fischer into a small office on the ground floor. Firmly closing the door behind them, Fischer showed the men to the two chairs in front of his desk and then sat down himself. On the wall behind his seat was a framed swastika pennant.

Josef glanced up at it.

"Yes, it is the very same flag that was photographed on the summit of Siniolchu. The expedition leader Paul Bauer presented it to me for my support of German mountaineering," Fischer said, as if reading Josef's mind. He paused before adding, "In fact, for my support of Germany in general in this region. Actually I must admit to being surprised that Bauer is not supervising this operation, given its very nature, but I understand that it is a private SS venture, and, of course, I have every respect for that. My nephew is a panzer-grenadier in the Second SS Deutschland, currently in training in Berlin. The reichsführer knows that I am a man who can be fully trusted with his interests in this region."

Fischer eyed Josef up and down.

"Well, how are you feeling after such a long journey? Do you really think that you, one man, can do it?"

"Fine. Yes, I do," Josef answered, returning Fischer's hard stare until he looked away to speak to Schmidt.

"Well, I hope that the reichsführer has the right man for the job, even if I am inclined to think that perhaps things may not prove to be quite as simple as imagined. Turning to the business at hand, there are some things that you should know. Firstly, I have identified the porter who will go with you. He is excellent at altitude, a Tiger Sherpa who has been above twenty-seven thousand feet on Everest. He has an ongoing grievance with the British, whom he hates and who have blackballed him in return, which is obviously beneficial to our cause. He speaks some German, as he has worked not only with German expeditions but also lately for me here at the hotel. He already knows that he is to personally assist Obergefreiter Becker on this expedition but does not yet know that he is to accompany him to Mount Everest. I am trusting that his loathing of the British is such that he will jump at the chance when he does. He is called Ang Noru, and I will introduce you tomorrow morning."

Fischer stopped for a moment, as if considering some unspoken detail.

"I have absolutely no doubt that Ang Noru will help you. For the reasons I have already explained, he is the best you could hope to find. However, I should warn you from the start that he does, like many of the local people here, have one big weakness: drink. As long as you keep him away from that stuff, he's as good as gold.

"Which brings me on to another warning, Becker. Darjeeling is a village, a British one at that. You must not do or say anything that might give anyone the faintest idea that you are here for any purpose other than Schmidt's expedition. The Sherpas are very wily. Any clue that you are up to something different will undoubtedly find its way back to Karma Paul's ears. He is the local middleman who organizes all the porters, particularly for the British expeditions, and he most definitely knows on which side his bread is buttered, as his masters would say. If he hears what you are up to, it is inevitable that sooner or later the English will find out, and then we will all have some explaining to do."

Schmidt turned to Josef. "You heard the man."

Josef ignored him, looking back at Fischer to say, "Anything else I need to know?"

"Yes. We have arranged some old Tibetan clothes

for you to wear when you start your journey to the mountain. You will need to check they fit. Later tonight when the others have retired to their rooms, we will separate the loads and prepare the small amount of equipment that is to go with you when you leave the main expedition. This you will hide on the approach to the Zemu Glacier for retrieval when you exit alone. I have already sent your other equipment through as part of a resupply to Ernst Schäfer's expedition in Tibet. I personally checked each of the ten boxes marked 'OS' that Obersturmführer Pfeiffer sent here and they are complete.

"I understand that one of Schäfer's men will be bringing them directly to Rongbuk Monastery at the foot of Mount Everest to meet you there. I will admit to being nervous about this transfer because the British mission officer in Lhasa, Hugh Richardson, is watching Schäfer's team like a hawk. There is little that the British can do about them being there, now that they have the permission of the Tibetan leadership, but it doesn't mean that they like it. Richardson is looking for the slightest excuse to have the expedition expelled. Schäfer is undoubtedly a determined and resourceful man, a favorite of the reichsführer for good reason, so I think he will get the equipment through to you. However, until he does, you will have few provisions. Your journey to the mountain will be very basic but I think it will permit you to cross the country far more rapidly than the British Everest expeditions with their hundreds of porters and endless provisions. Fast and light is the only way that you will succeed with this venture. My nephew says his Panzer regiment is training with the very same philosophy.

They call it 'blitzkrieg.' For now, that's all I wanted to say. Professor Schmidt, do you have anything more you wish to add?"

"Yes," said Schmidt. "Becker, I had some of my travel photographs developed when we were in Calcutta and I thought you should see them to ensure that your mind is focused only on the operation ahead."

From his cotton safari jacket, Schmidt pulled a wax paper envelope and passed it to Josef.

Opening it, Josef's breath caught with shock; he saw that they were all of him and Magda walking along the *Gneisenau*'s rear sundeck. All the photographs had been taken from the inside of the ship through a window that looked out onto it. His recall of the time he had spent with Magda was still so vivid he could even remember the actual day from the clothes she was wearing. It was the third to last day of the voyage.

Watching Josef look at them, Schmidt said, "Did you think your ship-born romance with that *mischling* would go unnoticed? That she was the only one snapping away with her little camera as we voyaged east? I must say that it gives me very great pleasure to advise you that I telegrammed Obersturmführer Pfeiffer about all this in Calcutta. He replied that I should give you one of the photographs so that you can look at it whenever you want and imagine all the others attached to the inside of the Operation Sisyphus file."

Josef took the clearest photograph of Magda just before Schmidt snatched back the others and said, "The rest are mine. Run along now, Becker."

Josef left with the photograph in his hand to the sound of Schmidt's laughter.

In the hotel lobby, Frau Fischer was at the reception counter. Seeing Josef, she asked, "Becker? Josef Becker?"

"Yes, I am."

"I have a telegram for you from your family in Berlin. How exciting!"

Josef took the folded paper she offered him.

It was indeed from Berlin.

```
1530.150339.PRZRIB8-BERLIN

JOSEF.
DELIGHTED TO HEAR ABOUT
MAGDA-SHE SEEMS FAMILY
ALREADY.

WE ARE ALL ON A KNIFE EDGE JUST
THINKING ABOUT THE COMING CLIMB.
YOUR DEAR UNCLE,

JURGEN.
```

44

JALAPAHAR BARRACKS, DARJEELING, NORTHEAST INDIA
March 16, 1939
6:00 a.m.

Lieutenant Charles Macfarlane scraped the sharp safety razor over his chin, thinking of the day ahead. He was delighted to be finally going up into the high Himalayas, relieved he was getting a chance to do so before returning to England and his regiment, the Coldstream Guards. He'd hoped for a possible turn as a liaison officer with a foreign mountaineering team before leaving Darjeeling, and, with his year-long attachment to the 2nd Gurkha Rifles now almost over, something had finally come up.

While he shaved, Macfarlane reminded himself of what his local commanding officer, the irascible Colonel Atkinson, had told him about the expedition he was joining that morning. "Bunch of Jerry hobbyists, really. No serious mountaineering ambitions, certainly not for Kangchenjunga itself, but they are Germans and so we do need to keep an eye on them. It will give you a chance to get up into the snow for a bit of a look before you head back to Blighty. You might even be able do a bit of hunting while the gentlemen of the swastika are doing their hill walking. Bharal, tahr, argali, wolves, even snow leopard can be found near the Zemu Glacier where you'll be. That surly SS chappie Schäfer bagged quite a bit when he was up there, I hear. Anyway, look on this trip as bit of a reward, old man; your fellow officers here have given you very favorable reports, and I am only disappointed we can't persuade your regiment to let us keep you for a little longer."

Macfarlane was going to miss the eccentric colonel, India too. His time there had absolutely flown by. The region fascinated him and he was incredibly impressed by the brigade's cheery-faced Gurkha troops. They were an indomitable group, strong and humorous, hardworking and loyal, traits that tended to distract you from a deadly streak of savagery they could tap into in an instant. It took little to imagine the stories of them in the Great War volunteering to crawl through no-man's land to the German lines to slit a sleepy sentry's throat or retire an off-duty machine-gun team with their long, spoon-bladed kukri. Macfarlane's razor caught with a sting. Wiping the small trail of blood that ran off his chin, he told himself to stop daydreaming, or he'd cut his own throat.

The next hour he spent packing his rifles and his kit bag. The expedition was due to head out from Darjeeling at 11:00 a.m., and Ernest Smethwick, the secretary of the British Himalayan Club, was going to introduce him to its leader, a Professor Markus

Schmidt, at 9:00 a.m. sharp, so he left to breakfast with Smethwick at the Windermere, and afterward they walked together up to the Hotel Nanga Parbat.

They arrived to a whirlwind of activity. Porters were hauling boxes and bags from every direction to furiously load three old tea lorries. A motor coach with "St. Michael's School for Boys, Darjeeling" painted along the side was parked beyond them awaiting the expedition team itself. Nearer the front door, another, smaller group was being addressed by a dapper-looking local man wearing a trilby with a long pheasant tail feather waving from its brim. Upon seeing Smethwick and the English officer, the man instantly stopped talking, stood almost to attention, and enthusiastically shook Smethwick's hand. Smethwick turned to Macfarlane, then back to the man, saying, "Lieutenant Macfarlane, let me introduce you to Namgel Sherpa. He is the sirdar for this expedition, and these good men around him are the climbing Sherpas."

With a nod to each, Smethwick greeted the others by name. "Dorge Temba, Nima, Sen Bhotia, Lobsang …" He looked at the last and hesitated before finally saying, "Ang Noru." Macfarlane thought Smethwick gave the man a rather severe look—a look that was returned in kind.

After Smethwick had said, "Good luck, you chaps; we must go in to meet Professor Schmidt," he confirmed Macfarlane's observation, saying under his breath, "Keep a close eye on the last one, Ang Noru. He's trouble. Wouldn't be on any English expedition, that's for sure."

Inside they sought out Schmidt, who was with Hans Fischer. Smethwick introduced Macfarlane, and all four sat to consider the objectives of the expedition. A large map was unrolled, and Schmidt explained in slow, faltering English how the team was to go north by road into the tiny kingdom of Sikkim, then to its capital, Gangtok. From there, they would journey still further north, up the Tista Valley, following the old trade route toward Tibet as far as the monastery town of Lachen. West of that they would establish a camp at the foot of the Zemu Glacier.

The professor stressed that the expedition was as much a wildlife and geological endeavor as it was about mountaineering, but then, with a puff, pronounced, "But we are not without alpine ambition. We might try for a repeat of Siniolchu or possibly attempt Nepal Peak to remind you what we Germans are made of." Abruptly standing up, he looked down at the English lieutenant to say, "We will be leaving at 11:00 a.m., following the taking of an official expedition photograph for which you will not be required. I will introduce you to the team now, and then you will check our paperwork for passage into Sikkim. I do not want any delays from the authorities at the border, and it will be your job, Tommy, to ensure that doesn't happen."

Schmidt smirked to himself and walked away without so much as a by-your-leave. The man's use of the German nickname for a British soldier grated on Macfarlane as he was forced to get up and follow. By the time the professor had introduced the lieutenant to his companions, all bar one, Macfarlane knew that he was going to dislike Schmidt intensely.

The obnoxious professor appeared in no hurry to track down the absentee, so Macfarlane quickly excused himself to consider the expedition's paperwork. He reviewed the name of each team member again as he studied the completed forms noticing that the man he hadn't yet met was called Josef Becker. He was twenty-seven, from Elmau in Bavaria, and for his profession Schmidt had written *"lanwirtschaftlicher arb."*

The lieutenant asked Fischer's wife for a translation and then, crossing it out, wrote "farmworker" alongside it in English so the border authorities would know what it meant. It sounded rather odd as he inked it in, but his mind was already occupied with wondering exactly how annoying and difficult Schmidt was going to prove to be.

45

**WUNDERKAMMER GRAF ANTIQUITÄTEN,
THEATINERHOF, MUNICH, GERMANY**
September 18, 2009
5:15 p.m.

The gold-embossed letters across the main window announced Quinn's arrival at his destination: Wunderkammer Graf Antiquitäten. The shop was set to the far side of a courtyard that made Quinn think more of Italy than Germany. The square's elegant cobblestone piazza was surrounded on all sides with full-height, arched windows and doors, set within mustard-yellow, plastered walls below pitched roofs of overlapping orange tiles. Overlooking it all were the encrusted, rococo towers of an ornate Catholic church; the courtyard must have once been adjoining cloisters.

The music that had followed him across the square to the shop's dark windows further contradicted the location. The Magyar polka of the five Hungarian buskers, huddled against the early evening cold in the courtyard's entrance, was an infectious, toe-tapping groove of guitars and violins racing to keep up with the rattle of the cimbalom at the quintet's center. It pushed Quinn east, making him think of gypsies, not Nazis, despite the small sign he had just passed that identified the exact place where Adolf Hitler's original putsch in 1923 had come to a bloody end.

Quinn's first view into Graf's shop was obstructed by the reflection of his own tall body in his black wax-cotton motorcycle jacket. The head of the old axe, wrapped in a piece of sheet and looped with an off-cut of climbing cord, projected above his right shoulder like a Franciscan crucifix. Cupping a hand over his eyes, he leaned in closer to the glass in order to get a better view. The sights within instantly assaulted him.

An aging king cobra, splitting and flaking from the rusty wire frame that supported it, reared up as if about to strike at him through the glass. Below it lurked a small stuffed crocodile, black and polished with age like carved ebony. A fully distended puffer fish was keeping the grinning reptile company, a look of surprised agony on its bloated face telling of a final brief moment of understanding that it was never going to be allowed to exhale. Interspersed with the varnished taxidermy were bones of all shapes and sizes, some reassembled into the complete skeletons of reptiles, birds, small mammals, even a hollow-shelled turtle. Behind them, a fossilized fish skeleton lay within a slab of cream limestone. Another, smaller fish skeleton was visible within the curved cage of its spiny ribs, a secret cannibalistic shame laid bare in stone for all to see in eternity.

Raising his gaze a little, Quinn's eyes met the cobalt glass stares of two stuffed crows. They looked down their sharp jet-black beaks at him from either side of a bony human spine to which their feet were bound with barbed wire. The sight instantly took Quinn back to that desperate gorak scratching and clawing at him on the Second Step. Quickly looking away to break the recall of the oily bird, his eyes were drawn to an array of other artifacts that warped and disassembled the familiar of human life. A compartmentalized wooden box contained fifty glass eyes staring, lidless, in every direction, each iris a slightly different shade of blue or green or grey. Two large glass domes stood to either side, one filled with severed antique dolls' heads, the other crammed with detached legs and arms, each limb chubby and porcelain white. Last, and most disturbing of all, an array of jars containing fetuses in yellowing, syrupy formaldehyde behind peeling, handwritten labels. The realization they were actually baby sharks swept Quinn's body with a physical surge of relief.

It didn't last long.

Suddenly Quinn saw not the black crow but a ghost staring back at him.

He jerked away from the window's glass.

When he looked again, he saw that it was actually a human skull, hovering between the glass bell jars of amputated doll parts, studying him in return with hollow eye sockets. Its two rows of teeth, long to their roots, began to open and close as if laughing hysterically at his fright.

Slowly, the grinning skull lowered on unseen hands to be replaced by the head of a man of about seventy. The image of the skull lingered within the face that replaced it, a shadowy outline beneath the pale skin, little flesh to hide it. A shaved head showing patches of grey stubble above each ear revealed the precise, round curve of the cranium. The faint outline of a short white beard in no way hid the pointed jawbone. Only the eye sockets were obscured as white light reflected off small round glasses, masking the eyes within. Quinn watched as a pair of thin lips exaggeratedly mouthed "Boo!" at him and then vanished from the window.

A glass door within the next arch opened, setting off a brass bell that clanged with an irritating racket, vibrating violently on a coiled leaf spring as if determined to wake the dead. When it finally quieted, Bernhard Graf, patiently standing to the side of his now-open door, said in the same elegantly fluent yet accented English that Quinn recalled from the telephone call, "Mr. Neil Quinn, for I can only assume it is you, do enter. I am, of course, Dr. Bernhard Graf."

Quinn hesitated.

"Come in," Graf urged with a smile of reassurance. "Whilst it is my deliberate intention to deter the loitering teenager and the ignorant tourist with the somewhat disturbing nature of my shop window and, should that not suffice, with my unnecessarily irritating doorbell, I am most keen for you to enter. I have been looking forward to meeting you all summer. I see you have brought the ice axe as I asked. That is exciting indeed."

The collector retreated before him into the shop. Everywhere Quinn looked there were glass-fronted cases full of objects. Every inch of free wall space was covered with more artifacts, some even suspended from the ceiling. His eyes adjusting to the subtle backlighting, Quinn was assaulted by the sheer variety of the items. Antlers, daggers, fossils, spears, swords, bones, surgical tools, helmets, false limbs, effigies, skins, feathers, tribal masks, battle flags, gods, devils—it was endless, all of it sinister and disturbing.

Instinctively Quinn tried to seek safety in the familiar. He identified a pair of wooden skis and then some big snowshoes, lattices of taut gut pulling on curved ash frames like vintage tennis rackets. In an umbrella stand filled with fencing swords, walking sticks, tribal clubs, a sawfish blade, and a narwhal tusk, he noticed two wooden ice axes, much like the one he was carrying, the sharp edges of their metal heads covered in wrinkled brown leather covers. In one display case there was another group of alpine items. He wondered if it contained the oxygen cylinder he had sold to Graf. Squatting down to get a closer look, he tried to further settle his mind with recognition of the old metal pitons, the snow daggers, the long-toothed crampons like animal traps arranged on the glass shelves within.

"Mr. Quinn, I hope there will be plenty of time for us to study old climbing things together in the coming days. But for now, let us take a seat, share a schnapps, perhaps?" Graf raised his eyebrows in wry recognition of the rhyme in his English question. As if reading Quinn's mind, he then said, "I am afraid you won't find your oxygen cylinder which I am sure you have regretted selling to me many times. It was a beautiful piece but sadly proved irrelevant to my specific interest. I too received an offer for it that I could not refuse. Please take a seat and permit me to pour you a drink so I might study your famous ice axe. Dirk, bring out the Williams Birne."

Graf pointed Quinn to two chairs with a small glass-topped table in between, while a man in his late twenties, dressed in a black suit and a black silk shirt that both precisely matched the color of his parted hair, appeared from a room to the rear of the shop. Bringing forward a crystal decanter filled with a clear liquid and three small glasses on a silver tray, the thin white Dirk placed them on the table and waited as if ready to join them.

"Time to disappear now, Dirk," Graf said dismissively. The younger man's face hardened, his eyes narrowing as he looked first at Graf and then at Quinn unslinging the axe from his shoulder. Graf stopped Quinn from unwrapping it with an outstretched hand, saying to Dirk, "Later. Okay?"

Without another word, the man turned precisely on his heels, collected a leather raincoat and a briefcase from the back of the shop and left. As the hideous racket of the doorbell settled for a second time, Graf poured two full glasses of schnapps, saying, "Poor Dirk, he'll be in a sulk now. It'll cost me a trinket or two, I imagine. The boy is a poltroon but he has his uses. Now let me trade you a glass of schnapps for a look at this famous ice axe."

Exchanging the drink for the axe, Quinn turned to sit but immediately stopped himself short.

The chair before him was a spiky black metal frame constructed of the eroded barrels and pitted firing mechanisms of what must have once been bolt-action rifles and simple machine guns. The joints were the steel skeletons of small pistols and revolvers, the feet, long-finned bombs that ended in small black metal pineapples. The other chair was made in exactly the same fashion, as was the frame that supported the glass table. The ensemble crouched in front of him, almost pulsating with past murder.

"Oh, come now, a big, brave Everest climber like you surely can't be scared of a little chair. They are magnificently evil though, aren't they?" Graf chided, his lips curling in delight. "They were made by an Italian artist, a delightful young man. He hikes the high Italian Alps looking for the rusting remains of the war waged there between 1915 and '18. The fighting up there was as unrelenting and brutal as anything that happened on the Western Front. The 'White Hell,' they called it, and I am sure it was. Anyway, whatever my charming boy finds he now converts into furniture. I think he successfully conveys his obvious message, don't you? We are, indeed, all sitting on hell, Mr. Quinn, be it black or white."

Graf then deliberately sat down heavily on the nearest of the two chairs and rocked back on it roughly. Its back metal feet scraped in protest before the front feet then fell back with a bang onto the shop's flagstone floor. The sudden movement and noise alarmed Quinn, just as Graf intended, the German laughing back at him.

"Do you know sometimes I amuse myself with the idea that perhaps my young Michelangelo with the welding iron hasn't properly deactivated one of the little bombs? So I sit in delicious anticipation that the chair will blow me and my little shop of horrors to—how do you say it in England, smithereens? It would be deliciously ironic, wouldn't it? The very few people who would attend my funeral would have to endure the entire proceedings trying to stop themselves laughing. The thought of suppressed humor arising from my own demise does so greatly appeal."

Quinn sat down gently on the other chair's uncomfortable seat, taking a gulp of the schnapps as if in preparation for a major explosion, but all that happened was the clear alcohol scorched his throat with a taste of cooked pear. Sipping some more, he watched as Graf began to study the axe head with a large magnifying glass, twisting it around and nodding to himself as he spoke.

"I considered it inevitable you would not have supplied me with all the details of the axe in your brief description, and I'm delighted to see you didn't. These markings on the shaft of '99' and 'J. B.' and, of course, the tiny eagle and swastika that must have sent you scurrying for cover in the first place, are really most interesting. They will require us to take a little day trip to Garmisch tomorrow if our relationship develops as I hope it will."

He turned his head to look directly at Quinn, all trace of a smile now gone.

"When I called you I started a mental stopwatch ticking that stopped the moment you arrived at my window. I told myself that the brevity of the time elapsed would reveal how high the axe was when you found it on the mountain. Given you are here in Germany so soon, it leads me to believe it was above eight thousand meters? Or perhaps it just suggests that you are completely broke?"

Even though Graf was right on both counts, Quinn was reluctant to reply, wary of any more of his secrets being sucked out of him by the strange man.

Graf put down the axe and stood up. When he looked again at the still-seated Quinn, his smile was restored.

"Neil Quinn, you are right not to reply. You are currently feeling disadvantaged. I understand. I act as if you already know me when it is still only the other way around. From afar, I have studied you at some length over the summer and therefore feel I already know you quite well. I take liberties with what I identify as your better nature. I need to remedy this presumption before I go any further."

He passed the axe back to Quinn.

"Like a car salesman with a conscience, if there is such a thing, I am going to give you some more time in order for you to decide whether you wish to trust me. If you will join me, we can have dinner together during which I will try to convince you that, despite all the appearances to the contrary, I am actually a potential ally. Something I know you British like." As he concluded his suggestion, Graf removed his spectacles and cleaned them with a handkerchief. Without them, Quinn noticed the man had surprisingly kind eyes.

46

It had rained a little while they were in the shop. Quinn followed the collector, now clad in a long green bergstock coat and a Bavarian hat with a pinch of spotted feathers pinned to one side, as he quickly led them across the wet cobblestones of the courtyard and out onto the Theatinerhof. To sidestep the snakes of homebound office workers and shoppers slowly moving through the wet, shiny center of Munich, Graf quickly guided Quinn up a narrow side street and on through a maze of alleys and small squares until they arrived at a crowded beer hall.

The huge, vaulted room was filled with such a fog of warmth, food, and people that it made Quinn appreciate how cold and hungry he was from the day's long ride from Saas Fee to Munich. They took seats at the vacant end of one of the long, crowded tables, and Graf quickly ordered for the both of them, having confirmed that Quinn accepted his recommendation of the spit-roasted knuckle of pork with potato dumplings. Tall steins of weissbier arrived soon after. While

Quinn took his first eager gulp, Graf began to talk again. "I was born on the night of November 9, 1938." He stopped for effect, but the date meant nothing to Quinn. "You might know it better as 'Kristallnacht.'" He paused again.

This time Quinn nodded, querying, "The night of the broken glass?"

"The very same," Graf answered. "As I came mewling into my new world, it was, at that very moment, unleashing horror on the Jews of both this country and Austria. That evening the full extent of what the Nazis intended for them was revealed without hesitation or remorse. Many were killed, and thousands more were imprisoned. Synagogues were burned. Jewish businesses destroyed. Quite a night to be born, don't you think?"

Quinn looked back at Graf and shook his head in what he deemed a silent yet sympathetic reply, but still felt uncertain as to where the conversation was going.

"I will give you further food for thought as we await our meal when I tell you that my father was an officer in the SS, and my dear mother was very proud of him. He was doing well for himself and his young family, which now included me, alongside my two elder siblings." After an almost preparatory sip of the weissbier, he added, "I have often wondered, when I consider the many sins of my existence, if the biggest might have been that my parents were actually proud I was born during the Kristallnacht. I sometimes try to imagine it: the shattered shop windows, the Stars of David daubed in still-wet paint on the walls, the dead Jews on the pavements, my parents inside, with me—the innocent newborn, swaddled, oblivious to the insidious—"

Graf's voice was suddenly lost amidst a deafening cheer from a group of soccer fans assembled at a number of tables on the far side of the beer hall. Bedecked in the same blue and white harlequins worked into the designs on the beer hall's painted ceilings, they all stood collectively toasting success in that evening's coming game with a clanking of huge, full beer glasses before breaking out into a clapping, call-and-response chant from the terraces. With a look of irritation, Graf waited until they settled and he could be heard again.

"My father was destined to die somewhere in the Ukraine in 1944. His bones must still be there, I suppose, slowly crumbling into the angry ground of that much-abused country. At the end of the war, as the family of an SS officer, we were interned in a former concentration camp. A typhus breakout during that first brutal winter of 'peace' took both my brother and sister and crushed what was left of my mother's broken heart. She had hung herself by the summer. It is still somewhat disappointing to me that my own robust survival was not enough to inspire her to pursue her own."

He stopped and took another drink.

"I will not depress you further with additional details of my suitably tragic start in this world as it is not courteous to completely ruin your appetite. I only wish you to get a glimpse of why I grew up naturally attracted to the darker sides of life. It is not because I am a diabolist or a Nazi or a pervert. Whilst I will admit to having tried to be all three at various times in my life, ultimately such devotions prove impossible if your horrific early life is a daily reminder of their inherent futility."

Seeing Quinn's glass was empty, he called for it to be refilled.

Quinn made no attempt to stop him, content to simply drink and get warm as the collector continued to talk.

"I do, however, admit to greatly envying the single-mindedness of such fanaticisms. They offer an envious simplicity, do they not? Take those soccer dullards, for example, living only for the next game. It anesthetizes them entirely from their unloving wives and spoiled children, their daily disappointments and failures. How pleasant must that be?

"I see it and envy it also in you, Neil Quinn. You are a fanatic for the mountain. You go to it. You start at the bottom. You get to the top. You go down again. You go home. Then you start all over again with the next. What could be a simpler, less-cluttered existence than that?"

Feeling the beer beginning to lift his spirits, Quinn replied, "Yes, well, that certainly used to be the case, even if I am not so sure now. However, like those Bayern fans, I'll drink to such simple past glories in the hope that it might inspire them to return." He raised his refilled glass to the collector. "Cheers!"

"*Ein prosit der gemütlichkeit,* as we say here, Mr. Quinn." They both drank before Graf continued to speak. "I personally gave up trying to lose myself in cults and creeds a long time ago but strangely my attraction to the items related to them remained. I found that the objects from such worlds were heavy with traces of previous sufferings or sacrifices that, in some cases, were dark enough to better my own. Surrounding myself with such things gave me an unexpected comfort, so I set about amassing a personal collection sufficient to drown out my own inner demons with the screams of their own ancient traumas. It is my pride and joy, at more difficult moments, my salvation."

The arrival of the waiter with their food broke Graf's flow. For a while they quietly ate, allowing Quinn to also digest what Graf was telling him. Only when their plates held just a pair of stripped bones did Graf resume his monologue.

"As you can see from my successful shop, I am not alone in my passion. My eccentric collecting has become a profitable business that keeps me well. I am the darling of Munich's rent boys with my odd tastes and my full wallet, much to the faithful Dirk Schneider's continual disappointment." He looked at Quinn as if hoping for an expression of shock. "My shop thrives, Mr. Quinn, because many people now look to the esoteric and the profane to try and explain their increasing confusion with our modern world. They desperately seek lost civilizations, ancient races, alternative religions, alien beings from other worlds—the 'occult' in the truest sense of the word, the hidden, the secret, the obscure …

"Some say it is evil, others that it is nonsense; yet they all miss the real point. It is the trend itself that presages the new nightmares yet to come. The very same ingredients I have described underwrote many of the Nazi beliefs that brought the world to its knees and killed more than sixty million people. Despite the benefits my business brings me, I would be lying if I did not say that it worries me that we are starting to walk such a tightrope again. Europe is financially bankrupt, yet the gap between rich and poor grows daily. Its countries resent each other bitterly behind their feint of unity. The religions hate each other even more. People, good and bad, migrate without control. Old recipes for new disasters—wouldn't you say? Never forget that 'civilization,' when all is said and done, is only a thin veneer."

He waved a slightly crooked finger around the room.

"Look around you at this very pleasant restaurant full of happy, smiling people, full of the *gemütlichkeit* of my toast to you. 'Coziness' is, I think, the correct translation. Munich is famous for it." The same finger then stabbed up at the ceiling of the beer hall. "You should know, Mr. Quinn, that Adolf Hitler made his first major political speech here, upstairs, in this very beer hall. Think about what happened to the coziness then. Much more recently we saw in the Balkans, not more than a few hundred kilometers from here, how we are all still just fifteen minutes away from anarchy. And anarchy can never be a constant. It is, by its very nature, a lawless vacuum that will soon be filled with extremism of one form or another. Every time we build a pyre of alternative beliefs and kindle it with anarchy, it always ends up burning with dictatorship and racism. History has shown them, time and again, to be very violent flames."

Graf stopped to draw a breath and stared at Quinn through his sparkling eyeglasses.

"I am lecturing, aren't I? But, then again, so I must. Despite the fact that you are nearly two meters tall, you remind me of a small boy playing with a box of matches in a hay barn."

Even though the remark piqued a little, Quinn

replied amiably, "Dr. Graf, you are undoubtedly a fascinating man, and you order a good dinner, but perhaps your own experiences are causing you to read more into my climbing and the old ice axe than is really necessary."

"I disagree completely. Whilst I myself gave up going to the mountains to hide long ago, for me they remain, alongside war and the occult, as a place where I can always find the bleaker dimensions of the human experience. Think of all the people who have died on them and for what? You even call the upper reaches of the very highest mountains, that ghost world above eight thousand meters where the air is so thin no human can survive long without bottled oxygen, 'the death zone.' Originally that was a Swiss-German term, *die todeszone*, which, now I think about it, sounds even more sinister.

"Whatever way you look at it, mountains offer a rich vein of despair and misery; that is one of the reasons they so captivate us. Mount Everest especially carries more than its fair share of desperate memories and, as such, has long been worthy of my particular interest. In fact, its status as the highest mountain in the world means it can easily hold everyone's attention. So why don't we play with that idea a little?"

Quinn thought the man was irrepressible, but, despite all his talk of death and destruction, he was actually enjoying listening to him. With a smile, he conceded, "Well, I am sure we are going to, whether I want to or not."

"It is thus, I am afraid. Do you know, Neil, that one of the earliest Himalayan climbers was none other than Aleister Crowley, the greatest diabolist your country, perhaps the world, has ever produced, the self-proclaimed 'Great Beast'?"

This was news to Quinn.

"The pioneering Mr. Crowley went to K2, or Mount Godwin Austen, as it was more often called in those days, in 1902 with Eckenstein and then on to Kangchenjunga three years later with Guillarmod. It is hardly surprising, given what we now know about Mr. Crowley, but evidently he was a somewhat disagreeable climbing partner. He carried a pistol with which he threatened anyone who annoyed him. Apparently, on Kangchenjunga he refused to give the porters any boots, saying they were unneccessary as he had protected their bare feet with satanic spells. You should try both techniques on your next trip to Everest."

"The gun might be useful, but even if the Sherpas are very superstitious, they wouldn't buy the one about the boots today," Quinn joked in return.

"I suspect you are right, but remember these were very different days. When, during the Kangchenjunga expedition, the remainder of Crowley's team insisted on climbing in the afternoon, something our wicked wizard correctly objected to because of the greater risk of avalanche, they fell, and one climber and three porters were killed. Crowley is reported as having said, 'A mountain accident of this sort is one of the things for which I have no sympathy whatsoever,' and proceeded to continue sitting in his camp, drinking his tea and writing. An amusing little anecdote, nothing more, and soon after Crowley gave up on the mountains to turn his attention to full-time necromancy and sex magick, to which he was obviously much better suited."

The collector drew breath for a moment as if searching for space to conjure his own spell.

"But let's just imagine that instead Crowley had directed his attentions to Everest, and then through some strange combination of luck and ability, perhaps even with a bit of a push from Beelzebub himself, had actually become the first person to reach the summit. What would that have done to our perception of him, of his abilities, of his beliefs? More importantly, what would it have done for his acolytes? Imagine how it would have inspired them. A ridiculous example perhaps, but it raises an interesting point, don't you think?"

The waitress served yet more beer, even though Graf's glass was still mostly full.

"So now, as they say in Italy, I come to the *dunque* of my little soliloquy. Here I am, Dr. Bernhard Graf, unlimited in twisted fascinations, seeking the dire in everything, including Mount Everest. A person who has always wondered why it took my people until 1978 to put one of their nation on the highest point of the world—a reticence to dominate that is strangely out of character.

"Then there is you, Mr. Neil Quinn, the high-altitude climber who sells me old things he finds high on Everest, who asks me about a German ice axe a few days after he returns from climbing to its summit once again, at the same time feeding alpine forum sites with leading questions, clearly blundering his way toward a story I have long suspected—a secret that, like all the best secrets perhaps, should not be told or, at least, not too widely. A secret that also, if true, would be the pride of my collection.

"I know you will have considered it, so let us imagine another scenario together: the image of a climber on the top of Everest raising a swastika flag. Think of it. Think also of what it could have done before the war. If you need help imagining it, we can actually consider another of your beloved Seven Summits to help. The mountain of Elbrus is in the Caucasus and, I understand, now a sought-after climb as the highest peak in Continental Europe and therefore one of the seven you climbers seek to collect."

"It is."

"Well, did you know that during Operation Barbarossa, Hitler's ultimately ill-fated attempt to invade Russia, his elite mountain troops, the very same Gebirgsjäger who, surprise, surprise, bore an ice axe identical to the one now in your possession, climbed Elbrus and planted a swastika on its summit?"

Quinn shook his head as the collector continued.

"Hitler was actually said to be furious when he heard about it. He considered it a waste of effort when the Russian tide was beginning to turn so unfavorably for him at Stalingrad. But a few years earlier, I suspect, it would have made him somewhat happier. Wouldn't he have greeted them with handshakes and medals as he did the conquerors of the Eiger Nordwand? Surely a picture of the swastika on the summit of Mount Everest would have delighted him even more. It would have been the greatest example of the force of Nazi will imaginable, a tool of incredible power in the hands of Goebbels and his ministry of propaganda. Think further. Imagine what such an image might even do today in the wrong hands. It might not kill sixty million people, but it could inspire further mayhem in certain quarters somewhere out there in our increasingly anarchic world. You need to consider this, Mr. Quinn."

"But there is no record of such a thing ever happening. No mention, in fact, anywhere. I have looked hard."

The collector reached down and opened his attaché case. Pulling out a thin file, he opened it onto the table to reveal pages of handwritten notes and an old newspaper cutting inserted in a clear plastic sleeve. Passing the sleeve to Quinn, Graf explained what he was handing over.

"I stumbled on this editorial many years ago by accident. It is the reason why I have always suspected that the Nazi leadership attempted to climb Mount Everest in 1939 and why I too have searched since, mostly in vain, for the tiniest further detail. It is the very reason why I buy old oxygen cylinders from people like you who regularly visit the high parts of that mountain, hoping that it might one day produce another clue, and finally, it did."

Quinn looked at the old cutting. Through the clear plastic cover, heavy black print was blocked all over the browning newspaper. Even though the text meant nothing to him, it appeared sinister and perverse. In a grainy photo at the foot of the article, he slowly recognized the faces of the two men pictured meeting a stern-faced Adolf Hitler: Kasparek and Harrer, the first to climb the North Face of the Eiger.

"I took the liberty of quickly translating it when I knew you were on your way to see me," Graf said as he handed across another sheet of paper covered in elegant copperplate handwriting.

Quinn quickly read the collector's translation of the article, entitled "An Insult of Mountainous Proportion."

Digesting the contents, he put down the notes and asked, "So you think that Hitler would have listened to an appeal such as this and responded with an attempt on Everest?"

"Hitler? Göring? Goebbels? Who knows? The only thing that I have always been sure of is that by 1939 the Nazi leadership were capable of anything. Lozowick called them 'the alpinists of evil,' and I have always suspected it was more than metaphor even if further proof eluded me."

"Well I'm sorry to disappoint, but the only thing I found was the axe and anyone could have taken that up there."

"I suspect not, actually, and that is why I have brought you here. I would like to pay you handsomely to go back and retrieve whatever else is there. I am hoping particularly that you might find one of these."

Reaching again into his case, Graf lifted out a bundle in red velvet cloth and put it on the table.

Opening it as if unpeeling a fruit, he revealed a vintage Leica camera.

47

OLAV HOTEL, AVENUE DU MIDI, CHAMONIX, FRANCE
September 19, 2009
1:55 a.m.

Soraya closed the back door of the Olav's public bar behind her and locked it. Outside, the streetlights were fighting a losing battle against the small hours of the night. It was freezing so she tugged the hood of her sweatshirt out from under her fleece jacket and over her baseball cap.

Retreating into the little cocoon it created, she set off through the now deserted streets. It had been a busy Friday night, a busy summer season, in fact. It would be over soon and the next few months would be slower. She could kick back a bit and relax, and then, when the winter ski season began, she could get back to using every bit of her spare time snowboarding. Chamonix had some of the best off-piste skiing in the Alps. Soraya reminded herself that was why she was there. It would be good.

Life is good—or is it?

Walking down the hill at a near trot to escape the cold, she tried to imagine where Neil Quinn was at that very moment. He should have finished his booking in Saas Fee and would, she guessed, be in Munich visiting that antiques dealer he had mentioned. Once again, she asked herself what he was doing there. It seemed a bit odd. She wondered if it might actually be another woman even if she had to admit to herself that he'd made no effort to hide the screen of his phone in the bar when he scrolled through its address book to text that he would be visiting after his next job in Switzerland. On it, she briefly glimpsed a name, Graf, before he started to type. It had made her think of the German tennis player her father used to watch on TV when she was a kid in Australia. Still, it rankled her more than it should for someone who was meant to be playing by her own "no commitment" rule …

Striding on, she reflected on why she was even so concerned. Was Neil Quinn getting to her?

Turning into the narrow alley where she had a small studio apartment on the second floor, Soraya pulled her backpack forward to feel inside for her keys. As she did so, a dark shadow suddenly grabbed her left shoulder and the back of her neck from behind and slammed her against the side of the building.

Soraya instinctively twisted away but was unable to prevent the side of her face from impacting on the rough brickwork. There was a white flash of pain as the soft skin of her cheek and two teeth instantly broke, something deeper in her jawbone cracking. She heard the noise it made just before the inside of her mind folded in on itself.

She was out for a second or two, somewhere else.

When she came back, too stunned to scream or shout, her attacker flipped her around. With one viselike hand covering her mouth, the other ripped down the hood of her sweatshirt and knocked off her baseball cap before grabbing her by the throat and pushing her hard back against the wall a second time.

The new impact of her bare head on the brick wall split her scalp, immediately unleashing a flow of blood into her long, straight hair.

A voice screamed, "Please no!" and, from deep within the pain of the two blows against the wall, Soraya recognized it as her own.

A dreadful realization anticipated what was going to happen next. It sparked a desperate fight in her.

She tried to bite at the hand that covered her mouth, but her broken jaw offered no strength, only pain.

She scratched wildly, but the man was strong and his body positioned to negate every move she tried to make. Her attacker's face was wedged hard into the crook of the left arm that covered her mouth, and his right shoulder was pushed in behind the hand around her throat, the elbow jutting outward to lock against the wall. In this way, he was pinning her against the brickwork, yet protecting his head. His groin and his legs were also pushed tight into the wall to the side of her. There was nothing she could do to connect with him.

With utter horror, Soraya understood that the man had done this before. She attempted to scream again, but this time no sound could emerge from her blood-filled and obstructed mouth.

The man didn't move. He simply held her head hard against the wall and, as she slowly became exhausted from her ineffectual efforts to twist away from him, finally he said, very quietly, *"Ça suffit."*

Soraya could hear his panting breath, see his incensed light-blue eyes glaring into hers as he then almost whispered, "Stop struggling and listen," with a slow and deliberate precision, giving a squeeze of her throat with every word, as if forcing each one down into it.

When he was sure that she was complying with his instructions, he said in a faster, louder voice, "I am told that you are fucking Neil Quinn. I am already pissed off that I have wasted a lot of time in this shitty little town trying to find him. If you give me any more trouble, I will fuck you myself, do you understand me?"

Soraya writhed and tried to shake her head from side to side, but her defiance turned to panic as she felt herself beginning to choke on more blood and saliva. She tried to cough it up but couldn't, her body convulsing as she began to drown in it.

Sarron released his grip slightly so her head could move forward, loosening the hand over her mouth to let her breathe and swallow for a moment, before banging it back again, hard. As her eyes rolled back into her head from the third impact, he spat, "I repeat myself, bitch! 'Do you understand me?'"

Her resistance disintegrated with that final blow. Sobbing, she attempted to nod her head within the lock of the man's renewed grip.

"Okay, good. Now I am going to take my hand off your mouth, and you are going to tell me where I can find Neil Quinn. If you try to scream, I will instantly squeeze your throat again like this." He gripped her neck tight once more and then, just as quickly, stopped, saying, "Now tell me!"

Soraya struggled to get any words out whatsoever, violently coughing up more bloody sputum, gasping for air.

"I said, 'Tell me!'"

"Not here," was the eventual, faint response.

"Where the fuck is he then?"

She hesitated until a new tightening on her throat squeezed out the words, "Switzerland ... working ... no, Germany."

"Which fucking one is it?"

"Germany ... Munich."

"Are you sure?"

"I think so ..."

"Why is he there?"

"Don't know."

"Try again!"

"Antiques dealer."

"What?"

"He's seeing an antiques dealer. Please believe me."

"Then give me his name."

"Graf."

"When did he go?"

"Today, yesterday, whatever it is."

"How?"

"By motorcycle from Saas Fee in Switzerland."

The hold on her instantly released and Sarron disappeared from the alley as the broken girl folded to the ground, unconscious. Five minutes later, as he raced the stolen Renault out of Chamonix, intent on getting through the Mont Blanc tunnel and into Italy as fast as he could, Sarron punched the redial on his cell phone. It took some time to answer while the car sped up the hill, wallowing and sliding around its sequence of switchback bends. When someone did answer, all Sarron said was, "Change of plan. Munich—as soon as you can get there."

48

THE ZEMU RIDGE, NORTHWEST SIKKIM—18,750 FEET
April 3, 1939
6:30 a.m.

Namgel's words cut through the canvas skin of the sagging Schuster tent. "Sahibs. We go summit. Breakfast tea." Within, Josef laboriously crawled forward to receive the two tin cups he knew the Sherpa, crouched outside in the deep snow, was waiting to pass in.

Moving in the limited space of the cramped two-man tent, Josef could feel the altitude holding his body back, making him unnaturally slow and awkward. It was a new sensation to be so high. Unfastening the entrance, the cold beyond the tent instantly assaulted his outstretched fingers. It stabbed into the tip of the one damaged by the gestapo, painfully reminding Josef why he was really there.

Quickly pulling the two cups back in, his movements dislodged a shower of rime ice from inside the top of the tent. The flakes caught the back of his neck and slid down under his shirt collar, causing him to shudder involuntarily and spill some of the tea. Shaking it off, Josef began to drink what was left. It faintly heated his insides and filled his stomach with a feeling of optimism. Despite everything, he was looking forward to going still higher.

"Time to go," he said to the other occupant of the tent, invisible within his long, eiderdown bag. Leaning closer, Josef tried to determine if Schmidt was still sleeping. It was difficult to tell now that he wasn't snoring like a pig.

The bag's exterior was still, encrusted with a thin layer of ice, giving it the appearance of a fat brown slug frozen to death by a hard morning frost. Looking at it with loathing, Josef told himself that the man was probably still out cold. Despite the long trek across Northern Sikkim, the heavy, overfed professor was nowhere near the condition necessary for what they were attempting, even if that obvious fact hadn't stopped him from engineering everything so that he, and only he, would accompany Josef on this, the first ascent of the expedition.

Josef suspected—no, he knew—that Schmidt was using him to ensure that he got to the top of at least one mountain and that he did so with Josef by his side. If Operation Sisyphus proved successful, it didn't take much to imagine the professor dining out forever on the story of how he had climbed a Himalayan peak with the man who stole Everest from the British. Ever the organizer, once the Base Camp had been established, Schmidt had neatly divided up the team to take some separate first looks at the higher snowfields above the Zemu Glacier. Undoubtedly, this was a good tactic to permit Josef and Ang Noru to make a first climb together and then make their subsequent exit from the expedition, but Josef was concerned that theirs was the only group attempting an actual summit. Even if the peak was low compared to the monsters that surrounded it, not even meriting a name on their maps, he still thought it would attract too much attention from that British Army officer, Macfarlane. The man was no fool, always watching them.

"Sahibs, sun coming. Necessary faster," Josef heard Ang Noru shout this time.

Short of breath, Josef had to pause before he could answer with a simple, "Yes."

Drawing in some more deep gulps of air to build his strength, he gave the inert sleeping bag next to him a hard kick with the heel of his double-stockinged foot. Schmidt exploded upward in a paroxysm of coughing before looking around with puffy, blinking eyes, saying breathlessly, "What was that? What time is it?"

Josef looked at Schmidt's altitude-swollen face and, shrugging his shoulders, said, "Nothing," as he passed him the cup of tea. Through the slit entrance of the tent beyond the bewildered professor, Josef could see that the snowy plateau on which they were camped was already beginning to glow golden from the dawn sun. He could hear also the low chatter of the two Sherpas as they made ready to leave the camp. "Drink the tea, eat some biscuit, and get ready as quickly as you can. It's time to go up."

In the cramped confines of the tent, Josef began his own preparations to go out into the cold. After twisting his woolen scarf around his neck and up over his head and ears, he struggled back into his windproof outer jacket and boots. He smeared his face with zinc cream, pulled his scarf up around his head, and then reached inside the deep ammunition pocket of the snow-troop jacket for his snow goggles. Looping them around his neck, he opened his rucksack to retrieve something else he had specially packed for that moment. From deep inside, Josef pulled out his army field cap tied in a tight roll since Germany. He had kept the cap hidden during the expedition's long trek into the glacier, wary particularly of that English army officer, but if he was going to the top that day he was going to wear it instead of the woolen one he had been using. He always wore it on his big climbs.

Untying the string, he beat the cap against his knee to loosen it for reshaping. As he did so, he felt the metal of the skull and crossbones badge that Pfeiffer had attached. He looked at it. The sight instantly took him back to Wewelsburg, but his thoughts didn't stop there. They traveled on further to that tramping file of nine Jews, the black woods dripping with rain, the blast of the wind carving down onto them from the snowy chapel ridge, the glint of that same badge on the cap of the SS officer who had taken all their lives away, one way or another. *That badge has got to go,* Josef told himself as he pushed the cap down onto his head and then himself out of the tent into the freezing air to join the two Sherpas.

The sun was climbing in the east by the time Schmidt was finally ready to leave. Together the four of them began to wade through the deep snow to reach the narrow ridge that led to the summit. Ang Noru broke the trail, followed by Becker, Schmidt, and then Namgel. They moved forward well until they roped together and filed up onto the narrow, snowy ridge. There, Schmidt immediately started to make the going painfully slow.

Every few steps they had to stop for the wheezing professor. Josef could feel the Sherpas growing frustrated, even if they said nothing beyond a questioning, "Sahib?" each time they halted. He quickly instructed Namgel to move ahead of Schmidt and shorten the rope between them all. He knew it would have the effect of the three of them almost pulling the professor along but he didn't care. He just wanted to get Schmidt to the top as soon as possible and then back down so the real purpose of his journey could start.

The way was not difficult, but the exposure grew extreme as the ridge narrowed, the faces to each side of them falling away vertically to vanish into thick cloud lying far below. To the west, the huge, multiple peaks of Kangchenjunga reared up from the flat base of the same low-level cloud. Beyond, the summit pyramids of other great mountains appeared like atolls emerging from a calm but grey sea. Ang Noru and Namgel pointed to them in turn, mumbling unintelligible names until Ang Noru, his hand held above his round snow goggles, pointed to one in particular in the far distance and said pointedly to Josef, "Look, Sahib Becker. Mount Everest."

Josef immediately looked at the black wedge that broke the far line of the horizon. A thick plume of cloud was blowing from the summit as if the distant mountain was steaming slowly off the edge of the world. He expected, any second, for it to vanish, consumed by the curvature of the planet, but it remained, fixed to the horizon, bleak and severe, so much higher than all the other peaks in between. The more he looked at it, Josef began to realize that this, his first real view of Everest, no longer in a photograph, was filling him with dread. He felt foolish that he had ever thought he could climb such a mountain.

It's imposs—

Schmidt, struggling back up onto his feet and coughing as if he was about to choke, broke the moment, preventing the silent admission.

Josef quickly wrenched his gaze back from the immense mountain to say to the two Sherpas, "He's on his feet. Let's go."

Ang Noru, who had been watching Josef as intently as he had been looking at Everest, said only, "Yes, Sahib Becker," and when Josef stepped forward, instantly moved with him.

Namgel however stayed stock-still, as if frozen in his tracks, the rope between them all straining until it pulled them to a halt once again.

Turning back to see what was wrong, Josef saw Namgel's eyes fix on the badge sewn to the front of his cap. His usual smile was missing. When he tugged angrily on the rope to get the Sherpa moving, Josef glimpsed him hastily perform a sign against the evil eye and start mumbling something continuously under his breath before he would follow.

49

THE ZEMU GLACIER, NORTHWEST SIKKIM—15,250 FEET
April 3, 1939
8:45 a.m.

Lieutenant Macfarlane was finishing his breakfast in the otherwise empty mess tent of the expedition camp. There was a thick fog outside and it was unusually quiet now that the raucous Schmidt and his equally noisy team were exploring the mountains above. He was happy to have the place to himself that morning with just the cooks and some of the porters for remote company. It was even better that it was his first without one of the splitting headaches that had dogged him since their arrival at the glacier. Opening the copy of Douglas Freshfield's *Round Kangchenjunga* that Smethwick had lent him as they were leaving Darjeeling, he called for some more tea and biscuits. *Appetite's back too.*

Studying the pictures of the hidden mountains that surrounded him, Macfarlane tried to imagine what it must be like to be up there above the clouds.

He was not a climber and Colonel Atkinson had been emphatic that he was not to try to be. His role, as the colonel put it, was "to be supervisory, not participatory," something he had immediately reinforced when he arrived to see them off and saw Smethwick hand over the mountain book to the lieutenant as a parting gift.

"Read that book, by all means, old fellow, but make sure you stay off those bloody mountains," Atkinson had cautioned. "It's the only place where the Hun won't be able to get up to any mischief, and I have been ordered to send you back to London in one piece as a condition of your presence on this expedition. Once that fat führer and his cohorts take to the snows, let them get on with it. Go and bag some of that wildlife I mentioned. It should be fine hunting."

It was true. Macfarlane did like to hunt. When time permitted from the busy routine at the barracks, he had made trips with some of the Gurkha to track the wild pigs and the small, nervous antelopes that picked their way through the tropical forest below the hill station. He had been invited twice by other officers to try for tiger, but, beyond the impressive sight of some big, splayed paw prints in the soft orange mud of a jungle stream, they had never found one, which had been a dissappointment.

On the long trek from Gangtok to the Zemu, he fleetingly saw some of Atkinson's wildlife but with no desire or capacity to shoot any of it. From the moment they entered the upper Tista Valley, Macfarlane had been absolutely pummeled by the effects of altitude. At times it had been so bad his only wish had been for someone to shoot him. He could only look on with envy at the porters and the likes of Becker, who seemed totally unaffected however high they went.

Becker ...

He still hadn't fully worked that one out, even if he thought he was now closer to an answer. The "farmworker," as Schmidt had labeled him, was elusive, ephemeral even. He floated silently on the margin of Schmidt's team, detached from its brutish camaraderie and enthusiastic lack of serious purpose. He actually seemed closer to the Sherpas and the porters, more at ease moving with them along the tracks and trails that had led them into the hills. Becker was usually accompanied by one Sherpa in particular, Ang Noru. They didn't seem to say much to each other, but they were never far apart. If they did speak, it appeared to Macfarlane to be in a very simple German. He didn't have the ability to follow what they were saying, although he did detect the occasional word of English being thrown in, particularly by the Sherpa. Any time that he himself tried to engage Becker in conversation, he was met with an immediate shrugged response of *"Kein Englisch"* before the German quickly moved away with a shake of his head. It was a pity because of Schmidt's team, Macfarlane suspected that Becker was probably the best of the bunch.

For that matter Ang Noru was also equally reticent to speak to him. This was unusual because the majority of the porters, particularly the climbing Sherpas, were chatty within the limitations of their rudimentary English. It made him recall Smethwick's warning about the man, even if, at first, it was difficult to see why he merited it.

The Sherpa Ang Noru, although tough and

undoubtedly dour, was an indefatigable workhorse. Soon however he had heard from the other climbing Sherpa about how Ang Noru had been higher than all of them except for Namgel, that he had even been to Everest, proving to be one of the strongest on the mountain until his feet suffered frostbite. Ang Noru had made the mistake of blaming the English sahibs for it, they said, because they gave him boots that were too small and refused to change them when he asked. He had lost all his toes as a result and now only the Germans would give him work. When Macfarlane tried to imagine what it must be like to suffer such injuries yet still have to continue to use your feet to make your living, he understood that it could make a man somewhat bitter. In fact, the English officer thought that Becker and Ang Noru complemented each other. They were both quiet loners within the current company, which was probably what pushed them together.

But why had Schmidt described Becker as a "farm-worker"?

At one communal meal in the mess tent, Macfarlane had taken the opportunity to study Becker's hands. He didn't have the rough, thick-fingered hands of the farm laborer. They were wiry and thin, moving with a delicate dexterity and precision more suited to a piano player or a watchmaker. Yet one of his fingers had been caught in some form of accident. A long, still-livid scar pushed from the very tip back to the first knuckle. It had no fingernail. Maybe Becker did work with machinery, but Macfarlane didn't think that it was a thresher or a plough. There was something else about Becker that suggested his background wasn't farming. His climbing clothes were much more specialized than those of the others in Schmidt's party. Becker's equipment was equally purposeful. He was never without his ice axe, his backpack, and a coil of rope once they neared the glacier.

When Schmidt announced that Becker and Ang Noru would be accompanying him on a first trip to bag a peak, it had all become a little clearer to the English officer. Becker was obviously some kind of professional mountain guide from the Bavarian Alps, brought along by Schmidt to ensure that the fat man made it to the top of a mountain so he could brag about it on his return to his beloved Nazi Germany. If Ang Noru had Everest experience and was as good as the other Sherpas said he was, toes or no toes, then Schmidt must have instructed Becker to team with him.

That has to be it.

Leaving the mess tent later, his breakfast over, Lieutenant Macfarlane looked up into the blanket of thick cloud and wondered how they were doing up there. Schmidt was a big man, always red-faced and out of breath at any altitude. Becker and the Sherpa were going to have their work cut out to get that man to the top of anything. If the day cleared, he would use the expedition's telescope to see how they were progressing. Firstly however, he was going to have a chat with the porters to see if there was word of anything worth hunting down the valley.

50

**THE SUMMIT OF UNNAMED PEAK 23A,
NORTHWEST SIKKIM—20,376 FEET**
April 3, 1939
11:47 a.m.

Arrival on the summit gave the utterly spent Schmidt just enough of a boost to pull a swastika flag from his pack and insist that Josef take photograph after photograph of him holding it. As Josef squinted through the viewfinder of Schmidt's camera, the image sickened him. It was a sham. He, Namgel, and Ang Noru had virtually dragged Schmidt to the top, and there he now was, waving his damn flag as if he had run up there. To make matters worse, when Schmidt was finally satisfied he had enough photos of himself on the summit, he told Josef to pass the camera to Ang Noru to photograph them together with the flag. Josef knew why Schmidt wanted that photograph and just as quickly told himself that he wasn't going to have it.

To Josef's relief, even though it was something he

needed to remedy, it was obvious Ang Noru had no idea what to do with the camera. But then Namgel, saying a sahib had once showed him how on Everest, took over, pointing the camera at them expertly as he clicked and wound. When he finished, he offered the camera back. Josef quickly took it, telling Schmidt he was going to take some views of the other mountains, turning away from them all as if to scan the horizon. Feigning that he was taking long-distance shots, he actually released the base cover of the camera within his hands to let the brilliant high-altitude light leach in. Only when he was as sure as he could be that the film inside was ruined did he resecure it and return the camera to Schmidt, saying to them all that it was time to go down.

It was a long and slow descent all the way to the upper edge of the glacier that took most of the afternoon. There, drained from having almost dragged the ever-weakening professor back down the mountain, Josef and the Sherpas could do little more than just sit for a while. Eventually Josef suggested they brew some tea. He knew that Schmidt needed it badly if he was to go any further and the time to prepare it would ensure it was night when he did arrive back at the camp. The cover of darkness was essential for the deceit ahead.

Ang Noru instantly broke out a small metafuel burner from one of the packs, while Namgel took a pan and his axe to collect some ice from within the glacier.

When he was sure Namgel was out of earshot, Josef whispered, "It is time now, Ang Noru. We will make tea, and then you and Namgel must take Schmidt on to Base Camp. Carry him if you have to. I stay here. You will tell the others that I am sick and that they must send people to bring me down."

The Sherpa nodded as he battled to light the burner. He already knew the plan. When Fischer had taken him aside with Schmidt and Josef in Darjeeling and explained Operation Sisyphus in his own language, Josef had watched Ang Noru listen intently without a flicker of emotion. Afterward Fischer had told them that when he had asked the Sherpa to swear to secrecy on the spirits of his ancestors, the reply had been that it wasn't necessary, that he wanted to do it as much as they did.

Josef looked across at Schmidt. He was a mess, collapsed against a large rock that projected from the snow, dragging slow, shuddering breaths into his lungs. His eyes were closed. He was drifting into sleep. Leaning closely into the side of his head, Josef said slowly and firmly, "Do you hear me, Schmidt? You need to stay awake. We are making some tea. It will help you make the last few hours down the glacier to the camp. It is easier going from here. Ang Noru and Namgel are going to help you. You need to pull yourself together if you are going to be the one who sends me away. Do you understand me?"

Schmidt grunted unintelligibly in reply as Namgel reappeared with the pan full of broken ice and water. When the Sherpa set the pan onto the sooty burner and huddled down alongside Ang Noru to wait for it to boil, Josef stared directly at Namgel and forced himself to cough violently.

The Sherpa immediately looked back at Josef with an expression of horror, his eyes glancing repeatedly upward at Josef's SS cap badge. He pointed to it as he muttered to Ang Noru. He then began mumbling to himself, turning his eyes down to stare worriedly into the faintly steaming pot while Josef continued to force himself to cough and groan.

The combination of the tea and the lower altitude of the glacier basin slowly put a little life back into Schmidt, even if it took another ten fits of coughing from Josef before Schmidt finally took the hint.

"Sahib Becker is sick," he eventually slurred to the two Sherpas. "We must go on and send help back for him."

Upon hearing Schmidt say this, Namgel became instantly alarmed, raising his voice as much as he dared. "No, Sahib, no. We cannot leave him. I will stay. He must not be left alone here."

Namgel continued to plead to Schmidt causing Ang Noru to say something to him in their own dialect. The conversation between the two Sherpas became heated until, with difficulty, Schmidt broke it up, saying between deep gasps for air, "Look, you two ... I give the orders ... And I say we go now ... We will leave Sahib Becker with what he needs ... Then send help for him when we get to the camp."

While Ang Noru made an elaborate display of making Josef comfortable, he said to him under his breath, "Namgel says you are the strongest sahib he has ever seen on the mountains, strong as the Sherpas, but that you carry the mark of death on your head. He says the bones have attracted mountain devils. He says they will come for you if you are left alone, and they will eat your heart and lungs to take your strength for their own. He says you must rid yourself of the bones, or you will die."

"Tell him, Ang Noru, he is right. I will die if he

doesn't get back to the camp and bring help as soon as possible. Now go. You know what to do. It is time."

"But the bones …" Ang Noru began to question.

Josef cut in. "Ang Noru, think about it. You know the plan. It is not the bones."

"Yes, Sahib Becker."

When Josef watched them leave, Namgel was still protesting, wanting to stay. He looked back at Josef with fear in his eyes, Ang Noru pulling him on until they disappeared with Schmidt into the broken ice towers of the glacier.

The bones, indeed.

Alone, Josef told himself that now was the time to be rid of them but for his own, not Namgel's, reasons. He reached for his pocketknife and, with the point of its blade, delicately unpicked the stitching that held the metal skull and crossbones badge to the front of his cap.

For the next half hour, as the sky darkened and the cold closed in, Josef occupied himself by placing the badge on a rock and hammering it with the pick of his ice axe. It gave him a strong feeling of satisfaction to finally cast its mangled shape onto the snow. He then turned his attention to preparing for his rescuers' return.

First he retied his army cap into a roll and hid it back inside his jacket. Then he reached into his pack and pulled out a small tin of baking soda. Opening it, he emptied a handful of the powder into the pocket of his wind jacket. Putting his woolen hat back on, he pulled it down over his eyes and the sleeping bag up over his head to settle in for the long wait. He would bite the inside of his lip to draw some blood and put some of the baking soda in his mouth to create a foam when he heard them returning. There was no need to suffer yet. It was going to be a long night.

51

PARKHOTEL KOBLENZ, SCHILLERSTRASSE 5, MUNICH, GERMANY
September 19, 2009
4:48 a.m.

The green glow of a battered digital clock radio illuminated the dark of the room like a sickly full moon. The beer of the dinner and the cheap whiskey of a solitary bar crawl back to his cheap hotel pushed down on Quinn's forehead with a dull throb, a ripple of nausea turning his stomach when he raised his head from the spongy foam pillow to check the time.

4:48 A.M.

Needing some water to wash out the heavy funk of too much alcohol, Quinn got up, squeezing himself into the minuscule bathroom to fill a plastic beaker at the sink. The extremely cold water tasted brackish as it rinsed his rough throat and chilled the tops of his spine and lungs. Returning to the bedroom window, he pulled aside a curtain and looked down on the wet, deserted street below. It was empty, a temporary silence having finally fallen on the run-down, trashy Hauptbahnhof district.

Quinn had seen it all after he refused the collector's offer of a lift back to his hotel at the end of their dinner and walked instead. He had wanted—needed, in fact— to be alone, to let his mind turn over all that Graf had said. Enjoying the buzz of the beer from the dinner, he stopped for more in a sequence of good-natured bars along the way. At some point, he couldn't precisely recall when, he'd left beer behind and made the switch to cheap whiskey and then, at the last bar before the hotel, the Café Istanbul, he also left Graf's "coziness" behind.

To the tinny blast of overly loud turbo-folk, he found himself within a maelstrom of other cultures, a dislocation of Turks, Eastern Europeans, Southern Italians, the darkest of African girls, all talking and drinking at the same time as if desperately trying to savor every hard-fought second of their lives. Through the windows, the neon signs of their world blinked back at him: "Casino," "Internet," "Sexy World," "Handy Phone," "Tabletop," "Laptop," "Non-Stop." When finally he left its sweaty smog after one last drink too many, the fresh air hit him like a cold shower but still left him feeling dirty. His head spinning, Quinn had heard Graf's dinner conversation all over again as he stumbled back to his hotel, the social and racial tinderbox the collector had described on the streets all around him.

Awake now, in the darkest hour before dawn, he could only lean his aching forehead against the cold glass of the window and think about Graf himself. The collector was odd and fanciful, no doubt, the ringmaster of his own inanimate freak show, but for all his doom and gloom, his slightly barbed comments, Quinn couldn't dislike him. There was an almost confessional honesty, a repressed gentleness to the man that kept him hovering above the abyss that so clearly fascinated him. Quinn even found himself in agreement with much that Graf said about the world, about its history, about him even. His was, indeed, a simple life, pursuing the interest he loved as Graf had pointed out. Yet it hadn't been so simple since that last summit. Death, coma, murder, cremation, legal harassment, recurrent nightmares—his mind cascaded through it all until stopped by a stark realization.

Graf is collecting me.

Quinn chided himself for being so melodramatic and tried to reassure himself that he was merely a source for a somewhat eccentric antique dealer. Quinn's ice axe, bearing its tiny swastika to Mount Everest, was a significant item for such a man, or so he said—one that could lead to more interesting finds that the man had coveted for years.

That's all—or was it?

He turned back into the room and saw the old axe on the desk sat alongside the Leica camera that Graf had urged him to take and look at.

Was he correct in his recall of the sum of money that Graf was offering to pay him if he could find a similar camera on the Second Step? It was crazy if he was. Impossible to refuse even if he wasn't sure there was anything else up there.

Quinn reached for his phone to text the collector that he would come by his shop at 9:00 a.m. to continue their discussions. He'd switched his phone off during the dinner and, as the alcohol flowed afterward, forgotten it. Turning it back on, it chimed its irritating welcome and immediately began a manic, beeping vibration of incoming data that sent the black plastic clam dancing in his hand. Multiple missed calls and messages; some names he recognized, some new numbers he didn't, but they all said the same thing. "Call as soon as possible."

He immediately tried to ring them. With a growing sense of frustration and then panic, he got voice mail after voice mail, but no answer until a hesitant female voice finally said, "Hello?"

Quinn took a breath of relief at someone finally replying. "This is Neil Quinn speaking. I think you rang me earlier."

"Yes, I did. I'm Nikki, a friend of Soraya. Doug Martin gave me your number. Look, we've not met, although actually you were … Look, shit, none of that matters. You should know she's been attacked. I am actually in the Chamonix hospital now. She's pretty badly beaten up. They are keeping her under sedation at the moment."

The shock of the girl's words twisted Quinn's insides. "What? When did this happen? Who did it?"

"We don't know much yet, but she's in a really bad way. We think it happened on her way home from work at the bar, maybe around two in the morning, two-thirty. We're not sure. She was found by a couple of guys at about three. The police were only briefly able to speak to her as she was drifting in and out of consciousness. It seems that it was some crazy French guy, and he was looking for you. But she was really messed up and couldn't say any more than that. The doctors stopped the police from having any more contact with her."

Quinn couldn't believe what he was hearing. "Fuck. Could she describe the guy that did it?"

"I'm sorry, but I don't know any more than what I've told you. I think the Cham police are trying to get in touch with you. You should call them."

"Okay, but how is she now?"

"A real mess. I'm staying here until the morning. I'll call you when the doctor's been around again."

The call ended. Quinn had no doubt that it was Sarron, Henrietta Richards' words at the cremation ringing out in the silence of the hotel room: "He'll be back for you, Neil ... sooner or later."

If Sarron had attacked Soraya demanding news of Quinn, it was inevitable that she would have told him what she knew, and she knew he was there to see an antiques dealer. If he drove through the night, the Frenchman could be there later that day. However Quinn didn't remember telling Soraya the name of the antiques dealer. Sarron was going to have to find him first and Munich was a big city, surely with many antiques dealers.

Still unnerved by the news about Soraya, he typed a text to Graf: "Something has come up. Meet at shop early. 8:00 a.m.?"

His phone almost immediately announced a response: "*Jawohl, mein* führer!" A winking, smiley emoticon followed.

"Shit, that guy really is a piece of work," Quinn said to himself as he sat back on the bed, trying to work out what the hell he should do next.

The phone bleeped again.

"Bring the axe and the camera."

52

At the glass door of Graf's shop, Quinn braced his hangover for its cacophonous doorbell, only to be startled by the blast of a car horn exactly as his hand touched the handle.

Cursing loudly, he turned to see the collector behind the wheel of a black Mercedes 500SL, the coupe's long nose poking out from an arch on the far side of the courtyard. The powerful car immediately rumbled out onto the cobblestones, making a circle to stop beside him. The passenger door clicked open, and the collector beckoned Quinn into the car as he got out, saying, "I need to get a few things from my shop before we go."

Quinn folded himself into the low-slung seat, inserting the old ice axe and his daypack with the Leica camera inside behind it. The sickly sweet sound of Julie Andrews singing "Edelweiss" from *The Sound of Music* surrounded him as he closed the door and waited.

After a few minutes, Graf returned, placing his attaché case behind his seat.

Quinn raised an eyebrow at him. "Julie Andrews? Really?"

"Not a favorite? Oh dear. I thought it might get you in the correct mood to think about mountains and Nazis."

The collector touched a hidden button on the steering wheel.

The music jumped to the husky voice of Dietrich singing "Lili Marlene."

"Easier on your hangover perhaps?" he said, smiling at Quinn then pushing another button. The large, multicylindered engine reawakened and the car began to roll forward, wide tires rippling on the stones and crunching on the salt already cast in anticipation of the icy winter months ahead.

"I am impressed that you wanted to make a start so soon after our dinner, if not a little excited, I must say. In the event you did correctly determine that I was only a pretend prince of darkness, I took the liberty of planning a little trip for us to meet someone in Garmisch. I think he will finally rid you of your secret hope that the axe belonged to some brutish Ivan or Chinaman with a penchant for secondhand climbing equipment. You did bring the camera?"

"Yes."

"Good. We'll need that this afternoon."

The sleek Mercedes began to travel quickly through the central Munich traffic.

"Despite my little jokes and tales of the macabre, I feel that I have been very open with my proposition to you, Neil. Now it is time for you to be the same with me. I'd like to hear the full story of the ice axe.

We have a while before our first destination, so spare not the tiniest detail."

Quinn paused and then, pushing through his fatigue, proceeded to tell Graf the whole saga from beginning to end.

The collector listened, quite still, with the attention of a heron studying a pond. As requested, Quinn did not spare anything, telling Graf not only about finding the axe but also about Nelson Tate Junior, Pemba, Dawa, Soraya, and his suspicion that Sarron was on his way to Munich at that very moment. The only thing about which he was deliberately vague was the original location of the axe, being no more precise than saying it was found on the Second Step as things unraveled with the kid.

By the time he was finished, the Mercedes was punching its way down the fast lane of the autobahn, passing all other cars as if they were standing still, the Bavarian Alps rising up in front of them. Thinking on what he had been told for a few minutes, Graf said, "Your story is actually stranger and more violent than I expected but I can't say that disappoints me. *Abyssus abyssum invocat,* as they say. Am I right that you mentioned that there was the string of a flag on the shaft of the axe? I don't recall seeing that when you showed it to me yesterday."

"It was very weatherworn. I think it came off when Sarron's thugs beat me with it in Kathmandu."

"Ouch. It spoke to you of the summit, didn't it?"

"Yes."

"So what I was imagining in the beer hall last night is actually possible: a swastika flying over the summit of Mount Everest. It presents a most exquisite irony, don't you think? The Everest world fixated on finding Sandy Irvine's body and the camera that could finally prove that he and Mallory gloriously made it to the top in 1924, when you could have found proof of a somewhat different and distinctly less palatable first summit, long before that of Hillary and Tenzing. Beautiful."

"It's possible, but as I have said, I only found the axe."

"But perhaps there is more still waiting up there on the Second Step?"

Quinn pushed his mind back to the gorak cave and his desperate struggle to save Nelson Tate Junior. He saw again that mound of snow and ice rising inside it, the glimpse of something dark within.

"Maybe. I'm not sure."

"Well I am," Graf replied, "and I am taking you to meet someone who might be able to tell us some more about all this. Dieter Braun is his name, a rare individual these days, Neil Quinn, because he is an eyewitness of those times. He must be at least ninety years old, maybe more, but he's still mentally alert. He says it is only because he is cursed. But his curse may be our fortune."

"How so?"

"At night he begs for old age to take his memories."

"And it doesn't?"

"No, and some of them are very bad indeed."

"How do you know him?"

"He returned to Garmisch in the late '50s when he was finally released by the Russians. He became somewhat of a historian for his regiment and their role in the war. He says he owed it to the many who didn't return. Dieter is not so active now, but occasionally he contacts me with an item he wants to sell or a story he wants to tell. I don't think he has much longer to live."

Graf accelerated the car still harder as if fearful that Braun might die before they could get there.

"But then again, he has survived so much. He went into Poland in '39, followed by the Low Countries and France. He even trained to scale your White Cliffs of Dover until Operation Sealion was abandoned and they were sent to take Yugoslavia through the mountains instead. In the summer of '41, they arrived at the *ostfront*, the worst front of all. By the time Stalingrad finally collapsed onto the remains of the one million soldiers that died there, the war was lost, even if Hitler didn't want to admit it. Braun was one of the few from his regiment who survived the rear guard action all the way back to the mountains of Southeastern Austria. There, they finally surrendered, only to be transported back to Russian prison camps and used as slave labor to rebuild what they had destroyed, easily forgotten by a world that had no desire to remember them. Even fewer returned a second time."

Quinn said nothing, considering the misty German countryside flashing by, taking in its soft green farmland dotted with small animal sheds like dollhouses, feeling the weight of all the death and suffering that had sprung from such a gentle-looking land. His thoughts drifted on to Soraya, Dawa, Pemba. Involuntarily, he sighed aloud before saying, "But if there really is anything else up there, shouldn't it just be left alone? Too many people have been hurt already."

"Perhaps, if we could be sure that sooner or later it would not be found by someone else. You know very well that they are still looking all over the North Face for the body of Sandy Irvine. How long until the searchers arrive at the same place as you?"

"Perhaps, but why are you really so keen to get your hands on it?"

"Because I not only want to possess this discovery for myself but also to keep it away from others, to stop it becoming an icon to people who should receive no encouragement or further inspiration."

"But are there really that many today?"

"Neil, I have heard it said that here in Germany, one in ten under the age of twenty now regularly visits some form of neo-Nazi website. Maybe this is inaccurate, but even if it is only one in a hundred or even a thousand, surely that is still unacceptable given our past? And it is not only here—Greece, Bosnia, Russia, the Ukraine—they are all experiencing revivals of the far right in some form or another. If certain people within those groups became aware of what we might have, they would stop at nothing or no one to use it to their advantage. If that were to result in the persecution of a single person, then we would hold responsibility for that. Sometimes outwardly insignificant things become difficult to stop. You, of all people, should understand the dangers of rolling a small snowball down a large hill …"

53

The car turned off the autobahn and descended a slip road into Garmisch where it slowly drove down the town's picturesque main street. Continuing past an immense red brick barracks garrisoned by the US Army, the Mercedes finally turned down a side street to stop in front of a squat, chalet-style house.

At its door, they were met by Dieter Braun's daughter, a neat, handsome woman who appeared younger than the midfifties she must have been. She greeted Graf in the Bavarian dialect, seemingly cordial yet formal. The pair talked on the doorstep and, after Graf had glanced a couple of times at Quinn without breaking the conversation, she switched to a simple yet well-structured English, holding his outstretched hand for slightly longer than was necessary. "I am pleased to meet you, Mr. Quinn. My father is in the sunroom. I will show you in. He is pleased you are coming. We do not get many visitors these days."

She showed them into the immaculately tidy house. Not a single light was on, making it lonely and dark until they entered a bright sunroom to its rear. The room's main window shone with a spectacular view of the jagged Wetterstein mountains. The Zugspitze massif and the spiky Waxenstein peak pushed up from pine-clad slopes, bleak and savage despite the almost suffocating warmth of the sunroom.

Turning back into the room, Quinn saw an ice axe identical to the one he was holding mounted on one of the walls. It was displayed with a coil of rope, an army field cap, and a tarnished metal plaque of a large edelweiss flower. Dieter Braun was sitting below it in an upright wicker chair pointed toward the window, his legs covered in a blanket. The old soldier looked all of his ninety-plus years. His remaining hair was white, combed back. His face was thin and proud, blue eyes still clear but red-rimmed, the skin a faint cream color, almost translucent. Transparent nasal cannulas were piping oxygen into him from a cylinder on a trolley set to the side of his chair. His breathing was labored, a faint rasp emitting from within his lungs. Quinn noticed that part of one of Braun's ears was missing but the old soldier didn't seem deaf. With their first steps into the room, the ancient man had immediately turned in his chair to take in the arrival of the collector with his battered attaché case. A faint smile had come to the corner of his lips as he looked at it.

Braun's daughter gestured for them to sit and have coffee. She served it to Quinn and Graf from a round glass pot that was placed on the windowsill above a small burner that infused the room with a smell of coffee and methylated spirit. "Please don't tire him too much. Even Papi is beginning to feel his years now. I have to go and get some things from the shops, his medicine too, so I will leave you to talk until I get back. I think then that will have been enough," she said to them both. As she started to leave, she spoke somewhat more brusquely to her father, who waved her away with a dismissive, *"Ja, ja, ja."*

Graf immediately started talking to Braun until he heard the front door shut; then he stood to remove a new bottle of Stolichnaya vodka from his case. He quickly poured the coffee from his own cup into a pot of geraniums and, taking a tissue from a box on a side table, wiped it out before filling it with the clear spirit. He passed the cup to Braun, who took a long, slow draught. As he did so, his eyes rolled up into his head, and he shuddered. When he opened them again, he stared straight at Quinn and began to speak to him in German. The voice was soft but still clear, broken only by Braun's heavy breathing. Quinn couldn't understand a word, looking to Graf and hunching his shoulders a little as if in question.

"Dieter is apologizing that he doesn't speak English," Graf responded. "He said that if they had won, you would be speaking German now, which would be easier for an old man like him. He says that a lot of things would have been easier if that idiot hadn't sent them to Russia."

The old soldier rolled his eyes at the delay of translation, taking another swig from the cup of vodka before his German filled the room again. He began to talk about the war, Graf's accented English over Braun's voice reminding Quinn of a Second World War documentary series he used to watch on TV as a child. When Quinn gave a sideways glance at the fact that Graf was already refilling the cup with vodka, the collector instantly translated the old man's response to his look of concern: "Don't be alarmed, Britischer. It won't kill me. Dr. Graf always brings me a taste of Russia when he comes. I spent ten years in their gulags. A love of vodka was the only thing those bastards gave me that I wish to keep. I have often longed to be able to return the dust of their godforsaken roads and buildings that fills my lungs."

Braun pointed to Quinn's ice axe. "That's an aschenbrenner. You know of him, of course, Aschenbrenner, the man known as 'Himalaya Pete.' He left two legacies, disgrace on Nanga Parbat when it was said he skied away from his Sherpas, leaving them to die, and his design for the ice axe, which we all used back then. It was Gebirgsjäger standard issue. I have one up there on the wall." He raised his shaky hand to point back over his shoulder to the wall behind him. "They worked well in the hills and, with a few modifications, could be useful in hand-to-hand combat, although a sharpened trenching spade was always better."

He moved the wavering hand to his side to reach for his spectacles, which were resting on a pile of black, leather-bound ledgers on a small table. He put them on with difficulty and then gestured to be given the axe. Passing it across to the outstretched hand, Quinn saw that on his ring finger Braun was wearing a silver ring, the design on it also an edelweiss.

Graf spoke some more to Braun before explaining to Quinn. "I have told him that we want to know if this axe brings back any memories. I said that we think that the '99' on the shaft stands for a regiment, that the 'J. B.' on the other side are initials. Also that the swastika dates it to the Nazi years."

For a while Dieter Braun just held the axe in both hands, slowly rotating the head and looking at it, lost in thought. Then he looked up at the savage mountains that filled his tall window. Outside, it had started to snow, the first hesitant flakes of autumn floating down into the garden.

Braun began to speak again, Graf translating as he went. "The 99th was one of our regiments. I was in the 98th, and with the 100th, the 79th, and the 54th, we made the 1st Gebirgsjäger Division based here in Garmisch. The Americans still occupy our barracks to this day. You passed them on the way here."

Dieter Braun smiled grimly before continuing.

"I joined up when the 1st Division was formed in April 1938. I was twenty years old, a naive city boy who chose the Gebirgs because he wanted to do some skiing. Can you imagine how stupid that felt a few years later?" He shook his head slowly as if answering his own question.

"But the individual regiments were older than that. The 99th had existed since the Great War. It was a proud regiment, Bavarians mostly, tough mountain folk. They had little time for people like me from the city."

He studied the initials "J. B." again by holding the axe shaft almost against the tip of his nose and then pointed the collector to the stack of leather ledgers on the side table, Graf making a comment to Quinn that Braun said he couldn't remember so many names these days, but the ledgers were old regimental rosters that might help.

The collector began to study the first of the books as the old soldier fell silent, content to drink his vodka and look out at the falling snow, the axe lying across his blanketed lap.

After ten minutes of silence, Graf looked up from the second of the ledgers and asked Braun something in German, conversing with no translation until he finally turned to Quinn. "In October 1938, three Gebirgsjäger were court-martialed for Treason against the Reich. Their names were Kurt Müller, Gunter Schirnhoffer, and Josef Becker. They were all Heeresbergführer within the 99th. A Heeresbergführer is an army mountain guide, Neil. Dieter says that although he didn't know them personally, he does remember the scandal. It was a huge disgrace for the entire division. SS troops were assigned to their barracks for a long time after to keep an eye on them all. Evidently the three were working for a smuggling ring based in Munich. Whenever they could get away from the regiment, which was often as they did a lot of mountain training, they moved contraband in and out of Switzerland. They did it by going over the highest, most inaccessible mountain paths in the Alps. He thinks there is a detail of their charges in another of his books."

Braun looked at Quinn and, with a finger, beckoned him to move close. Taking the Englishman's arm, he pointed it weakly to the sheer north face of the mountain that rose dramatically up beyond the sunroom's window and spoke directly to him. Quinn followed his raised hand to consider the treacherous wall of rock himself. Even with his experienced eye he struggled to make out a climbable line.

"Dieter says that now that he thinks about it, he recalls that one of the three was an outstanding climber. Not long after he had joined up, he and the other new recruits were permitted to break from their drill to watch the man climb the face he is pointing you to. He did it totally alone without any ropes or support. He says it was an incredible feat to have witnessed."

"Which of the three was it?"

"I am surprised you need to ask. J. B., of course … Josef Becker."

Looking again at the sheer wall of rock, Quinn said aloud, "That would be a very extreme climb even today," before asking, "What were the three smuggling when they were caught?"

"Oh, they were efficient with their time—they were German, after all. Jewish refugees on the way out; mostly foreign currency, some cigarettes on the way back in."

"What does he think happened to them?"

Graf turned back to Braun, asking the same question in German.

The old man laughed before replying.

"Dieter says whenever the scandal was referred to within the 1st Division, it was always said that the three were sent to put a swastika on the top of Mount Sinai as punishment."

Quinn raised his eyebrows in question.

"It's schadenfreude, Neil Quinn. I thought that was a German concept with which you British were familiar. It was their black joke for the fate of the three."

"Which was really?"

"Either the firing squad at Dachau or the guillotine at Stadelheim Prison for crimes such as theirs. They were never sure which."

Dieter Braun said something more, as if asking Quinn a question, forcing the Englishman to look again to the collector for translation.

"Dieter says it's likely that he'll be seeing them again soon. He wants to know if you would like him to ask which it was."

54

HEILIGGEISTRASSE 67, MUNICH, GERMANY
September 19, 2009
12:00 p.m.

Sarron entered the crowded bar on the narrow Heiliggeistrasse. Pushing his way roughly through its noisy patrons, he quickly picked out Hagen Kassner's hard, lean face projecting above the bar counter. It had been some years since he had last seen him, but the man hadn't changed, still every bit the legionnaire Sarron remembered soldiering with in Africa.

Kassner pointed him to a door at the side of the bar and, taking a bottle of cognac and two glasses from a shelf, followed him through. In the quiet of the private back room, he first saluted and then poured two full glasses of the brandy, passing one to Sarron.

"Vive la mort, vive la guerre, vive le sacré mercenaire," they toasted in unison, downing the contents of the tumblers in one.

While Kassner quickly refilled the two glasses, his face broke into as much of a smile as it ever permitted itself. "Jean-Phillipe. It's been a long time. It was good to get your call. I expected you here earlier," he said, offering Sarron a seat and returning his full glass.

"I took the long way round. I had to avoid Switzerland. Can't risk border controls at the moment." Sarron knew well that he could easily have cut three to four hours from his journey by going through Switzerland, but their border checkpoints were the only ones that now remained in the center of Europe. By slipping south through the Mont Blanc tunnel into Italy and losing himself in that fast flow of traffic that continually pounds eastward past Milan and then up through Austria, he could move between countries without risk of scrutiny but at the expense of a much longer journey.

"My friend, there is no need for explanations here. It is only that I was looking forward to remembering some of our old times together. Later, when the bar is closed perhaps?"

Sarron nodded. "Have the others arrived?"

"Yes, this morning. They were here off a private plane, but they had a meeting arranged with some *Serbische*. Yugo Mafia guys, I think. They said to tell you they were feeling a bit—how did they say it?—'naked' and wanted to sort it out before you arrived. They should be back soon. Wait here for them. Enjoy the brandy. I will send in some food. I need to get back to the bar for now."

"The Englishman?" Sarron asked as Kassner was leaving.

"Nothing so far, although I do have this for you." Kassner stopped and took a folded piece of paper from a back pocket that he passed to Sarron. "It will get you started. I'll send the others in when they return."

"Merci, mon ami," Sarron said, raising his glass to the tall man.

He opened the fold of paper. It was a printout of the home page for Wunderkammer Graf Antiquitäten, the shop of Bernhard Graf. He first noted the address, Theatinerhof 6, Munich, locating it on a street map of the city hung on the wall. It was not so far away from the bar and he had to fight the urge to go there immediately.

Telling himself to slow down on the brandy and wait for the others, Sarron studied the paper's photographs of the type of antiques the shop sold. It was instantly obvious that it was an expensive, if strange, antiques store in the very center of what he knew to be an expensive city.

Maybe Quinn had found something linked to Mallory and Irvine. This Graf he was visiting certainly looked like the kind of person that might be interested in such a story. If so, perhaps it really did have enough value to get Sarron back from the brink. He was going to need to play this slow and get the full details before he could deal with Quinn the way he intended.

* * *

Half an hour later, the parlor door swung open, and Oleg and Dimitri Vishnevsky came into the room.

Sarron was instantly surprised at their appearance. He hadn't seen them since they'd fled Nepal eighteen months earlier. Although they always looked fit and strong, the tall blond twins were no longer the scruffy, disheveled mountain bums he knew but now were immaculately dressed in dark designer clothes and well-cut black leather jackets.

"Where have you two been? Robbing Hugo Boss?" Sarron asked, recalling Kassner's comment.

"No," they said as a pair.

As each took Sarron's outstretched hand to shake it, he noticed the expensive gold watches on their wrists. "You both look well. Richer too. Things must be good."

"When we returned, we found the new Russia more friendly to a couple of deserters than it might once have been," Oleg Vishnevsky replied with a hard smile. As he spoke, his brother dropped a hand-tooled, leather Gucci overnight bag onto the table with a heavy thump.

Unzipping it, Dmitri lifted out a bundle of white cloth from which he unwrapped an Uzi submachine gun. "On loan from our Yugo friends here," he said, passing the weapon to Sarron.

Reaching in again, he produced an AKM rifle with a collapsible stock.

"*Qu'il est beau*," Sarron responded as he rapidly stripped the first gun of its magazine, cocked it, and then let the mechanism strike on the empty chamber with a click.

Oleg Vishnevsky sat down and helped himself nonchalantly to a brandy using Kassner's empty glass. "We are here, Sarron, because you called and because we owe you. You gave us a chance when we were lost, with nothing, and we don't forget something like that in Russia."

He drank from the glass and then passed it to Dmitri, who also took a swig before he said, "And because, despite everything we now have, we sometimes miss the Himalayas."

He raised the glass up as if in a toast to the mountains.

"So what now?" demanded Oleg.

Sarron handed him the piece of paper he had been studying. "I think we should make a start here."

"Okay, let's go."

"Patience, boys. Patience."

SS

BREITENAUER STRASSE 21A, GARMISCH-PARTENKIRCHEN, GERMANY
September 19, 2009
1:00 p.m.

Visibly tiring, the old soldier directed the collector to more books and albums of photographs stored in a stacked bookcase, requesting that he also turn on a tape recorder on one of the shelves. A marching tune began to play, instantly turning the room's clock back to a different time.

"*Es war ein edelweiss, ein kleines edelweiss,*" long-dead mountain troopers sang as Braun, his cup empty once more, began to doze. Fearing the cup would drop from his hand, Quinn put it on the table and then studied the sheer face of the Waxenstein again.

It really is a hell of a climb.

Graf interrupted his contemplation of what it would be like to solo such a wall by passing him a sepia-tinged photograph. "That's a group photo of all the Garmisch Gebirgsjäger's noncommissioned officers being officially reissued Nazi Heeresbergführer badges in the spring of '38. See if you can find Becker in the photograph. There's a magnifying glass in my case. Next to it, you will also find another batch of my own photographs; they show the different German expeditions that went to the Himalayas in the late '30s. See if you can then identify Becker in any of those."

When Quinn opened Graf's attaché case, he was shocked to see a black Luger pistol lying in the main pocket of the case. Carefully taking out the photos and the magnifying glass alongside it, Quinn began to study the lines of Heeresbergführer arranged in the old photograph. It took some time to match the face to the name from the many listed on the mount below but eventually he found it.

Quinn analyzed the details of the young man that bulged out at him through the thick lens. Compared to the others standing alongside him, Josef Becker appeared to have been quite short, slight even. About twenty-seven or twenty-eight, Quinn thought, but possibly younger. He was fine-featured and tanned, his eyes noticeably bright. A shock of light-colored hair pushed from under the peak of his field cap, which was tilted slightly back off his forehead and combined with a faint smile to give him an irreverent, almost humorous look: the look of the typical, happy-go-lucky climber in fact.

Moving on to the Himalayan climbing team photographs, Quinn finally stopped at one labeled, "Schmidt, 1939." There, standing at the end of a row of very amateur-looking climbers assembled in front of a building called the Hotel Nanga Parbat, was the same Josef Becker.

"Yes, he's here with Schmidt's expedition in 1939."

Quinn studied this second image of Becker. He was without either his cap or his smile this time. Stood slightly apart from the others, he looked cold and determined, his face thinner, much older than the year between the two photographs.

"So he went with Schmidt," Graf said. He thought for a moment. "Go back to that original Heeresbergführer photo, find Schirnhoffer and Müller, and see if either of them also made it to Darjeeling with Schmidt's expedition."

It took some studying, but Quinn could only conclude that they hadn't.

"I am thinking that perhaps Becker might have gone to Everest with only that Sherpa you mentioned, just as Maurice Wilson did a few years before," Graf said as he continued to read from a large, black leather–covered folder. "What an impossible task."

"Yes, I know. And it killed Wilson. Becker must have known it would probably kill him."

"But, think about it, Neil. Becker had been caught smuggling Jews. In those days Treason against the Reich meant automatic court martial followed by the death penalty, whoever you were. Normally there would have been no possibility of a reprieve, but maybe someone high up did offer him a deal to climb the mountain instead. As I have said, anything was possible, however horrible it may seem to us today. I have his charge sheet here in this ledger. It lists the family of Jews that Becker was caught smuggling. The youngest, Ilsa Rosenberg, was only seven years old. What a fucking time it was."

Graf's use of the expletive shocked Quinn, who had grown accustomed to the man's considered eloquence. It brought a darkness into the room.

"What would have happened to them?"

"Shot, I imagine. Men, women, children, it wouldn't have mattered. Maybe they were brought down and sent to a camp. The Bone Mill—Mauthausen, the Austrian concentration camp—opened around that time, although I think that one was more for political prisoners. Whatever, their ultimate fate would have been the same. Death. Talking of concentration camps, we should be going. I want you to see the Dachau Memorial Site on the way back to Munich. If that doesn't make you understand what we risk with this matter, nothing will."

The sound of the front door opening set the collector moving quickly to pour a new drop of coffee into Braun's cup, swill it around to mask the vodka, and then hastily return the now two-thirds-empty bottle to his case with the ledger and the Heeresbergführer photo. After, he leaned down behind the old soldier's chair to click his oxygen up a notch.

"It will help him sleep a little better," he said to Quinn, who was looking again out of the room's wide picture window for a final view of the cliff that Becker had climbed. It was rapidly disappearing, the top already lost in the low cloud that was now pushing down into the valley.

Braun's daughter seemed disappointed when Graf told her they couldn't stay longer as they didn't want to be caught by the snow. It was a thin excuse. Her face dropped its guard for a second, revealing to Quinn a hopeless, faintly pleading look. She was trapped in her duty to her father.

It won't be for much longer, Quinn thought as she quietly waved them on their way.

56

THE ZEMU GLACIER, NORTHWEST SIKKIM—15,250 FEET
April 4, 1939
9:45 a.m.

Macfarlane had watched the drama of Schmidt's return to the camp unfold, unsuspecting that the whole thing was as contrived as the Oberammergau Passion Play. The first act, the previous evening, was the arrival of a very exhausted Schmidt alone with the two Sherpas and rambling about the need for a rescue. The second was the subsequent sight of Becker being brought back to the camp in the small hours of the morning on a stretcher.

Even in the dark, Macfarlane could see the bloody foam drooling from the man's mouth and hear his labored breathing interspersed between the spasms of horrendous coughing. The Sherpa Ang Noru said that the German was going to die. The lieutenant knew little about mountain illnesses, but it did seem highly possible so he was somewhat relieved when a message from Schmidt was delivered to the mess tent during breakfast that announced Becker was going to make it as long as he was taken to lower ground as soon as possible.

Now, as he stood in a semicircle with the rest of Schmidt's team, he was observing what was actually the third act—the Sherpas pushing and pulling the seriously ill Becker up onto one of the two small ponies that Ang Noru would lead back down the valley, the other already loaded with their equipment. Their expedition was over. They would return to Darjeeling and then, when Becker was able, he would make his own way back to Germany. The thought that Becker had been so damaged getting Schmidt to the top of a mountain only made Macfarlane detest the fat führer even more.

***

Although shaken up for a few days, the expedition slowly resumed its business and the British officer's interest was turned elsewhere when one of the cook boys, eager for a tip, sought him out to say that the tracks of a "ghost cat" had been sighted further down the glacier. Macfarlane knew from his long reading sessions in the camp that "ghost cat" was the local people's name for the snow leopard. The thought of even seeing one, let alone taking a shot at it, excited him immensely, especially after his earlier disappointments trying to hunt tiger. It would be a fitting finale to his time on the subcontinent.

The lieutenant quickly sought leave from Schmidt to take a couple of the climbing Sherpas to see if he could find it. At first Schmidt seemed a little nervous at the idea, but when the Sherpas explained that it seemed be staying near to the glacier, he acquiesced. They left the next morning, Macfarlane, Sen Bhotia, and Dorge Temba intent on combing the rocky flanks of the glacier's valley with the first objective of finding a small flock of bharal. The blue sheep had been seen with a number of recently born young, the Sherpas saying it was the lambs that would have attracted the snow leopard down from the high hills.

Macfarlane liked the plan because even if they didn't see the snow leopard, he could at least shoot a bharal ram for his trouble. However, the day tracking them proved to be as hard as any he could remember. The two Sherpas were incredibly strong, and he struggled to keep up with them as they searched high and low for the elusive bharal. Only as the sun was setting did they finally spy them grazing on a patch of stunted spring shoots pushing up amidst the blasted rocks at the very snout of the actual glacier.

As it appeared the sheep were going to settle there for the night, Macfarlane and the Sherpas set up a makeshift camp in the boulders above, the Sherpas taking the first watch so that the lieutenant could rest until midnight and recover. After eating a little, Macfarlane could do no more than collapse into his sleeping bag. When a bitter cold pushed into it, waking him just before 11:00 p.m., he saw that a rising full moon was casting a grey light on the hillside, illuminating the tumble of rocks that descended below. The conditions were perfect to view the beast if it appeared, so, even though it was earlier than agreed, Macfarlane got up to join the Sherpas.

Quietly approaching them from behind, he saw

that they were having a hushed but animated conversation about something.

Sen Bhotia was holding up a small silver object, his hand twisting it to catch the moonlight while they both looked at it with an intense concentration.

"What have you got there, boys?" Macfarlane whispered as he silently arrived next to the two Sherpas.

The pair jumped in obvious surprise, Sen Bhotia plunging the object of their attentions into a pocket with such speed that it instantly aroused Macfarlane's curiosity.

"Come on, let me see it," he repeated amiably.

The Sherpa feigned ignorance.

The English officer asked yet again but still Sen Bhotia ignored him forcing Macfarlane to hiss, snow leopard or not, "Give it to me, man. Now!"

Even then Sen Bhotia did so only reluctantly, eyeing Dorge Temba nervously as he handed it over.

In the half-light of the spring moon, Macfarlane first thought it was some form of native talisman. But as he studied it, he saw that it was a fragment of beaten metal.

Turning it over in his hand, he asked the two Sherpas what it was.

They looked at each other but said nothing.

"Tell me right now what this is, or I will write this disobedience up in your chits when we return to Darjeeling," Macfarlane threatened, knowing full well that the chits, the written reports of their performance and behavior on an expedition, were extremely important to them. Just one bad chit could keep a good Sherpa pulling rickshaws for the rest of his days—such was the competition for climbing work in Darjeeling.

At the mere mention, Sen Bhotia began to speak. "We find it when we return to rescue Sahib Becker. Namgel Sherpa speak of it, say that Sahib Becker only live because he killed the bones. They dead now."

Macfarlane was completely at a loss to understand what the Sherpa was hesitantly talking about. He looked at the other man, holding the crushed piece of metal up close to Dorge's face and saying, "Dorge Temba, you tell me what this is. Tell me everything now."

Dorge Temba shied away from the badge's proximity, looking down before replying. "Lieutenant Macfarlane, it is true what Sen Bhotia say, I swear it. It is a mark of death, the bones of dead men. Sahib Becker show it—here on his hat—when he climb peak with Sahib Schmidt. Namgel see it and tell to us."

The Sherpa anxiously tapped his finger against his forehead to show where the object had been placed on Becker's hat.

"Namgel says it make Sahib Becker strong, strong like Sherpa, stronger than any other sahib Namgel ever see in the mountains. But when they come down, they are all slow because of Sahib Schmidt. Namgel say the bones of the dead men attracted mountain demons that caught up with them because they were so slow. They start to eat Sahib Becker's lungs because they are strong, and the demons are jealous, and the demons want to take them. When they stop on the glacier, Namgel says to Sahib Becker, 'Destroy the bones or you die.' When we come back for him, we see he has broken the bones so he can live, but Sen Bhotia takes the broken bones. Sen Bhotia does a bad thing."

Pulling out his lighter, the lieutenant held the "bones" up to its flame. The crumpled, mangled metal glinted as its damaged edges caught the flickering yellow light. Intently studying it, Macfarlane saw that it had indeed once been fashioned as bones, a skull and crossbones; in fact, it reminded him of a cap badge not dissimilar to that worn by the 17th/21st Lancers, one of the most famous British cavalry regiments, even if it lacked the words "Or Glory" that traditionally hung beneath its motif of death.

But Becker is a bloody German anyway, so what would...

The sudden realization that it was a death's-head—an SS soldier's cap badge—splashed adrenaline across the inside of the lieutenant's chest like acid. The shock made him gasp. Clenching the badge into his palm, he frantically began to ask himself what else he had missed, but his questions were immediately interrupted by a hideous squeal.

A cloud of dust exploded up from the rocks below them. From within there was a momentary scramble of twisting and writhing, snarling and bleating, before the bharal flock fled in every direction across the hillside. When the dust settled, Macfarlane could see, in the silver moonlight, a snow leopard crouched at what had been the center of the disturbance. The ghost cat had seized a bharal lamb by the neck.

The three men watched in silence as the leopard's viselike jaws suffocated the short life out of it with little effort, the baby bharal's pathetic kicks and stifled grunts slowly diminishing until the only movement was the end of the snow leopard's long tail flicking rhythmically in anticipation of the coming meal. Only when satisfied that its prey was dead and the taste of its sweet blood was too much to resist any longer, did the beast effortlessly slink off into the darkness, the small lamb hanging like a rag doll, loose and lifeless in its mouth.

Watching the incredible scene below them unfold, Lieutenant Charles Macfarlane never once thought to get his rifle. All he could think of was that if Becker was more snow leopard than mountain goat, then his impeccable military record was in serious jeopardy. He needed to get a message back to Colonel Atkinson as soon as possible.

57

PARKHOTEL KOBLENZ, SCHILLERSTRASSE 5, MUNICH, GERMANY
September 19, 2009
7:55 p.m.

The Mercedes pulled up outside the hotel entrance.

Graf stopped the car, catching Quinn's arm to prevent him from getting out.

"Some things. You need to check out of this hotel. Your French friend will have arrived in Munich by now and if he has the right connections he'll quickly find you in a hotel like this. Nightly guest rosters are easily hacked and I am sure you innocently checked in under your own name and passport. Well, that has to stop now. You need to keep moving, be elusive. Go in, pack everything onto your bike and I will send Dirk by at nine p.m. He drives a black BMW M5. Just follow it to my warehouse and store your bike there. After, he will take you on to my apartment. You will be safer there."

The collector pulled out a small tin from inside his attaché case and handed it to Quinn. "In the meantime, like your good Mr. Crowley, you should probably have this."

Inside the tin was a small black pistol. Quinn quickly closed it and thrust it back at Graf. "I don't need that thing. It looks more like a bloody starter pistol than a weapon anyway."

Graf squeezed Neil's forearm still tighter. "Believe me, Neil Quinn, if you need to use it, you'll soon be running as fast as you can. It's a Mauser WTP. Luftwaffe pilots used to keep them in their flight boots to defend themselves if they were shot down. From what you have told me, you may well need to take it from your boot if Sarron catches up with you."

Saying nothing more, Quinn pocketed the tin with its pistol.

"I need to go to my shop now to catch up with what Dirk has sold today. I'll see you later."

Quinn reached for the ice axe and opened his daypack to put the tin with the gun inside. Before he could get out of the car, Graf handed him the old Leica camera as well, saying, "Don't forget this too. A souvenir of our day together perhaps?"

Taking the camera, Quinn left the car and went into the hotel, crouching from the rain that had replaced the snow on their drive back, cursing to himself that the last thing he wanted to do was go back out in it again on his motorcycle.

* * *

From the window of the crowded Istanbul Café across the street, Dmitri Vishnevsky watched Quinn's return.

Calling his brother Oleg, Sarron immediately took the phone. Hearing that Quinn was back at the hotel and Graf had left, he said, "Good. Stay on him, Dmitri. Just as planned. Does he have the ice axe with him?"

"Yes."

"Okay. Remember, I need Quinn and I need that axe. As soon as we have got the story from the antiques dealer, we will join you and go in later when Quinn is sleeping. We have got to wait, but there's time enough. We'll do one at a time. Just stay on him, Dmitri."

58

WUNDERKAMMER GRAF ANTIQUITÄTEN, THEATINERHOF, MUNICH, GERMANY
September 19, 2009
8:50 p.m.

Sarron watched Dirk Schneider cross the courtyard talking animatedly into his cell phone. Only when certain he was gone did the Frenchman silently emerge from the shadow of the church and follow the arched walls of the square to approach the shop entrance.

Gesturing Oleg Vishnevsky to stay back, he clenched his fist around the door's handle, determined to open it as gently as possible. He must have moved it only a centimeter, but instantly an old-fashioned but very loud bell began to clang like crazy.

The Frenchman could only freeze in the doorway as Vishnevsky slipped back into the shadows of the courtyard.

"Come in, Monsieur. I have been expecting you," a voice said from inside the shop.

As Sarron warily moved in through the door,

Graf stepped forward, pointing his Luger pistol straight at him.

"*Hände hoch*, as they say in all the best war films."

Raising his hands half in the air, palms forward to show they were empty, Sarron edged forward into the shop's unholy menagerie until Graf pointed the short barrel of the weapon to the side, saying, "Take a seat in one of those chairs. From what I have heard, they could have been made especially for you. Would you like a schnapps or do you prefer pastis? We should be civilized, after all. You are, I assume, Jean-Philippe Sarron?"

Sarron didn't reply. He just stared back at Graf as he slowly stepped toward the first of the chairs. He eased down onto it, noticing that the arm holding the pistol over him was beginning to waver slightly in its aim.

It won't be long.

Sarron regulated his breathing and waited in silence.

"Nothing to drink or say? Oh well, so be it," Graf said as he stared at Sarron. "I must say that my first impression of you is rather disappointing. I had a clear premonition while I took a walk around Dachau this afternoon that you were going to be my nemesis, but perhaps it is not to—"

A tapping on the glass of the shop door interrupted Graf, who instinctively turned to the source of the noise.

There was a moment's silence before the door exploded open in a blast of glass fragments, its old bell flying deep into the shop.

Instantly, Sarron lunged for the distracted man,

slapping the pistol from his weak grip and jumping onto him.

Locked together, they crashed back against a tall glass display case. It shattered under their combined impact, a long shard of glass skewering Graf's upper arm before they both fell back to the floor. The collector passed out from the shock, blood pooling under him.

Sarron quickly pulled himself free as Oleg Vishnevsky stood above, pointing the Serbians' AKM down at the unconscious man. "Put the gun away, Oleg. We won't need it now," Sarron ordered, checking Graf's neck for a pulse. "Turn off the main lights and find something to tie him with. We'll take him into the back of the shop and put a tourniquet on his arm. I need him alive."

The Russian went to work cutting some lengths of electrical flex with a long ceremonial SS dagger that had fallen from the broken display case, while Sarron pulled one of the two heavy metal chairs to the very rear of the store with a screech of its bare metal feet.

Holding the knife and the lengths of cable in one hand, Vishnevsky then dragged the still-unconscious, bleeding Graf along the floor after Sarron. After lifting him up into the metal chair, he bound Graf's hands to it and twisted another length of flex high around his upper arm in an attempt to slow the bleeding from the wound.

With the collector where he wanted him, Oleg ripped a moth-eaten battle flag from the wall and, bunching its fabric in his hand, took hold of the shard of protruding glass and pulled it from Graf's arm as fast as he could. Dropping the fragment, he forced the flag's red, white, and black material into the wound instead before binding it with more flex.

The searing pain of the glass blade's removal shocked Graf back to consciousness. He groggily angled his gaze up at Oleg Vishnevsky, whose cell phone began to ring.

Vishnevsky answered it, conversing rapidly in Russian.

"*Russisch*. Of course," Graf said faintly to himself, as Oleg passed the phone to Sarron, saying, "Quinn is on the move."

Sarron listened intently and shouted, "Well fucking well follow them! There's nothing we can do now, we're busy."

Passing the phone back and seeing the collector was conscious again, Sarron stepped forward to put his face close to Graf's ear.

"Listen to me, Graf. I don't want to kill you. You're not worth the trouble. I just want you to tell me about the ice axe. I know it has value. Tell me why."

The collector, missing his spectacles and with a thin dribble of blood running from the corner of his mouth, turned his head to stare back at Sarron and said, "The biggest wound you inflict on me is that you deem me not worth the trouble."

"What? Look, old man, you need to be smart about this. You are going to tell me whether you want to or not and if you make me extract the information, I warn you, it will not be pleasant."

Graf looked again at the Russian. "This beauty undoubtedly has the capability to make me tell you what you need to know, but I should warn you: I have the capability—the need, in fact—to necessitate that you kill me in the process."

"Shut up with your nonsense, Graf. You're wasting my fucking time!" Sarron screamed, slapping the collector so hard across his face that it twisted to hit the metal back of the chair. The old firing mechanism of a rifle dug into Graf's cheek, lifting a flap of skin that quickly released a stream of crimson down the collector's face.

"It is not in my nature to shut up with my nonsense," Graf weakly slurred, straightening his head back to look again at Sarron.

Spitting blood from his mouth, Graf appeared to savor its taste before speaking again, this time with a greater strength.

"By dwelling within the macabre, surrounding myself with it, embracing its artifacts, its twisted people, its inherent evil, I often wondered if all along I wasn't really just courting a gruesome fate. Perhaps simply seeking to put myself on an equal footing with the rest of my family for when I meet them in the next world. It would save the embarrassed silences and inevitable recriminations as we caught up on what I had been doing for the last sixty-five years, don't you think?"

"I don't think anything, you fool. Just tell me about the ice axe."

Oleg Vishnevsky pushed past Sarron to grab Graf by the throat, pushing the point of the SS dagger against his chest.

"You will tell us everything, old man, or I will cut out your heart."

"Then you should treasure it, Ivan, because, to my immense inconvenience, it's always been a good one."

59

LANDSBERGER STRASSE, MUNICH, GERMANY
September 19, 2009
9:10 p.m.

Quinn was thrashing the old motorcycle to keep up with the new BMW sedan, the wild ride beginning to unnerve him. Raindrops and spray from the speeding car's tires lashed the scratched visor of his crash helmet, causing it to refract the city lights into blinding yellow stars. Every time they sped across tramlines set into the street, the bike's front wheel slid on their greasy metal, threatening to spit him off. Other traffic was following too close behind: if Quinn did fall it would just go straight over him. With a shudder, he remembered how Pemba had been killed.

When the BMW's left indicator began to flash bright amber and they turned into a side street, Quinn hoped it signaled their arrival at Graf's storage unit. Following the car, he watched it stop in front of a metal roller door and flash its main beams twice. Schneider quickly got out, and, hunched against the rain, unlocked a side door to disappear inside. A metal roller door wound itself up enough to permit Quinn to ride the motorcycle straight inside, its headlight briefly revealing an array of stacked and covered furniture before he hit the kill switch.

Getting off the bike and arranging it on its center stand, Quinn moved to start taking off his bags.

"You won't be needing any of that," Schneider said as three other men stepped into the storage area from the street outside. "Just step away from the motorcycle and get into the back of the car."

"What?"

"You heard exactly what I said, Quinn. Do it now."

Quinn looked at the men closing in on him, taking in the black bomber jackets, the faded jeans and high-laced boots beneath, the shaved heads, and most of all, the clubs two of them were carrying. Ducking his head, still clad in its white crash helmet, he tried to plunge through them to the street only to be floored with multiple blows across his helmet and back. Hands seized him, pushing him down as they tore off the helmet and dragged him relentlessly out to the car. Forcing him into the backseat, Quinn was sandwiched by a skinhead on each side.

When Schneider got into the driver's seat, he had Quinn's ice axe, taken from the kit bag strapped to the motorcycle. He passed it to the third man getting into the front passenger seat.

Quinn tried to struggle only to be elbowed hard in the face by the thug on his left. The contact set his head reeling, his eyes flashing white against the wet darkness.

"Stop, Quinn," Schneider said. "You're not getting out."

"What the fuck?" Quinn slurred in reply.

"Quinn, I know that you and Graf are working on something to do with this old ice axe and he is mistaken if he thinks he can keep it for himself. He thinks he's so rich and clever, that he can buy me, but my loyalties are with Stefan Vollmer now. This is his time, a new beginning for the true German to kick out the immigrants that stink up our streets, to have a currency that is our own, to rebuild the army we are denied …"

Schneider continued to rant as the car raced west from the center of Munich. Heading into the outskirts, it sped past monotonous housing projects and massive illuminated warehouse buildings to pull into a crowded parking lot. Groups of people were emerging from the lines of parked cars to walk toward the shadowy hulk of a building at their center. In the dark it looked like a bunker, flat and low, but as Quinn was strong-armed from the car toward it the headlights of other arriving cars revealed a dilapidated framework that projected above the roof to read, "Saturday Night Fever." It must have once been some sort of nightclub or disco. Nearing the main entrance where there was a queue to get inside, Quinn saw a smaller, newer red neon sign that shone, "Das Weisshaus." The *s*'s were shaped as lightning bolts, the two in the middle repeatedly flicking to white to flash "SS." The blinking lights showed that those waiting to enter were also predominantly skinheads.

Quinn was hustled in through a side entrance, Schneider going on ahead with the old ice axe in one hand to disappear into the depths of the building while Quinn was stopped by the three others from the car and told to wait. Inside, the house PA was obscenely loud. A deep guttural voice distorted over a sonic feedback of thrashing guitars and pounding drums so deafening that something popped within Quinn's right ear. He could hear it whistling when the drilling music stopped, but the quiet only lasted a second as a huge roar erupted from a crowded dance floor. The cheer quickly mutated into a repetitive chant of "Oi! Oi! Oi!" as two hundred right arms began to drive from chests to the ceiling in a uniform Nazi salute. In their center, a large swastika flag rose up on a long, flexible pole. As it began to wave from side to side, the chant changed to "Sieg heil! Sieg heil! Sieg heil!" until the thrashing guitars and beating drums broke into another crazed anthem and the seething mass began to pogo again.

Quinn took in the building around him. It was a huge, matte-black barn that stank of stale beer, body odor, and leather. Condensation was falling in large drops from the ceiling as if the very structure itself was sweating. On the far wall, a film of total war was playing. He stared across the bouncing, crazed crowd at the grainy, black-and-white images being projected. Stuka bombers hung momentarily in the air before diving down vertically to drop bombs like defecating birds. Tiger tanks rolled past burning farmhouses and dead livestock. Lines of thin prisoners were shot in the back of the head to fold forward into deep pits already lined with dead bodies.

When the portrait of a blond SS officer filled the wall, it set off another cheer from the crowd; more followed in rapid sequence. Some were studio shots, perfect blond haircuts and tight, humorless smiles staring back from above that infamous black uniform. Others had been taken in combat. Dirt-streaked, battle-weary faces now set above mottled, almost modern-looking camouflage jackets. The one constant throughout was the death's-head insignia, the skull and crossbones of the SS leering back from every picture.

The images began to be accompanied by the shout of a name on the house PA that set off more shouts and straight-arm salutes from the crowd.

"Kurt 'Panzer' Meyer!"

"*Sieg heil!*"

"Sepp Dietrich!"

"*Sieg heil!*"

"Michael Wittman!"

"*Sieg heil!*"

The SS roll call went on and on until a number of pictures of the same man began to overlap. The first showed a young officer in a ceremonial uniform, another next to Heinrich Himmler studying a map, a third receiving an Iron Cross from Adolf Hitler.

The pictures of the man multiplied all over the wall as the officer's name was drawn out in a long raucous scream.

"JURGEN PFEIFFER!"

The name was met with the biggest cheer of all.

"*SIEG HEIL!*"

Quinn looked on as yet another photo of Pfeiffer appeared. He was standing in a court, wearing simple fatigues shorn of any insignia. A large number "42" on a white card was hanging around his neck.

The picture grew ever larger until it covered all the others. It incensed the crowd, driving it wild, until the image began to burn from the center to reveal more film of flaming villages and racing Panzer tanks, and the music launched into another thrashing song dedicated to the SS officer. "Jurgen Pfeiffer! Jurgen Pfeiffer! Jurgen Pfeiffer!" the chorus screamed, the crowd picking up the new chant and starting to bounce maniacally once more.

A push in Quinn's back signaled him to move. With more shoves, he was directed to a private room beyond the bar. When its heavy door was shut behind him, a quiet fell, pierced only by a residual squealing in Quinn's ear. The walls of the room around him were decorated with old Nazi propaganda posters set in heavy metal frames and triangular black flags that each displayed a different white rune of an SS regiment. A man in his midthirties in a black suit with a white open-collar shirt sat at a table in its middle with Schneider to the side of him. The old ice axe was lying on the table to their front. The lean-faced man looked up at Quinn.

"Hello, Mr. Quinn, my name is Max Schalb and I work for Stefan Vollmer. I understand from Dirk here that you know something about this old ice axe that might interest my boss. Take a seat."

Quinn said nothing in reply, staying standing.

Schneider, agitated by Quinn's silence, spoke. "Come on, Quinn. I know from the Internet work I have done for Graf that this Nazi axe is, in some way, linked to Mount Everest, that you found it there. Tell us what you know about it."

Quinn ignored Schneider to say directly to Schalb, "Look, it's just an old axe, whatever this weasel might have told you. There is absolutely nothing more to it for you or your boss, whoever the hell he is."

"Tough guy, huh? Dirk, perhaps a little dance might warm him up, then we'll try again."

Schneider got up from the table and motioned to the two skinheads standing at the door to take Quinn from the room. Seizing his arms, they pulled him out and to the edge of the heaving dance floor. There, for a second, Quinn was able to pull back and stop himself. As he did so, he could have sworn that the lights dimmed slightly, and the volume of the thrashing music increased.

A flickering image of a burning building crumbling as German storm troopers ran for cover filled the far wall as a boot rammed into the small of his back. The kick flung him into the slam-dancing mass. Hateful, grimacing faces began to scream and spit at him. He caught snatches of shouts, fragments of words and sentences in harsh German as he began to be spun around by grabbing hands pulling him still further into the crowd.

"Du hurensohn!"
"Schwuchtel!"
"Jude!"

A straight-arm punch hit Quinn hard in the side of the head. Others immediately followed to send him reeling to the floor where a kick hit him full in the stomach. It winded him totally.

Quinn couldn't compress his chest. He couldn't even choke, his lungs and diaphragm paralyzed. Panic flooded his brain as he lay on the floor. Above him, in the black of the ceiling void, a huge disco mirror-ball hung motionless.

Finally able to draw a breath, anticipating more stamping and kicking, Quinn curled himself into a ball, pulling his legs up into his groin, hugging his ankles with his hands.

But the new onslaught never came.

Everything stopped—the music, the shouting, the screaming—everything.

The house lights went on and the crowd, pulled back, leaving Quinn lying at its center. Twisting his bleeding face upward, he squinted into the unfamiliar light to see two figures push out from the crowd. It was Max Schalb, with Schneider standing a little behind him, holding the ice axe.

Schalb stepped further forward until he alone was standing over Quinn. Making a tutting noise as he shook his head, he held up a hand in signal to the crowd to remain silent. When he had their complete compliance, he lowered his arm and started to slowly take off his suit jacket. He carefully folded it lengthways and handed it back to Schneider. Schalb then undid his silver cufflinks and unbuttoned his crisp white shirt before taking that off also. Beneath was a tight, long-sleeved white T-shirt that he pulled up and over his head to reveal a pale yet intensely muscular torso completely covered in tattoos, an intricate pattern of Germanic script, SS runes, the numbers "18" and "88," and, over his heart, a single black swastika.

At the sight of the tattoos, the crowd began chanting and shouting until the man quieted them once more with another wave of his hand. He exchanged the shirts with Schneider for the ice axe as he motioned others to pick Quinn up.

Strong hands wrenched Quinn from his ball, pulling his hands from his legs and tugging him onto his feet. When he was upright, the tattooed Schalb feinted a head-butt into his face, stopping a few centimeters before he made contact. Quinn instinctively flinched back and when he moved his head forward again it met the man's face close in to his.

"Still not ready to talk to me?" Schalb asked, his lips almost touching Quinn's bruised and bleeding face. "Well, you will be soon."

The man stepped back to address the crowd in a tirade of German, constantly turning to direct his words equally to everyone around him, raising the axe into the air like a sword to reinforce what he was saying. The crowd cheered in response, edging in ever nearer as if readying to rip Quinn to pieces.

Schalb continued to goad them, whipping them into even greater frenzy until gesturing for silence once more. When he had it, he stepped toward Quinn again, the wooden shaft of the axe still above his head, leaving no doubt that, this time, he was going to hit him.

The man brought the wooden shaft down onto the side of Quinn's neck as if trying to cleave his head from his shoulders.

Just before it impacted, Quinn closed his eyes and, in desperation, squeezed the trigger of the small pistol he had concealed in his right hand.

At the same instant, Dmitri Vishnevsky, who had been watching everything from near the main entrance, unloaded the magazine of his Uzi into the ceiling, aiming for the old mirror-ball hanging from its center.

The heavy blow snapped Quinn's head back.

His body followed it, released from the grip of captors startled by the violent burst of machine-gun fire showering plaster and broken glass onto the crowd.

The tiny automatic fired three times as he fell backward.

The first bullet projected sideways into the leg of an onlooker.

The second grooved Dirk Schneider's neck, severing the carotid artery.

The third bullet disappeared into a ceiling now sparking and smoking with exploding lights.

Hitting the floor, the back of Quinn's head smashed against the concrete and the little pistol spun from his hand just as the mirror-ball fell, exploding like a nail bomb when it met the floor.

There was total panic and mayhem. People scattered wildly, ducking for cover or trying to escape. Amidst them, Schneider spun and spun, gagging and clutching at his throat as it sprayed a jet of arterial blood.

Quinn made a weak effort to get up and away. He felt someone grab at him with one hand and try to pull him through the crowd but, broken from the kicking and still senseless from the blow of the axe, he was a dead weight. He heard the man shout something at him in a language he didn't recognize and then let go.

Quinn tried to get up again only for Schalb, slick with Schneider's arterial blood, to slam himself onto him. Pinning him to the ground with his wet tattooed body, the German screamed instructions until help came to pull Quinn back onto his feet once more.

Without ceremony this time, the axe forgotten in the confusion of the gunfire, Schalb immediately drove a fist into Quinn's stomach.

The punch doubled the Englishman over, breathless again, as the other men holding him began dragging Quinn to the side of the club through the screaming, panicking crowd.

Double doors sprang wide open, and the cold night air rushed in. Through swelling eyes, Quinn made out the rear of a Mercedes panel van reversing toward the open doorway, grey fumes billowing from the tailpipe as the engine revved frantically. When the van was nearly touching the building, its wheels skidded to a halt, spitting gravel into the club like bullets.

The van's rear doors split and opened. Quinn began to struggle desperately at the sight of the two men inside tugging black ski masks down over their faces. They moved forward to pull him in, Max Schalb following and closing the doors behind them.

The vehicle began to speed away, a burst of machine-gun fire from the club chasing it.

60

TSANG PROVINCE, TIBET
April 11, 1939
11:45 a.m

Squinting his eyes against the harsh sunlight, Josef began to pick out the sharp point of the fortress of Kampa Dzong in the far distance, the castle rising up on its own narrow crag, dominant and dangerous in that otherwise empty, silently hostile land. At Wewelsburg, Josef had told himself that Tibet would be a land of snow and ice but what he encountered on the long descent from the Sepu-La was very different. The snow of the high pass quickly vanished, and the country that stretched out below soon became an ochre desert of blasted rock and gravel, dust and mud.

Tramping ever further into it, Josef knew why he had conjured something softer and more hospitable in his mind's eye. It had been easy, comforting even, in the fearful uncertainty of Himmler's castle to conjure Tibet as a mountain land permanently in the thrall of Christmas, a place of pine branches bending beneath balanced slices of new snow, of long, sparkling icicles, of brooks covered with sheets of clear ice that trapped air bubbles, a place where he, as a mountain man, would be at home. But it proved to be just one more deceit. The arid, barren plain they followed offered none of those things.

With every heavy step a desperate loneliness grew in Josef as he and Ang Noru forced themselves ever onward under the pale blue sky, constantly fighting against a bitter northwest wind that robbed the land's harsh brightness of any heat, feet being pummeled by the rocks and rubble of the faint pathway marked occasionally by small towers of rocks or the bleached bones of long dead yaks or mules. Ang Noru worked tirelessly, as did their two ponies, but none of them offered much companionship. When they had first set off together from the Zemu, Josef had tried to converse with him more as a friend but soon gave up when the Sherpa showed little inclination to do the same. He suspected that Ang Noru didn't really trust him. Josef didn't seek to change the situation. It was enough to focus on the demands of their brutal trek, to follow the way that Ang Noru sullenly indicated, to wonder why the hell he sometimes struggled to keep up with a man who had lost all his toes to frostbite …

Nearer the fort, Josef began to make out far beneath, a low, flat village kneeled on the valley floor as if in subservience. Josef wished they could avoid them both but knew that would not be possible. They had to stop there. Increasingly nervous at the prospect, he repeatedly told Ang Noru that they must be careful. The Sherpa nodded in serious agreement, adding only that such places were full of eyes and ears, all eager to earn favor with the dzong pen.

Josef already knew something of the overlord of the region. When he had studied the route with Fischer in Darjeeling, the German had identified it as the only place where they might be able to get new supplies in Tibet. He had gone on to explain that its *dzong pen* ruled both the town and the desiccated region with a harsh feudal order that squeezed everything it could into his coffers. Fischer had been grave in his warning that if caught by the overlord then there would be nothing anyone could do. Their only hope, he had said coldly, would be that the dzong pen would probably value selling Josef to the English higher than the entertainment of beheading him.

Uncharacteristically, as they approached the town, Ang Noru began to talk some more. He recalled how the British expedition with which he traveled to Everest six years before had feted the dzong pen with gifts, as was customary to buy the man's favor and hospitality when they passed through his land. Delighted, the lord had responded the first night with a feast of rice, blood sausages, and freshly roasted mutton.

But, of course, it had only been for the English sahibs. The smell had made the Sherpas' mouths water while they guarded the supplies outside in the fort's courtyard. Ang Noru even smiled when he recounted how, in revenge for this torture, the Sherpa had angrily concocted a plan to tell the sahibs that they had eaten all their *tsampa* and that bad crops in the region were making purchasing unexpectedly more expensive. The morning after the banquet they had demanded an additional cash advance of four rupees a man to make up the difference and ensure they had enough food to be fit and strong to carry on to the mountain.

The sahibs, fearing anything that might hinder their progress to its top, had fallen for the story completely and the Sherpas had spent their ill-gotten windfall on *chang* and *rakshi,* the local beer and firewater, the very next night. "Big party with many chang girls, we make. Even bigger headache next day," the Sherpa said, his eyes gleaming at the memory. "Sahibs very cross with us blokes. Long silence on walking days after," he added, laughing at the irritation they must have caused.

It was the first time that Josef had heard Ang Noru really laugh. It showed a warmer, friendlier side to the normally distant, angry man who accompanied him. It hinted at what else had been taken from him when they cut off his toes. Josef was reluctant to stop Ang Noru's rare amusement, but, recalling Fischer's words of warning once again, he took the Sherpa's arm, stopping him to look directly in his eyes. "Ang Noru, no chang this time. Very dangerous. Do you understand?" There was no reply.

* * *

Well before the outskirts of the town, they separated, Ang Noru leaving Josef to wait with their two loaded ponies while he found a lodging for the night. Attracted by a cairn of rocks at the foot of the hill of scree that led up to the steep cliff wall below the fort, Josef hobbled their ponies so they couldn't wander and went to investigate.

Reaching the neatly stacked pile of yellow and ochre rocks that reminded him of a beehive, Josef saw set into the side a stone plaque. Expecting another Buddhist text or design, he was surprised to see it was carved with letters and words he could read.

A. M. K.

5 June 1921

Om Mani Padme Hum

It was a gravestone for a European that must have been engraved by one of his countrymen. Staring at the memorial, Josef tried to place the initials and the date from his studies of Everest at Wewelsburg, but, beyond understanding that the death must have happened during the very first British expedition to the mountain, he failed. The words engraved beneath the date were also lost on him, but as Josef repeatedly shaped the letters with his lips, he recognized the sounds as a phrase that Ang Noru often repeated over and over to himself as he walked.

"*Om Mani Padme Hum.*"

He said the words to himself, training his own mouth to utter the phrase. Quickly losing himself in its rhythmic sound, Josef repeated it over and over like the Sherpa. It relaxed him as he quietly contemplated the gravestone. The mantra and the memorial pushed him back to Gunter and Kurt, to the nine Jews, to little Ilsa—all dead, their passing unmarked. It made him worry for the lives he still held in his hands, his mother, his sisters, the beautiful Magda. They could not be allowed to go in the same way.

I have to get to the mountain.

A faint grumbling noise interrupted his reverie.

It grew into a growl, rising in intensity, occasionally checking itself before continuing, each time becoming louder and stronger.

The source revealed itself; a huge black and tan mastiff dog rose up menacingly from the dirt beyond the stone cairn.

The beast, thick fur matted with solid clumps of filth, was covered in dust. Its yellow eyes fixed on Josef with a mean hatred, its mouth curling up at the sides to reveal two rows of heavy teeth set within pink-and-black-streaked jaws, strong enough to crack yak bone.

The dog shook its shoulders and then, swaying its heavy head a little from side to side, hunched forward, preparing to lunge. In return, Josef could only slowly pull his ice axe from his pack and hold the pointed tip of its shaft out in front of him as he began to very deliberately step back.

Seeing him make a move, the mastiff sprang.

Josef stuck out the end of the axe to fend the creature away, but the dog angled its head as it leapt, seizing the wooden shaft of the axe in its teeth.

With a muscular twist of its neck and a tug, the mastiff easily pulled the long axe from Josef's grip. Furious, it shook it violently between its jaws, instinctively seeking to snap its spinal cord.

Only when satisfied that the axe was dead, did the dog drop it and move toward Josef again.

Its body lowered once more.

Josef turned to run.

The dog jumped a second time.

As it flew into the air, a small rock hit the dog in the side of the head with a resounding crack.

A bigger stone followed, thumping into its ribs.

The two well-aimed stones diverted the dog in midleap, sending it crashing into the dirt in an explosion of dust. Knocked senseless by the blows, the mastiff staggered back up onto its feet and shook itself, groggily seeking its target once more.

A second barrage of stones instantly struck it, their bruising accuracy leaving the dog no alternative but to turn tail and run.

Breathing heavily, his heart racing, Josef watched Ang Noru shout at the retreating dog and hurl yet another large stone after it. Beside him was a small boy of about six or seven dressed in little more than grimy, torn yet thickly padded rags. The twisted leather thong of a sling was hanging from the lad's small right hand, another stone already suspended in its cradle.

The boy's perfectly round, dirt-stained face creased into a huge smile, and his eyes closed to become little more than slits as he expertly spun the sling three times above his head and then sent its rock, bullet quick, into the dog's fast disappearing backside.

Josef could only stutter, "*Danke schön*," to the grinning pair as Ang Noru picked up Josef's chewed ice axe and handed it to him.

"You must have a care for Tibetan dogs, Sahib Josef. If not, you as dead as old Sahib Kellas there," the Sherpa said, pointing to the cairn of stones. "Yak herder dogs more dangerous even than chang! Let us go now. We stay at the house of young Phurbu here; his mother once most famous chang girl in all Kampa Dzong. So good she own her own hostel now."

Watching the unlikely pair saunter off to retrieve the two ponies, Josef heard Ang Noru say, "Phurbu, good boy, son of Sherpa, I think, perhaps," as he tussled the child's mop of jet-black hair.

61

KAMPA DZONG, TSANG PROVINCE, TIBET
April 11, 1939
9:45 p.m.

The atmosphere in the crowded caravansary was charged with noise and heat and excitement. Pungent smells of filthy clothes, unwashed bodies, and animal dung mixed with sweeter fumes of food, tobacco, incense, and a huge juniper log fire to clog the thin air of the long communal room. Josef, just sitting on a bench against one wall, was finding it hard to breathe but he was enjoying the enveloping warmth from the fire and the feeling of satisfaction of having eaten a hot, rich meal.

Josef knew well that they should be hiding in the tiny room they had been shown to by little Phurbu's mother, but Ang Noru had insisted that, for once, they eat properly, in some warmth, arguing that there would be so many people in the main hall that no one would even notice them. It was a thin argument, but in the chilly, claustrophobic room, still shaken by his encounter with the dog, Josef had found it impossible to refuse. He was as exhausted by loneliness as he was by the arduous journey with the surly Sherpa.

The hostel's hall was indeed full. Half of the people in the room were Tibetan: tall, wild-looking men with hooded eyes and long, jet-black hair strung with heavy plaits of red wool, their fierce oval faces in no way softened by the small lumps of turquoise and coral that hung from makeshift earrings and necklaces. They were all drinking, intent on a noisy betting game at their center. Each had a long knife tucked into his belt, almost small swords with broad scabbards of turned metal inlaid with colored stones. Josef recalled Fischer's warning that the Tibetan always carried two knives: one bold and visible in front to draw your eye as he embraced you with open arms, the other hidden, smaller and sharper, with which he would stab you in the back. Interspersed with the Tibetans were smaller men—hardy Sikkimese muleteers; skinny, malnourished Lepcha porters; plumper, moonfaced Asian traders; even shaven-headed monks in saffron and magenta robes. All of them were watching the Tibetans with quick, darting eyes, mouths full of bad teeth and the taste of easy money from the game at their center.

Josef had to acknowledge that Ang Noru was right. That game was the only thing attracting any attention. Each and every play inspired a crescendo of shouting and waving, until a silence fell and one of the players indulged in a highly theatrical shaking and casting of a handful of bones across a sturdy table. The pronged segments of the backbone of what was once a small animal would skitter and dance before coming to rest in configurations that were immediately clear in their implications to everyone except Josef. The shouting would instantly resume, accompanied by a frenzied redistribution of money. Ang Noru had found his way into the middle of it all, a grin on his face and a growing wad of dirty paper money in his hand.

The exhausted German took a swig from his wooden bowl of chang as he observed the scene. The thin, watery barley beer was not unpleasant to the taste even if it made him yearn for a stronger, smoother Bavarian *weissbier*. He had been surprised at the weakness of the chang, finding it difficult to deny Ang Noru after the Sherpa had told him to taste it and see for himself how harmless it was. He knew that it was probably time to reel the Sherpa in, but once again recalling his deliverance from the dog and enjoying the rare feelings of warmth and good food, Josef decided he would let him play a little longer.

* * *

Every time Josef's chang bowl was near to empty, a young Tibetan woman would refill it before he could say no. When the girl poured the chang, she did so slowly, deliberately brushing his arms with hers and looking into his eyes, holding his gaze through long eyelashes. With a broad, brown face and doelike eyes, she was old enough to be a woman yet young enough to still have perfect, clear skin beneath her glossy, tied-back hair. Once his cup was full again, she would linger over Josef until he drank, or rude shouts demanded her attentions elsewhere.

When she moved away, Josef could see at the head

of the room the proprietor, little Phurbu's mother, surveying the scene and directing her chang girls here and there, pointing them to pay particular attention to various people in the room. She was continually gesturing the same girl to return to him. The more he drank, the more Josef forgot his worries about being there, about Ang Noru, about the chang. He even stopped thinking about getting up, leaning back instead against the wall and letting himself relax as the beer kept flowing, the Tibetan girl kept fluttering her dark lashes, and the game got louder and louder.

Occasionally he caught a glimpse of the boy Phurbu, the little tyke weaving between the legs of his mother's patrons, quick, picky fingers reaching up into pockets and purses above, alert to every opportunity. It was amusing to watch him at work. Seeing a bamboo cage placed for safekeeping alongside a number of other bundles, the beady face of an unrecognizable small creature peering out, the boy crouched in front of it and began prodding at it with a thin black and white stick.

A loud bell rang.

It snapped Josef from his soft contemplation of the room around him to see that it was Phurbu's mother ringing it. Immediately the girls began urging everyone to drink up, hurrying to collect the wooden bowls.

It must be time.

Josef was relieved that the evening had passed so peacefully. Standing to leave, he was surprised to find that the floor swayed a little before settling. Chang was stronger than it tasted. Shrugging the realization aside, Josef leaned into the crowd of gamblers and tugged Ang Noru by the arm, gesturing they should go.

The Sherpa wasn't having any of it. When Josef insisted, hissing at him that the chang was finished, he was met with the immediate response that it was only because the rakshi was arriving.

Even as Ang Noru spoke, Josef saw indeed that the girls were now handing out smaller clay bowls and theatrically filling them from high above with a stream of clear liquid poured from narrower, taller bamboo jugs.

The gambling Tibetans cheered with approval. The instant their new bowls were full, they each stuck a finger in and flicked some of the spirit into the air three times before proceeding to drain the contents in single gulping draughts. They immediately called for more and repeated the action.

Josef felt a wave of panic ripple down his spine. He had to get Ang Noru out of there. Intent on keeping the Sherpa from the rakshi, he pushed deeper into the gamblers, but the more he strained to reach the Sherpa, the more he had the sensation that he was being held back from him. Pairs of hands were clutching his arms and pulling him away.

Ignoring his protests and laughing at his attempts to escape them, Phurbu's mother and the chang girl tugged Josef back to the place where he had been sitting. Putting her finger on Josef's lips, Phurbu's mother quietly silenced him while the girl gave him his own full bowl of rakshi. She too then murmured something to him, putting down her jug and leaning forward to dig her nails into his thighs until he started drinking.

Even though he knew it was a mistake, Josef drank it down, telling himself just one and then he and the Sherpa were out of there.

The rakshi hit Josef straight between the eyes.

The buzz from the chang instantly became a howl.

People merged and melted, their actions slowing to become unrelated snapshots with faintly anticipated yet seemingly unimportant consequences.

The girl leaned her mouth close to Josef's and whispered something he didn't understand.

Her lips brushed his.

Magda.

Magda's face appeared before his.

She was smiling and laughing.

He had to leave, but the rakshi—or was it Magda—was telling him it was all right to stay.

Stay, Josef. Stay.

Wild shouting, singing, and dancing were erupting from every corner of the smoky, half-lit room.

He looked again for Ang Noru.

There he was, still taking part in the game.

Only he and the biggest Tibetan were actually playing. The frenzied crowd surrounding them had taken the side of one or the other, waving their money behind either man in proof of their allegiance. Those behind Ang Noru were shouting, "Chomolungma! Chomolungma! Chomolungma!" over and over, clapping their hands in time to urge their champion on.

Through the warping blur of the rakshi, Josef slowly told himself that they were shouting the Tibetan name for Mount Everest. He thought that wasn't such a good thing.

The Tibetan girl came back and, putting down her jug of rakshi, straddled Josef's lap and leaned in on him with both of her hands around his neck. She started to massage his aching neck, stiff from carrying his heavy pack so far; it felt good. She began to tease his cheeks with the tip of her soft, wet tongue, her breath scalding his already burning face. She smelled like bonfire smoke. When she moved down to start biting his neck, Josef told himself that it wasn't Magda. He knew that wasn't good either.

Josef looked down at the ground in a last attempt to resist the alcohol, to avoid the advances of the girl, only to see that little Phurbu was opening the cage he had discovered. He was absolutely sure that the large spiny porcupine the boy was releasing into the room was going to be the worst thing of all.

From somewhere distant and remote, Josef registered that the big Tibetan and his supporters took Ang Noru's final victory in the game as badly as the porcupine, which someone stepped on at the exact moment the backbone segments settled to reveal that the Tibetan's half of the room had lost all its money.

With a roar, the Tibetan lunged across the table for Ang Noru's throat.

With a piercing squeal, the porcupine lunged its long, black and white quills at the legs of everyone else.

The room ignited as surely as if it had been doused with gasoline and a match thrown into the center.

In the midst of the screaming, brawling mass, the big Tibetan pulled both his knives on Ang Noru.

Josef stood to help the Sherpa but the room was spinning so violently he could barely stand. He thought he was going to be sick.

A man with a dagger in his guts staggered into him, knocking him to the floor.

Josef got to his knees, only to be flattened again by another falling body.

He was sick.

When he raised his head again a small hand caught his and tugged.

Josef crawled after little Phurbu out of the door.

PART III

IN THE DEATH ZONE
IN DER TODESZONE

62

THE WEISSHAUS CLUB, ALLACH CARGO PARK, MUNICH, GERMANY
September 19, 2009
11:47 p.m.

Police Inspector Martin Emmerich was intelligent. Could have been a lawyer or a doctor; should have been, his parents still said. That wet night in the dark of the Weisshaus parking lot, Emmerich almost wished he had listened. A soft, comfortable office or consulting room seemed eminently preferable to the rattle of the rain on an unmarked police Audi growing chillier by the minute. But yet, as he peered out at the grey, scabrous outline of the building holding his attention, he knew that it couldn't be any other way. He was exactly where he was meant to be.

Emmerich had been only thirteen, walking alone to his favorite model-making store in Munich, the afternoon he was pulled into a narrow alley and repeatedly kicked and beaten by four teenage skinheads because he "looked like a Jew." He was released from the hospital three weeks later, already decided that he was going to devote himself to ensuring that, in Germany's case, history did not repeat itself. His family and friends said he was being ridiculous; that the new generation skinheads were just young fools, more about fashion than fascism. They urged him instead to do just as they did: prove with good, honest careers, through leading respectable, civilized lives, that the dark days of the Nazis were a unique abhorrence, something to be forgotten.

Martin had ignored them all, dedicating himself from that moment to understanding what created the Third Reich and how best to use his time to prevent any possibility of a fourth. It was even the topic of his final paper in modern history at the University of Munich. His entry into the Bavarian State Police was immediate and, after training and the monotony of a mandatory period in traffic, he got the transfer to the Group Crimes Division he desired from the outset. There, he was assigned to work alongside Gustav Klein, a twenty-five-year veteran of the department, and told to learn everything he could from one of the most knowledgeable and experienced officers in Munich.

Doing exactly that, within two years he had been given responsibility for monitoring all the region's youth gangs, quickly becoming one of the leading experts in the country on neo-Nazis, his chosen specialty. Senior voices in the department were already tagging him as destined for the very top after he had proven, almost single-handedly, that the high-profile German businessman and financier Stefan Vollmer had been making significant donations to the far-right NPD party and actively sponsoring other, more extreme underground neo-Nazi youth groups.

Still only thirty-two, Emmerich's vocation had been somewhat hampered at first by the fact that his face looked even younger than its years. However, recently he had aged. The dark bags beneath his determined eyes and the frown lines increasingly etching his forehead were beginning to betray the severity of his chosen profession. Even his slightly olive skin, the cause of the attack that set him on the course of his life, was becoming paler from too many long nights like that one, peering into the underbelly of the "New Germany" and asking himself if, despite his best efforts, he wasn't fighting a losing battle. Neo-Nazi activity was on the rise wherever he looked …

Emmerich was glad Klein was alongside him that evening. Even if Gustav was now more mentor than partner, the Weisshaus had a bad reputation and officers always went there in pairs. A tip-off from an informant that Max Schalb was expected at the club had pulled him there even if he knew it would be impossible for him to go inside. It didn't matter, he felt that any proximity to the next neo he was determined to take down might prove advantageous. Martin knew well that Schalb was now Vollmer's representative in Germany and, sitting there, he could only wonder what was going on inside and hope that their informant could get close enough to see and report. It would probably be difficult, judging by the huge crowd that had filed into the hateful nightclub earlier.

There were no clues for Emmerich in the parking lot. Wedged with empty cars, it was totally still—the only sounds the patter of rain on the car roof and the distant buzz and thump of music from the club. Klein interrupted the calm. "I need to stretch my legs and have a cigarette."

He moved to get out of the car, saying, "It's quiet," as he opened the door.

"I know," Emmerich replied.

"No, Martin," Klein insisted, raising his index finger to focus Emmerich as he leaned back in through the door. "Listen. It's too quiet for that cesspit."

It was indeed now totally silent. The rain had stopped, as had the dull pounding that always came from within the building.

Feeling his senses alert to the unusual, Emmerich replied, "You're right, something must be hap—"

His words were interrupted by a rapid drilling noise.

"Was that machine-gun fire?"

"It was!" Klein shouted, grabbing for the car's radio receiver.

"*Scheisse!*" Emmerich swore, jumping from the car to see people already running from the club's exits, heading for their cars. In seconds, the first vehicles were fleeing the parking lot, skidding and sliding on the dirt and gravel to get away as fast as possible.

Closely followed by Klein, Emmerich began to run toward the building, unholstering his pistol as more shouting, screaming skinheads poured from the exits.

He grabbed one of them by the jacket and shouted into the wild, panic-stricken face, "What happened in there?"

"Shooting," was all he heard before Klein dived to push the pair of them from the path of a blue Mercedes panel van that was reversing wildly toward the club.

Regaining his footing as the terrified skinhead

scrambled away, Emmerich caught a glimpse of the van's driver as it sped back from him. A black balaclava was masking the face, its two ghostly eyeholes looking straight back at him while the van's reverse gear whined in even greater acceleration.

"Halt! *Polizei!*" Emmerich shouted, brandishing his pistol at the retreating vehicle, but the Mercedes didn't slow. It continued to race backward to the building where it skidded to a stop just centimeters before crashing into the club's cinder-block wall.

For an instant, Emmerich thought he saw struggling shadows in the strips of bright light that surrounded the van filling the exit, but, just as quickly, the vehicle was accelerating toward him again.

A burst of machine-gun fire from the club doorway ripped into the back of the escaping vehicle as the rear doors swung shut.

Stray bullets cracked into the cars around Emmerich, who fell to the ground just as a red Volkswagen Golf, reversing out from its parking space in blind panic, smashed into the side of the van.

In an explosion of red and white taillights and crumpling bodywork, the force of the impact rocked the van wildly, the left-side wheels rising high into the air and causing it to veer to the right before crashing back down again.

The vehicle stalled.

Emmerich and Klein rushed forward again, badges in one hand, pistols in the other, screaming at the now stationary van, "Stop, or we shoot!"

The masked driver looked out at them from the side window and ducked down to restart the van.

Emmerich began pumping bullets into the front

wheel directly below him as the engine desperately tried to turn.

On the third attempt, it caught.

Frantically pumping the accelerator to build the revs, the driver cleared the motor before gunning the van forward again.

The shot tire spun violently and then exploded into shreds, leaving the bare wheel rim grinding and sparking on the gravel.

The masked driver lost steering control but still didn't stop.

His arm suddenly thrust from the window to point a large caliber revolver at Emmerich.

Seeing the silver firearm, Gustav Klein coldly aimed three bullets into the van's cockpit at head height.

The van swerved into a row of parked cars and flipped onto its side, the dead driver wedged on its horn.

Approaching the rear of the van, Emmerich motioned Klein to cover him as he tentatively reached forward to open the rear doors.

Lifting one he looked in to see a dark mess of blood and bodies. The light of a departing car briefly curled around him to illuminate the body on top, its bare torso was covered in tattoos and punctured by bullet wounds. Martin Emmerich realized that it was Max Schalb. He didn't recognize any of the others.

63

HEILIGGEISTRASSE 67, MUNICH, GERMANY
September 20, 2009
1:05 a.m.

Sarron was in the back room of Kassner's bar drinking slugs of brandy, washing the taste of torture from his mouth, cursing Graf as he did so.

What a fucking crazy old man.

He had never seen anything like it—almost as if the man really did want a violent death in exchange for giving up the information about Quinn and his axe. Graf had goaded them continually, taunting Oleg Vishnevsky particularly to the point that the Russian had lost all control. It was ugly long before the end, a lot of blood and pain only to find out that what Quinn had discovered was not related to the Mallory and Irvine story.

Initially Sarron was furious that the axe promised less than he hoped, incensed that they had wasted so much time to extract the information. It wasn't even the right man tied to that metal chair. Quinn was the one he wanted to make whimper and bleed, the one who deserved to die so horribly. To make matters worse, he didn't even know where the Englishman was now. All Oleg said was that Dmitri had called and reported he'd lost him.

Sarron's eyes snapped to Oleg as he asked, "Did Dmitri tell you any more about what happened? Call him again."

"No need. He says he will tell you everything when he arrives. For now, we wait and drink," the Russian said, refilling Sarron's glass and unscrewing a bottle of vodka for himself.

Drinking back more brandy, Sarron thought some more about the story Graf told about the axe. The antiques collector was convinced, quite literally on pain of death, that it revealed a very different first summit of Everest, one where the first man to reach the highest point on earth had actually been a Nazi German. It seemed impossible, but there was no way that Graf could have been lying.

It has to be true.

Sarron began to think that perhaps that would be major news to certain people, people who would appreciate it for what it was, a shocking rewrite of history. He knew that there were fanatics who would welcome such a discovery, particularly in Germany.

Maybe, but I don't have Quinn and I don't have the axe.

Also Graf actually didn't even know what else was up there, despite being convinced that more could be found. He had talked of finding frozen bodies, of equipment, of cameras, of undeveloped summit photos …

Can that really be possible?

It was several years since the Frenchman personally had climbed the Second Step, but he did remember that there were a lot of hidden nooks and crannies on that part of the mountain. They were largely unexplored. Off the main route, something or someone could well have lain undisturbed for years. They found Mallory and everyone said that would be impossible.

But even if I can find it, what value does it really have?

Sarron racked his brain as he sat there, sifting through ideas and alternatives until the door to the back room opened and Dmitri Vishnevsky entered.

"Where the fuck have you been?"

"In a club full of Nazis," Dmitri said in his heavy Russian accent. "I brought you something."

From the inside of his long overcoat, he took out the old ice axe.

Sarron stood up and grabbed it, demanding, "Tell me everything."

Studying the pick, Sarron listened as Dmitri Vishnevsky described Quinn's kidnapping and what happened when he followed him to the Weisshaus.

"So the Nazis already want the story of this axe?"

"Yes. And, from what I saw, they didn't get it. Probably why they started to beat the Englishman on the dance floor."

"Did they kill him?"

"No."

"Did you kill him?"

"Possibly. I shot the van pretty good as it tried to get away. I aimed high to try for just the guys pulling him in. Police officers stopped the van soon after so I had to go. I don't know the rest."

"So we now have what they want and, if Quinn is dead, only we know the details?"

Kassner walked back into the room.

"There is a lot of talk in the bar that Stefan Vollmer's right-hand man in Germany, Max Schalb, was one of the people killed at the Weisshaus."

"Who is Stefan Vollmer?"

Kassner explained.

When he finished, Sarron raised his glass to him in thanks and then to the two Russians.

"Boys, I think we might have found a customer to take us all back to the Himalayas."

64

LACHEN MONASTERY, NORTHWEST SIKKIM
April 13, 1939
4:30 p.m.

The noise of men outside the Dak Guesthouse in Lachen broke the silence of the valley alerting Macfarlane to the arrival of the patrol Colonel Atkinson had dispatched. It was a huge relief as the days waiting for them to arrive had been interminable. Quickly looking out the low door of the drafty bungalow where he had taken up residence after his hasty exit from Schmidt's camp, Macfarlane was immediately disappointed to see that there were only five men. He had expected more.

Four were uniformed Gurkhas. Behind forced smiles of arrival and determined salutes to their senior officer, they were exhausted, drop-shouldered, and stretched thin from traveling too far and too fast into the highlands. The fifth man accompanying them was not a Gurkha but a taller local man dressed in the almost medieval, heavy black-and-red robes of the

Tibetan nomad, a long knife hung from his belt. The hood of his cloak was raised over his head, obscuring the man's face but not the long, black beard that hung down to his breastbone.

Macfarlane beckoned the sergeant in as the three riflemen unpacked and the Tibetan, offering them no assistance, walked instead to the bank of the small stream that ran in front of the little hunting and trekking cottage. Entering, the Gurkha sergeant saluted again and handed Macfarlane a dispatch pouch from the colonel. The leather case felt thick and heavy in his hands.

Seeing that the sergeant was struggling to catch his breath, Macfarlane put the pouch to one side. "Thank you, Sergeant. Take a moment, and then tell me if you saw any sign of the two missing men on your journey north."

The small man looked pained, firstly, at having to wait to speak in order to regulate his breathing, and then, secondly, at having to reply in the negative. "No, Lieutenant Macfarlane, sir. Nothing at all."

Drawing another long breath before he could continue, he added, "We have been vigilant and made inquiries all along the route, but there has been no sight or word of them."

"Disappointing."

"Yessir."

"I was expecting more men, Sergeant?"

"We traveled up under Lieutenant Bailey as a patrol of nine. But we separated earlier when he took four men to go directly to the Zemu Glacier to escort the Schmidt team back to Darjeeling. Their expedition permit has been revoked. We four are to remain under your command."

"So who then is the fifth man with you, Sergeant?"

"He is called Zazar, Lieutenant Macfarlane, sir."

Macfarlane repeated the name to himself before asking, "Tell me more about this Zazar."

"He is a Tibetan, sir, a tracker assigned to us by Colonel Atkinson. He joined us in Gangtok. It is said that he has worked as a man hunter across Tibet for many overlords. I think that it is true. He …" The sergeant hesitated.

"What is it, Sergeant?" Macfarlane asked.

"I think that you will need to talk to this man, sir. Throughout our journey, he has complained to Lieutenant Bailey that Colonel Atkinson is not paying him enough to track wanted men and then bring them back alive all the way to Darjeeling. He says it is far, and 'alive' makes more work than returning only with heads as the dzong pen favors. He says that all sahibs are rich so they can pay. You must be careful of him, sir. Zazar has no love of the sahib. No love for any man, I think."

"I note what you say, Sergeant. Does this Zazar have any idea where the men we seek might have gone?"

"Zazar says they have gone north into Tibet. He says that if they had gone south he would have found them already."

Macfarlane walked away from the sergeant to look out the door at the Tibetan. A sinister, solitary presence, Zazar was squatting on his haunches and silently staring into the running water of the mountain brook as if willing it to stop. The hood of his cloak was now thrown back and his head, long hair tied back into a plait like something from the Boxer Rebellion, was slightly angled as if he was sniffing the air.

Seeming to sense that Macfarlane was looking at him, the Tibetan slowly turned his head to stare straight back. His eyes bore into Macfarlane's. They were narrow and dark, deep set within the cruelest face the young lieutenant had ever encountered. The Englishman broke his gaze away from the Tibetan immediately.

"Sergeant, send Zazar down into the town to see what he can find out," he quickly ordered, turning back into the room. "Then you and your riflemen should make camp and rest, as we will need to make some sort of start early tomorrow, even if I have not yet decided which way we should go. I will study Colonel Atkinson's orders and make a decision tonight. We have to find these two men, Sergeant, and quickly too."

The sergeant saluted and left the bungalow, leaving Macfarlane to unseal the pouch he had delivered. Within, he found a long handwritten order from Colonel Atkinson. There were also some detailed survey maps of Sikkim, copies of more rudimentary hand-drawn maps of the Tibetan borderlands, and passe-partout documentation for him and the patrol, allowing them to travel onward into Tibet if necessary. Macfarlane glanced at it all before returning to his instructions from the colonel. Hastily written, they were rambling and lengthy, little attempt made to hide the colonel's fury with the whole matter, which he clearly saw as the lieutenant's failure.

The diatribe revealed that Atkinson was convinced that the German, accompanied by a Sherpa who, he added, was already known to be anti-British, must have slipped away to stir up trouble for British interests in the region. At best, it was Sikkim, at worst, Tibet. If it was Sikkim, Atkinson stated he was fairly confident that British control of the tiny country was such that Becker's whereabouts would be revealed quite easily, possibly before the patrol even met Macfarlane and delivered the very document he was reading. However, if they had gone into Tibet, then matters would be far more difficult. The country was huge, and the British, while influential with the country's rulers, had little actual authority, particularly beyond the country's capital, Lhasa.

The letter continued with the information that, although nothing had been proven, the British authorities in India were already wary as to the true purpose of Himmler's ongoing expedition to Tibet, especially now that it had established itself in Lhasa. Schäfer and his four team members were all known to be SS officers, and the fact that another suspected SS man was now on the loose only made matters more suspicious.

It was on this subject that Atkinson saved his best for last. If Macfarlane could prove that Becker was in Tibet deliberately seeking to damage British interests, then beyond apprehending him, which was to be his priority, it would have the added bonus of allowing the British authorities in India to demand that the Tibetans also expel Schäfer's team. As the colonel put it, such a "result" might go some way in restoring Macfarlane's sullied reputation for vigilance and endeavor.

* * *

A gentle shaking pulled Macfarlane up from the depths of sleep.

His watch told him it was 3:35 a.m.

"Lieutenant Macfarlane, sir, Zazar has returned. He says he has news of the two men we seek."

Macfarlane bolted upright, instantly awake.

"What news, Sergeant? Where are they?"

"I will bring him in, sir."

Macfarlane got up and lit a candle as the sergeant returned to the door of the bungalow, leaned out, and summoned the Tibetan.

Zazar's shadowy form stepped inside to dwarf the stocky Gurkha. Macfarlane could smell the man now that he was close. It was a rancid, heavy smell that turned his guts as Zazar began to speak in a low growl to the sergeant.

The sergeant translated it for the benefit of Macfarlane. "Zazar says he has been up in the town's monastery speaking to the last monks and traders to arrive from Tibet for news. Some monks tell him that they met a white-skin and a Sherpa on the Sepu-La."

"What?"

"It is a mountain pass due north of here. It is the most direct route into Tibet—much more difficult than the one Zazar thought they might take."

Macfarlane felt his heart jump with this first report of their quarry. The hunt was on.

"We will leave at daybreak," he said to the sergeant. As he spoke, Macfarlane could feel Zazar staring back at him as if he had already found his prey.

65

**KLINIKUM GROSSHADERN,
NUSSBAUMSTRASSE 20, MUNICH, GERMANY**
September 25, 2009
10:12 a.m.

When Quinn opened his eyes and saw someone who looked remarkably like Henrietta Richards standing at the foot of his bed, his first instinct was to close them again. In the next seconds, he questioned whether he was actually dead, but the pain was too real, he couldn't be. It left him instead to ask himself what Henrietta Richards was doing there—*if it really is her?*

His brief glimpse had showed her engaged in conversation with a younger, dark-haired man. He was standing between her and the end of his bed, talking in an agitated manner, gesturing at her with his hands. Henrietta was slowly nodding her head in return, as if saying to a small boy who'd fallen off his bicycle that things would be all right, that there was absolutely nothing to worry about. It was doing little to mollify the irate man.

Looking again to check that he wasn't hallucinating, Henrietta's eyes caught his over the man's right shoulder. Instantly she turned toward the door of what Quinn now realized was a hospital room. Drawing the young man after her, he heard her say, "Of course, Martin, of course. As soon as he regains consciousness," and they both stepped out into the corridor.

Left alone in the room, Quinn took in the banks of monitors and wires and tubes that fanned around him. An image of Dawa's tortured coma flooded his mind before morphing into a flickering recall of his last moments in the Weisshaus Club. The memory made him wince.

Henrietta returned.

It's definitely her.

"Florence Nightingale, at your service," she whispered, standing at the end of Quinn's bed, looking down on him and putting a finger up to her mouth. "Don't say a word. If you see anyone else coming in, close your eyes immediately."

Quinn resisted the temptation to wish he really was dead and raised his right hand up from the bed in acknowledgment. The difficulty of moving it surprised him. A shot of panic made him curl his toes to check he had movement in the rest of his body. He did. *Thank God.*

"Good," Henrietta said, moving to the side of his bed to sit on a chair she must have been using before. Picking up a book from it, she sat and, pretending to read aloud, said instead, "Neil, you don't need to talk. In fact, you shouldn't. I would prefer everyone here to think you were still out for as long as possible. Close your eyes."

He closed them.

"However, you do still need to listen to me. It is no accident that the hospital staff here think I am a mad Englishwoman. If they see me mumbling at you from a book while you are still unconscious, they are unlikely to think anything of it. Do you follow me?"

Quinn slowly nodded once, every bone and muscle in his body hurting with the slight movement.

"Okay. So, other than telling you that you have been more or less comatose for the past four and a half days in this very clean and modern Munich hospital, I will let the doctors advise you of the injuries you have suffered. Suffice it to say you will live, although you won't be running up a flight of stairs, let alone a mountain, for a few months.

"Once again you've been lucky, Neil. You should be dead. Possibly you deserve to be, but I will let that go for the moment. We have more important things to discuss first."

Turning a page, she continued.

"The rather agitated young man you saw me talking to is not a doctor but actually Inspector Martin Emmerich of the Bavarian State Police, Group Crimes Division. He undoubtedly saved your life when he pulled you from the bottom of a pile of bodies that had been riddled with machine-gun fire by your accomplice ..." As Henrietta said the word "accomplice," she stressed its three syllables and raised her penciled eyebrows in question at Neil, awaiting a reply.

"Henrietta, there was ... no accomplice ... I was taken there ... alone ... by force ..." Quinn struggled to reply, intent on denying that anyone was with him.

"Neil, I'm using Inspector Emmerich's words, not

mine. However, it does appear that you did have some sort of 'guardian angel,' even if I suspect its intentions were no more angelic than those of the neo-Nazis who beat you senseless. Actually, I must say that I find Inspector Emmerich to be an intelligent and honest young man. He seems very good at his job, passionate about it even. Reminds me, in some ways, of a younger version of myself, which is a little frustrating, but, so be it, I have my work to do also."

Quinn reopened his eyes to see Henrietta staring at him intently.

"I imagine you are probably asking yourself why I am here, Neil."

"Thought … at first … you'd got St. Peter's job …"

"Well, Neil, it's good to see that the skinheads didn't kick all the humor out of you. Whilst I may well be increasingly aged and sanctimonious, I can assure you that I am not yet a rival for St. Peter. However, you are correct in that I do still have a job. Now and again, I undertake work for Her Majesty's Government, namely the Foreign Office, who rather euphemistically refer to me as a 'private contractor.' More specifically, I specialize in matters pertaining to the Himalayas, which has always been a sensitive frontier. I also have a bit of a track record of getting people who have made a considerable mess of things back home to dear old Blighty, and, I must say, you most definitely qualify for that category." Hearing the click of heels in the corridor, Henrietta instantly stopped talking, returning her gaze to her book as Quinn reclosed his swollen eyes.

A nurse briskly entered the room and took a look

at a motionless Quinn. She glanced at Henrietta, who looked up and gave a sad little shake of her head that quickly diverted the nurse to fuss with a suspended IV bag, tapping its tube and adjusting the flow into the back of Quinn's left hand. After observing a bank of electronic monitors, she then jotted something onto a clipboard at the end of the bed before leaving, saying only, in an abrupt, accented English that sounded like an order, "Summon me as soon as he is the waking."

"Of course," Quinn heard Henrietta reply.

When the nurse was gone, she resumed her quiet explanation. "I was over on one of my rare visits to England when someone from Legoland tracked me down to ask why I thought a well-known British Everest climber called Neil Quinn might have tried to get himself killed in a neo-Nazi nightclub on the outskirts of Munich. I have been asked many questions about Everest but that was really one of the best in a long time. As soon as I heard it, I realized that the very question itself answered a number of questions that I have had for a very long time."

"Legoland? What questions?" Quinn asked, increasingly confused.

"Yes, Neil, Legoland—our rather too obvious military intelligence headquarters on the south bank of the Thames that looks as if it was designed by a focus group of preschoolers. It is the home of MI6, who thought me best qualified to provide an answer to the question of what the hell you were up to. If the answer was one that might interest them further, given the fact they are becoming somewhat alarmed at the resurgence of the far right across Europe, then I was to help in getting you to a hospital in England where you might explain it to them in person. By the way, if the answer is unsatisfactory, I am instructed to leave you here to rot."

She studied Quinn for a minute.

"It is actually a fine question. What were you up to in there?"

"Long story," Quinn slurred in response.

"Well, it is one that you are going to have to tell me, with no omissions this time. However, I am going to give you the benefit of the doubt for now assuming you confirm one thing."

"Which is?"

"Over the last few days the very dedicated Martin Emmerich has been doing a lot of research into you. He is developing some interesting theories that include you, the renowned Everest summiteer currently somewhat embittered and down on his luck after the tragic death of his last client, being employed by some of the lunatics in that club to climb the mountain and plant a swastika flag on the top as some sort of publicity stunt. He has concluded that there must have been a somewhat emotional breakdown in the negotiations, financial or otherwise, that in fairly rapid succession led to you being beaten up on the dance floor and the shooting of at least ten people inside and outside of the club by an unknown person armed with an Uzi submachine gun, and, possibly, also you, armed with a smaller caliber pistol. Inspector Emmerich rather eloquently describes the Weisshaus Club as a 'human hornets' nest.' One that you most definitely stuck a stick into, or rather, as one witness seemed to suggest, an old ice axe …"

She paused to let everything she was saying sink in. "Funny how that old ice axe keeps turning up, isn't it?"

Quinn could say nothing in reply.

"Actually, Neil, I think young Emmerich's intuition is quite good about the swastika on the summit. He's just about seventy years too late—am I not right?"

This time he did try to say something, but still no words came out. All Quinn could do was nod in reply to her.

"Thought as much. Good. That's enough for now, Neil. You need to sleep because, be assured that when you next wake up, a lot more questions are going to start arriving, thick and fast."

Still talking, she began to collect her things. "When they do, you must, and I repeat must, stick to the following line: You were visiting Germany on a motorcycle trip after a summer season mountain-guiding in Chamonix. You drank too much beer in a rough bar near to your cheap hotel by the station which resulted in you, in a fit of macho curiosity, taking a solo trip to what you had been told by a couple of Hell's Angels was the wildest, most dangerous place in town. Inside, a fight broke out, and when people realized that you were English, they got somewhat annoyed and took some delight in including you in it. Sadly, you don't remember anything after that, absolutely nothing at all. Have you got it?"

Quinn looked at her and responded with a whispered, "Okay."

"Good."

Quinn stopped her from leaving by saying, "Henrietta …"

"What, Neil?"

"The axe?"

"It's lucky for you, Neil, that it's missing, just

like your 'accomplice' and both of the guns used. The eyewitness reports as to what happened are generally unsound, particularly as the one police informant in the place remembers little after he thought you shot him in the thigh. With little evidence beyond a heap of bodies, Emmerich is struggling to accurately piece together what happened. I intend to exploit this uncertainty for as long as I can and you must stick to that story while I do."

Turning to leave, she added, "Just one more thing. Be aware that Emmerich is also trying to work out the connection between you and the horrific murder of an elderly antiques collector called Bernhard Graf. Given that it took place more or less whilst you were being set upon in the Weisshaus Club, even he accepts that you have an alibi, but the fact that Graf's boyfriend, Dirk Schneider, was one of the people shot in the club has not gone unnoticed. Be careful, Neil. Emmerich is no fool. He'll work it all out but hopefully not before I have made a deal to get you back to England. In the meantime, just stick precisely to what I have told you."

The shock of Henrietta's final news put Quinn under again.

66

KAMPA DZONG, TSANG PROVINCE, TIBET
April 14, 1939
4:20 p.m.

Josef was losing hope. Nearly three days had passed since the brawl in the caravansary, and there was still no sign or word of Ang Noru. It was time to face up to the fact that the Tibetans must have taken him. Without Ang Noru, he realized he was lost. He had no chance of arriving at the mountain alone. Repeatedly cursing himself for his stupidity, for letting the alcohol get the better of him, for taking a risk that would kill more than just him and the Sherpa, Josef could do little more than pace the small stable where Phurbu had shown him a hiding place.

Whenever the tyke or his mother appeared to bring food or items of his personal equipment, he would ask "Ang Noru?" to no reply, until, just as he was deciding that he would have to go on alone the next morning, little Phurbu raced back in and pulled him to the doorway. Pointing into the sky, the boy said repeatedly, "Ang Noru, Ang Noru." Wondering at first if the boy was in some way trying to tell him that the Sherpa was dead, Josef soon realized that the youngster was actually stabbing his small finger toward the outline of the old fort on the hill above. When Josef nodded back to the boy that he understood, Phurbu continued to mime. The first gestures were impossible for Josef to decipher until the chopping motion of Phurbu's left hand on his right wrist followed by a slicing motion across his throat left no scope for confusion.

Josef retrieved a pair of binoculars from his things to better scrutinize the medieval-looking structure. The ancient castle's tall, flat-fronted façades grew directly upward from the rock of the long, narrow ridge on which it was perched. On one side, the towering building trusted its protection entirely to a sheer cliff, seemingly safe in the certainty that no army would ever approach from that side, that no archaic cannon they might possess could ever fire that high. On the other, the building was defended by a stacked mass of swollen towers and battlements that dominated the gentler hillside that sloped back down to the valley. With an outstretched hand, Josef traced the twists and turns of the track that led up that hillside to the great entrance gates. The approach from that side was guarded from every angle, impregnable.

The young boy, seeing Josef do this, pulled Josef's arm down and shook his head. Mimicking the firing of flintlocks and cannon at any unwanted visitor who sought to use that route, he pointed Josef back to the side of the fort above the cliff. Then, before Josef's eyes, he transformed his small hand into a grubby spider whose curling, flexing legs commenced to climb diagonally up the cliff face.

* * *

Josef waited until midnight before he and Phurbu slipped out of the silent town and started up the steep scree slope that led to the cliff. He moved quickly but cautiously, unwilling to risk a noisy slide back down the steep, loose rocks or another encounter with a dog, the boy following close behind.

At the foot of the cliff, they stopped. Josef looked down through the clouds of his own breath at the young boy. In the faint light of a quarter-moon, he saw only a toothy grin and two big eyes. When the small head that contained them started nodding and bobbing back at him, seeming to urge him on in its own guttural language, Josef pushed him down on a rock to sit and wait while he pulled the coil of rope from his rucksack. He wanted to share the child's enthusiasm, but he knew that the ancient leader who built the castle had been correct to have confidence in the cliff. It was a treacherous and difficult wall, no easy climb in daylight, far worse in the dark.

The rope uncoiled, Josef picked Phurbu up, gripping his narrow chest between his hands, mentally weighing him. The boy felt incredibly light, little more than a birdlike frame beneath his ragged yet thick clothes. For a moment the boy's feathery weight made Josef think back to little Ilsa. The memory sickened him. Quickly setting the child down, Josef took one end of his rope and tied it around his own waist before knotting the other around the child's tiny middle. Looping the remainder of the long rope over his shoulder, he then tied it off so that only a short length remained between them. He next took the boy's face between his two hands and, staring into his eyes with as stern an expression as he could make, said slowly and emphatically, "You follow me. Near. Understand?" The boy wouldn't understand the words but Josef hoped that the severity of the gesture and the short, tight rope that now joined them would make his intent clear.

Roped together they set off parallel with the bottom of the cliff. When he'd studied it through the binoculars, Josef had identified two fault lines that ran up the cliff. One was to the left of the rock face's center, a dark scar that ran almost vertically from the top to the bottom. The second, commencing slightly further to the right, rose up in a fainter stepped diagonal to the very top right corner of the cliff. The two fissures were the only two natural climbing lines that Josef was able to discern on the otherwise sheer wall. Of the pair, the vertical crack was the more pronounced from a distance and Josef wanted to explore that one first, even though, when he had pointed it out to Phurbu, the boy had held his nose and feigned retching in reply—somewhat confusing Josef at the time.

Moving across to the point where he thought that crack started, an overpowering stench of human waste began to engulf them until the little boy stopped and, after tugging at Josef's sleeve, began to hold his nose again and spit vehemently at the ground. Josef sternly yet quietly told him to stop it, but understood what the boy meant. The line of the fissure was being used as a drainage chute from the castle above. The runoff ahead of them was slick with decades of partially frozen filth. Far above, Josef could even make out the boxy outline of the latrine that projected from the smooth wall of the fort.

The boy tugged at the rope and pointed further along the cliff toward the second line, so Josef allowed Phurbu to lead them both down and around the icy tongue of effluent that ran down the hill and then back up to the bottom of the cliff face to approach the other fault. When they reached it, Josef saw to his relief that it was dry, also set back deeper in places than it had appeared from a distance. It was climbable.

The boy immediately sprang onto the rock and started upward, forcing Josef to grab him by an ankle to stop him. He pulled him back down. Enough was enough. Josef was going to lead from now on. He didn't second anyone on a climb, even if they knew the way. After checking his rucksack was tightly cinched and his axe was secured, Josef paid out some rope between them and then began to climb himself, the boy following a little way behind.

The German moved up the diagonal break in the rock, slowly and positively, checking each handhold twice before putting any weight on it and, wherever possible, wedging himself as much as he could into the crack he was following. With each upward move, he hung the short length of rope that ran between him and the boy over any projections in the rock he could find. It might hold them if one of them started to slip or fall. Wherever the broken groove in the rock widened sufficiently to present a natural ledge, Josef would, as quietly as possible, knock in a piton, a necessary precaution for what would be a hasty descent.

It was slow, precise work to climb the groove in the faint moonlight, but gradually Josef felt the emptiness of the cliff growing beneath them and the heavy presence of the castle growing above.

* * *

The upper third of the wall began to tax even Josef's climbing ability. He slowed, increasingly having to feel in the dark to find anything that felt like a good hold. The delays were starting to put too much tension into his legs, tiring them. Reaching up for another handhold, he told himself to speed up.

With a surge of relief, his fingers touched the hard edge of another ledge.

We can rest here for a little.

But before his hand could even close on the sharp stone, a hawk suddenly exploded from the rock above.

The female peregrine startled Josef, the surge of air from its rigid wing feathers pushing dust and dirt from its aerie into his eyes. Temporarily blinded and disorientated, his feet scrambled for grip as he grabbed at the ledge. The boy below screamed, a hail of small rocks raining down on him. He slipped and fell until jerked to a sudden halt by the rope that made him cry out again.

Josef held on to the edge of cold rock as tightly as he could, the rope taut below him, the small boy swinging on the end like a pendulum. Slowly the German regained his footing, until, with one arm, he was able to pull the rope back up to him and connect the thrashing boy with the rock face once more. When they were both secure, he listened apprehensively for any reaction to their disturbance from the castle above but heard only the boy cursing and complaining from below. Josef tugged sharply on the rope and growled at the boy to be quiet, even if the mistake had been his.

Silence returned only to be interrupted by a scratching noise close to Josef's head. He pulled himself up to see two downy hawk chicks peering out at him from their bare nest within the rock. One of them edged forward, determined to peck at the monster invading its tiny world. Josef pushed it back into the little alcove and, when he was satisfied that the chicks were the only living things watching them, started to climb again until the rope tightened once more and stopped. He instantly gave it a strong pull to tug the small boy past the distraction of the peregrine's young.

After another long sequence of climbing moves, Josef was finally able to clamber over the very top of the cliff onto the narrow ledge that jutted out from the base of the castle. He cursed silently to himself when he felt its wall. It was completely smooth. It offered no holds. Any windows were set far above, no possibility of climbing up to them. Nailing in another piton to secure the rope, he waited for Phurbu to join him, asking himself how the boy knew they could gain access to the castle from this point. He saw no immediate answer.

When the boy arrived, he seemed sulky from his near fall and squatted, distracted, on the ledge, offering no clues when Josef pointed at the castle. Josef wondered if the rope around his middle had hurt him in some way when it arrested his fall. He asked quietly and reached down to poke Phurbu's stomach to see if there was any injury, but the boy just batted his hand away. Tying him into the piton instead, Josef gave up on an answer and moved to the very end of the ledge to the right to see if he could find a way from there.

There was none.

Returning to the boy, Josef saw that he was sitting hunched forward, nonchalantly dangling his legs over the edge while he looked down into his jacket. A faint squeaking noise was coming from within. Sensing Josef's approach, the boy quickly closed the jacket and folded his arms in front of his chest.

After Josef had sat back down alongside him, he held out his hand to the boy.

Little Phurbu feigned ignorance.

Grasping the lad's jacket, Josef forced it open to reveal one of the peregrine chicks cowering inside.

Seizing the writhing, downy chick from the struggling boy, Josef had an idea. Swatting away the boy's grabbing hands, he put the chick into his rucksack and closed it up. He then unclipped the child from the piton and pointed to the castle.

Phurbu didn't move, holding out his hands for the chick, but Josef just shook his head, saying, *"Nein, nein, nein,"* as he waved a finger at him. He then pointed up into the castle again before nodding positively and smiling. Understanding quickly, Phurbu gave up on the bird and scampered away along the ledge. In an instant, he was climbing up and under the latrine that projected out from the castle wall and then, with his feet wedged on the wooden framework below, squeezing his way up through its foul hole to disappear into the castle.

Josef followed as the rope between them snaked up the sewer until he was forced to stop. Although the latrine's hole was no impediment for the small boy, Josef's body was much too large to pass through it. Taking the pick of his ice axe, he knocked in another piton to secure himself and then spent the next thirty minutes gagging on the stench as he perched on the frame below and broke away the wood perimeter of the opening with his axe. When eventually Josef had created a hole big enough to squeeze up through, he also finally emerged inside the castle walls, disgusted and stinking.

Scheisse!

Once inside, Josef quickly untied the rope from the boy and pulled the peregrine chick free from his rucksack. As it flapped and clawed, he held it above the reach of the small boy, who jumped and snatched at it from below. *"Nein,"* Josef whispered down at him again before lowering the chick almost into his outstretched hands and then lifting it back up, repeating, "Ang Noru, Ang Noru, Ang Noru" and smiling some more to initiate the game.

The boy kicked him in the shin, grinned cheekily, and then vanished into the black of the castle, leaving Josef with only the young hawk for company.

67

GUY'S HOSPITAL, SOUTHWARK, LONDON, ENGLAND
October 5, 2009
6:15 p.m. (British Summer Time)

Martin Emmerich had been a serious challenge to Henrietta, but she prevailed. With every questioning, Quinn had stuck to his "no memory" line, more often than not with Henrietta sitting alongside him as a representative of the British authorities. With a serene smile etched onto her lips, she similarly deflected Emmerich's every attempt to get to the truth of what Quinn had really been doing in Munich.

Once, in his fury at their constant stonewalling, Emmerich, a patient man, completely lost his temper. Screaming at them both, he pointed out that it was only because of him that Quinn was even alive. "And for that I will be eternally grateful to you," Henrietta had replied, "particularly, I must say, as it gives me the possibility to kill him in the future, which may well be necessary if he doesn't stop causing me so much trouble."

Her comment had only enraged the German police officer even more. Emmerich did not find Henrietta Richards quaint or amusing. He didn't understand who she was, what she was even doing there. Beginning to suspect that Quinn must be an undercover British operative and she was some sort of handler, he was not particularly surprised to finally receive a phone call from the Federal Police commissioner informing him that there had been a deal with the British and he must let the matter go. Within minutes Martin Emmerich had been standing aside to watch Quinn transferred to London by air ambulance, realizing that he had been totally outplayed by Henrietta Richards at every turn.

That day's trip home had been long and painful for Quinn. Henrietta had warned him on the way that it was no coincidence that the hospital chosen for his return was in Southwark, fifteen minutes from the MI6 HQ. Preparing him for the fact that they were going to be frequent bedside visitors, Henrietta suggested that the first thing Neil do after their arrival was tell her the full story of the ice axe. Despite being tired from the journey, as soon he was installed in his new private room he did so, much as he'd done for Graf, recounting every twist and turn, leaving no detail out, not even the gorak cave.

Henrietta took the news calmly, listening silently, jotting specific points down in a notebook. Particularly, it seemed to Quinn, those that he had learned from Graf; the *Der Stürmer* editorial, the recollections of the old Gebirgsjäger Dieter Braun in Garmisch, the fact that Becker had traveled to the Himalayas with Schmidt's expedition.

Finishing his explanation, Quinn said to her, "You don't seem so surprised?"

"I'm not, Neil, even if the detail of what you learned with Graf is fascinating."

"How long have you known?"

"'Known' is too strong a word: 'suspected' is better. Since the early '70s, I suppose."

"Really?"

"Yes, I stumbled across it working in the embassy filing room one afternoon just as my interest in Everest was growing. It was only a few old papers really, marked as transferred to Kathmandu from the British Mission in Tibet, which was fairly hastily abandoned after the Chinese invasion. They were dated to 1939 and one of them raised suspicions of an SS plot to climb the mountain whilst another gave details of a British lieutenant being sent with a patrol of Gurkhas to stop it. Sadly, I made the mistake of casually raising the matter with the ambassador at a diplomatic event the very same evening. Not only did he deny it all vehemently but all the papers had vanished by the time I could return to the filing room."

"Why do you think that was?"

"I used to think back then that it was because climbing Everest was seen as so exclusively ours. It was a British narrative with no space for mention of any other nation. But actually it was much more specific than that. The British authorities must have known that the Germans, or I should say now, the German Josef Becker, got too close to success for their comfort and became desperate to hide the fact. Even though the papers disappeared, I knew I hadn't imagined the whole thing because I was able to track down the records of the British Army officer involved."

"Who was he?"

"A Lieutenant Charles Macfarlane of the Coldstream Guards. There was actually no reference in the regimental archives of him ever visiting Tibet but I did learn that he was demoted to second lieutenant at the end of a secondment to the 2nd Gurkha Rifles in Darjeeling in the summer of 1939. No reason was given. He was killed five years later at Anzio with the rank of acting captain, posthumously adding the Military Cross to a series of decorations won during the course of the war. The regiment's wartime almanac remembered him as a 'brave and, above all, utterly honorable man.' A statement I always thought at odds with the fact that he had once been stripped of rank. From what you have told me we can probably assume that it was as a punishment for failing to catch Becker. And if he didn't catch him, then Becker may well still be up there as Graf believed."

"The collector was definitely convinced of that."

"Well, we can't be sure until we go back. Don't forget there is a Tiger Sherpa to add to the picture. It might even be him that's still up there."

"Really?"

"Yes. As you can imagine, after the name Ang Noru came up I was intrigued. I asked Dawa about it as soon as he was better. He told me his ancestor Ang Noru was possibly the strongest porter at altitude of his day, but suffered severe frostbite when he climbed on Everest in 1933. Ang Noru blamed the British, who, in return, labeled him a 'troublemaker' and never invited him to work on another of their expeditions. After that he only worked for Germans until he disappeared in 1939. At the time most people in Darjeeling said he must have drunk too much one night and wandered down into the valley river and drowned, but evidently there were other whispers that he was killed on the order of the British who wanted him silenced. Dawa, however, doesn't believe any of these things and suspects that actually Ang Noru went back to Everest one last time.

"I think I would have enjoyed comparing notes on all this with your collector. Although he approached the truth from a very different starting point, his objective sounds the same as mine—to discover it, to protect it, and above all, to stop it from being used for harm. Together I believe we would have worked the whole thing out quite quickly."

"I think that's true. He was an interesting character. I was only with him for a few days yet it seems now that I knew him all my life. Is that odd?"

"Not really, Neil. As Graf believed, there is a darker side to the mountains. It feeds on the risk, the ambition, the inherent potential in aspiring to reach the highest summits for failure, for betrayal, for lies instead." She hesitated, her face momentarily revealing to Quinn a fatigued sadness she normally kept hidden. "Also the extreme loss and sorrow caused by the deaths on those mountains; that never-ending feeling for those left behind of having been robbed by the mountain of something beautiful and irreplaceable to your lifetime. I think Graf manifested something that subconsciously accompanies giving your life to the hills as you have done."

Neil lay back in the hospital bed, the weight of all the mayhem and suffering that had followed him since his last climb forcing his spirits down and making his wounds from Munich ache. "Well, it doesn't feel so subconscious now."

Henrietta ignored the remark. "The only other time I seemed to get a hint about Germans and Everest was somewhere totally unexpected. I always kept an eye open for any stories of Germans in the region dating back to those prewar years in the hope that they might provide a clue. I combed the obvious ones like Harrer's *Seven Years in Tibet* and also the writings of his colleague Peter Aufschnaiter but there was nothing.

"However in the memoir of a German doctor called Magda von Trier, I thought I did feel a connection to Everest. Her story was one of coming to India and helping its poorest people as a personal amends for the horrors her country had inflicted on the world. She often described herself as feeling like a modern-day Sisyphus and made many allusions to the Himalayas and Mount Everest. This struck me as odd as her work was predominantly in the South of India.

"At first I thought perhaps it was whimsy but the more I read it, the more it struck a chord in me that in some way that mountain had affected her deeply. She died in the early '80s before I even found the book so I couldn't ask her why. I wrote to her daughter but got no reply beyond a thank-you for the donation I made to the charitable institute the family still runs in Hyderabad."

Henrietta stopped for a moment before continuing. "I will dig that stuff out when I return to Kathmandu and have another look at it in light of all this. Anyway enough of that, I need to get you ready for the scrutiny of MI6."

"What will they want to know?"

"Everything. I want them to see that you are a straight shooter so just be open and honest with them. I will manage the process."

"What will happen then?"

"We'll get you back on your feet so you can return to Everest and fix all this."

"From where I'm lying that doesn't seem very likely even if I think it is down to me to put this matter to rest once and for all."

"Neil, if Dawa can now make it up to my apartment unaided to get his monthly money from the fund organized for him, then, with a bit of work this winter, I think we can get you back to your gorak cave."

"It's not my cave."

"Well, it's time to find out who it does belong to."

68

KAMPA DZONG, TSANG PROVINCE, TIBET
April 15, 1939
3:51 a.m.

Josef retreated into an empty room opposite the latrine, leaving the door slightly ajar to listen for the boy's return. Sitting there alone in the stink of his filthy crawl into the castle, he tucked his chin down into his chest to evade the vile odor only for his nose to be met by the sour but slightly less offensive smell of the falcon chick he was still holding.

Warily he began to stroke its soft down, alert to the threat of its needle-sharp beak and the small black sickles of its talons. Relaxed and warm, the young bird went to sleep in his hands with a faint, repetitive whistle of slow breathing. Its rhythm settled Josef also. Gently pushing the sleeping chick inside his jacket, he closed it up and dozed lightly himself until disturbed by the patter of the boy's soft footsteps tripping up and down the corridor. Quietly getting up and reaching out of the door, Josef pulled him into the room. "Ang Noru?" he whispered.

The boy nodded. He pointed back out the door but then down at Josef's hobnailed boots, making a clicking noise through his teeth as he shook his head from side to side. Understanding, Josef took his boots off and stuffed them into his rucksack alongside the climbing rope, squeezing it tight. When he was positive there were no rattles from within, he put it back on, picked up his ice axe, and gestured for the boy to lead the way.

The fort was a labyrinth of close, dark walls, the air inside stale and musty. Phurbu darted ahead, skirting the sides of each passageway like a rat, stopping at every corner or the slightest hint of a sound. Whenever he sprang forward, Josef almost had to break into a trot to keep up with him. They moved at their quickest when they had to pass through the molten glow of burning butter lamps. Their passing would cause the smokey flames to flicker, bending light and shadow up the walls, momentarily illuminating their ancient painted detail: rolling brown hills stood sentinel before jagged lines of snowcapped mountains; billowing cloud faces with bulging cheeks blew blue lakes into rows of cresting waves shaped like horses' heads; wide-eyed demons with massive teeth and blood-red curling tongues chased white-faced sahibs down steep hillsides; a huge, silver-haired ape reared up on its hind legs atop a mountain ...

The boy stopped at the last one, raised his hands in the air with a quiet growl, and whispered, *"Migou,"* to Josef as he pointed at the beast.

"Schneemensch," Josef mouthed in reply, more to himself, before urging the boy onward. Heading ever deeper into the sleeping castle, they came to a set of

steep stairs that dropped straight down through the bowels of the building, seemingly continuing into the very rock of the hill. The temperature fell with every step, the cold stone chilling Josef's stockinged feet. At the last, the boy motioned that they stop. Together they craned their heads around the wall to see a small guardroom, little more than a lobby, lit with more flickering butter lamps. A low corridor beyond was lined on each side with heavyset wooden doorways. The cells.

In the center of the guardroom was a table, to the side a low wooden bunk. At the table, a guard was leaning forward onto his crossed arms. The tall bamboo jug and two rakshi bowls to the side of his head instantly gave Josef hope that the man was in a drunken sleep. In the bunk a second guard most definitely was sleeping, head thrown back, open mouth emitting a guttural snore that ebbed and flowed up and down the stone walls.

With the point of his ice-axe pick, Josef lightly tapped the stone of the staircase wall.

Neither of the guards stirred.

He tapped again.

This time the guard at the table did move to raise his head groggily, look around, and then slump forward onto the table.

Silently pulling out the smallest metal piton he could find in his pocket, Josef also turned his axe around so as to hold it by the neck like a club.

He waited for a few minutes before tossing the piton across the lobby into the cell corridor. The metal nail briefly clattered across the stone floor.

The guard at the table raised his head again,

turning to the source of the noise. Slowly he got up and staggered into the corridor.

Josef crossed the lobby behind him in three long yet silent strides to bring the wooden shaft of his axe down heavily on the back of the guard's neck. The man gave a brief grunt under the force of the blow, falling forward until Josef caught him with his other hand and slowly let him sink to the ground.

Dragging the prostrate guard further along the cell corridor, Josef pulled his rope from his pack and cut three short lengths. He tied the unconscious man's hands and feet and gagged him with the third piece. Picking up the rest of the rope he returned to the lobby to find the second man still sleeping soundly.

Stepping silently over to the snoring man, he knotted one end of the climbing rope to the end of the bed before weaving it around the frame of the bed and the guard's ankles, knees, waist, chest, and arms. Leaning over the guard's snoring face as he worked, Josef smelled the foul alcoholic odor of the man's breath compete strongly with his own stinking jacket. It made his eyes water.

Tugging the scarf around his neck free to plug the gaping mouth, Josef suddenly felt a point sear into his chest as if the material of the scarf was secured to it by a fishhook. The sharp, slicing pain made Josef jerk forward, involuntarily slamming a hand down onto the sleeping guard to brace himself. The man beneath him instantly awoke. Utterly confused, he emitted a short-lived shout of alarm before Josef could force the scarf into his mouth and pull hard on the rope to clamp the bucking man to the wooden bedframe.

The shooting pains within Josef's jacket continued

from the stabbing beak of the awakened peregrine chick that had remained still and silent during his delicate journey through the castle. Doubling the rope into the hand already pushing the guard's twisting, thrashing face, he desperately reached inside his coat to pull out the forgotten bird. As he held it away from his body over the wide eyes of the terrified, drunken guard, the hawk squawked and writhed in his hand, pecking furiously at the air, flapping its featherless wings, and clawing at Josef's wrist with its taloned feet. A squirt of white excrement splashed into the guard's wild eyes.

The young hawk and the man were squirming so violently, it left Josef with no option but to throw the eyas toward Phurbu, who scooped it up from the stone floor. Both hands now free, the German circled one last loop of rope around the guard's neck and pulled it tight onto the man's Adam's apple. Gagged and immobilized, he could only blink up through soiled eyes at Josef in horror.

Josef searched for keys on both of the bound guards. They weren't there. He looked back at the boy, who was sitting cross-legged, stroking the bird in silence; he hissed at him to get his attention. When the boy looked up, Josef made a turning motion with his hand.

Phurbu smiled back and, with one hand, pulled a tight bundle of old cloth from inside his jacket. Shaking it open, he triumphantly revealed a ring of keys that he must have taken during his search of the castle for Ang Noru. Josef guessed they had been intended for use as a—now unnecessary—bargaining chip for the hawk. Josef took the keys, running to open the cell that revealed the shadow of

Ang Noru through the window of its barred door.

The Sherpa was sleeping on the bare stone floor, oblivious to any commotion. Shaking him awake with a hand over his mouth so that he didn't cry out, Josef pulled him to his feet. His face scabbed and swollen, Ang Noru started to say, "Sahib Becker, you …" but Josef silenced him and pushed him quickly from the cell. There he gestured for the Sherpa to help him drag the unconscious guard back in.

That done, they returned to the guardroom where Josef pointed to the guard trussed to the bed, saying quietly, "We need the rope that holds that one to descend. We must tie him with something else and then leave them both in the cell." Finding some lengths of webbing, they retied the guard's hands, feet, and mouth before releasing the main rope and carrying him immobilized into Ang Noru's vacant cell. All the time the guard just stared at them in mute terror. They relocked the door and, with Phurbu leading the way, fled back up through the castle to the latrine. One by one they wormed their way down through it and moved back along the ledge to where Josef had set a piton when he first climbed up onto it.

Looping their rope through the eye of the anchor, Josef cast both ends down the cliff face. While he waited for Ang Noru and the boy to climb down the rope to the next small ledge where he had prefixed another piton, a red tinge to the horizon silently announced the new day. Shadowy mountains began to appear in ever-increasing ranks just as he had seen painted on the walls inside the castle. To the east, the way he and Ang Noru had come, their heights were lost in ominous grey cloud. But, to the west, their summits were slowly sharpening against the dawn sky. One summit was higher and, at first, blacker than the rest. The horizontal lines of its snow and rock layers caught the faint rays of light as if the mountain was veined with gold. A great plume of cloud blew back from the peak as if that gold was really fire.

Josef stared at Everest until a tug on the doubled rope told him it was time to come down. Descending, he paused only once, the remaining peregrine chick fluffing itself and pecking at him anew as Josef cast the bundle of cell keys into its lonely nest.

69

MONTE CARLO HARBOR, PRINCIPALITY OF MONACO
October 20, 2009
10:45 a.m. (Central European Time)

Walking alongside the harbor in Monte Carlo, Sarron was immersed in the extreme wealth of the Riviera. To his right, the street was lined with Ferraris, Lamborghinis, Maybachs, and Rolls-Royces like a luxury car show. Yet they were mere accessories when compared to the line of multimillion-euro yachts moored to his left. If he wanted money, then he had certainly come to the right place. It had taken a month to arrange a meeting with Stefan Vollmer. In the end it had been the Vishnevskys' access to a Russian oligarch that moored near to Vollmer who arranged an introduction through a terse, late-night telephone call that was going nowhere until Sarron told Vollmer he had the ice axe from the Weisshaus Club.

Vollmer's yacht wasn't hard to find. At over seventy meters long, the *Hyperborea* was significantly larger than the majority of the other boats docked in the crowded harbor. As Sarron approached, it rose up out of the water before him, blindingly white against the perfect blue of the sky. It was moored from the stern, revealing three visible decks, each broad in the beam to house the extensive living space within before narrowing to end in an aggressively sharp, angled prow that pointed out to sea like a grooved bayonet. The roof was a cluster of satellite dishes and communication domes—high-tech bumps and blisters that suggested greater purpose than the simple desire to follow the money markets or the latest game of the owner's Bundesliga soccer team in HDTV.

Sarron stepped onto the gangway that led to the lower rear deck of the yacht. It was narrow and unstable. Deliberately so, he thought, as, holding the rope barriers, he began to walk across, the gantry flexing beneath his feet similar to a long ladder over a crevasse in the Khumbu icefall. When the Frenchman was exactly halfway across, two men in immaculate white suits and dark glasses appeared from the rear of the boat, motioning him to stop exactly where he was, the bulges in their jackets indicating they were both armed. The little bridge to the boat bowed some more as Sarron stood there.

One of the men stepped forward to where the gangway met the boat. "Name?" he demanded as the other stood to the side, clearly covering his colleague should anything happen.

"Jean-Philippe Sarron."

"Shoe size?"

Sarron was momentarily confused by the question.

The security guard repeated the demand.

"Forty-one," he replied, slow to understand the purpose of the query.

"Okay. When you step onto the boat you will immediately hand me the bag you are carrying. Do you understand?"

Sarron nodded and deliberately held it forward to show he intended to take nothing out.

The guard motioned him forward onto the deck. There he exchanged the kit bag for a pair of slippers, saying, "Take off your shoes, put these on and then follow me." They then quickly ushered Sarron across the deck and through two sliding black glass doors into a security room. One side was lined with a myriad of camera screens that monitored every approach to the boat, even green-tinted underwater views of the ship's hull.

Once inside, both men motioned Sarron to stop again. One told him to remove his watch and belt, hand over his wallet, and then step through a metal detector followed by a pat down. Meanwhile, the other guard opened the kit bag to remove the only thing it contained, the old ice axe: its presence a condition of Sarron being allowed onto the boat to see Vollmer. The whole process was putting the Frenchman on edge. His mind automatically began to run moves and scenarios to evade them, to take them down, to kill them with the axe until he reminded himself that he was there at his own request. He needed to calm down if this was going to work.

Eventually satisfied that Sarron was unarmed and the ice axe was exactly as described, one of the two guards picked up an intercom and, after a few words, motioned Sarron to follow the other up a chrome spiral staircase. When he asked for the ice axe back, the guard curtly said no and told him to get moving.

Growing angry now, Sarron emerged up into an elegant reception room to be told to take a seat and asked if he would like a drink. He requested a brandy. While the drink was being prepared, he remained standing, looking at the room around him.

It was not what he had anticipated. He had expected something harder, edgier, but the room transported him away from the modern lines of the boat and the bright crystalline sea, to a softer, cooler country house seemingly somewhere in the Alps. There were sofas and chairs of the smoothest leather, polished wood sideboards and tables decorated with exquisite marquetry, antique Asian rugs, gleaming silver ornaments. Hanging on the walls were mountain scenes of the Argentinean Andes, interspersed with those of the Bavarian Alps. Handing Sarron the drink, the guard gestured once again for him to sit, waiting until he did so before leaving.

Still no one appeared. Sitting there alone, Sarron recalled what he had learned about the man that Kassner said many in Germany believed was going to lead the Nazis back to power one day.

Vollmer's extreme wealth was rooted in a steel business in the Ruhr Valley, built by his family over many generations. During the credit squeeze of the Great Depression, the family threw their hat in with the fledgling Nazi party, quickly becoming one of Adolf Hitler's most fervent benefactors. When the demand for steel rocketed during the rearmament, their loyalty was rewarded. At the end of the war, Vollmer's grandfather fled with his family to Argentina where, within the network of Nazi escapees and investments masterminded by Martin Bormann, they continued to be active in international business until the family could return to Germany in the midsixties. Once home, Stefan Vollmer's father, Rudi, was seemingly able to pick up exactly where his own father had left off some twenty years before, quickly reestablishing the family's steel interests.

Rudi Vollmer would die in 1993—a single-vehicle accident in the Simplon Tunnel that had "Mossad" written all over everything except the official police report. A week later, the *Yedioth Ahronoth* newspaper in Tel Aviv ran a story that reported an unnamed source in the Israeli government as "confident that Saddam Hussein's attempts at obtaining the materials of reconstruction and rearmament were being thwarted wherever he turned." Stefan, still a young man of thirty, had immediately picked up the reins of the family's interests, and did so with aplomb, taking them to even greater heights, expanding into all areas of modern commerce: real estate, energy, telecommunications, information technology, media, even sports club ownership.

In doing so, he was as discreet in his political affiliations as he was with everything else about his private life. However, in 2007, a young policeman in Munich had revealed that, through a series of dummy companies, Vollmer had been making significant financial donations to the German far-right NPD party and possibly sponsoring other underground neo-Nazi groups. The revelations had sent Vollmer running to Monaco, where he now lived full-time, the *Hyperborea* both his home and, by the look of it to Sarron, his fortress. There he abandoned his former discretion, vowing publicly to rebuild the far right across Europe and prepared to use his vast fortune in any way necessary to do so.

* * *

The entrance of his host interrupted the Frenchman's contemplation. Blond, tanned, wearing a red polo shirt and white slacks, Vollmer moved effortlessly into the room, more tennis professional than businessman, holding the old ice axe in his right hand as effortlessly as if it was a carbon-fiber framed racquet.

"*Bonjour*, Monsieur Sarron, welcome to the *Hyperborea*."

Sarron rose from his chair to meet the German. They shook hands with a firm grip, both making deliberate eye contact until Vollmer stood back and deliberately turned the axe upside down to hold it like a golf club. Taking a step back, he gave a practiced swing at an imaginary ball and said, "This old axe has already cost me much more than it is worth, so I hope that you are here to offer me something better?"

"I am," Sarron coldly replied.

Both sitting, Sarron proceeded to explain what he had learned from Graf about the axe in his hands.

Vollmer listened carefully saying only, "Interesting," as he pulled his face close to the steel axe head to study its tiny swastika.

"Then you might be even more interested to hear that, despite what happened in Munich, it seems that the Englishman who found that axe on Everest is still alive," Sarron continued. "It leads me to believe that others will soon want to find out what else is up there and, if it is as I suspect, will do everything to stop people like you getting their hands on it."

"People like me? What does that mean?"

"You know well what that means, Vollmer. I am not a policeman and you are not a communist. You are someone that could use such a story to promote their own stated interests and intentions."

"That is indeed true but do you think there is really more waiting up there? It seems a long jump from this ice axe to a frozen camera full of summit photos …"

"Perhaps … but is that a risk you can afford to take?"

"Sarron, I can afford anything, which I am sure is the principal reason why you are here."

"No, I am here because I am the one person, beyond the Englishman, who can retrieve whatever else is up there and, if it does prove to be a photograph of an elite Nazi climber on top of Everest in 1939, I am also sure that you are the one person that would like to own it."

"Okay, Sarron. I'm listening. What's your proposal?"

Sarron outlined his plan and its financial terms while Vollmer looked out on the Monaco harbor through the dark-tinted windows. When the Frenchman had finished, Vollmer said nothing for a few minutes before turning back toward Sarron and raising the axe up in the air as if imagining it flying a swastika on a distant mountaintop.

"That's a very expensive offer given that I have little interest in the contents of the pockets of some frozen Wehrmacht soldier; I could easily find similar myself if I were to dig around in the permafrost of Norway or Finland.

"No, the only thing that interests me is the rare chance, as you have explained, that you could find the climber's camera with actual summit photos still preserved. Such photographs would indeed have a high value to me and on that basis alone I am prepared to make a counteroffer. However it will have to be an 'all or nothing deal,' one that places the risk, as you call it, back onto your shoulders."

Sarron stared at Vollmer as he silently listened.

"I propose to fund you to go back to Everest," Vollmer continued, "and will pay you an additional 2.5 million euros for a bona fide summit photograph if it exists. If it doesn't, I will pay you nothing more than the initial expenses."

Sarron opened his mouth to negotiate but Vollmer quickly stopped him. "Take it or leave it, Sarron, you won't get a higher offer. And one more thing, I want this axe now as a sign of good faith."

"Okay, Vollmer, I'll take the deal but you can't have the axe. Well not yet anyway."

"Why?"

"I need to kill someone with it first."

70

WEWELSBURG CASTLE, NORTH RHINE-WESTPHALIA, GERMANY
April 18, 1939
7:30 p.m.

"Enter."

Pfeiffer stepped forward into the shadows of the reichsführer's circular office in the North Tower.

"Please sit," Himmler said, his head still turned down to the papers he was working on.

Pfeiffer walked toward the desk to do as he was ordered. For five minutes, he waited in silence, taking in the medieval room around him, the intricately carved heavy oak desk he was sat before, even the granite stand adorned with iron skulls and SS runes that served as a paper knife holder. Above him, the doglegged spokes of the black sun painted onto the circular ceiling radiated out to the tower wall like some form of antenna.

Something was wrong. What information had been sucked into that office? How was he involved? Trying to anticipate what it might be, Pfeiffer questioned his recent actions. They had all been in service of the reichsführer, all successful. He appreciated he had been heavy-handed in dealing with that group of Czech intellectuals agitating against increased German control in Bohemia and Moravia but it was no worse than anything Reinhard Heydrich was doing.

A final signature and the closure of the letter blotter signaled Pfeiffer was about to find out what was the problem.

"The British know about Operation Sisyphus," the reichsführer said reaching for another file. Opening it, he took out a letter. "I have heard from Hans Fischer in Darjeeling. Evidently, the British Army liaison officer on Schmidt's expedition sounded the alert not long after Obergefreiter Becker left for Tibet."

"This is disappointing, Herr Reichsführer. Do the British know where Becker is going?"

"At the moment it seems not, but I suspect that in time they will work it out. I have called you in as I wish to invoke the contingency detailed in your file note WBB12/125a should this operation be compromised."

"But it is not yet compromised, Herr Reichsführer. Becker could be climbing the mountain as we speak."

"He could be, but on the other hand, he could also be in the hands of the British. His family, the mother and two sisters, should be immediately moved into protective custody in Lichtenburg. Next month we will be opening our first facility solely for women at Ravensbrück. They are to be transferred there as soon as possible. Have them terminated twenty-four hours after their arrival and make a report to me of how well Director Koegel handles the process. He needs to get that camp to maximum efficiency as soon as possible. It will be an interesting early test of its readiness."

"But—"

"No buts, my dear Jurgen. What about the *mischling* in India?"

"Magda von Trier is in Hyderabad now."

"Our reach is long. Send an agent from our embassy in Calcutta to deal with her."

"All this can be done, but if Becker climbs the mountain, won't we have some explaining to do when he returns?"

"We will explain nothing. I always considered that your plan had a fatal flaw and these actions are also appropriate to its remedy should Operation Sisyphus prove to be successful."

"Herr Reichsführer?"

"You can't make a common criminal one of the most famous men in the Reich. Even if Obergefreiter Becker succeeds, his moment in the sun will be extremely brief. I suspect it will end in a fatal climbing accident in the mountains of Bavaria that he loves so much, not long after his return."

"I understand, Herr Reichsführer."

"I knew you would. Now tell me about what you have been up to in Bohemia. I have heard good things from Reinhard."

71

TSANG PROVINCE, TIBET
April 21, 1939
3:00 p.m.

It had taken Macfarlane's patrol two attempts to cross the Sepu-La. The first, inspired by the urgency of Zazar's news that the German and the Sherpa had passed that way, rushed them headlong into a fierce whiteout five hundred feet below the top of the pass.

It was the Tibetan who had led them back with frozen fingers and feet to collapse exhausted and hypothermic in the very same cave where the monks at Lachen Monastery told Zazar they had met Becker and Ang Noru before they had crossed the pass. The weather forced them to spend four miserable nights there. Unable to go on but without the possibility of turning back empty-handed, Macfarlane could only wait and watch with impatience and frustration as his patrol disintegrated into three units: Gurkhas, Tibetan, and Englishman.

The Gurkhas were brave fighting men, utterly loyal to their leaders and fearless in battle, but they were also tribal, spiritual men who were wary of the elements, assigning such matters to higher powers whom they did fear. In the cave, they presented him with brave, eager faces, yet otherwise kept their own company, sullenly whispering to each other as if defeated prisoners of the weather, aware that no simple stroke of their kukri knives could resolve their predicament.

The Tibetan, on the other hand, simply withdrew deep into the overhang. Draping a heavy blanket over his hooded cloak, he became utterly immobile, as if conserving every ounce of energy for when it might be better used. Macfarlane envied the hateful man's detachment. It was a skill that eluded him. Only once did Zazar approach him, and, when he did, he said nothing but just handed him a piece of foil paper he had found in the cave. It had come from a European cigarette packet or chocolate wrapper.

Macfarlane needed no words of Tibetan to understand what the man hunter was proving. With every paralyzed day spent under that rock wall, he could think only of his quarry moving further from him and the effect failure would have on his army career. Lonely beneath the cave's shadowy walls, decorated with other people's gods and goddesses, Macfarlane turned in on himself, replacing the ancient images with the paintings of his own ancestors lining the walls of his stately family home. Resplendent in red coats, decorated with rows of medals and clusters of stars, generals and brigadiers, grandfathers and great-grandfathers looked sternly down on him over thick waxed mustaches to demand explanation as to why he was going to be the one to ruin their family's long tradition of military glory and honor. He had to find the German.

To do so, through the mediation of the Gurkha sergeant, he tried to agree to new terms with Zazar for their capture, terms that would see both Becker and the Sherpa returned alive to Darjeeling. Each time they approached the Tibetan to propose a new fee, he would look up at the British officer as if he was a complete fool before pulling his hood forward again to hide his face, saying nothing. Some hours later the sergeant would then report, with obvious embarrassment, that the Tibetan's demand had actually increased. It was like some perverse Dutch auction.

That morning, when the lieutenant awoke finally to a brighter world of white and blue beyond the cave, they left quickly to slowly break a trail through the now deep snow up to the pass. It was backbreaking, torturous work, but Macfarlane would be denied his chase no longer. Arriving at the flags that jutted up from the new snow to mark the Sepu-La Pass, Macfarlane had looked down at a bare world of humpbacked mountains and valleys that stretched into infinity. The day was so clear and the country so vast that he almost expected to see Becker and the Sherpa walking the far horizon.

Descending from the ridge, following Zazar's lead, Macfarlane saw that the deep, soft snow was streaked with red, as if it had been sprayed with a thin mist of blood. The Gurkhas pointed to it and talked amongst themselves, becoming agitated, until Zazar stopped, turned back, and tersely shouted something. There was further discussion among the Gurkhas, and then the sergeant stepped out of the narrow trench that they were breaking to wade back through the deep snow and stop next to Macfarlane. "Not omen, sir. Not blood, sir," he stuttered with an unconvincing smile. "But sand, sir, sand. Red sand blown from the great Asian desert by the north wind during the storm."

"Of course, Sergeant. Thank you. I am aware that such a thing can happen in the high mountains," Macfarlane replied. He was telling the truth; as soon as the Gurkha had spoken, Macfarlane recalled reading in the *Times* of such a phenomenon in the Alps. He had been amazed that the mistral wind could carry sand from the Sahara all the way across the Mediterranean to deposit it on the snowy flanks of the highest Swiss mountains. But on that day, before the Gurkha had spoken, it was not the first explanation that had come to mind.

Zazar didn't wait for the conversation to conclude. He stamped on ahead into the stained snow at the same driving, relentless pace with which he had led the way since Lachen. Watching him, Macfarlane understood that the man who should have been the most suspicious of omens and portents ignored them all. He was as practical as he was cruel. The lieutenant dug deep, forcing his tired legs to follow.

72

FOREIGN AND COMMONWEALTH OFFICE (MAIN BUILDING), KING CHARLES STREET, LONDON, ENGLAND
November 5, 2009
12:05 p.m. (Greenwich Mean Time)

"Well, it all seems fairly straightforward to me. Mr. Quinn here will go back up and sort out this mess as soon as conditions permit, which I understand will be this coming spring. Her Majesty's Government would obviously have preferred it to be sooner, but evidently winter is not the best time to try and climb Mount Everest."

Quinn mouthed, "You don't say," quietly to himself as the civil servant continued to talk. "As you already know, Ms. Richards," the man emphasized the "Ms." with a drawn-out nasal burr, "we have found someone with previous Everest experience to accompany him—a Captain Mark Stevens. He was in the Paratroop regiment and undertakes sensitive security projects for us on a regular basis. The pair of them will go up to the"—he stopped to glance at a document on his desk—"Second Step. Once there, they will investigate the site where Mr. Quinn says he found the old ice axe and retrieve or dispose of any additional articles of interest depending on what is practical. The retrieved articles will then be couriered to London to be destroyed to the satisfaction of both the British and German authorities. This process will be coordinated by our representative in loco, which will be you, Ms. Richards, and also a representative of the German authorities." He consulted the paper again to read, "Inspector Martin Emmerich of the Bavarian State Police."

The civil servant raised a bushy eyebrow at Emmerich who was seated alongside Quinn and Henrietta.

"Which is you, sir, I trust?"

Martin Emmerich nodded in return, slightly bemused by the combination of the man's plummy Old Etonian voice and his archaic, chalk-stripe suit. The permanent undersecretary immediately turned his attention back to Henrietta.

"By undertaking this exercise, Ms. Richards, I am assuming that we can put this irritating little matter to bed once and for all and permit Her Majesty's Government to focus on more pressing world matters. I can't imagine that there is anything particularly complicated to any of this. People climb Everest all the time these days, don't they? It is not even as if they have to get to the top."

The horse-faced man gave a desultory shrug of his shoulders, clearly convinced that arriving at the Second Step on Everest was as taxing as his morning walk to Cobham railway station to catch the 7:26 into Waterloo. Quinn opened his mouth to correct the error, prompting Henrietta to kick the side of his ankle before he could utter a word. Turning to look at her, Quinn saw her head shake ever so slightly as if to say, "Don't you dare."

Biting his tongue, he looked instead through the immaculately clean window of the old ministry building. Outside, Whitehall was cold and grey, damply making its way into winter. The trunks of the trees lining the street were black and greasy from years of traffic fumes, the leafless branches above disfigured from decades of pollarding that had rendered them miserable and sore like over-chewed fingernails. Quinn too felt miserable and sore. He had only been discharged from the hideous concrete tower of Guy's Hospital a few days before. He still hurt like hell when the painkillers wore off. A walk of more than a hundred yards was a struggle. A return to Everest seemed impossible.

His attention was brought back into the room by the civil servant speaking to him directly. "Mr. Quinn, you will need to sign a confidentiality agreement bound by the Official Secrets Act to cover your participation in this matter. There are obviously to be no subsequent books or slideshows about this little Everest escapade. You do understand that?"

"Obviously," Quinn replied in sarcastic repetition.

The civil servant's face twitched a little at the cold stare that followed, forcing Henrietta to jump back into the conversation in her most enthusiastic headmistress voice. "Yes, it really will be quite routine. Mr. Quinn and Captain Stevens will be joining a British commercial climb organized by Bill Owen, an expedition outfitter I know well. He's ex-army himself, and we can trust him to be totally discreet. It will be explained to the rest of the team that Mr. Quinn is acting in the capacity of private guide to Captain Stevens, who, after a failed attempt on the difficult West Ridge with the British Joint Forces team in 2006, is returning to make the summit this time by the Northeast Ridge route.

"They will acclimatize with the team but set off slightly earlier than the others for their 'summit attempt' even if they will actually be stopping at the Second Step to make the investigation. As this is happening, I will be visiting the Base Camp with Martin. We estimate this is likely to be some time from mid-May onward. Between us, we will then deal with all necessary matters once they have descended. It will be really quite exciting to go there, won't it, Martin? Martin tells me he hiked Kilimanjaro once, so it won't be an entirely new experience for him."

She smiled at Emmerich and then abruptly closed the file of papers she was holding to prompt an end to the meeting.

It worked. The civil servant rose from his chair and showed them to the door.

* * *

Exiting the austere Ministry, Quinn began to rant at Henrietta as he slowly and painfully walked down the building's steps to the street. "I'm glad that pompous twit seems to think it's so easy to wander up to the Second Step, recover a few bits and bobs, and then head back down in time for bloody tea!"

Telling him to "Sssh," Henrietta lowered her voice

so that Emmerich wouldn't hear her over the passing traffic. "Neil, the man is not actually a fool. He has agreed to a very effective operation with the German authorities so that together we—and I mean *we*—can make what could be a major problem at a time of resurgent neo-Nazi activity quietly go away. Who do you think wrote the report that he was reading from? I did, and I hope you appreciate that, bar their inclusion of the ex-paratrooper, they are effectively permitting us to manage the whole thing."

Quinn knew she was telling the truth. All the time he had been in Guy's Hospital, she had visited him daily and put the plan together.

"And another thing," Henrietta continued testily, quickly glancing at Emmerich to be sure he wasn't listening. "Why do you think you received no further legal letters on behalf of Tate Senior amidst the get-well cards?"

"I rather assumed that once you were able to speak with Dawa, you confirmed that his son's death was not my fault."

"Neil, I have made an entire career based on assuming nothing. I would suggest you start doing the same. Tate Senior will never forgive you for what happened to his son, whether you are innocent or not. However, his own need for a little forgiveness due to some financial naughtiness involving offshore funds in the British Virgin Islands has enabled us to persuade him to focus his ire on Sarron and leave you alone."

There was little Quinn could say to that, so they walked on in silence until Henrietta pointed Quinn and Emmerich to a small corner pub, saying, "I think that before we go our separate ways over the winter, we should have lunch and compare a few notes to be sure that we are all on the same page."

The pub was dark inside but warm. While they waited for their food at a table in a corner, Emmerich updated them on his subsequent investigations relating to Sarron. After their cold war in Munich, he was open and friendly to Henrietta. He knew that he had been totally outplayed by "Agatha Christie," as he had secretly nicknamed her, but was smart enough to know that he should learn from it. His inclusion in the recovery plan had been Henrietta's way of apologizing for the trouble she had caused him and, in return, he seemed satisfied that it gave him fair representation in the process ahead.

Emmerich told them that Sarron had killed Graf as suspected but that they also now knew he had been assisted by Oleg Vishnevsky, a Russian known to International Police as an enforcer for organized crime in Moscow. The German police officer continued to add that Oleg Vishnevsky always worked in tandem with his brother, Dmitri, so it was thought likely that he was the one who had followed Quinn into the Weisshaus Club. Since then, he added, Sarron had vanished, possibly going to Moscow with the Vishnevskys in a private plane owned by one of Putin's inner circle.

Henrietta was disturbed by the information. "If Sarron's back together with those two then that is very bad news indeed."

"But surely if the bloody man is wanted for murder in Europe now as well as Asia, he'll have been caught by someone before the spring?" Quinn said, looking to Emmerich for some reassurance.

"I would hope so," Emmerich said but with little

confidence in his voice. "However the Vishnevskys have established quite a reputation for themselves in Moscow, making a lot of friends in high places. It would be easy for them to get new documents, travel papers, whatever Sarron needs to move around under the radar. We do, at least, have some time to play with even if, in the meantime, Quinn, you will have to be very careful."

"Neil is going to be staying with a cousin of mine in the country over the winter. He will not be found," Henrietta replied to Emmerich.

"Can I at least have the address? We have closed the file on Graf's death and, once his lawyers finish settling his estate, we will be able to release the motorcycle and possessions you left in his storage unit the night you were kidnapped."

"No, I'm sorry, Martin, but you can't," Henrietta replied. "Until Sarron is caught only I will know where Neil is while he trains to get back to full fitness. It has to be impossible for Sarron to find him. You can send it all to this address marked for my attention."

"Just the bags," Quinn added. "Keep the bike in Munich for now, I'll come and get it when all this is over. I don't want Henrietta riding it around London."

73

RONGBUK MONASTERY, RONGBUK, TIBET
April 25, 1939
2:30 p.m.

To Josef's tired eyes, the Rongbuk Monastery was little more than a ramshackle cluster of dusty buildings sliding down onto the wide valley floor as if part of the immense slip of rocks and rubble that curved down from the towering hills above. Flat-roofed and meager, the place spoke only of supplication before the great mountain that punctured the bright blue sky ahead. Bursting from the two sides of the valley, Everest rose up before Josef, utterly massive.

With each step nearer, Josef felt his spirit weaken under the mountain's unfriendly gaze. A comment Ang Noru made during one of their long, cold nights huddled around a small fire returned to him: "Sahib Josef, to you, I think, all mountains are friends. You must understand that Chomolungma is not your friend. She is a goddess with no need for human friends. You are as important and interesting to her as the fly is to you. She will kill you just as readily if you annoy her."

Josef told himself to stop looking, that this view of the mountain, separated from the rest of the Himalayas, entire for the first time, was too much to contemplate when he was so tired and hungry. Instead he turned to look at Ang Noru to escape the magnetic pull the mountain had on his eyes. The Sherpa smiled grimly back at him, flicking his head up at the mountain, pulling Josef's eyes back to it, saying, "Only here in the Rongbuk do you feel her truly. This is the place where all sahibs begin to really understand her great height. Not good to do on an empty stomach, I think. Better to look at monastery instead and use slow walking time to ask your god to make kind words to the Mother Goddess for you. I will find place to stay and equipment supply."

Josef nodded, too exhausted to even talk, setting his gaze on the large chorten that stood before the main entrance to the monastery's cluster of buildings. The swollen, dirty white cupola thrust a golden mast, with emblems of the sun and moon, high into the air before them. Four strings of wind-torn, faded prayer flags arced down from the apex to be secured to the ground by small stacks of carved stones. His fatigued brain registered the sight as a big radio transmitter beaming messages to the pinnacle of the mountain, communicating directly between the monastery and the goddess on the summit. The surreal, rippling thought told him how much he needed to rest.

Arriving alongside the monastery, Josef let his heavy pack fall to the ground and slumped down onto the dirt, leaning back against the whitewashed stonework plinth that supported the chorten. Ang Noru walked on to tie their remaining pony to a loop set in the side of the main entrance. With a final, "Sahib Josef, rest here. Better when you have food, sleep," he disappeared into the dusty compound.

Josef could move no more. His only surprise, concern really, was that Ang Noru was not similarly exhausted. *How does he do it?* His energy, his endurance seemed limitless. The Sherpa made a mockery of Waibel's rambling discourses on Aryan racial superiority in the library at Wewelsburg. It was Ang Noru who was the superman, not Josef.

The Sherpa was also now his friend. He had changed toward Josef immensely since the rescue. He was considerate and talkative, at times humorous, even if he still used the title "Sahib," he applied it to Josef not Becker. It was only when Ang Noru spoke about the mountain, reluctantly, when pushed into necessary response by Josef's endless questions or another distant sighting of it, that he became dour again. The Sherpa's chopped, broken observations and warnings about how Josef should try to climb the mountain had become his mantra as he walked, particularly the one in which he saw his only possibility for redemption.

"Sahib Josef, your only chance is to pass unobserved. The British are noisy. They come with large expeditions like loud armies determined to conquer her. They are soldiers first and mountain people second. The Mother Goddess is not a castle to be stormed by a great force of men. You must be a mountain person first and a soldier second. Seek to live quietly on her sides, not fight her, and she will ignore you, allowing you to creep higher. The quieter you are, the higher you will get. You did it for me at Kampa Dzong; you will have to do it again for her, ten times over."

74

Josef awoke to find himself still leaning back against the chorten. His back and neck were aching and he felt feverish and weak. Before him was a semicircle of shaven-headed young monks. Seeing him surface, one said, "Aha," as the others smiled and pointed.

Another stepped forward from amidst the grinning faces to approach Josef. The monk stood in front of him, staring down, speaking without pause, a waterfall of language cascading from his smiling mouth. The novice pointed at Josef and then up at the mountain, his dialogue becoming just one word, "Chomolungma."

The others quickly followed his lead. Shuffling their sandaled feet, the monks began chanting the name in unison. The incantation grew, louder and louder. It reminded Josef of the gamblers chanting in the caravansary and began to fill him with the same dread of discovery.

Ang Noru returned to push through the monks and reach out a hand to pull Josef back up onto his tired legs.

The monks instantly fell silent, staring at Josef as if surprised to see that he could stand, almost wary that they had angered him.

"Do they know?" asked Josef, his head beginning to spin as he followed the Sherpa back to the pony.

"Of course. There are few secrets here. There have been messengers; the British are looking for us in Tibet. The monks know well that if we have come here it is only for one thing: the mountain. They have offered us a room. Let us go there, and I will tell you all."

The room was within a side building off the monastery's central courtyard. It was bare and simple, but it shut out some of the cold and was clean. The sight of the mountain through its solitary square window resembled the fearsome framed picture in the entrance of the Hotel Nanga Parbat. Josef quickly shuttered the window to hide it from view, but it did little to block the roar of the wind racing over the summit. It sounded like an out-of-control freight train.

They unloaded, then sat on the floor and ate a meal that two young monks brought to them. It was simple and without taste, but its warmth and variety after their daily diet of plain flour cakes and dried yakmeat reinvigorated Josef a little as Ang Noru explained what more he had learned in the monastery about the British.

But only when the meal was finished did the Sherpa reach into the front of his baggy jacket and pull out a sealed letter. "From your countrymen, there is only this, Sahib Josef. No supplies or man with it so I think may be better to give after you eat. You stronger then if bad news."

Josef opened the sealed envelope.

A formal printed letterhead across the top of the page inside read:

DEUTSCHE TIBET EXPEDITION ERNST SCHÄFER

Below, atrocious, hasty handwriting crammed the single sheet:

Sisyphus,

If you have made it to Rongbuk to receive this letter, then I salute you as a man of endeavor. I assure you that there is no one who understands better than I the difficulties of traveling through this savage and barren land. It is only out of respect for your possible arrival that I take the extreme risk of sending you this communication by native messenger. If apprehended, it could in itself compromise my entire Tibetan mission.

Be aware that from the start I expressed my fears to the reichsführer-SS regarding Operation Sisyphus. I considered it undoubtedly doomed—you do see the mountain before you?—but also bearing the potential to destroy the necessary business of my own SS expedition to Tibet.

While my opinions were ignored, my concerns have come to pass. It is apparent that the British authorities in both India and Sikkim have become aware of your illegal entry into Tibet. Their cadre, here in Lhasa, is already using the matter to increase pressure on the Tibetan government to terminate my expedition and expel me from the country.

As I write, it seems that the British are not yet aware of either the exact nature of Operation Sisyphus or your current location. It is only because of this that they have so far been unsuccessful in their lobby. If I recall correctly, our führer writes that "leadership necessitates uncomfortable burdens," and with this in mind, it is with regret that I advise you that, as de facto leader of the National Socialist Mission to Tibet, I cannot risk the issue of supplies or personnel to assist you as instructed.

Having to turn away when so near to your goal must indeed make you feel like Sisyphus himself, but I can assure you that it is in the best interests of our wider project for Tibet. I personally advise you to cross into the Kingdom of Nepal and make good your escape from there.

Heil Hitler!

Refolding the letter, Josef got up and reopened the window shutters to look at the the mountain again.

His eyes followed the line of the Northeast Ridge to the summit. Mouthing, "Berg heil!" at it and shaking his head in disbelief, he turned to Ang Noru to explain.

75

THE OLD FARMHOUSE, BETWS-Y-COED, SNOWDONIA, NORTH WALES
March 15, 2010
11:00 a.m.

The ring of the doorbell followed by a heavy welsh accent shouting, "Delivery. Three packages for a Mr. Quinn," announced the arrival of the bags from Munich that Martin Emmerich had promised. They had been a long time coming owing to the protracted legal process involving Graf's estate which was, inevitably, thought Quinn, as obscure and complicated as the man himself.

As Quinn ripped open the three boxes to reveal his big kit bag and the two plastic pannier suitcases off his motorcycle, his first thoughts were of the climbing kit they contained. It was just one month before he was due to leave Snowdonia for Tibet and the absence of his bags had begun to make him think that he was going to have to purchase much of it anew, something he could ill afford to do.

The delivery, same week that the Welsh valley

turned yellow with daffodils, signaled that his winter of recovery from the events of Munich was now finished. He had spent all of it at that whitewashed farmhouse, run as a small yet comfortable hotel by some distant cousin of Henrietta, rebuilding himself for a return to Everest. He refused to call it hiding.

During the cold, damp days, he progressively pushed himself out of the medical rooms of the local physiotherapist and back into the granite and heath peaks that surrounded the small town. In the evenings he recovered from the aches and pains sitting by a log fire in the local pub, immersed in the notes and maps of Everest that Henrietta had loaned him.

Quinn thought he knew a lot about the mountain, but Henrietta's information was so much more detailed than the well-known histories of Everest that he had read in the past. It opened up a new world to him, one of unpublished mystery and endeavor that made him appreciate for the first time how the mountain had been a magnet for many unknown adventurers over the years. The more he read, the more he thought about Josef Becker and Ang Noru, the more inspired he became to follow in their tracks. The more he wanted to resolve the story and keep it, as Graf and Henrietta desired, from those that would use it for harm.

Opening the bags, still sealed with German police tags, he unpacked the contents and began to assemble the things he needed. One of the alpine climbing boots he took out was filled by a green T-shirt.

The sight shocked him.

He had forgotten all about it.

Quinn gently pulled the cotton bundle from the

leather boot, feeling the hard lump within.

It's still there!

He slowly opened up the crumpled T-shirt to reveal inside the antique Leica camera that the collector had given him.

For a moment, Quinn just held it in his hands lost in thought about Graf. He had only met the man briefly, but his murder at the hands of Sarron had, in a way, wounded Quinn far more than the nightclub shooting. Even if he suspected that such an end might have appealed to the collector, it made him increasingly fearful for Henrietta. She had the same intense curiosity in the story of the axe, a curiosity that was tending to kill the cat.

He would have been lying if he'd said it didn't worry him that there had been no recent news about Sarron. Quinn knew that he was still out there, watching and waiting. To have hoped that the psychotic Frenchman would be simply apprehended by the police now struck him as ridiculous. With every hike up into the Welsh hills, he understood that he was not only preparing himself to go back to the mountain but also to finish this thing with Sarron once and for all. He owed it to many people.

Quinn looked again at the Leica III, imagining it lying with a dead body high on the mountain.

He turned it over in his hands, studying it in detail.

It was compact and strong. Such a dense metal body could easily survive seventy years frozen in ice.

Lifting the camera to his right eye, he pictured within the small viewfinder a climber on a summit raising an ice axe and a flag.

He pushed the small shutter release button to

capture the imaginary moment. It wouldn't move.

When he looked at the film indicator, Quinn remembered something else.

76

KAMPA DZONG, TSANG PROVINCE, TIBET
April 25, 1939
5:00 p.m.

At the imposing gates of the Kampa Dzong fortress, Macfarlane gladly let Zazar, Colonel Atkinson's official travel documents held upside down in his big hand, do the talking. Entry was quickly permitted through the immense stone walls into a courtyard full of people. Tibetan noblemen, monks, paupers, soldiers, even small children were all standing in a circle, looking in on a cleared space writhing with colorful motion, a halo of dust hovering above.

The young lieutenant presumed they must be watching a fight, but as he pushed nearer, he saw that it was actually a dance. Curtained in brightly embroidered yet tattered ceremonial robes that draped from their arms and legs, every participant wore a tarnished copper mask beneath a headdress of horn, feathers, and long plaits of matted, woven yak hair. The bear, the yak, the fish, the wolf, the horse, and the pig strutted and spun violently around a smaller yet wilder dancer thrashing desperately in their middle. Holding out silk-swathed arms, flapping them like wings, it pecked back with its sharply hooked metal beak and clawed at them with long, hooked, wooden claws.

"Tibetan devil dance, sir. The spirits are being summoned to kill a hawk demon," the Gurkha sergeant whispered into Macfarlane's ear as he watched. Even through his fatigue, it was an amazing sight to witness, as if the long trek to get to that forsaken place had distorted the barriers of time and deposited them into the Middle Ages.

The British officer looked around at the spellbound crowd, only slightly less strange than the dancers at its center. He noticed a small urchin, wedged between the legs of the spectators on the opposite side of the square, staring at the scene. Transfixed with a look of total horror, the boy was holding a small animal in the front of his filthy jacket. Macfarlane thought the grey, fluffy bundle was a baby rabbit or a cat, but then he saw that it too had a sharp, hooked beak and black shiny dots for eyes. It was a hawk, a kestrel or peregrine, still very young, downy and round, only recently taken from the nest. Sensing he was being watched, the boy broke his gaze from the gyrating hawk dancer to look straight at Macfarlane. Slipping back between the legs around him, he vanished.

Goaded by vibrating blasts from long horns arranged on the battlements, the dance gathered in intensity, the hawk dancer beginning to fail, dwindling before the other triumphant dancers until it spiraled into the dusty ground. One final earsplitting cacophony announced its symbolic death, and the other dancers, victorious over the hawk god, mimed hacking it into invisible pieces with which each creature fled back into the castle.

* * *

The symbolic sky burial over, the crowd dispersed quickly, and guards became attentive in leading the patrol inside to meet the dzong pen, the governor of the region. Four fur-capped soldiers, looking to Macfarlane as if they were part of Genghis Khan's Mongol army, accompanied them through wide but dark corridors until they came to a big hall.

At the far end, a large chair stood alone like some rudimentary throne and a small man, dressed in a high-collared, woven, crimson silk jacket that caught the glow of the butter lamps, was seated upon it. He was listening without reply to the competing comments of a group of advisers sitting cross-legged before him on an immense yet threadbare carpet. His eyes were tight shut, his face screwed up in intense concentration.

One of the soldiers approached the nearest adviser who, in turn, rose to approach the dzong pen and whisper in his ear. The overlord immediately opened his eyes; ratlike, they fixed on the British officer.

The small man immediately stood up from his high-backed chair and summoned a waiting servant who stepped forward to bring him a wide-brimmed fedora. The dzong pen slowly lowered the hat onto his head with both hands on the brim. It was far too big for him. Relinquishing his throne, he stepped through the still-seated councillors to meet Macfarlane.

He stopped silently before him as if struck by some deep thought. "*Ingleish prezent*," he said as he took the fedora off and offered it to Macfarlane. Uncertain, the lieutenant took it, flipping it over to see the white hatter's label within. There was an address for Savile Row; beneath, in black ink, the previous owner had written, "Gen. C. G. Bruce." Macfarlane was familiar with the name. General Bruce was a legend in the Gurkha Rifles. He must have gifted it to the dzong pen on the way to one of his attempts on Mount Everest some years earlier, for which he was equally famed.

Handing the fedora back, Macfarlane said, "A worthy hat," but the dzong pen, his knowledge of English already exhausted, instead turned his attention to Zazar. He greeted him warmly. Zazar, in return, handed him their travel papers, the dzong pen studying them with feigned comprehension as he questioned his countryman. Zazar's answers were long and convoluted. Macfarlane had no trust in the rapid stream of conversation until, unable to stand it it any longer, he told the Gurkha sergeant to stop Zazar from speaking and translate what had been said. With an insubordinate look at the officer for interrupting him, Zazar responded angrily to the sergeant, who relayed the content to Macfarlane.

"Zazar says the Sherpa Ang Noru was here. He caused a great fight in the town in which three men died. The Sherpa was sentenced to lose his cutting hand as penalty for starting the fighting and then death for the death he caused. The night before he was to be punished, he summoned a hawk god to the castle. The hawk spirit stank of a thousand hells and regurgitated its young onto the prison guards before switching them into the Sherpa's cell by magic. The Sherpa then escaped by changing into a bird demon and flying with the hawk god off the high cliff. Every day since, the dzong pen has ordered a devil dance before sunset to slay the hawk spirit."

"A highly unbelievable story, Sergeant. Is there any mention of the German in this fairy tale?"

"No, sir."

"Sergeant, can Zazar ask the dzong pen if we can stay here before we continue our journey?"

"He has done so already, sir, although you will have to give him some gifts in return. Zazar also says that the dzong pen believes that the magic of the devil dancers is now growing so strong that the Sherpa will soon be found."

"Let's hope so, for all our sakes, Sergeant."

77

Macfarlane spent the next day in the castle as the quickly abandoned guest of the dzong pen. Welcoming the rest and the solitude, he explored the castle. It was fascinating to Macfarlane, a piece of living history. From one window, he thought he could even see Mount Everest itself. The sight made him shiver. He thought again about General Bruce leading those first British expeditions to the mountain, and then of that famous British climber, George Leigh Mallory, who first went with him and then ended up vanishing so high on its flanks.

Is it really possible that he could have stood on the summit that day, as some of the newspapers still speculated?

Looking at the immense mountain, the lieutenant imagined the honor and courage that Mallory must have had to attempt such a feat, knowing full well that with every step he risked death. It was a humbling thought.

Returning to his room to rest, the Gurkha sergeant approached him with Zazar standing alongside. "Zazar wishes to make a transaction with you, Lieutenant Macfarlane, sir," the sergeant announced.

Macfarlane ignored the Tibetan's stare to reply to the Gurkha. "Does he indeed, Sergeant. And why should he feel the need to make a transaction with me now?"

"He says that it is you that has the need and, if you don't, you will never find the German you seek, returning to your countrymen empty-handed and in disgrace."

The accuracy of the Tibetan's understanding of Macfarlane's position caused the officer to involuntarily glance at Zazar. Their eyes momentarily locked.

"Go on. I'm listening."

The Tibetan and the sergeant talked some more until Zazar gestured that the man relay the conversation to Macfarlane. "Zazar wants you to pay him what was agreed with Colonel Atkinson when he leads you to the German and the Sherpa. He says that you can then take the German but the Sherpa must be allowed to stay in Tibet with Zazar." The sergeant paused before adding, "I am thinking, sir, that Zazar has sold the Sherpa's head to the dzong pen. The dzong pen will pay much money for it to show everyone that he is stronger than a hawk god and that no man can escape his castle."

Macfarlane was outraged at the Tibetan's gall.

"Absolutely not!" he shouted in reply. "Tell that accursed man that the Sherpa Ang Noru is wanted by the British authorities for aiding and abetting a foreign agent in activities detrimental to the interest of His Majesty. The Sherpa is not a bargaining chip for this man hunter to demand at will."

The Gurkha relayed the response to the Tibetan. With a slight smile, Zazar stared back at the officer as he replied in his low, guttural voice, the Gurkha translating as he spoke. "He says then you should return to the very top of the castle and from a window look down the great cliff it stands upon. He says that if you can imagine yourself climbing up that cliff alone and in the night, then you will catch the German yourself and have no need of his help. If however, when you look down it, your stomach turns over, your palms sweat, and you know that you could never do such a thing, then he says that you are in no position to bargain, for you will never catch a man who can climb such a wall without Zazar's good help."

The Tibetan turned and walked away, indifferent to Macfarlane's shouts to stay exactly where he was.

* * *

Macfarlane held out for most of the next day but then reluctantly followed Zazar's suggestion. Returning to the window from where he had seen Everest, he pushed his head out, this time looking straight down.

The plummeting drop below him made him instinctively pull back. It felt as if the castle could topple off the edge of the cliff at any moment. Looking out a second time, the mere thought of the view down the sheer rock face made him involuntarily brace his knees against the wall and lock his hands onto the window frame. Only then could he study the cliff below.

It was precipitous, sheer, and, although seemingly

impossible to climb, the officer understood Becker must have somehow gotten up it to enter the castle and free the Sherpa. If so, it was a feat of incredible skill and bravery. The realization forced Macfarlane to tell himself that if he didn't want to return to his regiment and his family a disgrace, he was going to have to use every tool in his power to find such a man. He must swallow the bitter pill and accept Zazar's offer for the greater good.

Even though he immediately sought out the Gurkha sergeant and told him that he would accept the Tibetan's terms, it wasn't until the evening that Zazar reappeared. When he did, he was pulling a small child after him. The boy was struggling to free himself from the tight grip on his hair, twisting and screaming like a snared cat, kicking out without effect at the man's long legs. In the flickering lamplight, Macfarlane saw that it was the boy with the hawk chick he had seen watching the devil dance.

Stopping before Macfarlane and the Gurkha sergeant, Zazar kicked the boy's feet from under him so that he fell to his knees. The Tibetan instantly squatted alongside him, tugging his head back, forcing him to look up at the officer.

The boy glared fiercely into Macfarlane's eyes before spitting up into the air.

Zazar immediately slapped the boy hard on the side of the head. The small child reeled from the blow and screamed back at the Tibetan so piercingly that Macfarlane's ears whistled.

The boy then spat up at him again. This time the frothy saliva was streaked with blood.

As Zazar raised his hand to strike the child

again, Macfarlane shouted at the Gurkha sergeant to intervene. "Sergeant, stop him. What is this, for God's sake? Who is this?"

The sergeant did as he was ordered, the Tibetan slamming the boy forward hard onto the flagstones, his face giving a crack as it struck the floor. Then, wedging his knee across the back of the boy's neck, he pulled the hawk chick from his own jacket and spoke back to the Gurkha.

"Zazar says this boy helped the German climb into the castle to free the Sherpa. He stole this young falcon from its nest on the great cliff."

"So where are they now?" Macfarlane demanded.

The Gurkha and the Tibetan spoke again before the sergeant responded, "Zazar says the boy knows, although he won't say."

"Sergeant, tell this boy that no one wants to hurt him, that I can make this stop. Let him go with his hawk. He only has to tell us where the German and the Sherpa are now."

When the Gurkha completed the translation, the boy struggled violently against the heavy pressure of Zazar's knee before shouting desperately back at Macfarlane. As the last word escaped his lips, the manhunter smacked the boy across the back of the head with his free hand.

"I cannot translate his reply, Lieutenant Macfarlane, sir. It is too disgusting to repeat to an officer," the Gurkha sergeant said.

"Repeat my message to him, Sergeant."

The sergeant did as he was told, but the boy just spat again.

Enraged by his continued insolence, Zazar pulled

the child back onto his feet by the hair and flung him against the wall.

To Macfarlane's shout of, "For Christ's sake, man!" the boy's body crashed against the plaster and fell back hard onto the floor. For a moment he lay quite still. Then, like a crushed crab pulling itself back under a rock, he dragged himself tight into the foot of the wall, sobbing and staring at his torturer with fear in his broken, bleeding face.

Zazar raised himself up to stand over him, one arm holding the hawk chick by the neck so that the boy could see it dangling. Slowly and deliberately the Tibetan flexed his big hand around its neck.

The eyas' beak gaped open in a desperate reflex against the suffocation. It flapped its stubby down-covered wings pathetically, clawing weakly at the man's wrist.

The little boy looked at the hawk chick and then at Macfarlane. Staring at the British officer, he began to beg, screaming, *"Nein, nein, nein."*

Macfarlane instantly understood that the boy was appealing to him to stop Zazar in the only foreign words he knew—German words.

Zazar spoke again to the boy. Wiping the blood and tears from his face with the back of his hand, the boy shook his head and said, *"Nein,"* once again.

The Tibetan began to swing the chick as if preparing to spin its body from its neck.

The boy looked beseechingly again at Macfarlane before prostrating himself on the floor, facedown, sobbing uncontrollably.

Lying there, his body shuddering, his small hands beating the stone, one word started to emerge, "Chomolungma."

"What is he saying, Sergeant?"

"Chomolungma, sir. It is the Tibetan name for Mount Everest. The German and the Sherpa have gone to Mount Everest."

Zazar shouted triumphantly and, thrusting his arm high into the air, closed his hand on the chick's neck. The hawk chick's feet kicked downward three times and its eyeballs burst from their sockets. The tiny wings fell limp.

The Tibetan threw the dead bird at the boy's defeated body and then walked back to look Macfarlane straight in the eyes. As he did so, he said something to the British officer before turning and striding from the room.

"Hawk spirit dead now," translated the Gurkha.

78

EVEREST NORTH BASE CAMP, RONGBUK VALLEY, TIBET—16,980 FEET
May 7, 2010
3:45 p.m.

The team's final rotation up to the North Col camp at over twenty-three thousand feet had passed without problems. As he strode back into the Base Camp to await the "go" for a summit attempt during the course of the next week, Quinn felt stronger than he had ever imagined possible during his Welsh winter of recuperation. Even if the circumstances of his return were completely bizarre, it felt good to be back on the mountain that he had wondered if he would ever climb again.

Beyond maintaining the appearance that he was Stevens' "guide," Quinn actually had little to do with the ex-paratrooper during the long acclimatization phase of Bill Owen's "Everest North Climb, 2010." A sullen, mechanical man, Stevens said virtually nothing, making so little attempt to be friendly that Quinn assumed keeping his distance was part of his orders. Despite the silent tension between the pair, things were relaxed for Quinn with everyone else in the Base Camp. Bill Owen ran a tight yet good-natured ship. He had five clients, all with good high-mountain experience. Two well-qualified guides were assigned to them. The Sherpa team was one of the most experienced on the hill. They all went diligently about their business of preparing to summit the mountain, and Quinn enjoyed their company when they were together in the camp. On any rest days, he also tried to catch up with the other teams to hear the Base Camp gossip, always with one ear open as to the possible whereabouts of Sarron, but no one had seen him or heard of him.

Quinn had tried to discuss Sarron with Stevens but the ex-soldier showed little interest. When he attempted to impress on him the Frenchman's disturbed history of murder and violence, Stevens just shrugged his shoulders and said that he had been up against worse. When they talked about their upcoming journey to the Second Step, Stevens was equally noncommittal. "You're the guide, Quinn, so just lead me to the gorak cave," he would say, his face devoid of emotion. "We go up. We retrieve anything of real interest. We destroy the rest. We go home. QED."

Hearing an echo of the FCO official's orders in Stevens' description of their mission, Quinn took task with the word "destroy." Imagining what that might mean, Quinn said if they did find any mortal remains, they must be respected. He suggested that after they had made the search and recovered any artifacts, they should cover any remains with an old tent fly weighed down with some rocks, maybe even go as far as to leave it with some more modern clothing, some old plastic boot shells, in order to make it look more recent and less interesting. Even as Quinn said the last detail, he knew it sounded ridiculous. He'd overplayed it. Stevens just stared back at Quinn and said, "Yes, we could do that. Alternately, you could use that stuff to cover the body of that sixteen-year-old you left up there last year." They spoke even less after that.

Quinn knew that something bad was coming from the ex-paratrooper just as it was from Sarron. He tried to make sense of it all but came to only two conclusions. First, there was no trust. Second, given that he had Graf's old Leica camera hidden at the bottom of his kit bag, there probably shouldn't be.

* * *

At lunchtime the next day, Henrietta Richards and Martin Emmerich arrived.

Henrietta hadn't visited the Rongbuk for fifteen years. She refused to be driven the final part of the new Chinese road, insisting she walk into the camp instead. She made a triumphant arrival at the mess tent, the Sherpas rushing to greet her, bedecking her with silk *kata* scarves in expression of their welcome. Once inside she held court as they reverently served her tea and biscuits, her presence in the Base Camp the event of the season. Everyone came by to pay their respects to the world's leading expert on Everest, ostensibly there to research yet another book about the great mountain. When Quinn could finally enter the tent and greet her amongst the throng, she fixed a sharp eye on him and mouthed, "You need to speak to Martin. He has some news of Sarron. I'll catch up with you when all this brouhaha has settled down."

He quickly left to find Emmerich outside, being escorted to the tent allocated to him for his stay. The German was feeling the altitude with a pulsing migraine so severe it was making him squint and arch his neck forward as he stumbled along. Quinn took control of him from the Sherpa and asked about Sarron as he led Martin to his tent. Through short, panting breaths, Emmerich told him that he was indeed still free, and that a routine surveillance operation in Monaco had recorded an unknown man, later identified as Sarron, visiting the yacht *Hyperborea*. He struggled to explain what that meant but the Englishman got there before him. "Martin, you can save your breath," Quinn said. "I've heard the name Vollmer before. I think we can assume that Jean-Philippe Sarron has teamed up with the one person as eager to have proof of a Nazi summit as we are to hide it."

Quinn helped Emmerich into his tent, lectured him on drinking as much fluid as possible, and then just stood there looking up at the black mountain towering over him. He could feel the storm coming even if the forecast was good.

79

EVEREST NORTH BASE CAMP, RONGBUK VALLEY, TIBET—16,980 FEET
May 11, 2010
6:30 p.m.

All the talk at the climbers' dinner that evening was of the team's imminent departure for the summit. Neil Quinn and his client would be leaving the next day. The remainder of the team was to follow a few days later. Everyone was excited, the mess tent filling with an electricity of anticipation and suppressed fear that almost made its poles vibrate with static. Bringing in the various courses of the meal, Pani, the assistant cook boy, was listening carefully to the expedition members talking. The more he heard, the more excited he also became. He had to tell himself to be patient. He knew the climbers would want to eat huge amounts if they were shortly going up. The meal would take time. He just smiled back at them as he worked, thinking of the money.

The supper finally finished, table cleared, dishes

washed, Pani slipped away to the storage tent where he also slept. There, when he was absolutely sure that no one was in earshot, he quietly made one more call on the new mobile phone given to him by the two Russians in Nyalam. Waiting once again for that familiar voice message followed by the electronic beep that signaled he should speak, he thought of those two kind friends of Neil Quinn, so keen for news of how he was doing on the mountain. That evening, understanding its importance to them, he said his message twice to be sure they got it. "Your friend Neil Quinn leave Base Camp for Everest summit tomorrow morning. I say you again, Neil Quinn leave Base Camp for summit tomorrow."

Putting his precious phone away, Pani felt pleased with himself. He was sure that the two Russians would be happy to hear that their old friend was going to the summit once more; they had seemed so interested in news about the climb. He was also happy for himself because, even if at times it had been a bit difficult to keep it a secret from the other Sherpas, it really was a lot of money for nothing. All he'd had to do was leave a short message each time Quinn returned from the mountain to the Base Camp and then a final one for when he was going to the summit. The Russians had paid him a hundred dollars up front and assured him that he would get another fifty each time he left a message.

So that's another two hundred now, Pani thought happily. Plus the men had told him he could keep the phone and another present they would bring him if he kept it all a secret. *And I have!* Three hundred dollars was as much as his pay for the entire trip, and he would also be returning to Kathmandu with a new Chinese telephone. He only had to wait now for the Russians to visit him in the Base Camp and pay up as they promised they would do. Pani was a happy cook boy that night.

* * *

Sarron was also satisfied to get that final message. He knew the summit weather window was fast approaching, but until he received that last call, his plan couldn't start. For the last five days he had been waiting for it, holed up in a small lodge in the village of Tingri, fifty miles to the north of the Base Camp. That time of year the place was crawling with tourists, climbers, and Chinese soldiers. Keeping a low profile, he let the Vishnevskys go about the business that needed to be done. The hours had dragged, stuck in that simple room, wondering whether there was even going to be a camera. What if Graf had been wrong? Without it, Vollmer had been clear, there would be no more money.

The only way Sarron could break his mind from the uncertainty was by shifting it to how he was going to kill Neil Quinn. His hatred for the British guide was so intense that it made him pace the room, talking to himself, acting out an end game with hacks and stabs of the ice axe, its edges carefully sharpened with a whetstone in preparation. With Quinn dead and an old frozen camera in his possession, Sarron could finally move on. And there had to be a camera— why else would Quinn be going back up? From the moment that Wei Fang had emailed him the Everest permit requests for that season, which showed Quinn as a member of Owen's expedition, Sarron knew what he was returning for.

His plan now relied on that happening. Even so, he had found it a struggle to control himself as he spied on Owen's team coming through Nyalam on their way to the mountain. It took all his willpower to not go over to the team's hotel in the middle of the night and stab Quinn as he slept. But he needed the camera first. Quinn's death, although essential, could only come after, and when it did, Sarron promised himself, it would be more spectacular than just stabbing him in his sleep. Reluctantly, he had bided his time as the two Russians had dealt with the cook boy, setting up their eyes and ears within Quinn's camp.

When Owen's team had moved on to start acclimatizing on Everest, Sarron and the two Russians had gone in the opposite direction to the mountains west of Shishapangma. At first, he thought they should climb that mountain to prepare themselves for the trip to altitude on Everest, but, even there, the possibility of being seen by someone who might recognize him was too great. Anyway, they didn't need to go that high. As long as they could go once to at least twenty-three thousand feet, they would be ready to get up to the high camps on Everest and do what needed to be done.

The message signaled it could start at last. The next evening they would go to the Base Camp. Stopping only as long as it took to deal with the cook boy, they would then move on to the glacier, keeping themselves a day behind Quinn as he moved up through the higher camps on the hill. They were going to do it fast and light, taking only the minimum kit: high-altitude suits, sleeping bags, oxygen masks, and radios. Sarron knew that the high camps would now be totally stocked for the forthcoming summit attempts. All the oxygen and food they needed was already up there.

80

RONGBUK MONASTERY, RONGBUK, TIBET
April 30, 1939
4:00 p.m.

Josef spent the days after their arrival totally lost despite the fact that he was at his destination. He passed the time mostly walking the Rongbuk Glacier, desperately trying to process Schäfer's abandonment of Operation Sisyphus. Thinking alternately of climbing the mountain or escape, he knew that he could do neither. He had no equipment to go up, he had little possibility to get away. Even if he could, the risk to his family, to Magda was too great. There was no way out.

Returning to the monastery, exhausted by the hike and the painful uncertainty of what should be his next move, Josef saw the distant figure of Ang Noru approaching. When they met, the Sherpa said immediately, "The monks say a runner has come from Shekar saying that the British now know we are coming to the Rongbuk, that we wish to steal Chomolungma from them. The abbot of the monastery is greatly disturbed. He wants to see you. You must come back with me now."

Josef said nothing in reply, simply adding the British to his desperate situation as he followed wearily behind.

At the monastery's chorten, he wanted only to sit and drink some water, to recover a little from the punishing pace Ang Noru had set for their return, but it wasn't possible. A pair of older monks was waiting to take them inside immediately.

Following them into the main monastery building, Josef felt unsteady on his feet, the metal studs of his boots slipping and rattling on the stone floor, black flagstones rounded at the edges and polished smooth by generations of bare feet.

For a moment, he imagined he was stepping across the back of a giant tortoise. Josef told himself again that he really did need to drink some water and rest. But given no chance to pause, he and Ang Noru were shown the way through an ornately carved doorway hung with a heavy curtain of once rich but now dusty and faded silk. They stepped into a wood-paneled hall. To its center, a square roof opening let a shaft of white light fall to the floor, tentacles of sweet incense smoke wandering into it to slowly dissolve, bright dust particles hanging as if suspended on invisible threads.

Eyes growing accustomed to the half-light that surrounded it, Josef saw opposite a raised dais, also draped with embroidered silk. In its center was the silhouette of a cross-legged man in heavy robes and a tall curved hat that rose up and forward like the helmet crest of an ancient Greek warrior. The abbot,

Josef assumed, was leaning forward and staring down at the perfect square of light on the floor between them. He made no movement at their arrival, gave no acknowledgement that he even noticed their entrance.

Looking around at the dark sides of the hall, Josef saw many other monks sitting motionless on benches. Above, a gallery looked down from every side of the room, its balustrade lined with more monks. The silence was perfect except for the click of Josef's boots as he walked on toward the shaft of light. It was so strong, so sharply defined, he was almost reluctant to step into it, but, looking ahead at the platform, intent only on reaching the man who had summoned him, he lifted a foot to step through.

Immediately he felt Ang Noru's hand on the back of his jacket, holding him still. His boot hovered mid-air, penetrating the shaft of light, illuminated and amputated from the rest of his body. "Stop. Look. Mandala," the Sherpa whispered in fast succession as he pointed to the square of light on the floor.

Pulling his raised foot back, Josef looked down. His first thought was that it was a painting he had nearly trodden on. He could see the edge of a square wooden frame. Within, it was filled entirely with sand that had been dyed in bold colors, intense and vivid after his long journey through pale, broken shades of rock, snow, and earth. The bright yellows, reds, greens, purples, and oranges shone up from the floor, as if determined to remind him that their colors still existed in the world.

Looking back up toward the abbot, Josef saw the outline of a frail hand lift to point at him and then back at the floor. His eyes followed the pointing hand down again. This time, they traveled beyond the blocks of colors into its complex geometry. Breathing in the overpowering scent of the incense, he felt himself being absorbed into the mandala's every detail. He began to see intricate filigrees, every fine line laid out like the edges of an ornamental garden with beds full of flowers, jewels, crowns, and stars. The patterns confused his already tired mind, the shapes and forms twisting and turning until, with a stab of shock, he recognized the four swastikas that pinned each corner of the grand design's outer square. He quickly turned his gaze from their marks into the center of the composition.

It was a perfect circle entirely filled with a flower. A ring of eight rounded petals fanned out, each holding an eyeball. The eight lidless white spheres, every iris a different color but each with an identical black pupil, stared unblinkingly up at him. The very center of the flower contained an image of a goddess sitting cross-legged. Her left hand was cradling a globe in her lap. Her right palm was raised in warning, as if demanding Josef stop and look. Behind was a triangular mountain edged in black. It was the great mountain outside. Her mountain. The mountain he had thought he could climb. *My mountain.* From each of its three sides projected the triangular summit of a smaller mountain. The effect was of a six-pointed star—a star he recognized as readily as the swastikas, a star he had seen vilified in newspapers, daubed on the walls of shattered businesses, on the abandoned documents of terrified people he had guided over the mountains …

The memory of it all brought Josef's fatigue and

misery crashing down onto him. He almost buckled under it, but held himself upright to stare into the picture yet more. The mandala began to speak to him, telling him that it wasn't even a painting. He saw every individual colored grain of sand arranged before him. They poured into his body like an hourglass, slowly filling him, images of his journey to that place rising to their surface: the fight in the chang hall, the cliff below the fort, the hawk chick, Schäfer's letter. The images turned darker, colder: Magda crying on the boat, the SS dagger on the table, Kurt sliding to his death, Gunter's bandaged hands drenched in blood, the little girl Ilsa, the shots ringing out over the valley, the explosion of the chapel.

With each new memory, Josef felt an overwhelming desire to make amends, to right the wrongs, to bring the dead back to life, to keep those still living alive. The wave of pure compassion submerged his heart until it overflowed into his arms and began to drip from the ends of his fingertips. It pooled around his feet to form small red rivers of blood that raced away from him into the woods as a distant pair of light beams began to twist and turn up the hill …

Josef passed out.

When he came to, he was already sitting up on the stone floor, supported by two monks. Ang Noru immediately gave him sips of the coldest water from a brass bowl. Its chill revived him as a low bench was brought forward. The monks helped Josef up onto it, sitting each side to support him as he continued to drink.

Slowly recovering his senses, Josef reached up and felt the side of his face. It was coated with sand. With horror, he looked again at the mandala and saw the damage his fall had wrought on it. Brushing the grains from his cheek, he hung his head in shame until a bell rang out, the chime clear yet gentle.

Josef lifted his head at the sound to see the abbot now standing before him on the other side of the broken mandala, two young monks also supporting him. The man looked impossibly old, his paper-thin skin loose around his skull, his eyes cloudy. Shakily, he raised his right hand and clicked his fingers together to issue a strong snap that belied any weakness. Immediately four monks approached the damaged sand picture and knelt, one on each side. They reached into their robes and brought out short, coarse-bristled brushes, waiting.

A second finger snap even louder than the first set them instantly into motion. In perfect time they each placed the brushes on the edge of the picture and began to slowly drag the stiff bristles through the colored sand. Each brush continued the destruction of Josef's collapse, pushing through the remaining design like tanks driving through ripe cornfields. Josef watched as the picture dissolved in on itself until it became only a swirl of sand they brushed into the center to stand like a small grey mountain between him and the abbot.

The abbot began to speak, very quietly.

Josef strained to listen to words he didn't understand until Ang Noru began translating.

"The Rinpoche asks if you are now feeling better."

Josef nodded.

The abbot spoke some more and then smiled.

"He thanks you for starting the destruction of the sand mandala. It has to be so. Everything is temporary, beauty, life, our world itself, everything. He says that you are tired, that you have come a long way to be here."

"Tell him it is true. I have."

The abbot spoke more, pausing so Ang Noru might repeat what he was saying.

"They tell him that you are here to climb Chomolungma alone. He says to tell you that there was such a man before who wished to do this, the Englishman Wilson. That man told the Rinpoche that he had seen the horror of total war and then went to the mountain never to return. They say he did not go far up the mountain, but the Rinpoche thinks that perhaps he didn't have to in order to find what he was really seeking. He asks if you think you can go to the top and return? Is that what you are really seeking?"

"I did believe it, but I don't any longer."

"Why do you not think so now?"

"Because my countrymen have forsaken me. I have no equipment, no supplies. I am too weary. Even if I wanted to go to the summit, without such things it is impossible. The British will arrive soon to find me."

The abbot nodded slowly.

"He says those British sahibs have already sent word to him that you are here to steal the mountain and ask that he stop you until they arrive to capture you. But he think it is difficult for you to steal something so big."

The abbot's face broke into a smile as Ang Noru began to speak to the abbot in Tibetan, his normally taciturn voice growing agitated and emotional.

The monk closed his eyes as he listened. There was a long pause before he responded, also at some length. When he had finished, he gestured to one of the monks supporting him to relay his reply to Josef. The monk did so in perfect German, slowly, word for word, so that Josef understood as if it was coming from the mouth of the abbot himself.

"The Sherpa says you are a man able to climb the mountain and that I should help you. But you should know that I have never wanted the mountain climbed. The triumph of the man who first treads the summit of Chomolungma means nothing here. It is as vain and temporary as the mandala. But I have thought much about your arrival, and perhaps this time it is not the case. I may be old, my spirit waning, but I can still feel that the world beyond the mountains is in great pain. Many are standing on the edge of oblivion.

"The Sherpa says you were sent by your masters to do their bidding, to make them even more glorious by climbing the mountain, but perhaps the Mother Goddess has deceived them and called you here instead to do her bidding. I think she wishes you to walk her heights to send a message visible to all the world to stop while it can."

With that said, the abbot called another monk to his side. He whispered something into his ear before motioning to the two monks supporting him to help him turn. Together they slowly walked away as the monk the abbot had spoken to led Josef and Ang Noru from the hall in silence.

They followed him deeper still into the dark warren of the monastery, finally coming to an ancient, studded wooden door. The monk produced a heavy iron key and unlocked it. Swinging back the door, the monk took a butter lamp from a niche in the corridor wall and entered. As the amber light filled the room, they saw that it was full of wooden boxes, baskets, and canvas bags. Everywhere they looked were bundles of tents, bags of clothing, rolls of sleeping bags, coils of rope, even a wall of brass oxygen cylinders stacked to one side. Stenciled lettering on the sides of the crates read, "British Everest Expedition, 1924"; "Everest, 1933"; and Everest Reconnaissance, 1935." Josef looked into some of them, finding can after can of food, rows of bottles, cups, plates, cooking utensils. In one there was an old gramophone with a stack of recordings, in another an artist's painting set with a collapsible easel.

The monk said something to Ang Noru who in turn spoke to Josef. "The sahibs always ask the abbot to look after best equipment after expedition until next visit but then return with even more boxes. The abbot thinks that you will find everything you need here. He says the decision of what you must do now is yours, but if you eat a lot of this food and rest, such a decision will come easier."

Ang Noru suddenly stepped away from Josef to a pile of new boots. Picking one up, he turned back to Josef and said, "See, my friend? I always know the English have extra boots." Cursing in his own language, the Sherpa threw it at the wall with all his force. Turning to Josef with tears in his eyes, Ang Noru said, "With these things I swear to my ancestors now that we will do what all those sahibs could not."

81

THE NORTH COL, MOUNT EVEREST—23,600 FEET
May 13, 2010
3:30 p.m.

When Quinn and Stevens pulled in to the North Col camp, there was a brief burst of radio from the Base Camp. The last thing Quinn heard Bill Owen say was, "Well tell them all to fuck off. I've got climbers on the hill!"

Quinn repeatedly tried to call back, but there was nothing. Exhausted from the long pull up the ice wall to the North Col, with the afternoon cloudily closing in and the temperature plummeting, there was little they could do beyond settle into their tent and set about melting the pots of snow needed to rehydrate and warm their bagged meals. Silently contemplating the pan stacked with slowly melting snow, Quinn wondered aloud why Owen had vanished off the air, imagining that Sarron was in some way behind it.

"Well, if he is, we'll just have to cross that bridge when we come to it," was all Stevens would say. But then, as if intended to settle Quinn's nerves, he pulled a small automatic pistol from inside his climbing suit. A vivid, blood-red dot of light instantly beamed up onto the tent's curved ceiling from a laser sight set beneath the pistol's stubby barrel. "Ruger, nine millimeter, steel barrel, polymer composite frame, integrated laser sight," Stevens said as he zigzagged the red dot across the yellow skin of the tent. "Perfect tool for this job."

The sight of the gun shocked Quinn. It was little bigger than the one the collector had given him in Munich. The recall of that night at the Weisshaus unsettled him still further. He saw again the jet of blood spraying from Dirk Schneider's neck as he spun to his death ... The thought of what even a small gun like that could do made Quinn recoil away from it, forcing him out of the tent with the excuse of making contact with any other team that might be up there on the North Col to see if they knew anything about what was happening in the Base Camp.

Many tents were dug into the high col but only one was occupied—three Spaniards on their last acclimatization rotation and due to go down in the morning. When Quinn pushed himself into the small lobby of their already cramped tent and explained about his loss of contact with his expedition leader, one of them, an impressive set of dreadlocks hanging from beneath his loose wool cap, began to work their radio to find out what was happening back in the Base Camp. Another translated the crackly bursts of Spanish that flicked back and forth.

Things were confused, he said, but the word seemed to be that a group of Chinese soldiers had arrived by truck out of the blue to aggressively search

Owen's camp. It was said that they had been tipped off that his team was going to film the raising of a Tibetan flag on the summit and then release it on the Internet as a "Free Tibet" protest. When the soldiers had found a packaged bundle beneath the cot of a cook boy and opened it to reveal some large Tibetan flags, they had gone berserk, arresting everyone in Owen's Base Camp. Beyond that, there was little more that anyone knew.

Quinn thanked the Spaniards and, in the growing dark, carefully moved back to his own tent. Nearing it, he thought he heard Stevens talking on their satellite phone. He tried to make out what the man was saying, but it was impossible. When he touched the zip of the tent, the talking fell silent. Crawling in, Quinn asked for the phone. Stevens gave him a sideways look that betrayed his suspicion that Quinn had heard him making the call. "Just phoned the wife in London. All fine there, whatever may be going on here," he said, trying to sound casual as he tossed the phone across to him.

Quinn didn't believe it for a second—the man wore no wedding ring—but he said nothing. Picking up the phone for himself, he tried to call Owen. No reply. It was the same with the phones of the team's other two guides. Nothing. Reaching for his radio again, Quinn scrolled through frequencies, trying to pick up other teams who were transmitting. He received some buzz in various languages until finally he heard an American guide he knew. Quinn asked him what had happened to their team in Base Camp.

The laid-back Californian confirmed the story that the Spaniards had told, humorously embellishing the details. "Henrietta Richards was ready to call in a napalm strike on Beijing she was so mad. Some German dude was ranting and raving he was from the Munich Police. He said he was going to have all the Chinese arrested, like they would give a shit. One of the soldiers pushed Henrietta Richards so Owen punched him out. That was the end of it, man. Within five minutes, they were all on their way to Lhasa in the back of army trucks."

The call ended with the American saying, "Neil, you're on your own up there now, buddy, and if you do have a Tibetan flag, I'd ditch it, and fast."

Switching off the radio, Quinn looked across at Stevens who had listened to every word. "We should eat and then sleep. We've got a job to do, whatever might now be waiting for us when we get back down," was all the ex-soldier said.

82

From early the next morning, the pair made their laborious way up the long, icy ridge that rose from the snow saddle of the col onto the broken rock of the towering North Face. With every heavy step, each retreated further into his own world, forgetting about what might be going on far below, what they must do high above, instead just digging deep into their legs and souls to slowly push their way to the next camp. There, the only luxury awaiting them would be the possibility to switch on to supplementary oxygen to sleep. Through the day their radios remained silent. Even the garrulous American knew nothing more, beyond confirming that Owen's entire team had definitely been taken away by the Chinese. They were on their own up there in every way.

Despite the bottled oxygen, Quinn slept little that night. When he did, it offered busy, surreal altitude dreams. He awoke frequently, gasping for air, claustrophobic from the oxygen mask, sensations of vertigo spinning his brain. All he could do was lie there in the dark, trying to regulate his breathing as his mind continued to stoke the fragments of his nightmares, a weight of something evil pushing him into the hard side of the mountain. His only response was to silently and quietly transfer the collector's Leica from the bottom of his rucksack into an inner pocket of his climb suit. It made him feel as if he was at least trying to fight back, but it brought no sleep.

* * *

The next day they moved on to the final High Camp at 27,400 feet. Once there, Quinn and Stevens behaved exactly as if they were going to the summit. They got in, went through the interminable ritual of boiling snow to rehydrate, tried to eat a few bites, and then rested until leaving for the Second Step at 1:00 a.m. Setting off, Quinn could feel Graf's old Leica in the mesh pocket inside his down suit. All the previous day, whenever he had thought about it, he had wrestled with whether he should try to switch it if they did find another. He still didn't know but a voice said that he should for Graf, for Henrietta, for the truth. But was that really correct? Hadn't this search for the truth already killed and maimed? Wasn't it for the best if it was all destroyed?

Quinn's mind continued to travel in circles as he gradually worked his way up the slope. The higher he climbed, the slower he went. The questions receded, his body subsuming his mind into the sole task of achieving upward motion until he settled into his usual summit-day rhythm of ten steps before resting. Each time he stopped, he leaned forward on his single ski pole, sucking in more air from his mask, his headlamp lighting only the ground before him. Nothing would exist beyond that roundel of illuminated snow or rock until the sun came. It was always that way beyond the High Camp.

By the time the batteries in his headlight had died and the sun was starting to rise, Quinn was pulling himself up onto the Second Step. To a yellowing dawn light, he slowly made his way up the rocky gully onto the step proper. There, he waited for Stevens on the same snow ledge where he had lost Nelson Tate Junior the year before. He looked for the boy's body. Dawa and Pemba had told him that they had moved it down off the climbing line, laying it to rest in a slightly lower rock crevice. It seemed that there had been a lot of snow over the winter. Quinn couldn't see anything, not even the older bodies below the step he remembered seeing after being hit by the rock fall.

Stevens' arrival stopped his search. Quinn pointed to the buttress at the end of the ledge and then slowly lead Stevens along the narrow ledge. There, at the end, they both edged their way around the rock buttress before ducking down into the entrance of the small cave. Entering into the darkness of the rock again, Quinn understood it for what it really was: a tomb. He was momentarily transfixed to the spot forcing Stevens to squeeze around him to get inside. "Okay, if this is the place, let's get on with it," he said as he passed. "Quinn, you will need to change the batteries in your headlamp and put it back on. We need all the light we can get to do this properly." Kneeling next to the snow mound, Stevens took off his rucksack and, from within, pulled out two small equipment cases.

Laying them on the cave floor, Stevens worked on his own headlight before using its renewed beam to light his opening of the first plastic case.

Quinn's gloved fingers felt thick and awkward as he fumbled to replace the batteries and switch his own light back on again. When he did, the smoky beam scythed into the shadows, ice crystals sparkling back at him from the black walls. For an instant, he saw projected onto them the image of him fighting, and failing, to save Nelson Tate Junior. Looking down at where he had first found the boy, the light reflected on something projecting from the ice. It was the syringe he had used. Seeing that Stevens was already concentrating on using his ice axe to hack away at the snow mound that filled the rest of the cave, Quinn gently put his hand flat on it and slipped it into his thigh pocket.

Turning back to look again at the snow pile, coursing the beam of his headlamp over it, the tube of light picked up the faint outline of something within. A shadow locked inside, a dark form that gave structure to the mound of ice and snow. Quinn tried to move closer but was blocked by Stevens. The ex-soldier was working as aggressively as the altitude would permit, smashing into the snow and ice with his ice axe without care or caution for whatever lay within. The sight revolted Quinn. As if sensing the disgust behind him, Stevens turned to shout at Quinn to help.

Pushing alongside to do so, Quinn began to pull away chunks of the snow crust in a gentler fashion. It was still laborious work. The snow broke easily, but the ice beneath was rock hard. For some time, they chipped and chiseled with the picks of their axes, gradually removing the cold chrysalis that had encased the frozen body for seventy years. When the chopped snow and ice accumulated, they kicked it out of the mouth of the cave down the North Face. Watching the wind tear it away, Quinn noticed that the new day was turning ominous. Beneath an iron sky, cloud was building in the valleys below, patches of it dense, with an almost purplish hue. It was a bad sign.

He mentioned it to Stevens but to no reply. Instead, the ex-soldier picked up the first case he had opened and took out a small handheld plastic wand. It was a metal detector. Quinn had seen similar, only bigger, at airport security. Connecting a small earpiece, Stevens pushed its bud under his thermal cap into his ear. The detector switched on, he ran the probe over the buckle of his own climbing harness as a test before proceeding to sweep it over the broken snow and ice before him. Quinn couldn't hear the detector's signal but could see the three green LEDs on the unit. They changed to a bright red when the wand hovered above what must have been the corpse's chest. The burst of scarlet light briefly illuminated a broken head above, as if bathing it with new blood.

Quinn saw two black holes where eyes had once been. Below, sharp projections of bone jutted through remnants of flesh and skin that had once been a nose. Lower still were two bare rows of teeth, stripped of lips, locked together in the permanent bite of death. The sight made Quinn swallow hard as Stevens unzipped the front of his thick down suit and, switching the wand off, pushed it inside. When the hand reappeared, it was holding a large black survival knife with a deep, full blade, jagged saw-teeth along the top edge.

With the tip of the knife's blade, Stevens immediately dug further into the remaining snow and ice at the point indicated by the metal detector. The excavation revealed a thick gabardine-type material, grey in the half-light of the cave. Lifting the knife, Stevens stabbed down into it. The ex-soldier then began sawing with the jagged back of the knife, moving upward to the nape of the corpse's neck, cutting through the frozen wind jacket. Putting the knife aside, he used both hands to rend the frozen material apart as if about to gut a deer. The sight within caused Quinn to struggle for breath. Even Stevens stopped short, seemingly forgetting himself in his surprise, twisting back to look at Quinn and say, "Fuck, there really is a camera. I thought it was bullshit."

Quinn was equally stunned by the sight of the silver camera suspended from a thin leather strap around the corpse's neck. It was a Leica 111, almost identical to the one in his chest pocket. Adrenaline flooded Quinn's body at the thought of what it could contain, of what he should do about it.

The collector was right.
Henrietta was right.
The truth was lying there in front of him.

Stevens cut the camera's leather straps with the knife and gently prized it from the frozen body with the tip of the knife. Pulling an insulated red plastic bag from his pack, he opened it and put the camera inside. Sealing it, the package went into his rucksack.

"Okay, Stevens, we have what we came here for," Quinn said. "We should properly identify the body, cover it, and then leave. I've brought some material we can use."

Stevens stared back, shaking his head. "You still don't get it, do you? You need to go. There is nothing more for you to do here." Reaching for the second equipment case, he removed a small package wrapped in black duct tape. Setting it on the corpse's chest, he started to hollow a cavity underneath the body with the blade of his knife.

Quinn, at a loss as to what to do next, could only stare at the time-stripped face in the ice. He couldn't even recognize if it was Becker or Ang Noru. It seemed dreadful that he didn't know. Reaching forward to try and find something, anything, that would tell him, Stevens aggressively pushed his arm back. "I said fucking go, Quinn. Now! Wait for me well beyond the bottom of the Second Step. The weather is closing in. We've been here too long already."

He started to reply, but Stevens interrupted him. "Quinn, there is nothing to discuss. My instructions are clear, whether you like them or not. I am going to blow your old Nazi out of his fucking foxhole, and if you don't get moving, you'll go up with him. I mean it."

"There is no bloody way I'm letting you do that. Even if you don't give a shit about the body—it may not even be a bloody German—what about the fucking avalanche risk?" Quinn shouted back.

In an instant, Stevens had reached back into his suit and pulled out the small pistol, the red dot of its laser sight igniting to settle on the center of Quinn's chest.

"I don't give a shit about that either." The red beam flicked twice from Quinn to the cave entrance. "I have my job to do here. I will do it and you must go. If you want to try and stop me, my orders are clear. Your only witness is long dead."

He gestured again with the gun for Quinn to leave the cave, waving the barrel slightly, the red dot now jumping up and down on Quinn's heart as if registering its beat.

With no alternative, Quinn slowly moved out and onto the rock buttress that led back onto the snow ledge. The clouds were now pushing in tight to the side of the mountain. He vanished into them as he climbed away alone.

At the foot of the Second Step he didn't stop to wait for Stevens or look for Nelson Tate Junior. Quinn felt that he had totally betrayed the body in the cave and just wanted to be away from the accursed place.

Fifteen minutes later he heard a muffled boom behind him like distant thunder. This time, he did halt. Quinn knew it wasn't any coming storm. Saying a silent prayer for the mortal remains of Josef Becker or Ang Noru, he then vowed that, even if it was the last thing he ever did, he was going to switch the cameras before they made it back to Base Camp.

83

RONGBUK MONASTERY, RONGBUK, TIBET
May 1, 1939
9:00 a.m.

Josef and Ang Noru did eat and sleep well the night they were shown the storeroom. The next morning, they awoke late at 9:00 a.m. feeling completely rested for the first time in a long time. Over a long, good breakfast they decided how it had to be, then set to sorting the equipment and supplies needed to climb the mountain, even if one of the first things Josef brought out from the storeroom was the gramophone left by the 1936 British expedition. He set it on a packing crate outside the small, whitewashed room where they were staying, its lid propped upward as if pointing to the summit beyond the monastery. A very young monk was instructed in the art of winding it whenever its music slowed and the jaunty, syrupy sound of Noel Coward singing "A Room with a View" varnished the stillness of the valley, making Ang Noru and Josef smile as they worked.

Their main difficulty, with so much choice from the storeroom, was in narrowing their selection. Every time he returned to it, Josef was further surprised at what he found. It was more lavishly stocked than the quartermaster's at Garmisch barracks. Opening more of the crates, Josef found that a lot of it was useless for the climb ahead—luxuries that might appeal to fat stomachs in London committee rooms but turned those that actually came to Tibet. He uncovered champagne, bottles of the finest French wine, and hundreds of small tins and jars of delicacies. He read their labels phonetically, trying to pronounce the contents within, only better understanding the true nature of "foie gras," "quails in aspic," "Carlsbad plums," "*patum peperium*" when he opened them and dipped the blade of his knife to touch the contents on his tongue. He saw no place for any of them on the mountain. As he roamed the dusky storeroom, Josef recalled again Ang Noru's words concerning the need to live quietly on the mountain, to work lightly up it with only the bare essentials.

Slowly, their own little room filled with new coils of rope, a stack of pitons and carabiners, the smallest tents they could find, four sleeping bags, sealed cans of fuel, tins of biscuits, bags of flour, can after can of food, even some English cigarettes and sweets. In one visit to the room Ang Noru had shouted, "We use air from England?" holding up one of the long oxygen cylinders.

Josef had shaken his head and laughed. "No, Ang Noru, English air only good for Englishmen. You and I will share Tibetan air." To Josef's surprise, the Sherpa stopped what he was doing to walk over and pat him on the back.

When Josef wondered aloud as to how they were going to get everything to the mountain, Ang Noru said that the abbot had instructed the monks and the villagers, such as there were, to assist. Later in the afternoon, a toothless man in thick, dirty clothes, a pendulum of turquoise and coral hanging from one stretched earlobe, approached them. He mumbled to Ang Noru that he had five yaks and two sons who would help them get up the glacier to the mountain. Two strong young monks then appeared to say that they were also to go with them. From that moment Josef broke the equipment into five big loads for the yaks and seven smaller loads for each of them. Stripped down to his shirtsleeves despite the cold, his field cap pushed back onto the crown of his head, he raced, with renewed energy, to get everything ready. When they started to tire, Josef switched the gramophone record to another by Benny Goodman.

The change of tempo to the blasting swing sound motivated him to reconsider every pile once again, discarding another round of gear he deemed superfluous. Finally satisfied that they had what they needed, they ate some more and rested before Josef unwrapped the new Leica camera he had been saving for the climb. Inserting a roll of film, he started to take photographs of the Sherpa around the monastery and up at the mountain, showing Ang Noru how to do the same until the roll was finished.

That evening they were summoned again to see the abbot. With difficulty, he blessed them, touching his forehead to theirs and placing cream-colored silk scarfs around their necks. His eyes seemed to show both joy and grief as he mumbled his prayers.

Leaving the monastery building, Josef tucked the scarf in close around his neck, taking comfort in its soft silk, the thought of what he was about to embark upon sending a continual nervous tremor through his body. Unable to sleep, he continued to work on into the dark of the night.

To the echoes of the abbot's words and watched by the ghosts of the journey that had led him to that place, Josef prepared the final items he now knew he needed for the summit.

* * *

They left at sunrise. A heavy frost lay on the ground, but Josef took heart from the sight of a cloudless sky. It made up for the lack of sleep and the pain of the cold in his fingertips as he tied the loads onto the yaks.

The sleepy beasts were reluctant to leave until a jab of a stick into each of their anuses provoked furious movement. Josef's small walking party followed behind, laden too under heavy packs. As Rongbuk Monastery receded, Josef thought that he heard the low drone of horns, but he couldn't be sure.

It took four long days for their strange caravan to arrive at the foot of the mountain where they stopped in the lee of the valley side and made camp in the snow and rocks. A few projecting pieces of wood and an old cairn of stones were the only indications that man had ever been there before.

The next morning, Josef and Ang Noru rested as they watched their companions depart, unburdened from their loads. They sat on the bundles left behind, drinking tea and smoking stale English cigarettes, watching the figures become little more than black ants in a universe of white. Only when they had completely vanished did Josef and Ang Noru turn their attentions to the North Col high up above them and the massive wall of ice they had to climb to reach it.

Drawing an imaginary line diagonally across it with a gloved finger, Ang Noru said, "Many porters die on this wall, Josef. Need for care." Josef realized that it was the first time Ang Noru hadn't called him "Sahib."

"We will be careful," Josef replied. "You should know that when we have a route to the top of the ridge, I consider that your work with me is done. From there I can go it alone."

Reaching inside his pocket he took out Schäfer's envelope and handed it to the Sherpa. "Inside this envelope I have put some money and the details of someone who will help you if you can cross into Nepal and get a message to her. You will be free."

The Sherpa looked at him quizzically. "But I am free already, Josef. Besides, who will take your photograph on summit? You should think less and drink more tea. Important here to drink much tea, even if you are not English."

Ang Noru tried to give the envelope back but Josef refused it.

"Okay, but whatever happens, you keep that envelope."

84

**BETWEEN THE FIRST AND SECOND STEPS,
NORTHEAST RIDGE, MOUNT EVEREST—28,090 FEET**
May 16, 2010
11:53 a.m.

With each pull of his straining lungs, Quinn bitterly contemplated the godless air burial he had just heard. Stevens' cleanup operation was complete. Even the smallest of blasts would have amplified within that rocky hollow to eject the body out into the void, the burst of explosives scouring the alcove clean of its seventy-year secret in an instant. If it hadn't been shattered by the blast, then it would have been by the contact it made with the sharp rocks on the long, long fall to the glacier below.

His breath steadying, Quinn told himself to put it all from his mind, to get going. It was too cold to wait any longer. The wind had increased dramatically. It was now barreling up the face, ripping and tearing at him. As far as he was concerned, Stevens could fend for himself. Setting off along the exposed traverse that led back to the ridgeline, Quinn hunched forward, forcing each leaden step, bracing his body against relentless punches from the fierce gusts that began to bring flurries of snow. His visibility soon dropped to only a few yards, making him search for the remnants of old fixed ropes in the snow and rocks at his feet to find the way.

With every new step, he bargained with the mountain, pleading for a release from the elemental beating. Validating the offers he was making, Quinn mentally removed the collector's camera from inside his chest pocket and wove complex, improbable scenarios of when and where he would swap it for the one now in Stevens' pack. He settled on the fact that they would both be exhausted when they made it back to the High Camp. Even Stevens would have to sleep at some point. He would switch it then. It had to be done, whatever the risks. It was the only pledge he could offer the mountain in exchange for his deliverance—a deliverance he wasn't sure he deserved.

Back up on the ridge, the wind was launching itself over the edge to twist and boil above the ten-thousand-foot drop straight down to the Kangshung Glacier below. One of the gusts was so strong it forced Quinn to fall onto all fours to prevent himself from being blown off the ridge. On his hands and knees, he clipped his fate into a blue nylon rope that led across the ridgeline. It looked the most recent of the tangle that lined the way. It was the only thing he could do.

In a stuttering stop and go, he began to follow its line, making his precarious way along the upper edge of the mountain. A bulb of dark rock began to fleetingly appear before him through the streaking snow and cloud. Quinn knew it was Mushroom Rock, the unusual three-foot-high formation that stood proud on the crest of that part of the ridge. The sight brought some mental relief from the weather's assault. They had cached extra oxygen beneath it on the way up. His current cylinder would be nearly empty by now and the thought of the additional oxygen was a comfort, pulling him onward. It would make him warmer and help him to move down faster. He could even permit himself the luxury of a few minutes' rest at four-liters-per-minute flow, double what he had been using all day, a much-needed boost to continue the treacherous descent.

Quinn dug deeply as he approached the bulb of rock, jamming his feet hard into the top of the mountain ridge, leaning his left shoulder out into the wind, occasionally having to tug the old rope he was following up and out of the snow to move his carabiner along it. Constantly working his fingers inside his down mittens and wiggling his cramped toes inside his double boots, he desperately tried to keep his weakened circulation moving to his extremities and stop the extreme cold from freezing them. When his goggles began to catch big snowflakes that congealed around the frames, he swiped them away to keep sight of that blue rope. It led the way to his survival.

With some relief, Quinn finally arrived at the rock to huddle down next to it, needing to recover from that last push through the fierce weather before he could do anything more. Feeling the hard rocks jabbing through the knees of his suit, their rough edges digging into his patellae, he was, at first, too tired to even alter his position. Wiping his ski goggles again with the back of his gloved hand, he twisted his head to search the base of the rocky projection for the two oxygen cylinders that they had left there on the way up. Orange and marked with two big black *X*'s, he told himself that they would be easy to find.

But, in those conditions, they weren't. Unable to see them, Quinn pulled up the goggles, squeezing his eyes against the icy blast to peer into the grey and white, desperate for a glimpse of orange. With his gloved hand, he probed in vain at a small mound of snow that had built up on the lee side of the column of rock even if he knew already that it was too small to be hiding them, that they hadn't even put them there. Quinn pulled his goggles back down with the realization that the cylinders had been taken. He recalled Stevens lagging behind him on the way up.

Did he move them to be able to control their descent?

Quinn wasn't in a position to wait to find out, determined not to if that really was Stevens' intention. Getting back onto his feet, he resumed his weary trek along the ridge, his experience telling him that he must push as hard as he could to try and get down over the First Step and past Green Boots Cave before his existing bottle gave out.

He did make it to the First Step.

Slowly climbing down the steep rocks, it was almost as if he could feel his oxygen flow gradually dwindle and then cease. He fought on, regardless. *Green Boots Cave, Green Boots Cave*, he started to repeat over and over in his head. It was the next identifiable feature of his path to safety, that rocky overhang that housed the body of a dead Indian climber whose green plastic Koflach boots still projected out for everyone passing to see. From there it would be on to the Exit Cracks. There the route turned down the face. Gravity would help pull him still lower through the yellow rocks of the Yellow Band and down to the High Camp.

Feeling his way along a low wall of rock like a blind man, his useless oxygen mask angrily pulled down from his mouth as if it was somehow to blame for his predicament, Quinn was slow to realize that he had made it to his first objective. He was even slower to notice the masked figure in the black down suit approaching him through the swirling snow. When it finally registered, he straightened up to see that the other climber was holding an orange oxygen bottle out to him, two black *X*'s on its side.

I have to have it.

Quinn stretched forward to take it, the cylinder his only desperate thought, no sense of awareness left for the second black shape uncoiling itself from beneath the overhang and rising up behind him.

Standing tall, the second figure raised the other double-X oxygen cylinder. It arced down onto the back of Quinn's neck, the Englishman going down like a felled tree, oblivious to the cause of his collapse.

85

RONGBUK MONASTERY, RONGBUK, TIBET
May 8, 1939
5:00 p.m.

While the Gurkhas busied themselves unloading their equipment, Macfarlane sat on the monastery's steps gazing in awe at the massive mountain that dominated the valley. Zazar, as always, had vanished inside.

The English officer, too tired to follow the formalities of his arrival, waited until the increased chill of the approaching night forced him to move. Stiffly getting up to go inside, he was met by the Gurkha sergeant.

"Zazar says the monks have told him there is a room for you to use while you prepare yourself for your return to Sikkim. Zazar also says the monks tell him that the German and the Sherpa have already escaped into Nepal by the Lho-La Pass and that you have no jurisdiction there, so your hunt is over."

Macfarlane muttered, "Zazar says, Zazar says," under his breath and followed the sergeant to the room, saying nothing more. All he wanted to do was rest.

Entering the simple room, the lieutenant was surprised to see a gramophone on the floor. Next to it was a bottle of Chateau Latour 1913 and an enameled tin mug, the initials "G. L. M." painted on the bottom. A piece of paper lay on the gramophone's disc, the playing arm pinning it down.

Raising the arm, Macfarlane pulled out the note:

> *Engländer,*
> *Schau aus dem Fenster hinaus.*
> *Solltest Du mich suchen, dort oben*
> *findest Du mich.*
> *Nichts für Ungut,*
> *Mad Dog*

The German was lost on him but the music hall reference wasn't.

Winding the gramophone, Macfarlane lowered the needle onto the now-spinning recording and reached for his pocketknife to uncork the bottle. It was a fine wine. Opening it, he thought he should let it breathe and smiled at the irony. After that he dug into his kit bag for the small German-English dictionary he had brought with him, originally to help his understanding during Schmidt's expedition.

By the time Noel Coward had trotted into his fourth chorus of "Mad Dogs and Englishmen," Macfarlane had finished his first enamel cup of wine and thought he understood the German's message:

> Englishman,
> Look out of the window.
> If you want to find me, that's
> where I am.

No hard feelings, Mad Dog

Pouring himself a second cup of the vintage wine, Macfarlane did go to the window and look out at Mount Everest towering above him in all its glory.

Josef Becker was up there, whatever the monks might be saying.

He wants me to know.

Another cup of wine accompanied the question of what kind of man could have the courage to face such a mountain. A little mad maybe, but Becker was no dog; he was as honorable and brave an alpinist as George Leigh Mallory, the man from whose cup he must be drinking.

And that Sherpa is with him.

A Sherpa, branded difficult and disloyal by Macfarlane's superiors, that Becker had gone back for at Kampa Dzong, knowing full well that he was risking everything, including his life, to free him.

The same Sherpa that Macfarlane had simply sold to Zazar in a pathetic attempt to save his own skin ...

The realization left Macfarlane feeling disgusted at the deal he had made.

It was little more than a devil's bargain, and it was wrong. Was his own honor not worth more than that, more than Colonel Atkinson's disapproval, more than blind loyalty, more than trying to prevent another country's man from achieving what his own could not, however hard they tried? Becker was neither saboteur nor assassin. He was only a climber, at worst a trespasser into Tibet, nothing more.

With resignation Lieutenant Charles Macfarlane

realized that if he was to be true to himself, rather than his superiors, his ancestors, his country even, then his hunt was indeed over, but not for the reason suggested by Zazar. He was contemplating a fourth cup when the Gurkha sergeant came to the door and said, "The Zatul Rinpoche wants to speak with you, Lieutenant Macfarlane, sir."

Feeling flushed from the wine on an empty stomach, he followed the sergeant out into the courtyard. There they met Zazar. The man hunter looked at Macfarlane, a triumphant smile creasing his leathery face as he spoke to the sergeant.

"Zazar says that a villager has told him that the German and the Sherpa have not gone to Nepal by the main glacier but took the smaller one that runs off to the east to Chomolungma. Zazar says that there is only one way in and out, that they won't be able to run up there. We have them, sir!" the sergeant reported.

Macfarlane turned away from both Zazar and the sergeant to enter the monastery, thinking, *There is only one mad dog in the Rongbuk.*

To his shame, he was the one that had brought it there.

86

GREEN BOOTS CAVE, NORTHEAST RIDGE, MOUNT EVEREST—27,890 FEET
May 16, 2010
4:53 p.m.

A mask over my mouth?
Oxygen?
Where am I?

Slowly twisting his head from side to side, Quinn understood he was propped against the rock wall of Green Boots Cave, a climber to each side of him. The shelter of the overhang was giving a temporary respite from the driving wind and snow.

An oxygen mask being held over his mouth was indeed bringing him back to life, but it wasn't Quinn's. It belonged to the climber to his left. His own mask, useless since he had run out of oxygen, was pushed down around his neck.

His goggles also removed, Quinn struggled to recognize his rescuers through frosty, blurred eyes. The only thing he could make out for sure was that they were too big to be Sherpas.

Drawing down hard on the oxygen, he told himself that he must have blacked out from a lack of it. He wondered if the two climbers spoke English. He began to say, "Thank you," as a third climber moved in front of him.

Pulling up his own goggles and unclipping his oxygen mask, Sarron revealed his face, saying, "*Ça suffit*. He is conscious now."

The oxygen mask over Quinn's mouth was abruptly pulled away by the other climber, who immediately pushed it back onto his own face.

"Save your English manners for those who might appreciate them, Quinn," the Frenchman said. "The only thing that you are going to be truly thankful for this day is when it ends. You will be envying the quiet fate of Green Boots here, much like your antiques-dealer friend."

At the mention of Graf, Quinn started to struggle.

Instantly, the two other climbers gripped him firmly, locking his body hard against the uneven rock.

Sarron lifted the old ice axe and, after holding it close to Quinn's eyes so that he could see exactly what it was, rested the sharpened metal end spike on the Englishman's cheek. "Stop. Moving. Stay. Still," he shouted over the wind, stressing each word with a push.

Quinn flinched each time the point pierced into his cheek.

Pulling the axe away, Sarron leaned in close to Quinn's bleeding face. "I heard that you like sticking ice screws into people's eyes. Not so much fun being on the receiving end, is it, fucker?"

Quinn could only stare back in silence.

"Huh, I thought so!" Sarron shouted. "I bet

you never imagined I would hit you so high on the mountain. Beautiful, for so many reasons. First, it permits me to take what I need with no witnesses. Second, it allows me to push you off the Kangshung face and give you a very long time to remember me as you fall. And, third, that *putain* Henrietta Richards can put it in her fucking record books as the highest ambush in history."

Sarron took a long Tibetan knife from inside his climb suit. He unsheathed it and slipped the narrow blade under Quinn's oxygen mask, which was hanging on his chest. Hooking it out and up on the end of the long blade, Sarron tensioned the razor-sharp edge to easily slice through the elastic straps. The mask fell loose.

The Frenchman lifted it up, slicing its red oxygen supply tube as he did so. For a moment he just held the severed mask in his hand, looking at it as if it was a surgically removed heart. "Remind you of Munich, Oleg?" Sarron asked before tossing it back over his shoulder.

"You won't be needing that anymore. I control your oxygen now," he said looking back at Quinn. He motioned to the person on Quinn's left. "Dmitri, give him some more of yours. I need him lucid for the next part."

The silent climber put his own mask back over Quinn's mouth.

Quinn was able to suck in five deep breaths before Sarron gestured for the mask to be pulled away once more.

"To be honest, it is very difficult to resist cutting your miserable throat right now, you English bastard. However, I need you to tell me some things first." He paused before asking, "Find what you were looking for up there on the Second Step?"

"No," Quinn replied.

"Sure?"

"Yes. Fuck you."

Sarron pushed the blade of the knife back up toward Quinn's face.

"No, Neil Quinn, it is I who will be fucking you with this knife if you don't answer me."

The blade stroked Quinn's face, his skin twitching at its touch.

"Now I ask again: What did you find? Did you find a camera up there?"

Quinn said nothing before a push of the blade produced an involuntary, "Yes."

"I knew it. Where is it?"

"I don't have it."

"Of course you don't. Oleg, search his pack."

The second figure pushed Quinn forward and pulled off his rucksack. Digging into the top, he pulled out the empty oxygen bottle on its severed tube and threw it down the slope of the hill. The Russian rifled deeper, discarding the other survival items inside before concluding there was nothing else.

"It must be inside his suit," Sarron said.

Quinn deliberately started to struggle.

"Hold him, both of you."

As the Vishnevskys forced Quinn hard back against the rock wall, Sarron moved the point of the knife down under Quinn's chin to his throat, pushing it into the skin to stop him from moving. With his other hand, he ripped open the wind flap to the front of the Englishman's suit and pulled down the zip inside. Lowering the blade of the knife, he pushed open the right side of the suit. It moved back easily. When he tried the left side, it was heavy against the knife. Sarron quickly pushed his hand onto Quinn's chest and felt the camera in the mesh pocket within.

"This is it, isn't it?" he said as he looked back up into Quinn's face.

Not waiting for any reply, Sarron reached into the suit and seized the old Leica. Once it was free, he nodded to himself, holding the camera up in his left hand.

"So you don't have the camera, huh? You shit!" he shouted at Quinn, pulling back his right hand and punching the hilt of the knife within his clenched fist into the side of Quinn's face. Quinn's head smacked back against the stone. He slumped forward, senseless from the blow.

Sarron put the camera inside his own suit, saying, "Get him up."

The two Russians each put a shoulder under Quinn's arms and pulled him to his feet.

Sarron, pointing beyond the overhang, shouted, "Up onto the ridge."

Quinn, head still reeling from the punch, blood flowing from his nose, was unable to stand.

Forced to use all their considerable strength, the brothers held him up and turned him back out into the blast of the weather. Sarron, his words now lost in the wind, followed, constantly gesturing for them to be faster, with the knife in one hand, the old ice axe in the other.

Quinn tried to collect himself as they moved, but the blow to his head and the renewed oxygen starvation made it impossible to think clearly. He had to do something, or he was going over the edge. In a vain attempt to slow the Russians, he raised his feet, dropping his full weight onto them.

It caused them to falter for a moment, but with another hard pull, they moved on toward the top of the ridge where a ramp of snow launched a grey maelstrom of cloud out over the abyss.

Just before the lip of the snow cornice, they stopped.

Sarron shouted something more, but those words too were lost.

Quinn tried to push back from the edge, only for Sarron to begin jabbing at the small of his back with the axe, determined to use it to send the Englishman over the edge.

In one last desperate effort, Quinn raised his right boot and brought it down as hard as he could. The sharp steel crampon ripped through Oleg Vishnevsky's down suit, stabbing through muscle and flesh to lodge into bone.

The Russian bowed from the pain as Quinn twisted around with the other brother. Both of them toppled forward over Sarron, beginning to fall down the mountainside. They left Oleg Vishnevsky behind them, collapsed onto his knees. He instinctively tried to stand up but his broken lower leg buckled and he fell, the snow cornice under him collapsing. The man vanished, the wind masking his screams, the swirling cloud consuming his plummeting fall.

Quinn and the second Russian continued to roll down the face, gathering speed until both were stopped by a black projection of rock. Dmitri Vishnevsky quickly forced himself on top. Clenching

Quinn's head between his hands, the Russian struck it back against the rock. The impact spiked into Quinn's skull with a white flash that left colored spots dancing before his eyes.

One of the spots remained, a point of bright red light that hovered on his attacker's chest. Quinn fixated on the firefly, questioning its brilliance, its persistence. Just as his addled, oxygen-depleted brain understood what it really was, the red light burst over him in a wet explosion of blood and feathers.

The Russian, killed in that instant, fell onto Quinn, cracking his head back once more onto the rock, knocking him senseless again.

Half opening his eyes, Quinn thought he saw Stevens approach and lean down to check that the Russian was dead.

He tried to say something to him, to warn him, but no words came.

Stevens looked at Quinn, reaching for him.

Sarron lunged from out of the cloud.

The long Tibetan knife disappeared into the side of Stevens' neck.

It was the last thing Quinn saw.

87

THE NORTH COL, MOUNT EVEREST—23,600 FEET
May 9, 1939
7:50 p.m.

For three full days Josef and Ang Noru slaved to make a route up the steep snow face to the North Col, cutting steps into the steepest ice with their axes and fixing rope along the most exposed sections. When it was finally complete, they ascended twice from their glacier camp with supplies and equipment, putting up two tents on the high col, much as they had on the Zemu. One tent they filled with supplies; the other was for themselves. Now huddled inside it on the evening of their second carry, they debated whether they should make a third. Ang Noru was in favor, but Josef disagreed. He could feel how much each round trip up the massive snow face was wearing him down. They had enough already for a push to the top. It would be lightweight, desperate even, but it was always going to be like that. They had to go for it while he still could.

They left at daybreak carrying everything they thought they would need to get to the top. Despite their heavy burdens, they made good progress across the snowy saddle of the col and onto the never-ending white crest that led to the rising black layers of rock beyond.

The day awoke bright and clear, but soon a haze veiled the sun, and fuller, thicker clouds began to rise up, their edges laced with hints of color, changing from yellow to orange to brown. The wind steadily increased as they struggled on, bowed under their packs, huddling into their thick clothes for warmth as the temperature plummeted.

Before long the cloud had thickened still further to become a grey-purple conveyor belt that drove relentlessly over them, completely blocking the upper part of the mountain from their view. When it started to lash them from the side with thick snow, they had no alternative but to turn around.

Descending through the worsening conditions, Josef's curses were insulated within the scarf that wrapped his face. His tired legs plunged into the ever-deepening snow, Ang Noru always two steps behind, until they made it back to their camp, where the pair dragged themselves inside their tiny tent. Ice-bound and exhausted as the storm raged around them, they lay there, unable to move, their world reduced to the drilling sound of flapping canvas, the numbing cold, and flurries of windblown snow that built up around them however much they tried to keep it out of the tent.

When the dark of the night began to close in, they reluctantly pulled themselves from the shelter of the tent to lash ropes over it to prevent it from being blown away. Then they collapsed the storage tent down on itself, weighting it with blocks of ice. Returning inside their pathetic canvas refuge, they wedged themselves against its sides, accepting that all they could do was shiver, endure, and hope that the little tent wasn't going to be blown off the ridge.

* * *

The raging storm continued on through that night and all the next day. Their extremities lost all feelings from the cold. They used every bit of energy they had to boil snow into water and make tea. They picked at dry food. They stopped talking, each retreating into his own frozen hell, hoping only for salvation from the weather.

During their second night, Josef told Ang Noru that, whatever the conditions, they must try to break out of that place in the morning or they would surely both die there. Josef had to get the Sherpa off the mountain if he could.

Digging up and out of the tent's entrance as the sun was rising, they saw that the wind was still pushing over the col, but the snow had stopped. The cloud looked a little brighter, as if better weather might be following it. They prepared themselves to leave, slowly, methodically, as if the act of kitting up momentarily reprieved them from their desperate predicament. Finally, they tied themselves together with a rope, silently accepting they were bound to the same fate, whatever their attempt at survival would provide.

Pushing themselves out of the tent, almost completely submerged by new snow, they stood in a white world without horizon. A hunched reading from Josef's small brass compass offered their only clue to direction.

Josef waded ahead through the snow following the trembling bearing to the tip of a tent pole tied with red tape they had used to mark the end of the rope fixed up the long exit gully.

Stabbing his ice axe down and working it around to make a hole, Josef finally saw the frozen, matted line of hemp within. He tugged it repeatedly upward, the rope slicing up through the soft snow, finally breaking through the white waves like a whale breaching.

Together they followed the rope down over the edge, gripping it tightly as they floundered and slid in the deep powder that now filled the path they had cut. Spindrifts of loose ice blew down on them. Occasionally the snow beneath their crampons broke away altogether to leave them hanging on to the rope, struggling to hold themselves against the soft side of the mountain as it crumbled beneath their desperate feet.

At the end of the fixed rope, they dropped out of the cloud to see what they had both already silently anticipated. Their painfully prepared trail down the immense ice face was gone. Josef, refusing to be defeated, immediately started breaking a new path.

They had completed seven rope lengths when they both heard a "crack" like a rifle shot. After a moment's hesitation, the whole slope started to slip with a growing roar.

Josef and Ang Noru were plucked from the hillside.

Accelerating downward, the snow beneath them began to fold and break, sucking them in.

Josef lost sight of Ang Noru.

He couldn't breathe.

Instinct said, *Twist your body over onto your front.*

He tried once.

Twice.

Each time he was wrenched back by the snow.

With one last lunge, Josef made the move stick, digging the head of his axe downward and automatically lifting his toes up and back so that his crampon spikes didn't catch and flip him down the face into a cartwheel that would never stop.

But still he continued to fall, the axe's pick slicing through the snow beneath him, refusing to bite.

More snow pushed down on him from above, heavy like wet cement.

For a few seconds, he was able to push his head up, spit snow, and gulp a breath.

Another even stronger wave of snow crashed down on him, forcing him back under.

The axe's pick scythed beneath him.

A flashed image of Kurt appeared.

He shook his head at Josef and released his grip from the roof once more.

The thought told Josef to surrender to the inevitable.

He commanded his frozen fingers to open and release the axe as he asked himself if Ang Noru was already dead …

His frozen fingers ignored the order, remaining locked tight on the axe head.

The pressure was becoming unbearable; his mind faded to black amidst the white that was crushing him.

* * *

Josef came to with Ang Noru, looking like some form of snow monster, digging the snow from his face and desperately shouting his name.

One of his hands was still clutching his ice axe, the pick caught in a loop of old rope pulled from deep within the snow and ice of the face—a remnant of a previous expedition long frozen into the side of the mountain.

Worming his way out of the broken snow, shocked and shivering, Josef looked up to see a trace of blue through the clouds above. Below, a new, perfectly white cloud bloomed from the valley as the avalanche hit the floor.

88

EAST RONGBUK GLACIER CAMP, MOUNT EVEREST—21,200 FEET
May 13, 1939
11:00 a.m.

When Macfarlane's view through his binoculars went totally white, he dropped their brass eyepieces from his face to see, firsthand, that the avalanche was now charging toward him. Looking back at the flimsy tents of the camp arranged around him and the wall of the valley rising up behind, he understood that he had nowhere to run even if the altitude would permit it. He ducked behind a boulder in preparation for the avalanche's arrival and waited for the impact. It never came. The approaching cloud of snow and ice slowed and collapsed in on itself, eventually stalling a few hundred yards away from the campsite, just as the more expert heads that had originally chosen that place many years before had known would happen.

Calm returning, Macfarlane stood up and urgently scanned the face again with his binoculars. When he saw the two dark shapes he had been watching slowly emerge from the upper part of the huge scar that the avalanche had rent across the mountain, he felt an unanticipated surge of joy. He also acknowledged that his relief at their survival made a mockery of his orders, that he was to be doomed by his own sense of fair play. Accepting it without remorse, he immediately ordered three of the Gurkhas and Zazar to the foot of the face to arrest the German and the Sherpa when they made it down and bring them to him. With a mistrustful look at Zazar, he stressed to the Gurkha sergeant that he wanted the two men "alive" before particularly urging the big Tibetan on his way, shouting, "Sherpa Ang Noru, Sherpa Ang Noru," at him to speed him there. He knew that Zazar was strong enough to carry one of them back alone if need be.

Watching them leave, Macfarlane unscrewed his nearly empty hip flask, took a much-needed sip of scotch, and considered his next steps.

* * *

The rescue party got back two hours later, Zazar carrying an almost unconscious Becker over his shoulders, the Gurkhas walking alongside the Sherpa. Laying the German at Macfarlane's feet, the Tibetan immediately spoke to the Gurkha sergeant who said, "Zazar says he has brought you the German, so the Sherpa, if you are a man of your word, is now his to take back to Kampa Dzong."

Macfarlane looked at the crumpled, ice-covered German on the ground before him and then at a similarly battered, yet still standing, Ang Noru. Shaking himself free from the hold of the Gurkhas, the Sherpa defiantly stared back at Macfarlane and, with a curse about the English, spat in his face. The British officer made no reaction at all, simply wiping his face with the back of his leather-gloved hand and coldly turning to the sergeant to say, "You can assure Zazar that I am indeed a most honorable man. He must also understand that there will be no killing here, whatever he has really agreed with the dzong pen. He must take this man back to Kampa Dzong alive."

The Gurkha sergeant and the Tibetan exchanged words before the Gurkha said, "Zazar has already promised the abbot of Rongbuk, who is the true master here, that there will be no killing in the shadow of Chomolungma. Beyond, he says it is soon the dzong pen's land, and there it is his laws."

"Undoubtedly, it is," Macfarlane said as he turned his head back to Ang Noru, who immediately started cursing at him again. Staring back at the Sherpa in return, he said to the sergeant, "Tell Zazar that for now, neither of these two men is in any condition to move anywhere. He can leave with the Sherpa tomorrow when the sun is up. I will permit him all the supplies he needs for his journey so he can prepare his pack tonight. We will have to stay here longer with the German for him to recover properly." Macfarlane then proceeded to help the four Gurkhas tend to Becker and Ang Noru as best they could, giving them water and hot tea, even feeding them a little before letting them sleep.

* * *

By sunrise Zazar was impatient to leave.

Macfarlane deliberately took his time before ordering the Gurkhas to awaken Becker and the Sherpa, bind their hands, and bring them out.

The Gurkhas led the Sherpa straight to the Tibetan, Zazar picking up a snake of rope already hung from his waist and tying Ang Noru to the end of it. The Sherpa, his hands bound, could only curse both the Tibetan and the British officer.

"Please save your energy for the journey ahead, Sherpa," was all Macfarlane said back.

Ang Noru responded by hurling himself face forward into the snow like an enraged small child. With a shout, Zazar tugged violently at the rope that held him, seemingly prepared to drag the kicking Sherpa on his way if necessary.

Seeing Zazar was ready to go, Macfarlane walked over to Josef, who was sitting on a rock under the watchful eyes of two of the Gurkhas. Nodding to the two soldiers that it was all right, Macfarlane beckoned the German to get up. "Walk with me, Becker."

With great effort, Josef stood, and together they stepped down from the rocky outcrop of the camp into the deeper snow around the Tibetan and the Sherpa. Slowly and precisely, so that he was sure the German understood him and the Gurkhas heard him, Macfarlane said, "Say goodbye to your companion. That Sherpa brought you a long way. A gentleman would shake such a man's hand one last time."

With that said, the British Army officer turned to Josef and took the German's bound hands, as if checking the ties, before saying something more under his breath and pointing him toward the Sherpa.

When Josef pulled his hands back, he found a

small bone-handled pocketknife had been placed in his right palm.

Macfarlane had quickly turned away to shout to the Gurkha sergeant, "Tell Zazar that he must permit the two to say their farewells, and then he can go."

Josef went to Ang Noru, who was still lying in the snow. He helped him to his knees and then, crouching down in front of him, shook the Sherpa's tied hands exaggeratedly as they exchanged their final words in German.

They both then got up from the snow while Zazar shouldered his heavy pack, crammed with all the equipment and supplies the British officer had permitted him to take for his journey. Despite the additional burden, the Tibetan was delighted with the haul, still surprised that when the British officer had checked the pack in the dark of the early morning he hadn't ordered him to leave some of it. Zazar would sell most of it in Shekar on the way back to Kampa Dzong. It would fetch a good price but nothing like the amount the dzong pen was going to give him for the Sherpa.

With a faint smile, Macfarlane watched as the big Tibetan buckled slightly under the weight of his pack before resolutely forcing himself to straighten up and bear the load.

Without any further words, Zazar tugged the rope and started tramping off through the deep snow, pulling the Sherpa along behind him. Josef watched them leave as Macfarlane stepped alongside him, saying quietly, "You should rest some more, Becker, but afterward I will want to talk to you about the direction of your next steps. As far as I can see you have two alternatives. You can either come with me to captivity or go back up. I suspect I already know which you will chose, and that is why I offer it."

89

UPPER EAST RONGBUK GLACIER, MOUNT EVEREST—20,750 FEET
May 14, 1939
10:25 a.m.

Ang Noru fought all the way, but Zazar was unbending, relentlessly pulling the Sherpa across the snowfield that stretched before them. The Tibetan paused once to go back and stop him struggling, but his pack was heavy and the snow so deep that he decided to save his energy with a different idea. Whatever the promises he might have made, he would simply kill the Sherpa when they were within the cover of the glacier's ice pinnacles. Carrying his head might increase his load still further, but it would be a lot easier than enduring the Sherpa's continued resistance all the way to Kampa Dzong. He tramped onward.

Slowly nearing the spiky horizon of ice that marked the beginning of the glacier proper, Ang Noru scanned the landscape for what Josef said he should seek, but the new snow and the bright morning sun made it difficult. Squinting into the light, squeezing his eyelids until they were slits, he tried to break down the view ahead until it was nothing more than light and dark. Eventually he thought it revealed what he sought: a faint line of shadow running straight across their path. Ang Noru dearly hoped that Josef was right as he stepped slowly toward it, pulling back on the rope whenever he could to keep Zazar roughly tugging him forward. The nearer they got, the more awkward he became, just as Josef had told him to be.

Enraged by the Sherpa's growing resistance, the Tibetan stopped again, shouting back at him, "You can try and delay all you want, Sherpa, but once we are in the ice, your head is mine. I will enjoy cutting it from your neck with you still alive to watch me do it. There will be none of your famous hawk spirits to save you there, only vultures to eat what remains of your body."

Zazar grabbed at the rope and pulled the Sherpa once again. This time Ang Noru did move, letting them both make easier progress through the soft snow, allowing the Tibetan to feel he was winning his battle. Following quietly behind, he waited until Zazar was stepping above the line of shadow, the faint depression in the snow he had identified. Then, with all his remaining might, the Sherpa tugged on the rope once again, throwing himself back into the deep snow as far as he could go.

The Tibetan lunged in instinctive response to the Sherpa's fall, stepping hard ahead to tug the Sherpa back up onto his feet. When his heavy boot touched the snow, it broke through the new crust.

It didn't stop. The surrounding snow splintered and collapsed to reveal a yawning crevasse that ripped open beneath the big man as he plunged forward, his heavy body and pack pulling him down into the narrow ravine of ice. The force of the Tibetan's unchecked fall snatched the rope, wrenching the Sherpa up into the air and onto his face, dragging him helplessly toward the gaping black hole that had sliced open.

Thrashing his legs and wriggling his body, his bound hands useless, Ang Noru tried desperately to stop himself from following the Tibetan down into the slot; but the rope dragged him relentlessly on until he heard the sound of something making hard contact with the ice below followed by a loud grunt.

In that brief moment, Ang Noru was able to turn his body, dig his heels into the snow, and bring himself to a stop just before the edge. For some minutes it was all he could do to sit there in the snow, breathless, as the Tibetan's shouts boomed and echoed from within the glacier and the straining rope that connected them cut into the snowy lip of the crevasse.

Slowly Ang Noru recovered enough to be able to lean forward and, with his teeth, open the small pocketknife Josef had secretly placed in his hands as they said their goodbyes.

Its cold blade stuck to his warm lip. Ang Noru ripped it away, tasting blood.

Gripping the knife in his bound hands, he forced the razor-sharp blade under the taut rope that led from his body down into the hole. Its tension pushed it down onto the blade.

Ang Noru rocked the knife slightly from side to side, the cords splitting and unraveling until the final strands burst apart and the frayed end before him vanished like a fleeing snake.

There was another heavy thump and a shout as the Tibetan's body slipped deeper down into the crevasse.

Pulling himself up, the Sherpa stood to look over the edge. Letting his eyes grow accustomed to the shadows below, he saw that Zazar's body was jammed between two sheer walls of ice about thirty feet down. The man's pack was still on top of him, but ripped open, the contents strewn over his horizontal form. To his surprise Ang Noru could see, amongst the many cans and provisions, two big rocks resting on the upper side of the Tibetan's body.

The Sherpa spat the blood from his torn lip down onto it. He then cut away the rope that tied his hands, listening as he did so to the man hunter's panicked curses becoming interspersed with the sound of the ice snapping and cracking as it closed ever tighter on the man's imprisoned body.

Tossing the remnants of the rope down into the crevasse, Ang Noru turned back up the glacier to return to Becker and the mountain. He walked a long way before the valley fell silent once more.

90

NORTHEAST RIDGE, MOUNT EVEREST—27,850 FEET
May 17, 2010
1:00 a.m.

Quinn is being crushed.

His body is caught within an iron vise that, sensing some final resistance, has stopped one millimeter before the breaking point—his breaking point.

A faint filigree of a cold blue fire intrudes onto the edge of his darkness, releasing a grey ash that floats down like snow.

It is the residue of a burned notebook, its ruled pages empty of writing.

As the cinders crumble over him, they demand a life story as yet unwritten, but he is trapped, paralyzed—he can't even talk to tell it.

Unsatisfied with his reticence, the dissolving embers cluster on his face to reveal an old photograph.

A hundred, or is it a thousand, people fill the picture—a lifetime of acquaintances frozen for the camera in one final image of remembrance.

The photograph begins to burn from the center.

The people bubble and dissolve as the expanding circle of blue flame incinerates them.

From within the burning, a single face appears.

It grows into a figure.

It is Graf.

With a faint smile, the German collector shakes his head as his long index finger beckons to Quinn repeatedly.

"Am I dead?" Quinn asks.

"Everyone who climbs Everest dies sooner or later, of that you can be sure. You need to get up, to get moving, or you too will become just one more color in the Rainbow Valley."

* * *

Quinn's mind forced itself up into consciousness.

In the freezing dark, he pushed himself from under the bodies of the Russian and Stevens. They were both completely rigid, suits and faces covered in a rime of frost, snow built up around them. Quinn had to fight to squeeze his way out on his back, digging hard into the ground with the heels of his crampons. Like a grub, he arched his body and gradually pushed himself from beneath the two dead men.

Finally free, Quinn lifted his head to look back at the outline of the human tunnel he'd left behind. In some way, he thought, it must have saved him, but his brain was unable to explain how. He stopped trying to understand it and lay back to look up at the stars. While he counted them one by one, an inner voice stated with authority that if the stars were visible then the bad weather had passed.

He tried to get up, but he couldn't.

He lay there instead and counted some more.

With no sense of time beyond night, constantly losing his place in the heavens, he closed his eyes and let his mind drift from its task.

He wondered how many toes and fingers he would lose.

He wondered some more.

Am I actually dead?

He knew the second thought in some way rendered the first irrelevant.

He told himself to stop thinking and count some more stars.

Opening his eyes, he saw that they were blocked.

A face was looking down at him.

Thinking it must be Sarron, Quinn flinched at the blow to surely come.

It didn't.

He looked again.

The peaked cap pushing out from under the baggy white canvas hood, the young, haggard face told him it was Josef Becker.

The realization came with no feeling of surprise, only relief.

Becker spoke to him in German. The words fused their meaning into his brain without need for translation.

"Come on, time to climb. We have to get this done. Ang Noru is here."

The Sherpa Ang Noru stepped out from behind the German, looked at Quinn and pointed back up the hill.

"We go top now, Sahib."

Quinn sat up to face his ghosts properly.

In turn the two shadows sat alongside him speaking of what they saw. They described the two dead bodies, becoming agitated about the Tibetan knife jammed into the vertebrae of Stevens' neck, the frozen fall of blood that hung from it.

The face of Becker peered in again at Quinn.

"Take the British soldier's pack. Find my ice axe. It's time to go."

"But I need oxygen. I need water. I need to sleep," Quinn heard himself pleading.

The German's voice grew inside Quinn's head. "There are not these things for you here. There never were. You must go up with us."

Quinn struggled to his feet, trying to push the hallucinations from his mind.

He failed.

"Get the things. Be quicker!" Becker said.

Quinn fought to free Stevens' pack from his rigid body. Discarding the heavy, empty oxygen cylinder within, he reached back further inside, seeking Becker's camera, still sealed in the nylon pouch.

"It's there," he heard himself say.

"Good. We go now."

Quinn shouldered Stevens' rucksack and began to move, step by individual step, back up to the top of the ridge.

There, outlined on the white snow, he saw the old ice axe.

He picked it up and leaned forward onto it as he looked up at the peak above. The clouds had receded. The wind had dropped. A bright moon outlined the snow and rocks of the mountain before him and he could trace the line of the route to the top.

He suddenly felt alone. The two shadows had disappeared so he contemplated what they had suggested. He could try to go up and over the mountain, traverse it from the north to the south. He understood that it would take him back into Nepal, away from the Chinese, away from Sarron. It was an elegant escape, one that would probably kill him.

Even as he worked to dismiss the idea as madness, he heard Henrietta say that he was capable of greatness if he set his mind to it. Her voice stung him into putting his left foot forward.

His right foot slowly followed.

Squeezing his lungs, he took another step.

Clenching his fists and his toes, he took five more but couldn't summon a sixth.

He leaned again onto the head of the old axe, gasping for air, head spinning.

His consciousness shuffled.

The two ghosts reappeared before him.

He followed, asking himself at what point he would accept that he was one of them. With no hope of a future, he climbed locked in the past. With each step he pushed down into the moments of his lifetime. He replayed old successes and enjoyed past happinesses. He was shamed again by old humiliations and felt the renewed disappointment of ancient failures. He acknowledged the wrongs he had done and made promises to do better. As he stepped forward, he continually made promises.

The steps became sequences, and the sequences became parts of the mountain. He passed the First Step and Mushroom Rock, and, once more, the Second Step began to loom large in his mind. A thought came with it that the shadows had tricked him, that they had set him up to return the camera to its rightful home, to leave his body next to Nelson Tate Junior's. The idea wounded him. He decided he was not going to listen to them anymore, but they were no longer there to ignore.

Lonely and betrayed, Quinn moved along the exposed traverse until the Second Step was rising up above him, black and sheer in the night. Feeling as if his lungs were bleeding, he looked up at it to realize that he had traveled further across the bottom of the obstacle than the normal route. He began to haul himself up, inch by inch, through the rocks and the boulders toward the exposed slabs above. He pushed through the pain, dragging himself upward with his hands, his elbows, his knees, his toe points, until, totally exhausted, he collapsed forward into the snow. As if surrendering to it, he pushed his face deep in.

It touched something.

With a gloved hand he clawed at the snow to reveal a frozen face.

It was Nelson Tate Junior.

The blue lips began to move.

"You let me die."

Something inside Quinn shattered.

"I didn't," he sobbed in reply. "I didn't."

He turned over, lying back on the snow and rock.

Looking up at the stars again, snippets of music began to play inside his head. A few chords, half a chorus, then a burst of static that stopped the melody as if an ancient valve radio was being tuned to another station. Even so he recognized it as the music that had journeyed with him through his life—rock, punk, reggae, rhythm and blues. It annoyed him that the dial never settled long enough to play the whole song.

He decided to turn off the radio and die.

* * *

The voice of the German climber startled Quinn from the slumber he had slipped into. "Okay, Englishman, enough rest. Make your peace with the dead. We go on now."

"But I thought …" Quinn said aloud, but before he could finish the sentence, Becker was gone.

The German and the Sherpa were moving up the rocks above. Quinn watched as they strenuously climbed the crack that split the rock face. Becker led, and then hauled Ang Noru up after him with a rope.

Quinn followed them, stepping up the metal ladder that was attached to the side of the fault.

Crossing the flatter ridge beyond, he thought that all three of them were moving too slowly.

They were definitely going to miss their cutoff time, that sacrosanct hour by which, if they hadn't summited, they would have to start to descend.

Shouldn't I turn them back now, get them going down?

He stopped himself.

There was no cutoff time, no down, for that matter, only up; so he continued after the pair as they tramped ahead of him through the new snow left by the storm.

Quinn crawled his way up through the rocks of the Third Step as the line of the horizon melted, red lava welling up behind it.

Dawn.

Ahead Becker had fallen into the snow. Ang Noru was helping him up.

Quinn watched as the pair staggered onward.

They no longer floated.

They continually stumbled and fell, every step an agony.

Quinn felt it too, but still he followed while the new day gained height in a swelling spectrum of orange, yellow, and white that hit the huge bulk of the mountain to project an immense triangular shadow to the west as regular as the Great Pyramid. Further on, the elongated heights of Makalu stared south like its Sphinx.

They skirted some rocks.

Moving out and around, only Quinn held on to the old, frayed ropes that lined the narrow path. To their right, it felt as if they were looking off the very edge of a flat Earth.

The path twisted back on itself to pick a way straight up through the rocks and ice that led to another snowfield above.

They were all gasping and failing now, their journey broken into groups of three steps, two steps, no steps.

When eventually they surmounted the steep climb to the top of the snow and stopped together, Quinn remotely studied the huge bulbous cornice of ice above that overhung the Kangshung face. It told him that they were near. He said the same to the German and the Sherpa.

They dragged themselves forward, each step a single one that had to be accommodated with rest and recovery.

An eternity passed in this way until a flash of color registered ahead.

More scraps of red, green, yellow, and orange poked out from the hard cap of frozen snow, signaling an end to their world of ice and rock and announcing the beginning of space.

The three linked arms and took the last steps to the summit before collapsing into the snow.

91

THE SUMMIT OF MOUNT EVEREST—29,029 FEET
May 17, 2010
9:30 a.m.

The five Sherpas coming up from the south side were jubilant. After the storm of the previous day, it was a perfect morning and their work of fixing the ropes along the Knife-Edge Ridge and up the famous Hillary Step had gone quickly and well despite the new snow. It was an unspoken privilege of preparing the route to the top that the Sherpas summited first, before any of the foreign climbers, and the Mother Goddess was showing her approval of the correct natural order by rewarding them with a beautiful day.

Traversing the slow diagonal from the top of the Hillary Step, the summit mound finally appeared. The Sherpas were extremely surprised, a little shocked even, to see a climber already sitting there, totally still, alone in the morning brightness on the top of the world. Approaching, they thought, at first, that the figure was dead, a forgotten corpse from the season before. But as they got closer, they saw the man was alive.

Kneeling around him, they peered at his broken and cut face. With a sense of horror, they remarked on the streaks of blood and ice that covered his suit.

The man did not move. He made no acknowledgement of their arrival.

Seeing that the figure lacked an oxygen system, one of the Sherpas unclipped his mask and, dialing up the regulator, passed the mask to the man. He very slowly took hold of it. The Sherpas would say later that he seemed to offer it to other invisible figures on either side of him before pushing it onto his own face. They thought, at the time, that the man was very close to the end, that his mind was gone.

For fifteen minutes he sat there, silently breathing the oxygen.

Another of the Sherpas then passed him a flask of warm tea. Again he appeared to offer it to others, invisible to the Sherpas but real to him, before drinking from it himself.

More time passed.

The Sherpas waited, not sure what to do next. They had to descend soon.

Finally, Neil Quinn beckoned the nearest Sherpa close to his face. He paused, looked from side to side, and then whispered through broken lips, "It's only me now. I think I should go down with you. But first I need to find my ice axe. I left it here last year."

92

SHAMBHALA HOTEL, LHASA, TIBET
May 23, 2010
2:30 p.m.

Sarron was growing impatient. He wanted his moment of victory. Even though he had retrieved the camera and left Quinn for dead high on the mountain, he couldn't celebrate until he had heard from Stefan Vollmer.

Drinking a warm beer from its shiny blue can, he looked down from his top-floor room in the Shambhala Hotel with intense frustration. On the bustling pavement below, a group of Chinese big-city tourists, each clad in a white face mask and an electric blue windbreaker, trotted hastily behind a guide waving an equally blue flag, desperate to not be left behind. Sarron raised his gaze to look across a group of old buildings seemingly sinking under the weight of their heavyset roofs into the brown-tinted smog that blanketed the city. Beyond, the improbable white mass of the Potala Palace jutted up through the haze.

Staring at it, he could feel his left eye flickering uncontrollably. He told himself that he was exhausted, that he needed to be on his way from that damn place. Pushing on his left eyelid with two fingers, he finally decided his destination. It would be Chile. He'd thought maybe Argentina like Vollmer's Nazi ancestors, but no, it would be Chile. He'd heard it was easier there. He could start again like many before him, far away on the other side of the world. He was finished with the mountains. He would get a place by the sea. But first, he needed money. He needed that call from Vollmer.

Turning back into the room, he looked at the silent cell phone lying on the unmade bed. He picked it up to check that it had a signal; four bars stepped up alongside a full-mast icon.

No new messages.

Vollmer's people must have received the camera by now. The international transport firm had been efficient. They had even sent a European representative to receive and package the camera to keep it at freezing temperature. The courier said he was taking the camera to Switzerland, where Vollmer had identified a specialist team to extract and develop the film. Sarron had been surprised and excited when the man said it would be there in less than twenty-four hours.

But that was three days ago now.

Sarron decided that he had to leave the room. He didn't want to; it was an unnecessary risk at this stage of the proceedings, but he couldn't stay inside any longer. He was mentally crawling up the walls in anticipation and suspense. He had to get out for a while.

Picking up the cell phone, Sarron pulled on a

wide-brimmed sun hat and dark glasses and went down to the street. There he pushed into the crowd, letting it sweep him along. He had no idea where he was going. Oblivious to the street scene, his internal vision flooded once again with images of what had happened high on the mountain: Oleg Vishnevsky falling into the Kangshung void; his brother, Dmitri, being shot. As he walked, he could feel his knife still lodged in that other climber's neck, refusing to pull free from the spine however hard he tried. He had winded himself killing that man. After, it had been all he could do to get away with the camera.

Reliving once again those murderous, bloody scenes, Sarron realized with a jolt that his phone was ringing.

He darted into a side street to take the call.

It was Vollmer.

As Sarron put the phone to his ear, his head spun with urgency as he heard the German say, "Sarron?"

"Yes."

"This is Stefan Vollmer. I have the pictures on my computer screen in front of me."

A burst of adrenaline made Sarron's heart leap. He clenched a fist and started punching at the air before getting control of himself. "*Fantastique!*"

There was a long pause before Vollmer spoke again. "I think that the only thing I can do, Sarron, under the circumstances, is to forward them to your email. You can take a look at them and then conclude how you wish to settle this matter with me."

"Yes, of course. How are they? Was the film good? Are they in focus?"

"Yes, Sarron, just like new, perfectly in focus.

Please be clear about one thing. We will find you."

The line went dead.

Sarron ran back into the main street and across the road, dodging traffic as his eyes searched the row of cafés and tourist shops that lined the pavement. Fixing his sight on the Mandala Internet Café, he ran in. Beyond the dim café bar at the front, a neon-bright room to the rear was filled with figures hunched before old computer screens set within individual, half-partitioned chipboard cubicles.

Every computer was occupied. Sarron bit his lip, pacing backward and forward, before noticing that a small, fat Chinese man in an electric blue windbreaker and a face mask was occupying one of the screens furthest from the door. He walked over and gently squatted down on his haunches alongside the truant. When he turned his face up, the man jumped in his seat, his concentration on the naked women on the computer screen shattered by the surprise of someone so close to him. With a look of terror, he jerked his hands from the keyboard to shield his face from the stranger. Sarron stared between the chubby fingers into the small, blinking eyes and hissed, "Fuck off, *Chinois*, or I will kill you."

The little man grabbed the effeminate satchel bag on his lap, jumped up, and fled, leaving Sarron free to sit down, clear the screen of Thai pornography, and log into an email account.

The connection was slow.

Finally, he got in.

A new email from the blind account that had been used by Vollmer throughout their deal was listed.

He rushed to open it.

It was a forward of another email from the photographic studio in Switzerland.

Ignoring the reams of text in German, he raced to open the attached photographs.

They took forever to download.

The waiting was interminable. Sarron scraped his fingernails frenetically at the edge of the cheap table on which the monitor was sitting. A piece of the table's hard plastic veneer split and stuck beneath one of his nails. It stung with a sharp pain and ran red with a rivulet of blood.

He cursed and sucked at the wound to stem the bleeding as the downloading symbol continued to make its snaillike trail across the screen.

His heart pounded.

His head distorted time.

Each second seemed to take a minute, each minute an hour, until finally the first picture signaled its arrival.

He opened it.

It was in black and white, crystal clear.

The image showed a black metal frame taken against the background of a featureless white sky. The frame's sparse diamond lattice was rigid with only the odd flourish in the metalwork to speak of a blacksmith seeking to impose some small signature of his skill on what was an ugly, brutal piece of ironwork.

The more Sarron studied the photograph, the more he understood that he was actually looking at a gate, in fact, set within a larger metal frame. It was slightly ajar. At its top, two separate metal rectangles were stacked one above the other. Within the rectangles were set letters. They stood out in strict silhouette against the white of the sky:

ARBEIT
MACHT FREI

Sarron had seen the words before, but couldn't instantly recall where.

Confusion pushed him to the next image.

Putting his hand back on the grimy mouse, now smeared with his blood, he scrolled and clicked.

The next photograph revealed cast concrete posts that stretched lines of barbed wire above a deep trench. The wire curled over at the top, turning back in on itself. The ceramic bobbins that secured the wire to the posts told him that it was an electric fence. They too faced inward. A fence designed to keep people in, not out.

With a growing sense of panic, Sarron opened all the photographs Vollmer had forwarded. One after another the images stacked the screen, photograph after photograph of unspeakable tortures, of human experimentation, of starvation, of death piled high, of ovens—a sequence of horrors dealt as randomly as a pack of cards. Sarron flicked through every image, shock burning his stomach, his left eyelid uncontrollable.

His attention froze on one. It was of a man in a long overcoat wearing a feathered Tyrolean hat standing in front of a large yet simple map that covered a wall. The map was actually little more than a grey shadow, but its shape obviously represented all of Europe. Sarron read the names arranged around the man—Mauthausen, Buchenwald, Wewelsburg, Sachsenhausen, Mittelbau-Dora, Ravensbrück, Bergen-Belsen, Auschwitz, and, at the very tip of the old man's pointing finger, above a dot for Munich, Dachau. He looked closely at the face beneath the hat. It was the same man that he and Oleg Vishnevsky had killed.

Graf.

The next photo was of a small display panel attached to a wall, the bottom left corner of a larger image showing rows of striped prisoners on parade visible above it. The white rectangle, the legend for the bigger image, showed only a phrase in German with an English translation set below.

Sarron pulled his face in close to the computer, his nose almost touching the hot screen as he read it.

> Fot. 15
>
> *"Ihr seid rechtlos, ehrlos und wehrlos. Ihr seid ein Haufen Scheisse und so werdet ihr behandelt."*
>
> **Aus der Ansprache des Schutzhaftlagerführers Josef Jarolin und die neuen Häftlinge in KZ—Dachau 1941/42."**

Sarron's twitching eyes quickly flicked to the English translation below, seeking explanation.

> "You are without rights, dishonorable and defenseless. You are a pile of shit, and that is how you are going to be treated."
>
> **From the address of the protective custody camp leader Josef Jarolin to the new Dachau prisoners, 1941–42.**

The final picture was of Graf again. He was smiling back at the camera, raising his feathered hat slightly above his head as if in a salute from beyond the grave.

Sarron's mind exploded like an egg hitting a concrete floor.

93

PUTRAPUR, ANDHRA PRADESH, INDIA
May 15, 1939
9:30 p.m.

Liebe Josef,

How are you? Where are you? I wish I knew. I wonder continually.

Today I am in a small village called Putrapur; the day after tomorrow I move on to Sihar. I would try and tell you precisely where they are but I am not really sure myself. All I know is that I have already traveled far into the dusty heart of this vast country and keep moving still. I have had no news of my parents since I left Hyderabad. My father said it must be that way.

I never linger anywhere long even though the people beg me to stay. They are so poor, Josef. Within minutes of my arrival, they form queues of illness and injury that would make me weep if I was not so busy treating it all.

Where do they all come from?

It makes me feel like I too am climbing a mountain alone, a mountain of pain and disease. It is as big as Mount Everest. You told me once that when you climb you just take one step at a time, put one foot in front of another. I try to do the same but I have no sight of any summit. I too feel like Sisyphus …

It is so hot here tonight. I wish I could lie next to you on the cold, cold ground where you are. Do you sleep on snow and ice now?

It is so dry here tonight. I wish I could walk with you in the green, fresh hills of Elmau. I would like to drink from the cool spring you told me you used to visit with your family. Will we go there together one day?

It is so sad here. I wish I could sit with you on the deck of the Gneisenau *and laugh as we once did. Will I ever laugh again?*

I am a person of questions with no answers.

I never have any answers.

I need you.

I can't do this alone …

Tears began to fall onto the paper.

The black ink they met dissolved and ran across the page.

Putting her pen to one side, Magda tore the note from her journal and crunched it into a ball in her hand. Holding it tightly, she stepped from the small hut out into the roar of the insects.

In the night shadows she could see the people already gathered for the next day's clinic. Walking through them she felt their patient suffering and let it smother her own.

Stopping at the embers of a dying cooking fire, she dropped the paper in. It briefly flared yellow.

The people began to stir, seeing Magda's face illuminated by the flames. Realizing who she was, they reached out to her.

Wiping her eyes, she turned back from the fire. There was work to do.

Just put one foot in front of the other ...

94

APARTMENT E, 57 SUKHRA PATH, KATHMANDU, NEPAL
May 29, 2010
11:30 a.m.

Quinn knocked on the door of Henrietta's apartment.

"It's not locked, Dawa. Sanjeev is ill today so just show yourself in," was the immediate response from inside.

"It's not Dawa, Henrietta. It's Neil Quinn."

"Well, you can come in also, Neil." Quinn stepped in as Henrietta's voice continued. "I was expecting Dawa to arrive first. I thought he should come to get his monthly money and then wait for you so that we could both talk to him about Ang Noru. I think he should know the full story."

Henrietta was seated in her usual chair. She looked up at Quinn over her half-moon glasses. "Well, I'm glad to see you back in Kathmandu and in one piece. I am also pleased to hear that you have finally done a half-decent Everest climb, a north-south traverse almost without supplementary oxygen. It doesn't make you a legend, of course, but it'll do under the circumstances."

She winked at him as she stood up. "I'll make us some tea. Sit down. What took you so long to get back here?"

Quinn put down the rucksack he was carrying, the old ice axe strapped to its side. "I holed up in Namche Bazaar for a while. I needed time to recover, and you were still locked up by the Chinese, so I thought it best to disappear until things settled down. I assume you heard from the Sherpa how I made it over the top."

Henrietta nodded as she walked to the small kitchen of her apartment. Filling a kettle, she shouted back above the rattle of the water. "Yes, evidently they were quite surprised to find you up there. Rather stole the thunder of their first summit of the season. One of them told me they thought you were pretty close to death, talking to yourself, seeing ghosts, covered in blood and ice. Evidently they had quite the job to get you down. I heard you wouldn't even leave until you got your original ice axe back."

"Yes. Its replacement was proving to be a bit troublesome. How was your stay with the Chinese?"

"Positively vile. It was very nearly a major diplomatic incident. Given the reason Martin Emmerich and I were there in the first place, it had to be handled with kid gloves by our chaps in the Foreign Office and their counterparts in the Bundestag. That's why it took us nearly two weeks to get out of the country. The death of Stevens and your disappearance didn't help matters, although I can hardly blame you for that.

"Martin's still here, you know. He's at the Tiger Hotel. He wants to see you before he goes back to

Germany. He's unhappy with the result but doesn't think that we could have done things differently. Sarron played a clever hand getting us all ousted from the Base Camp like that, but so far there seems to have been no shocking photographs of a first Nazi summit of Everest, so I guessed that none of you found what we were looking for up there. Perhaps it was all a bit of a long shot."

She returned with the tea set on a tray. She'd intended to put it on the small table between her armchairs, but Quinn had already covered it with items from his rucksack. Looking up at her, he said, "Henrietta, it's not George Leigh Mallory's handkerchief, but I brought down a few souvenirs."

She set the tea on another side table and looked at the lime-green oxygen cylinder from the Nelson Tate Junior summit and the medical syringe next to it.

"Wow, finally some evidence relating to the cause of the boy's demise," she said. "We'll get them looked at. Tea now?"

She turned back to the side table and poured two cups of tea. When she returned, Quinn had replaced the cylinder and the syringe with Stevens' red freezer bag and the old ice axe.

She looked at the case and back at Quinn.

"Is that what I think it is?"

"Yes."

"Now I really do feel like Pandora."

She unzipped the red nylon cube and pulled out a plastic ice block. Setting it to one side, she lifted out Becker's Leica, sealed within two clear plastic bags. As she turned it over in her hands, Quinn said, "I think it should live in your freezer until you tell me what we are to do with it. It needs to stay frozen."

Henrietta quickly replaced the camera back into the little nylon case and, holding it like a holy offering, hurriedly carried it into the kitchen. Quinn heard her freezer door slam shut on it.

There was another knock at the door as she returned.

"It'll be Dawa. I'll let him in."

Walking to her front door, Henrietta stretched forward to open it, saying in a loud voice, "Hold on. I'm letting you in."

Before she could turn the handle, the door slammed into her face, knocking her off her feet.

Sarron burst through it to immediately put a foot against the prostrate lady's neck.

Pointing a large kukri knife down at her, he screamed, "Don't move! You either Quinn, you bastard."

Quinn stared back at the deep curve of the spoon-shaped knife now being raised toward him. The blade was about a foot and a half long. Kukris like it were for sale all over Kathmandu. Even if they were made for the tourists, Quinn knew that it would still be strong and sharp.

He looked back at Sarron. He'd lost his oiled sheen. His face was lined, darkened, totally crazed.

"Make one move, and I will hack this old hag to pieces before your fucking eyes," he screamed at Quinn.

Raising the curved knife above his head as if preparing to carry out his threat, he demanded, "Where's the German's camera?"

"In the freezer in the kitchen—to keep it cold. Let her go, and I will give it to you."

"You are in no position to bargain, Quinn. Just get it and bring it out here now."

Quinn slowly backed into the kitchen, holding his hands up, watching Sarron intently with each step.

The incensed man remained where he was, swaying slightly, his left eyelid trembling violently.

Henrietta seemed to have passed out.

Stepping into the kitchen, Quinn quickly went to the fridge, shouting as he opened the door, "I'm getting it now."

Without removing anything, he slammed the freezer door loudly. He stood in front of it for a second, eyes racing around the kitchen, searching for any possible weapon, a knife, a bottle, anything, but in that moment, he saw nothing suitable. Totally desperate, he grabbed a large salad bowl sitting on the draining board next to the sink.

"Put it down, Quinn. That fucking thing is not going to save you."

Quinn froze, releasing the bowl. Turning around, he saw that Sarron had followed him into the kitchen.

He took another step toward him, pointing the knife's blade directly at Quinn's face. "Go back to the freezer, and this time get the camera out."

As Quinn did so, Sarron blocked the doorway, moving slowly from side to side, drawing a figure eight in the air before him with the long blade.

Quinn slowly passed him the freezer bag.

Sarron stepped forward to seize it with his left hand.

Quinn heard Henrietta moan from the main room.

Sarron twitched, hearing it also, but his eyes remained fixed on Quinn as he shouted back, "It's a pity you can't see this, since you like mountaineering history so much—the tragic death of Everest guide Neil Quinn here in your very own apartment."

Sarron lifted his right arm, rotating the knife's cutting edge toward Quinn, its razor-sharp blade catching the light.

Quinn readied himself to try and dodge its fall.

But it never came.

Instead he fleetingly glimpsed the steel head of the old ice axe rising high above Sarron's head before it chopped forward.

Momentarily, the raised kukri blade hung in the air separated from Sarron's stunned body until they both crashed to the floor.

Quinn looked up from the geyser of crimson blood erupting from the body at his feet to see Dawa, the end of the axe's wooden shaft still firmly clasped in his hands, its long pick wedged as far as it would go into the back of the Frenchman's skull.

95

THE SECOND STEP,
NORTHEAST RIDGE, MOUNT EVEREST—28,333 FEET
May 17, 1939
5:16 p.m.

Josef knew he was finished when he couldn't untie the knot that linked him to the Sherpa. He tried to squeeze his brain beyond the exhaustion and the numbing cold, ordering it to tell his fingers what to do. They fumbled at the rope, but it was hopeless. It was a knot that he had tied a thousand times. No recall. Gone.

Pushing his freezing hands back into his woolen mittens, Josef lay back, unable to respond to a faint internal command to get up and keep moving. The only thing he could do was slowly tug once more at the rigid rope tied around his middle. The effort to do even that sent him over the edge again. He drifted away to somewhere warmer, easier.

When he returned to the swirling cold of the mountainside, Ang Noru was looking down at him, shaking him gently by the shoulders. The Sherpa's snow goggles and blackened face beneath were encrusted with ice. His lips were trembling slightly. They moved, but no words came.

Josef pointed to the knot. The Sherpa untied it.

A remote thought reminded Josef of the strip of red tape with which he had marked their exit from the steep step on the way up. After their precarious, desperate struggle to climb up it, he had hammered a piton into the rock, reassuring himself that it would be an easier rappel on the descent, marking the spot for this very moment.

He couldn't see it anywhere. Pulling his ice-covered snow goggles down around his neck, he looked some more. Nothing. It was difficult to focus his eyes. His sight was going.

Slowly he reached into his wind-jacket pocket and pulled out his last piton. Taking the ice axe, he tried to beat it into the rock, but the side of the axe head continually slipped off the top of the piton. Ang Noru gently took the axe from him and pounded the nail in until it could go no further.

Josef laid back on the freezing rock, resting his head by the piton. His eyes tried to lock on its metal loop projecting from the black stone, the overexposed white snow beyond, but everything was a blur. Pushing his head against some loose snow, he imagined himself crawling into the mountainside, worming his way into the rock like the blade of the piton. It would be safe in there, away from the wind and the cold.

He started to cough again, huge coughs that twisted his body into knots, ripped at his throat, and filled his mouth with blood. With no adrenaline left to dramatize it, no energy to panic about it, Josef finally accepted that he was dying. It was almost a relief. He lay back again and looked up at the fast cloud passing over him. A long time passed before a contradictory urge made him search his pocket for a steel carabiner. Clutching it, he pushed it onto the piton at the fourth attempt.

Rope.

It was there, loose and untied, between him and the Sherpa.

He could see that Ang Noru was also now resting. It made Josef happy to see it. He needed to rest. He had done well. Josef told himself it was time to let the Sherpa go. Ang Noru was stronger. He might still make it down if alone. If he stayed with Josef, he too would surely die. While he looked at the Sherpa's still body, Josef told himself that he must work a little more, do one last thing, and then it could be finished.

Centimeter by centimeter, he threaded the frozen, coarse rope through the metal loop. When he faintly saw the black tape of the rope's halfway marker, his instinct pulled the two sides of the rope together. With one hand, he tugged the doubled rope down on the carabiner. The piton that held it didn't move. It was set into that rock for the next hundred years.

With his feet Josef heel-kicked the rope toward the edge of the cliff. When gravity finally caught it and pulled the coils of rope away from him over the edge, Josef leaned across to pull at the Sherpa's jacket. It was a shame to wake him, but it was time. Ang Noru awoke as if stuck with a cattle prod. He was on his feet in an instant. With a stream of apologies pouring from his lips, he reached down and pulled Josef up.

It was a hard pull. It told Josef he was right; the Sherpa did still have strength.

Josef unfolded upward from his icy seat, still holding the top of the doubled rope in one hand.

He could stand.

He could do what he had to do.

Josef turned to look back up the mountain and stepped over the double rope that hung over the cliff. From behind him he pulled a reluctant, heavy loop of it up and around his right hip and over his left shoulder. Pushing his ice axe back into the straps of his rucksack, he grasped the rope in front of him with his left mitten and the rear of the rope with his right.

Taking one last look at the Sherpa, he began to walk backward.

At the cliff's very edge, he stopped, leaning back over the huge void below. The rope that snaked around his body dug into his thick clothes as it took the strain. He thought for a moment about Magda and then told himself to count to nine and let go.

He knew only one of the Jews' names, but he remembered each of their faces as he took those last nine steps down the cliff. He saved the name he had for his ninth, final step, whispering, "Ilsa" as he released the rope.

He thought he would fall forever, but the drop lasted only a few seconds.

The sudden impact with the rocky ledge below snapped the bones of his lower left leg. The excruciating pain, the outline of the limb, his limb, bent strangely inward at the ankle, told him it was broken. A thought, *It's going to be much slower than you imagined,* grew from the agony.

Using his ice axe, Josef dragged himself into the little alcove that led off the ledge. Slipping out of his pack and pushing it to the side, he pulled himself around and up against the far wall. Leaning back he let the cold numb his pain, diverting his mind by replaying the climb, reversing it all the way back down to their surprising release from the valley camp. He heard again the British officer saying, "We will have to make it look like you both overpowered me when you were under my charge. The Gurkhas are honest, loyal men. I do not want to make them complicit in anything that might prejudice their futures, whatever it may do to my own."

The crunching sound of Ang Noru dropping from the rope onto the lip of the cave pierced the shadows within.

On seeing his horribly twisted leg, the Sherpa instantly ducked inside to crouch alongside the German, trying to tend to it.

Josef pushed him away.

"Go down while you still can."

"No," came the refusal.

Lifting his axe by the head with his right hand, Josef pushed at the Sherpa with the spiked end.

"Go away. It's over."

The Sherpa easily pushed the axe's shaft away with a hand and stared at Josef, speechless.

"It's all right, my friend. You must go. Someone has to tell of what we have done. I'll rest here."

The Sherpa hesitated.

"Go, please."

Ang Noru leaned forward to briefly touch his forehead to the side of Josef's head. As he did so, Josef heard him say only one word.

The Sherpa turned and left the small cave. Alone now, Josef tried to recall what the Sherpa had said but couldn't. It had gone with him. He remembered instead, for a moment, that there was something more that he should have given him, to take down, but that thought also dissolved, still incomplete.

He laid his ice axe down alongside his body. Its small flag was missing. It must have been torn away in the fall.

As he leaned once more against the cold stone of the cave, riding new waves of pain from his leg, he imagined that little flag caught by the wind, twisting and spiraling as it was blown away from the mountain. He flew with it into the air, back over the hills, over Tibet, Sikkim, India, the oceans, until they arrived at other hills, softer and greener. He wondered if Magda could see them as they flew.

I'm sorry.

A sudden fit of bloody coughing dragged Josef back down into the dark of the small cave. The walls around him closed in. He thought that the English army officer was actually there now, talking to him as he had for those hours before Ang Noru returned without the Tibetan. His final words to Josef filled the cave. "No man has the right to deny the destiny of another, whatever his masters might command. True honor is much more than blind loyalty. Good luck."

He must have fallen unconscious for a while. When Josef came to, he couldn't feel his broken leg anymore, only an intense heat burning inside his chest, violent like sodium reacting to water. Compelled to put out the fire, he forced the neck of his jacket open, pulling at the silk *kata* scarf within. He tugged the scarf away with his left hand and held it tight in his mittened fingers. He pulled it up to his face and held it over his eyes, catching a glimpse once more of the old abbot placing it over his neck before he set off, hearing again the mumble of his blessings, understanding again what he wanted him to do, acknowledging again that it was what he knew he should do all along.

A great weight bore down on him. It pushed his head forward, down into the opening of his jacket.

Josef felt his chin touch the top of the camera still hung around his neck.

He recalled what it was that he should have given Ang Noru.

It was too late now.

Tilting his head back up, he stared out at the faint white blur that was all that was now left of his world beyond the cave.

What was it the Sherpa had said?

Josef mouthed the word as he closed his eyes one last time.

"Summit."

96

THE BRITISH EMBASSY, KATHMANDU, NEPAL
June 4, 2010
3:30 p.m.

Henrietta was walking with Quinn down a basement corridor followed by Emmerich and Dawa. "The tests are back on the Tate oxygen cylinder, Neil," she said to Quinn as she looked from side to side, searching for a particular door.

"And?"

"Nothing, I'm afraid. I was expecting that they were going to tell me that it was porous but evidently the cylinder was not defective."

"Crap. So I'm not off the hook?"

"Well, not because of faulty oxygen, no. However, the syringe proved to be much more interesting."

"How so?"

"It was labeled as corticosteroid but actually it contained traces of a concentrated solution of street-grade methamphetamine laced with cocaine. It seems it was something cobbled together by Sarron and the

Vishnevskys to jump a client back onto their feet so that they could pull them down off the hill and sort them out at a lower level. It might even work for an adult, at the risk of a major heart attack. However, for a young man like Nelson Tate Junior it would have quickly proved fatal. As soon as Sarron heard that you had used his HA medical kit to inject the boy he would have understood what had happened. Attack was the man's only method of defense."

Quinn could say only, "Jesus," shaking his head and walking on until Henrietta, having found her doorway, motioned him to stop and wait for the other two to join them.

When they were all together, she said, "You do understand that we will never be able to talk about what we might see in here. Evidently the film in Josef Becker's camera was in very poor shape, hardly surprising when you consider what it went through. However, when I spoke to the specialist earlier, he did think he would be able to salvage something. We are going to sneak a quick look at it, then I will be making a final report to the British and German ambassadors and handing everything over for good."

The three nodded.

"I know that I am already going a bit far managing the development process in this way, but I think when all is said and done, we have each earned the right to see what really happened up there in 1939. It may well be the most bittersweet moment of my long career, but a summit is a summit, and the truth is the truth. Now is not the moment to shy away from the habits of a lifetime, whatever my fears at what will be revealed. At the end of the day, if Josef Becker made it then I must respect that, even if I condemn his politics."

Henrietta Richards knocked on the closed door before them.

From within, a delayed, "Come in," granted them access. They each filed through the door, pushing aside a black cotton sheet hung to mask the cracks. A filtered crimson light illuminated the windowless room with a visceral glow. The smell of chemicals was toxic: instantly overpowering everyone except the white-coated man already working inside. After a lifetime spent in such environments, the Leica technician no longer even noticed it. Finishing another sequence of adjustments to the skeleton of an archaic negative enlarger, he flicked his head from side to side in silent appeal for more elbow room, mumbling something only to himself. He clearly preferred to work alone.

The man made one further minute calibration then paused, arms dropping to his sides, eyes closing as he mentally counted down some required delay known only to his experience. The instant it was over, he quickly reached for the eight-by-ten-inch rectangle of photographic paper set within the base of the metal frame. Taking a corner of the white card in the long jaws of a pair of tongs, he then deliberately slowed himself to gently slide it into the first of four stainless steel trays of developing fluids he had so fastidiously prepared. He began to bathe the blank paper, lightly agitating it within the clear chemical bath, his soft, rhythmic movements setting the fluids lapping.

A dark smudge dirtied the white rectangle's center. Lines and shadows started to define themselves, growing in twists and turns like an aggressive black vine. The technician, completely and utterly absorbed in his task, carefully tweezered the sharpening image through the next three trays. With each transfer he leaned a little further forward, deliberately hiding it, still, at heart, the small, clever boy at the prestigious Karlsruhe Academy who would shield his impeccable schoolwork from the prying eyes of bigger, slower classmates.

The observers in the room tried to arch around him in response, each desperate for their own first look, but the diminutive man expertly blocked their every move. He didn't care who they were; he had a job to do. Only when he was completely satisfied with what he saw did he finally push back to lift the fully developed photograph from the last tray. Reaching up, he clipped it, with two small clothes pegs, onto the makeshift drying line strung in anticipation of that very moment.

The still-wet photograph hung above them all, soft like lychee flesh, swaying a little on the sickly air. No one in the darkroom said a word. They just stared up at it rigidly, as if brought to attention in unison.

The image was black and white, yet to its small audience it shone down through the blood-red haze with all the colors of the rainbow. It showed a mountaineer standing just a couple of steps below the pointed white apex of a mountaintop. The cloudless sky behind was almost black, yet the figure at the center seemed to faintly glow as if surrounded by an evanescence of a whiter, brighter light.

The baggy hood of the climber's white canvas wind-jacket was thrown back. A pair of round-framed snow goggles were pushed up onto the ice-encrusted front of a fabric-peaked cap. Beneath, a woolen scarf wrapped the climber's head, but it had been pulled down from the mouth to deliberately expose an exhausted yet triumphant face.

The figure's right arm was projecting forward and upward into the sky, its mittened hand gripping the bottom of a long, wood-shafted ice axe in a straight-armed salute. The T-shaped head of the axe was high above, hooking onto the very edge of the atmosphere. Below the axe's long pick was a small flag. At the very moment the photographer had released the camera's shutter, the wind must have gusted. In that fortuitous millisecond, the flag was perfectly unfurled, snapped back by the wind, its design unmistakable.

They all recognized it immediately. Neil Quinn smiled as he looked up at the rudimentary flag's ripped square of white cloth and the thick, hand-painted black lines of the Star of David it so clearly displayed. His lips moved slightly as he silently mouthed the two words written beneath the Jewish symbol:

FÜR ILSA

"Neil, I think we need to take a little trip together," he heard Henrietta whisper as they continued to look up at the photograph.

EPILOGUE

THE VON TRIER INSTITUTE, HYDERABAD, TELANGANA, INDIA
June 9, 2010
9:00 a.m. (India Standard Time)

Henrietta and Neil entered the small, white room. The window was open to let in the cool of the early morning. It brought with it the smell of jacaranda and the sounds of children playing.

The lady within was tiny, visibly older than her years, skin darkened and wrinkled by the relentless sun of the region. She sat in a wicker chair, a sheet covering her legs, her hands folded underneath. She looked up at her visitors with an alert curiosity.

"So you have come all this way to talk about my father?"

"Yes," said Henrietta.

"But he died in the mountains long ago."

"Did he or did he really end his days here with

you in Hyderabad?" Henrietta asked, slightly too hastily—overeager in her desire to get to the truth.

The birdlike woman just smiled at the quick fire question, if a little grimly, and then, shaking her head slowly, replied, "No, he died in the Alps in 1938. He was killed by the SS."

Henrietta paused this time before saying, as kindly as she was able, "But isn't that the official version? With the greatest of respect, wasn't the reality somewhat different?"

"No."

"But you are Ilsa von Trier, Magda von Trier's daughter?"

"I am."

"So wasn't Josef Becker your father? Didn't your parents meet on the SS *Gneisenau* when they both came to India in the spring of 1939?"

"No, but like my adoptive mother I did meet Josef. He was a kind man. He saved my life on the Paznaun when my family was trying to escape from Austria into Switzerland. He pushed me into a stone altar when the Germans surrounded the chapel where we were resting. I crawled out through a drain hole in the wall and jumped down the hill into the snow just like some goats I had seen on the way up. I disturbed the mules we had with us and the SS started shooting, but I fell so fast and so far they couldn't catch me.

"My mother told me how Josef thought I had been killed with the rest of my family on that ridge. I probably should have died up there but I kept going down that hill until I was found by a shepherd. Thinking that soldiers might be looking for me because of my family, I lied to him that my name was Ilsa Becker. You see, just before the SS came, I had asked Josef his name, and, even though he wasn't meant to, he told me. I think he did it because he was trying so hard to cheer me up and get me over that terrible mountain."

She stopped talking for a moment, her face freezing as she thought about something still painful to her.

"For years after, I truly believed that by asking I had, in some way, caused what then happened to everyone. Even so, I stuck with my lie, that name, the name of the person who had saved my life. It was a shield to hide behind, a reminder that I must never let my guard down, but also it spoke to me of the kindness of that particular German. It said that not all of them were evil.

"I took a long time to recover from that night without end. The shepherd and his wife thought at first that I was going to die from being so exposed to the cold. I lost all my fingers on this hand because of frostbite."

From under the sheet, she pulled out her maimed and scarred right hand as if in proof of her story.

"Josef had taken off my wet glove to warm it with his dry hands just before ..." Her voice breaking under the weight of her words, Ilsa paused, swallowed, and then, visibly steeling herself, continued. "I'm sorry, but moments like those never leave you. That shepherd and his wife looked after me for most of the war as one of their own. But then they were robbed and killed by a renegade band of army deserters in 1944 and I had to run for my life a second time. After that I was passed between a lot of people to stay free."

"So how did you come here?" Neil asked.

"In the chaos after the war ended, Magda tried to find Josef's family—his mother and sisters—searching high and low through the mountain communities and displaced persons camps of Bavaria. But it was all in vain; the Nazis had killed them in Ravensbrück despite the fact that Josef did what they wanted him to do. The SS were despicable. They even sent an agent here to Hyderabad to kill Magda, but her father was too clever for them. After the boat journey he knew she was in danger and sent her to work in the small villages helping people, so that she couldn't be found. She never stopped that work once she heard what had happened to Josef. Their betrayal of his courage and honor sickened her to her dying day."

"But how did she know he climbed the mountain?"

"The Sherpa Ang Noru."

Henrietta and Quinn looked at each other in recognition of that fact, both also silently acknowledging that it had been Josef Becker all along in that icy cave on the Second Step.

"Ang Noru made it down from Everest," Ilsa von Trier continued, "and then eventually here, thanks to a letter and a photograph of Magda that Josef gave him to deliver if he survived the climb. He was an incredibly strong and loyal man, as devoted to the memory of Josef as Magda was. He worked here until he died in August of 1964. He helped me a lot. Ang Noru understood suffering and he understood frostbite."

"When did you come here?"

"In 1946. Josef had told Magda all about me and my family on the boat. She noticed my false name, Ilsa Becker, on the roster of the Landsberg DP Camp, when she was searching for his family. Curious, she asked to meet me and soon worked out that I was actually Ilsa Rosenberg. She proved how she knew who I was by showing me some photos of Josef she was using in the search for his relations. Soon after she arranged for me to travel to India. I took her name, and we lived as mother and daughter."

Ilsa rang a small bell and an Indian orderly came into the room. "Yes, Miss von Trier?"

"Nerula, can you bring my mother's scrapbook from my bedroom table?"

They waited quietly until the man returned with what had once been an expensive photograph album. Its dark blue leather covers were old and battered, scarcely able to contain the bulging mass of press cuttings, letters, and photographs that crammed the huge volume. Wary of its weight, the orderly positioned it gently on the sheet that covered Ilsa von Trier's lap.

"There are some pictures in here of my mother and Josef on the boat to India."

Opening the album, she revealed some pages of small black-and-white pictures of a sea voyage. Most were views from the ship, but a few showed Magda on deck, others were of her parents. Magda von Trier was beautiful in the photographs, young and happy. There was only one of Josef. It was a close-up of his face in which he seemed to be laughing uncontrollably at something, the shine of tears showing on his creased cheeks.

As Ilsa turned the pages onward with her good hand, Neil noticed that she was wearing a silver ring with the relief of an edelweiss flower. Seeing him look at it, Ilsa stopped at a page on which was glued a single, very creased and tattered photograph of Magda and a handwritten letter.

"This is the photograph and the letter that led Ang Noru to Hyderabad. Josef Becker gave the ring you were looking at to my mother on the steamship. She wore it for the rest of her life, as I will too."

"Am I right in thinking you said Magda showed you more than one photograph of Josef Becker when she found you? Can I see the others?" Henrietta asked.

"Yes, here are some more."

Ilsa turned the page again, which to Neil's and Henrietta's delight, revealed shots of either Ang Noru or Josef in and around the Rongbuk Monastery with Everest itself in the background.

The pictures of Ang Noru were very sharp, clearly showing the Sherpa's strong, proud face, but the first ones of Josef were poorly taken. They dramatically improved, however, as Ilsa leafed further through the album until coming to a page that was completely empty of any images. After it, the photographs immediately recommenced, showing Magda and the work she did, many of them with a young Ilsa at her side.

Returning to the blank page, Ilsa tapped it three times with her damaged hand.

"My mother always left that page blank in remembrance of the photograph that Ang Noru took of Josef on the summit of Mount Everest. In his letter Josef told my mother that he would do what the Nazis ordered, summit and die on the mountain, if it would save his family and her, but he would never give them what they wanted, a picture of their flag dominating the entire world. Instead he dedicated his summit to the very people the Nazis were oppressing.

"Ang Noru brought here only a single roll of film, the one with which Josef had shown him how to properly take a photograph. He never stopped apologizing for not bringing the camera with the film from the summit. He said that the last thing Josef did up there was take pictures to the north, south, east, and west to show beyond a shadow of doubt that they had really made it to the very highest point on earth. After, he had kept the camera around his neck, pushing it deep inside his jacket to protect it. During the descent everything became so desperate and sad that the camera was forgotten."

Henrietta opened her briefcase and removed a brown envelope. From within, she took out Josef Becker's summit photo and placed it on the blank page. With a smile, she said, "Then, Ilsa Rosenberg, this is for you."

AUTHOR'S NOTE AND ACKNOWLEDGEMENTS

Summit is a fictional story that has fact in the foundations of its two imaginary journeys. The most obvious, of course, is that Mount Everest is the highest mountain in the world. The officially recognized height is 29,029 feet, or 8,848 meters, although you will often hear other measurements mentioned that give or take a few of each. None question that it is the highest, even if that is a slightly more recent presumption than you might suspect. As late as the early 1930s, there were still some, particularly an American explorer called Joseph Rock, who thought that there was another mountain called Amne Machin, located deep within a largely unexplored area of northeastern Tibet, that rose to "at least" twenty-eight thousand feet and, possibly, could be higher still than Everest. I mention this only because, during his second expedition to

Tibet in 1935, the German explorer, scientist, and SS obersturmführer Ernst Schäfer saw a "gigantic zeppelin" of cloud obscuring what he considered to be an immense mountain that set him to considering a possible return to climb it.

Schäfer's own ambition, when combined with the subsequent patronage of one of the most supremely evil men of history, Heinrich Himmler, would soon turn his attentions to other, still not totally understood objectives when he did revisit the country with an SS-sponsored expedition on the eve of the Second World War. Many stories can be found about Himmler's interest in race theory, mysticism, and the occult, and, in particular, his fascination with the racial and spiritual origins of Tibet. Schäfer's well-documented return to Tibet in 1938–9 undoubtedly gives some veracity to its core, even if the more fanciful myths are probably just that. Amne Machin was eventually proved to exist, although Rock's estimate of height was an exaggeration to the tune of more than eight thousand feet. As far as I know neither Schäfer nor Himmler ever showed any interest in an ascent of Mount Everest, even if I am sure it must have crossed the alpinist Heinrich Harrer's mind during his famous seven years in Tibet. He was a climber after all.

It is written that Western eyes first saw Mount Everest some time around 1847. In the age of a mountain estimated to be over fifty-five million years old, this is a recent date in a long and mostly silent history. It is significant however in that it marks the beginning of a time when an observer might have wondered precisely how high the mountain was, or what august superior's name they could attribute to it, or, just possibly, what it might be like to stand on the very top. Before the intrusion of Western ambition, observers would have assumed such a huge mountain to be the abode of gods, a place naturally beyond the reach of man, which already bore a name older than their ancestral time clock—"Chomolungma" for those looking from the north and "Sagarmatha" to those in the south—somewhere to be worshipped and feared by the hardy peoples who strove daily to eke out difficult existences in the valleys below.

Even today, these valleys offer few Western luxuries, particularly one of the biggest: risking your own life when not essential for survival. The fourteenth Dalai Lama, in his message for the book *Everest: Summit of Achievement*, applied his keen wit to the truth, as always, when he wrote: "George Mallory, who was the first man to nearly succeed in the quest, famously answered, when asked why he wanted to climb Everest, 'Because it's there.' I imagine that for most Tibetans, 'Because it's there' was a very good reason for not making an attempt."

It is said that in Sherpali, the Tibetan-based dialect used by the Sherpas, there isn't even a word for the top of a mountain. When you now consider their famed familiarity with the upper reaches of the world's highest mountains, it seems strange that they don't possess their own extensive mountaintop vocabulary, a subtle lexicon to define the infinite variety of such places, much like the Inuit in their need to properly classify snow. But climbing to the top of mountains is a recent thing for the Sherpas, not yet a hundred years old, younger even than the motorcar, far younger than language. When their outstanding natural abilities started to necessitate the regular use of such terminology, it is said that the Sherpa simply adopted the words used by the first Europeans they accompanied, the English sahibs of the British Empire, inserting the words "top" and "summit" into their own dialect.

In 1892, Clinton Thomas Dent, a past president of a still-youthful British Alpine Club already running out of unclimbed peaks in the European Alps, wrote an article for the October edition of a periodical called *Nineteenth Century*. It was entitled "Can Mount Everest Be Climbed?" It took sixty-one years to answer the question. On May 29, 1953, Sir Edmund Hillary and Sherpa Tenzing Norgay reached the summit for the first time. The crisp, unequivocal image of Tenzing on "top" that clear day is one of the most recognizable photographs ever taken. It is image number forty-five in *Time* magazine's "100 Greatest Images," the first within the selection to be in full color rather than black and white, thereby leaving nothing to the imagination in the sublime moment of human achievement it portrays.

In England, the news of the great mountain's first summit was headlined as the crowning glory of the nation's coronation of a new queen, fêted as the right and just conclusion of a string of eight official British expeditions to reconnoiter and/or climb the mountain that began in 1921. The only other official attempt to climb Mount Everest had been by the Swiss in 1952. Alarmingly, for the heavily invested yet still unsuccessful British, that Swiss expedition even had the audacity to be divided over two attempts: pre- and post-monsoon. It is reasonable to imagine that there must have been more than a few collective sighs of relief in London when they failed both times. The British undoubtedly knew that their 1953 expedition would be their last exclusive shot at the summit, for now they had to take their place within a queue of nations that desired to be first to place their flag on the top of the highest mountain on Earth. The world had changed dramatically since the end of the Second World War. Britannia no longer ruled the waves or the Indian subcontinent, for that matter. No longer could its regional power and influence keep the ascension of Everest its sole preserve, magnanimously permitting other countries other major mountains, such as K2, Kangchenjunga, and Nanga Parbat, but always keeping the biggest trophy for itself.

The stories of the attempts to climb those other mountains are just as heroic, tragic, and inspiring as those of Mount Everest. The German quest to be the first to climb Nanga Parbat commenced in 1932. With five expeditions and the cumulative loss of eleven Germans and fifteen Sherpas and porters, it, at times, more resembled a blood feud between a nation and a mountain than a climbing endeavor. Nanga Parbat was also finally summited in 1953, just thirty-six days after Everest, by the legendary Austrian climber Hermann Buhl. Although part of a larger siege-style expedition, Buhl, one of the few true rivals to another Tyrolean climber, Reinhold Messner, for the title of "Greatest Climber of All Time," soloed the final section to the summit without supplementary oxygen and then, on his descent, bivouacked for a night, standing up, at over eight thousand meters before returning alive. The outstanding climber of his generation, Buhl had also served in the Second World War as a young first-aider in the German Gebirgsjäger mountain troops, seeing action at Monte Cassino. After Nanga Parbat, Buhl would go on to make another first ascent of an eight-thousand-meter mountain, Broad Peak, before losing his life on Chogolisa, aged just thirty-two. His legacy still continues in the spirit of anyone who turns his back on the option of a big, organized expedition and heads into the mountains with the barest minimum.

During that thirty-year, presummit period of British expeditions on Everest, there were three unofficial solo ventures to climb the mountain, undertaken by an Englishman in 1934, a Canadian in 1947, and a Dane in 1951. They all failed, one of them, the Englishman, Maurice Wilson, dying in the process. In addition, it is said that in 1952, the six-man summit team of a clandestine Russian expedition led by a Dr. Pawel Datschnolian, also intent on stealing a first ascent, was blown off the Northeast Ridge, never to be seen or heard of again. The existence of this expedition is still unproven today.

In 1953, when Hillary and Tenzing safely made it down from the summit, the New Zealander and the Sherpa with Tibetan origins, for that's what they were, completed a journey for the British that could be said to have started with that first sighting of the mountain in 1847—a difficult and dangerous journey that lasted over a hundred years set against a backdrop of world history that saw the rise and fall of great empires, the most terrible wars known to mankind, and the birth of the modern, technological world. A number of times the journey had already come desperately close to reaching its destination. In 1924, the third British expedition to Mount Everest put the greatest climber of its day, George Leigh Mallory, and his younger colleague, Andrew "Sandy" Irvine, high on the Northeast Ridge, wearing early oxygen apparatuses, and, in the words of another team member, "going strong for the top." The pair never returned. Discussion immediately ensued as to whether they might have made the summit before they succumbed—a debate that continues, heated and passionate at times, almost as if chorused by the old pantomime refrain of, "Oh yes, they did! Oh no, they didn't!"

George Mallory's frozen body was found in 1999 in the very place where it finally stopped falling down the North Face some seventy-five years before. I have read that the internal mechanism of his broken wristwatch still partially functioned. Letters found on his body, wrapped for safekeeping in a still brightly colored paisley handkerchief, were as crisp and clear as the day they were written. Conspicuous by its absence within those personal papers was a photograph of Mallory's long-suffering and devoted wife, Ruth. Mallory had always said he would place it on the summit. "Oh yes, they did!" some cried once more. It had long been wondered whether Mallory's body, when found, would also offer up the borrowed Kodak Vest Pocket camera that the pair was carrying, the hope being that frozen within would be an undeveloped film that might finally reveal the truth of the greatest climbing mystery once and for all, but sadly, "Oh no, it didn't!"

The hunt for Sandy Irvine's body continues, determined in its desire to ascertain if it was he who was carrying the camera on that fateful day. Strangely, in all the analysis of the pair and their equipment, I have never heard mention of a "summit flag." But surely they would have had one? Possibly it too was left on the summit alongside that photo of Ruth Mallory or maybe it fell to oblivion, still attached to Mallory's ice axe, leaving him to claw painfully at the rocky slopes with his hands as he tried to arrest that final, fatal fall. But then again, perhaps Sandy Irvine also has the flag. If so, it must be folded in a frozen pocket or stuffed inside a frayed cricket sweater because it wasn't attached to his ice axe, which was found in 1933 lying on a rock slab at 27,760 feet (8,460 meters) on the Northeast Ridge, just below the First Step.

After that first summit in 1953, it took twenty-six years for the next one hundred ascents. It took another nineteen years to rack that total up to a thousand. There have now been over seven thousand summits by more than four thousand individuals. The youngest climber to have summited was just thirteen, the oldest, eighty. In 2011, the legendary Apa Sherpa summited for the twenty-first time and then finally retired. In 2013, Phurba Tashi equaled that record.

There are actually over twenty routes to the summit of Mount Everest. A number are still unclimbed. Each bears a history underwritten, and in a few cases unwritten, of the most extreme human endeavor imaginable. In the twenty-first century, the majority of these routes have been ignored by climbers who, more eager for success than originality, tend to take one of two tried and tested routes to the top: the Southeast Ridge route on the Nepali side, following that utilized by Hillary and Tenzing in 1953, or the Northeast Ridge on the Tibetan side, pioneered by those first British expeditions in the '20s. An industry has grown up around both paths to the top of the world.

Familiarity does indeed breed contempt, but either route to the summit of Mount Everest is still enough to tax a human body to its very limits. The ancient Eastern demons that guarded the summit for millennia may well have been vanquished by science and progress, but others from the West have replaced them. Overcrowding, global warming, commercialism, reckless ambition, human tragedy—all now haunt the mountain just as they do the rest of our modern world. But for all this, make no mistake, even today, climbing Mount Everest is one of the most incredible things you can do. Anyone who walks those heights gets himself or herself, for a few fleeting moments, slightly closer to heaven. Getting there will also have provided one or two quite intimate glimpses of hell.

Summit is unashamed fiction as big as the mountain at its center, yet it has sought to be faithful to any actual historic climbs it references and imposes no impossible actions or conversations on the participants. This novel's honest desire to transport and entertain should not be mistaken for a lack of the sincerest respect and appreciation for those who first did these things for real, especially Hillary and Tenzing's successful first ascent. If I have unintentionally trod on any other legacies, then please forgive me.

And yes, if you are wondering, I have also lived with that summit photograph of Tenzing for a very long time. I will go on doing so, having failed to insert myself into it one difficult day in 2006. When I think of my own Everest experience I am well aware of the irony in the title of this novel, *Summit*, because actually I didn't. They used to call climbing alpine mountains "slaying dragons." That is obviously Victorian melodrama, but it was a fact for me that if I summited a mountain it did tend to diminish and then fade from my life—I guess I was just a peak-bagger after all. Turning back from the summit of Everest created the unexpected by-product of the mountain accompanying me through life ever since. At first that wasn't easy, a daily reminder of a huge disappointment, but now I enjoy the companionship, the mountain's continued presence in my memories, my dreams, my imagination. I know it will stay with me forever, and I am happy about that. It's a magnificent and historic mountain, and I sincerely hope this book does it some justice.

Coming to a close, I am extremely grateful to Tad Shay, Ron Follmann, Rhys Jones, Justin Adams, Michelle Thornton, Ian Lawrence, Robin Maceyunas, Jennifer Jackson, Julie Heap, Pat Patel, Tony Schlegel, Bob and Mimi Graham, Eric and Bobbi Jo Engleby, Sam and Deb Sprayberry, Fred and Kelley Murray, Cookie and Harrison Jones, and John Jordan and Jane Farthing for all their enthusiasm for Summit from the very start. David White MD and Jens Klingenstein were generous with their time and knowledge in helping me with a number of medical and German language queries relating to the development of the story. A particularly big thank-you must also go to the "Mothers of Punctuation," Lucy Farthing and Marilyn Follmann, for pulling my initial narrative into pristine order. It was neither an easy nor a quick task.

The journey from self-published "bucket-list whim" to nationally published debut novel is as long and difficult as climbing Everest itself and only through the assistance of the following people would it have happened: John and Penny Coppedge; Linda Malcolm of Indigo Books on Kiawah Island; Paula and David Whisenant; my two "consiglieri," John Huey and Bill Barry; my agent at the Gernert Company, Will Roberts; my editor, Madeline Hopkins; and Josh Stanton, Lauren Maturo, Kathryn English, and all the team at Blackstone Audio and Publishing. I am indebted to you all for making this particular "summit dream" come true. To my three daughters, Hannah, Eden, and Isla, I say follow your dreams too because within them magic awaits. Finally, without the tireless support of my incredible wife and "compadre," Farrah, none of this would have been possible. To you I send my special love and complete appreciation for everything you have done to help *Summit* be the very best it can be and give it a visibility without which it would have undoubtedly remained hidden.

I'll admit to never being the strongest climber, but I had my moments—moments that two people, Italian mountain guide Massimo "Tambo" Tamburini and nineteen-time Everest summiteer Sherpa Mingma Tsiri, ensured that I would be able to enjoy for a long time after. Each of you gave me more than you can ever know, and I dedicate *Summit* to you both in return.

Harry Farthing, April 2016